SO BAD A DEATH

SO BAD
A DEATH

June Wright

INTRODUCTION BY
LUCY SUSSEX

**DARK
PASSAGE**

VERSE CHORUS PRESS

A Dark Passage book
Published by Verse Chorus Press
PO Box 14806, Portland OR 97293
info@versechorus.com

Cover design by Mike Reddy
Interior design and layout by Steve Connell/Transgraphic
Illustrations on title page and pages 8, 21, 54, and 190 by Frank Whitmore
Dark Passage logo by Mike Reddy

The publishers thank everyone who granted permission to reproduce copyright
material in this book. Every effort has been made to contact all copyright holders,
and we welcome communication from any copyright owners from whom permission was inadvertently not obtained. In such cases, we will be pleased to obtain
appropriate permission and provide suitable acknowledgment in future printings.

Printed in the USA

Library of Congress Cataloging-in-Publication Data

Wright, June, 1919-2012.
    So bad a death / June Wright ; introduction by Lucy Sussex.
        pages ; cm
    ISBN 978-1-891241-45-1 (paperback) – ISBN 978-1-891241-60-4 (ebook)
    1. Women detectives–Fiction. 2. Murder–Investigation–Fiction.
    3. Melbourne (Vic.)–Fiction. I. Sussex, Lucy, 1957- II. Title.
    PR9619.3.W727S67 2015
    823'.914–dc23
                                2014044271

INTRODUCTION

June Wright was one of a small but highly talented group of Australian crime writers, active in the mid-twentieth century, of whom some of the most significant were women. They published internationally, maintained their careers and detectives over a number of books, and enjoyed a high public profile. That June Wright achieved such success is particularly impressive in that she was raising six children—in an era when, unlike her nineteenth-century predecessors like Mary Braddon and Anna Katharine Green, she did not have domestic help. June Wright was a housewife superstar well before Edna Everage, and far more gracious in the role.

It is important to put her into context, firstly as an Australian detective writer. She belonged to a long tradition, hardly surprising given the country's origins as a penal colony. Crime appears in Australian writing from its beginnings, mostly in the form of what we would now term true crime. Fiction—and in turn the crime genre—slowly emerged over the nineteenth century, fed by reportage, the Gothic, and theatrical melodrama. Form and content began to coalesce in the 1850s, a period of intense interest from prospective colonists hoping for gold. John Lang (1816-64), the first Australian-born novelist—and a lawyer, troublemaker and expatriate—was also the first with a fictional detective. His 1855 *The Forger's Wife* included the secondary character George Flower, based on a real Sydney thief-taker, though his methods were more violent than deductive.

Lang's most significant followers came ten years later, in the colony of Victoria. For much of the nineteenth-century, police fiction was hampered by class issues—snobbery with violence. Victoria's brief creation of a cadet system, young middle-class men recruited for an elite police force, made the detective a far less problematic character for writers. The first Australian detective serials appeared in the *Australian Journal* in 1865, one writer being Mary Fortune (c. 1833-1909), who was married (bigamously) to a police cadet. She would write over five hundred stories in her 'Detective's Album', the longest early detective serial anywhere in the world. Also figuring in the early issues of the *Australian Journal* was Ellen Davitt's *Force and Fraud*, the first Australian murder mystery novel.

June Wright, although a Melbourne writer, knew none of these antecedents. What she did know was Fergus Hume's *The Mystery of a Hansom Cab*, a semi-self-published novel by a New Zealander that first appeared in 1886 in Melbourne (where it was set), and was reprinted in London the following year. It became the biggest and fastest selling detective novel of the 1800s, and a key text in creating the publishing genre of detective fiction. The connection for Wright was personal: her grandfather Daniel Newham had known Hume and had himself attempted a 'great Australian novel', never completed.

Following Hume's success, most Australian crime writers of the early twentieth century were expatriates. They lived in Britain, and wrote for that audience. Some, like the Geelong-born J. M. Walsh, even rewrote their Australian novels with English settings. As a teenager Wright did encounter a role model in Paul McGuire, who had moved in Catholic intellectual circles in London and continued to write Anglocentric detective novels after he returned to live in Adelaide. In contrast, her most famous peer, Arthur Upfield, was an English emigrant who celebrated the Australian landscape and, in his detective Bony, indigenous people. Other models came from Wright's preferred crime reading: the queens of crime fiction's golden age: Agatha Christie, Ngaio Marsh, Margery Allingham and the American Mignon Eberhardt. Although G. K. Chesterton was a fellow Catholic, she did not greatly care for his Father Brown stories.

Wright was a good student, but tertiary education for girls was not really an option in her family. Instead, she began working at Melbourne's central telephone exchange, which would supply her with a unique and interesting background for her first book. She married in 1941, and children followed quickly. When she drafted *Murder in the Telephone Exchange* in 1943, it was very much as an outlet, as solitary brainwork. She wrote it in six weeks during the intervals when her firstborn, Patrick, was sleeping. Pregnant again, she immediately started another novel, but did not have the energy to proceed at that point.

Upfield had been reprinted by Doubleday in America during World War II, to great success. This had reminded international publishers that, as with Hume, Australia contained crimewriting gold. Several other Australia-based writers found book publication in 1944, notably A. E. Martin (three novels) and 'Margot Neville', pseudonym of the sisters Margot Goyder and Anne Neville Joske. That same year, Wright chanced to see an advertisement for the 'United Nations Literary Competition' while wrapping up vegetable scraps in newspaper. She typed up and sent off her manuscript, and this led ultimately to the publication of *Murder in the Telephone Exchange* with Hutchinson in 1948, and a three-novel contract.

Murder in the Telephone Exchange was written from the perspective of a single woman, Maggie Byrnes, who detects and finds romance in the same narrative. *So Bad a Death*, published a year later, in 1949, again features Maggie, by now married with a small son. The novel is thus essentially a sequel, but it is in many ways a more skilled book, with Wright learning from the experience of writing. However, the time and energy she could devote to her work were now considerably limited: she had revised *Murder* in the maternity hospital after having twins. Her household comprised four children, with one twin proving severely mentally disabled, and this preoccupied her; in her memoir she could not recall much about the composition of her second and third novels.

Just as Wright's debut hit the target in its depiction of young working women—which proved a factor in its successful reception when reprinted last year—her second novel is similarly acute in drawing female lives. There is much in *So Bad a Death* that is autobiographic: a young mother seeking housing during a post-war shortage, as well as distraction from the domestic grind. Wright vividly and recognisably depicts the new suburb of Ashburton; in her memoir she recalls how people tried to identify the characters—unsuccessfully. Something else she captures is the tension of women returning to domesticity

The bland Ames was standing before the entrance to the drawing room, a silver tray of drinks in his hands.

So bad a Death

Third Instalment of the Australian Serial
by JUNE WRIGHT

SYNOPSIS OF PRECEDING INSTALMENTS

To mysterious Holland Hall come Inspector and Mrs. Matheson to buy, if possible, the Dower House, belonging to the Estate. Mrs. Matheson at once senses an emotional strain about the inhabitants of the Hall. Ruthless James Holland dominates his widowed daughter-in-law, Yvonne, and his sister's family, the Mulqueens, and although Yvonne's baby son, Jimmy, is his heir, "The Squire" refuses to take seriously Jimmy's faltering health. Mrs. Matheson meets the ubiquitous Ames — major domo of the establishment — and his quiet wife, Henrietta. While John Matheson probes the curious disappearance of Cruikshank, the surly estate agent, Maggie Matheson, taking her son Tony to the local Health Centre, learns from Sister Heather that Dr. Trefont is the nearest doctor. But Yvonne presses Maggie to have nothing to do with Trefont. Rather to their surprise, the Mathesons are invited to dinner at the Hall — Now read on:

When we arrived the house was brilliant with light. The front door stood wide open in spite of the inclement night. Music sounded — a sweet, hackneyed Strauss waltz.

Ames took John's coat, suggesting I retain my fur.

"Some ladies find the house a trifle draughty." His manner was perfect, but just the same I let slip my cape into his hands.

"I regret that Mr. Holland has not yet come in," he went on. "He is expected at any moment. Will you come this way, please?"

He ushered us into the drawing room, an apartment heavy with crimson and massive with mahogany. The Strauss waltz came from a panatrope situated on the far side of the room. Daisy Potts-Power, dressed in shapeless draperies of flowered voile, was standing beside it. Before I had time to greet her a deep voice spoke from behind the door.

"Again. Play it again, girl."

I swung round. An elderly woman of immense,

— (To page 55)

8

from war work, and finding it did not fulfill all of their needs.

An important point about Wright is that she was unselfconscious in using Australian settings—indeed she seems unaffected by the cultural cringe. Moreover, she based her writing on experience, which gives it a realist edge, even when her narrative is heightened by pronounced Gothic elements. All her novels are about women, chronicled with great acuteness. She does not subsume herself within the persona of a male detective, as did Marsh, or 'Margot Neville'.

So Bad a Death was serialised in *Woman's Day*, published at the time by the *Herald* newspaper group, between March and June 1949. (The magazine had previously, in October 1948, written her up under the headline "Books Between Babies".) Wright benefited here from the good local sales for *Murder*, and the novelty of being a young mother who managed to look glamorous on a small budget, and also to write. She was described as adopting "marriage and mystery-solving jointly as a career". The serialisation had illustrations—by colour-blind graphic artist Frank Whitmore—which skilfully evoke the story's Gothic mood, whilst also recalling Hollywood noir and Hitchcock. The images arguably reference Wright herself, whose publicity photos were striking. The *Women's Weekly* may have featured Margot Neville serials, with their Sydney detective, but here was a Melbourne counterpart. Only the previous year *Woman's Day* had serialised Christie's *Taken at the Flood*. In addition to Wright they also bought short stories from another young Melbourne woman, Jean Turnley, which they ran along with the overseas fare of Georgette Heyer and Alec Waugh.

Many of the tensions captured in *So Bad a Death* are also evident in the pages of the magazine itself. Food and fashion feature, but so do the problems of the 'obey' clause in the marriage vow and discussions on how to bring up children properly (Maggie is particularly severe on dummies*). Nearly every issue of *Woman's Day* featured a woman with an identity that extended beyond domesticity—Hollywood actresses, but also pioneering racing chemist Jean Kimble, and Wright herself.

---

* In the USA, a baby's dummy is more often called a pacifier

So Bad a Death is a subversive book: Wright had wanted to title it *Who Would Murder a Baby*, and delighted in telling interviewers how writing bloody murders was a good way to avoid infanticide. It also critiques the snobbism of the country house murder mystery with its depiction of an attempt to create a squirearchy in the Antipodes, a would-be Lord of the manor who plays god with the women around him. Patriarchy takes a pounding in the novel, as, more implicitly, does maternal dependency, the ideal of the stay-at-home mother. Like *Murder*, the novel resonated with women's lives, then and now.

After *So Bad a Death* Wright retired Maggie. It was just about possible to detect with one child, but if Maggie were to be consistent with 1950s norms, she would go on to bear an overwhelming brood. Wright also told me (after asking me to switch the tape recorder off) that Maggie had proved to be too much of a smartarse, and that she was sick of people assuming the character and her creator were the same. Yet they were similar: clever, competent women who managed homes, children and brainwork efficiently. Wright would subsequently create a character who could be a continuing strong detective: the nun Mother Paul. Since she was married to God, her professionalism was not problematic. But what Wright accomplished with Maggie was considerable.

Before June Wright, Australian detective fiction tended to focus on the male protagonists, the experiences of male detectives, even when it was written by women. Her work changed that, creating a writing space in which titles like *The Knife Is Feminine*, Charlotte Jay's 1951 debut, could flourish. Among Wright's followers into print were the superb psychothriller author Pat Flower (from 1958), Patricia Carlon (from 1961), and of course Jay herself, whose *Beat Not the Bones* (1952) won the first Edgar.

LUCY SUSSEX

SO BAD A DEATH

"So bad a death argues a monstrous life."

CHAPTER ONE

I

I am not a *femme fatale*. Crime does not dog my footsteps, as one garrulous friend assured me. It was she who applied the first loathsome sobriquet. Neither am I one of those sleuths for whom corpses crop up conveniently. Such individuals should, in the interests of public safety, be marooned on a desert island. Their presence in the community is an incentive to murder.

No claim is being made to the ranks of amateur detection. I am merely a police officer's wife who has certain reasons in recording impressions of a homicide case. One is to defend myself against further attacks by friends. The affair was bound to happen some time, and therefore it was just a coincidence that it synchronized with our arrival in Middleburn. Crime waits for no man, least of all for the super-sleuth.

It is strange to remember that it happened at that particular time of the year. One associates murder with a winter's wind whining in the trees, or with the electrically charged atmosphere that precedes a summer storm; indeed, our treacherous spring days would have been a more suitable setting. But the violence and mystery which emanated from the Hall, their breeding place, were played against a background of serene days and nights. The leaves of deciduous trees were yellow and starting to fall, and the smoke from chimney stacks rose as straight plumes through the unruffled air. Autumn was the backdrop.

Such days of glorious weather might bring a poignant nostalgia to some; to others happy memories. To me they are the reminder of the most terrifying experiences of my life.

One of those nightmare incidents becomes particularly vivid whenever I watch Tony playing in the sandpit John constructed. My heart will thud with a sudden fear of what might have been. I snatch his rotund little body hard against me to beat off the phantom. Then Tony complains plaintively of the uncomfortable grip, and the picture fades.

Tony makes me forget, but only temporarily. Often during the night I will waken sharply and think I hear his terrified baby call. I will slip quickly and quietly from bed and pad down the hall in my bare feet to the nursery. Each time I fully expect to see that dark-draped figure leaning over his cot once more. But the light from the passage shines on nothing more sinister than the black-stocking golliwog, clasped firmly in one striped-pyjama arm. Only after I lean over the high rail of the cot and listen for his quick breathing, with my own held, and take another look at the double screen on the nursery window, am I satisfied to leave him. I creep back to bed rather sheepishly, confident that I have not disturbed John with my midnight prowlings, until his voice comes deeply through the darkness.

"Well? No masked kidnappers?"

"Did I waken you? I thought I heard Tony call."

John rolled over. "Now listen, Maggie! It's high time you stopped this nonsense. Haven't you heard that lightning never strikes twice in the same place? Forgive the trite phrase, but it is about the best security I can offer you. I do wish you'd stop fidgeting and let us get some sleep."

I stopped thumping my pillow into shape and said meekly: "Sorry, darling. I won't offend again. Good night."

John gave a grunt of forgiveness and rolled back. The Holland case was closed as far as he was concerned. Such a prosaic attitude to the recent events which occurred in Middleburn could only be found in one to whom crime was an everyday affair to combat.

I lay straight and still in the darkness. Sleep was far away.

"I'll remember it all for the last time and then put it out of my head for good. I'll go over every fact, every little incident. That should cure me."

II

Tony had been with us for nearly two years when I decided that flat life was no longer bearable. We must have a house and plenty of yard space in which Tony could indulge his ever-increasing vitality without complaints from the neighbours.

John looked dubious when I told him of my decision. I would find it difficult to secure a place in these times, he said. The housing problem was acute, and so on. However, I had his permission to go ahead in the search; only make sure before doing anything final that there was an extra room he could use as a study. He wished me luck, with a pessimistic shake of his head.

"I'll find a house," I declared firmly, "even if I die in the attempt." Which, on the whole, was a rather ironic statement to make. Fortunately I did not know that then.

As usual John was right. But after many weeks of weary searching I triumphed.

"Middleburn," said my sceptical husband, poring over the rough diagram I had made of the house I had inspected that afternoon. "Where the devil is Middleburn?"

"And you a policeman! Give me that paper for a moment."

On the back I sketched a clumsy map showing two of the main highways leading from town which run through a couple of well-known outer suburbs. Between them, marked by large crosses, I made a smaller one.

"That is Middleburn."

"Looks very much out of the way to me. Is there a decent train service to the city?"

I assured him that there was, and went on to describe Middleburn itself.

Although classed as a suburb, it had more the aspect of a country village, so isolated was it from its neighbours. The homes and gardens were delightful, set in pretty, rolling country which from many parts commanded fine views of the city in the west and the hills in the east. The houses were small, modern and smart, and inhabited for the most part by young married couples. The tiny shopping centre, set in the main road on the crest of a hill, teemed with smartly dressed young matrons wheeling baby carriages. Strolling along High Street I had to sidestep now and then to dodge groups of young mothers chatting together gaily. My town suit and hat were glanced at curiously. I presented a rather incongruous figure among the tailored slacks and careless bare heads.

I had gone to Middleburn on the advice of a city estate agency, which had given me the address of a Mr Cruikshank.

This gentleman appeared to have many irons in the commercial fire of the village. His address was scribbled on the back of one of John's official cards. As I stood outside a shop in High Street comparing the numbers, I saw that not only was Mr Cruikshank the local estate agent, he also ran a lending library, managed several agencies for insurance, and was a depôt for a dry-cleaning establishment.

Looking back now, I cannot understand how I opened Mr Cruikshank's screen door, which was and still is badly in need of oil, without feeling some other emotion than a weary speculation as to whether he could assist me in my house-hunting. My feet were sore from tramping city and suburbs. If there is anything likely to break the spirit it is blisters on the heels.

Cruikshank was a short, stout man. When I saw him that afternoon he was in his shirt-sleeves with an immense black sateen apron tied around his protruding middle. This was his usual mode of apparel in the shop. He looked up from his job of rebinding battered library books when I entered. A keen, inquisitive look was cast at me.

"Ah, yes! Margetsons wrote to me about a Mrs Matheson," he remarked, after I had stated my business. He then added, a trifle patronizingly: "You're after a house. Well, now. That is rather a problem nowadays."

As I considered he was liable to start commenting at length on the housing position, a dissertation I had already heard many times, I cut him short by demanding if he had any vacancies on his books.

Mr Cruikshank put his head on one side.

"Yes and no," he replied, in an irritating fashion. "When I say yes, there is a vacant place in this district. On the other hand, it is doubtful whether the owner will sell it to you."

He stressed the last word, and I felt my irritation rising. But house-hunters cannot afford to offend estate agents. I asked for the owner's address, so that I could see him for myself. Mr Cruikshank gave a small derisive laugh.

"You had better wait for a while until I can take you along. Maud!" he yelled into a door leading from behind his counter.

I remained where I was, idly glancing through a pile of un-catalogued books. Mr Cruikshank's maiden sister appeared.

"I have got to go out," he told her. "Are you taking that one, Mrs Ames? Here, Maud, fix up Mrs Ames."

I had not noticed the young woman standing beside me until Mr Cruikshank spoke. She handed a book over the counter in silence, and then turned slightly towards me.

"You are looking for a house, are you?" she asked. Her voice was flat and toneless. She kept one hand on the turned-up collar of her coat, trying to hide the port-wine stain which disfigured one side of her face.

"That's right!" I said eagerly. "Do you know—"

The young woman shook her head disinterestedly. She turned back to the counter and picked up her book. The estate agent came bustling through the counter pulling on a coat.

"Yes, looking for a house. Hopeful, isn't she, Mrs Ames? I thought we'd try Holland again, but I don't like her chances. Are you ready, Mrs Matheson?"

I followed him through the shop.

"Do you mean to say there has been a vacant house in this district for some time and the owner won't sell?" I demanded, trying to shorten my stride to suit his. We became separated by a baby carriage, but not before I heard him start: "Yes and no—"

17

When I came within earshot again he was still talking.

"—many's the time I've taken hopeful young ladies like yourself to see the owner. Occasionally he has permitted them to look over the Dower House, but when it came to talking terms—a most uncompromising man. However, we'll see what happens today." Mr Cruikshank gave a little skip and started to hum a tune.

We followed the main road out of the village and up a steep incline. Houses had become more infrequent and soon gave way altogether to open paddocks. Now and then Cruikshank nodded to a stray pedestrian or waved his hand at a passing car.

"You seem to know everyone," I remarked pleasantly.

He gave another little skip. "I," he announced, turning his head towards me confidentially, "I am the most dangerous man in Middleburn."

"Indeed?"

"Ah, yes!" continued Cruikshank. "Not much that has gone on in Middleburn over the last thirty years has escaped my notice. I know such a lot about everyone. Why even you now—" He looked sideways. "You look a comfortably-off young lady. Not wealthy, but nice and secure. Am I right?"

"I suppose so," I answered, my dislike growing stronger.

"Well, now! That's good hearing. Let us suppose that I can use my influence with Mr Holland and secure the Dower House for you, perhaps there might be some little extra in it for me. Eh? What do you say?"

"There might be," I answered shortly.

Mr Cruikshank gave three consecutive skips. "We'll just see what happens today," he promised again.

III

Holland Hall was an immense estate, set on the rise of a hill and overlooking the village. The house, except for its square white tower, was rendered invisible from the road by the tall Lombardy poplars lining either side of the gravelled driveway. It was the length of this drive and the fact that just inside the elaborate iron gates was a small dwelling labelled "THE LODGE" that gave the whole property a pretentious appearance. The Hall was either an imitation or the manifestation of an ideal. An odd place to find in Middleburn, cheek by jowl, as it were, with five-roomed modern houses.

The agent Cruikshank swung open the path gate with a fussy gallantry, standing aside to let me pass through. Perhaps that was another time when I should have felt some overwhelming emotion that would warn me of the web of mystery into which I was to be dragged. But I didn't. Mentally I was girding my loins for battle. Although I understood that for some reason he was reluctant to do so, Mr Holland had a house to sell, and I was very, very weary of house-hunting.

The drive curved into an open oval area in front of the house. In the centre of the oval a marble female figure revealed her knees to the goldfish with one hand, while the other held aloft a spraying fountain. Beyond the lily pond, stone steps led down to a sunken garden. I turned my attention to the house itself as we mounted more stone steps to the surrounding terrace. It had had several years in which to became mellowed, but not enough to disguise its crudity. Gabled and gargoyled at every conceivable point, it presented a baroque example of mixed architecture.

"'The style is the man,'" Cruikshank quoted smugly. "Quite a showplace, isn't it?"

He pressed his broad-tipped finger on the bell for the second time.

A weak, fretful wail came from the side of the house.

"Surely that is not a baby I can hear crying?" I asked, surveying this fantastic dwelling in wonderment.

"That will be Mr Holland's grandson," Cruikshank nodded. "We'll go round and see if there is anyone there."

A middle-aged man dressed in baggy tweeds straightened up from bending over a perambulator which was parked at the far end of the terrace. He turned quickly at the sound of footsteps and slipped one hand into a shapeless pocket. The other clumsily readjusted the pale pink mosquito netting over the hood. The eyes that met mine held a certain expression of embarrassment, if not furtiveness.

"Well!" breathed Mr Cruikshank in my ear. "Well! I am surprised to see him at Holland Hall."

Before I could speak one of the French windows overlooking the terrace was pulled up with a jerk and a girl stepped over quickly. She did not notice us standing at the corner of the house. I was unable to observe the expression on her face, but her voice was charged with a cold loathing.

"What are you doing here? I did not call you. Why have you been looking at my baby?"

"Mr Holland's daughter-in-law," Cruikshank breathed again in explanation. "His son's widow."

The stranger smiled at the girl gently in a conciliatory way. His mild eyes came once more to rest on my face beyond her.

The girl wheeled around and gasped in such a frightened way that I retreated a step. I murmured something about ringing at the front door and no one answering.

She tried to disguise her agitation. Her face, though quite young, was lined and harassed. Her small hands fiddled incessantly with the belt of her green wool dress as though it was too tight about her slender waist.

"I didn't hear the bell. Baby was crying. Teeth, you know." She smiled in a tired fashion.

I nodded wisely, and watched the stranger trying to sidle past us unobtrusively. One hand remained in his pocket. He stepped off the terrace and walked unhurriedly down the drive. I glanced at Cruikshank. His gaze had been darting from the girl to the stranger with a bright curiosity.

"Yvonne," a voice called from the house. The girl started and went back to the French window at once.

"Yes, Mr Holland?"

I turned to survey this man who built himself pseudo-manor houses and was not disappointed. In appearance and bearing he was all that he should have been.

"Come nearer, Yvonne." Holland's voice was quiet, yet harsh and high-pitched. It demanded obedience. The girl advanced closer, her fingers entwined tightly. James Holland put out one hand and

gripped her thin wrists. She stumbled to her knees over the sill of the window.

"That fellow was here! Haven't I told you I will not have him in the house? My wishes must be respected!"

The girl looked up at Holland with a sort of weak defiance.

"I didn't want him here. Perhaps you can explain why he came," she said.

The old man held her gaze pitilessly until her eyes dropped. He released his grip on Yvonne's wrists so suddenly that she sprawled at his feet. I hated him most for the smile he gave when he saw the girl so. She moved away to her child, her shoulders rounded as though manifesting her beaten spirit. Holland turned to deal with the other two persons on his terrace.

He addressed the agent haughtily. "You've seen fit to answer my summons at last, Cruikshank. You will pay for your tardiness. Young woman with the inquisitive eyes, would you kindly leave my house?"

I gasped with indignation, conscious of the aptness of his description. Cruikshank, evidently accustomed to the vagaries of clients, completely disregarded the dismissal by ushering me through the window.

The room was James Holland's study; large, red-carpeted and impressive. There were two or three immense leathern caverns of armchairs. The bookshelves were packed with massive tomes of a variety that immediately make one wonder who would read them and why. Mr Holland's mahogany desk was of corresponding proportions. It lay angle-wise in one corner so that the light from the French window shone over his left shoulder. A beam from the late afternoon sun caught that side of his face, illuminating one eye, the tiny criss-cross veins on his cheekbone and the brown-marked hand tapping impatiently on the polished surface of the desk. I realized that unless my reluctant host was cross-eyed I was the object of his gaze and the cause of his tattooing fingers. I dropped my eyes meekly, thinking it might be pleasing, and swallowed my further indignation at being left standing.

At last Cruikshank drew up a chair and introduced me. I received a brief nod.

"Well, young woman, what is it? If you've come about my house, you're wasting your time. It is not on the market, and that is final."

I felt my heart sink, and cast an inquiring glance at the estate agent. He made no attempt to get up from his chair so I stayed put, ready to fight if the need arose. He merely put the tips of his fingers together and sucked in his breath through his teeth. He appeared to be enjoying some secret situation.

"Mrs Matheson is the wife of a distinguished Russell Street officer," Cruikshank told Holland. "You may have heard of him."

The old man shot the agent a startled glance. "What are you driving at, Cruikshank? Are you trying to intimidate me? You are scarcely in the position—"

"No one is in a position to intimidate the police," Cruikshank retorted ambiguously.

Holland was silent. He looked me over frowningly. The old man seemed to be debating some point in his head. I found it a tense moment.

"Very well," he said abruptly. "You may look over the house. But I promise nothing, you understand that?"

As the estate agent rose with me, Mr Holland added quickly: "A word with you, Cruikshank. My sister will show you through the Dower House, Mrs Matheson. Go along the passage to the east wing. You'll find Mrs Mulqueen there. Tell her I sent you."

IV

Dismissed as though I was a prospective housemaid he had been interviewing and then sent to the kitchen for further instructions, I wondered at the airy way in which James Holland permitted a strange female to wander unescorted through his immense home. Either he presumed that I was not the type to steal the spoons, or else his revenge would be so dire in any such instance that the punishment would more than fit the crime and therefore afford him greater gratification.

It was not to be the last time that I made a solitary journey through the Hall. Each one was to bring a stronger feeling that all was not well there. On every occasion there was some incident to support the feeling. That day it was a door ever so slightly ajar.

Someone had eased it a crack so as to peer into the passage, and then at my approach had fled, not willing to risk their surveillance being discovered by the sound of the latch going into place. It could have been one of the servants, curious as to who I was, yet timid in case I was an important visitor. But I know now that I had been watched right from the start.

I pushed the door wider and walked in. There was no one there. I paused, not knowing what to do next. I had hoped to find someone who could direct me to Mrs Mulqueen. I had been walking in an easterly direction for some time, but the lady remained elusive. I moved across the room to an inner door, and looked into a bed-room. Beyond it, through an archway, was a tiled bathroom. A tidy little suite. Then the thought struck me that this must be the east wing.

I cleared my throat loudly.

"Is there anyone in?" I called. "Mrs Mulqueen?"

There was no reply. I retreated to the passage and hesitated on the threshold. Time was passing, and I had no desire to view what might prove to be my future home in the half-dark. My abstracted gaze wandered over the sitting-room.

It was a deeply carpeted and luxurious room, fitted with many fine pieces of furniture. There was perhaps a propensity to over-decoration. Dresden figures and Lalique vases stood daintily on the dado above the countless paintings and portraits hanging at fre-quent intervals along the satin-striped walls.

One of these pictures caught my wandering gaze. At first glance it looked like a framed newspaper cutting. Then I realized that the picture proper was facing inwards. I went forward with what John described later as my inexcusable meddling to straighten it. The de-sire was far from me to start interfering where it was none of my concern, but I was curious to see why that picture was deliberately turned to face the wall.

Something flickered in the glass of a neighbouring portrait. I swung round, my arm dropping stupidly to my side, embarrassed and more than half annoyed at being caught so.

A girl of about my own age stood in the doorway. I surprised a rather speculative look before she smiled, baring an expanse of pale pink gum above her small teeth. She seemed disposed to be friendly, although she must have seen my abortive movement to the picture on the wall.

"Mrs Matheson? I am Ursula Mulqueen. Uncle James told me to find you. Mother is out, so I am to show you over the Dower House."

My mind took in this precise little speech while my eyes were noting the dark hair wound into cylindrical curls over the shoulders and the complete lack of make-up. With these went a sweet girlish manner that was as out of date as Miss Mulqueen's dress. It was a shade saccharine, and girlishness never did sit well on a mature figure.

"This is the east wing, isn't it?" I asked lamely. "I couldn't find anyone to direct me."

Again that considering look behind the wholesome façade.

"Yes, these are Mother's rooms. This used to be my bedroom next door until recently. Uncle James permitted me to furnish one upstairs. It's all in vieux rose. I love pink, don't you?"

Ursula Mulqueen tripped down the passage ahead of me.

"We can go through the conservatory door. It will be quicker. Just follow me, Mrs Matheson, and you won't get lost again." A playful laugh accompanied this, but I was sensitive enough to catch a certain significance in her words.

"Are you looking for some place to live, Mrs Matheson? But of course you are. What a silly question to ask! You're lucky Uncle James is letting you visit the Dower. He doesn't often do that. But he won't let you have it, you know. He never does. He was keeping it for Jim. I don't think poor Uncle James realizes yet about him. It was so sudden. Flying his plane and then crashing for no reason at all. It was terribly sad. Poor, dear Yvonne—mind the path, Mrs Matheson. Flags are pretty, aren't they? Especially with the sweet little flowers popping up here and there between them. But they can be slippery."

Ursula Mulqueen chatted on aimlessly as she led the way. The flagged path from the house developed presently into a narrow track which wandered in and out of thickly growing beech, poplar and oak trees. The effect of this artificial spinney was pretty, but the going was rather tedious. More than once I stumbled over a stunted growth from a gum tree which had been cut down to make way for James Holland's arboretum.

After a lot of unnecessary meandering of the path, we came out of the wood on a slight rise.

"There!" said my guide, pointing to the house below us. It was placed well back from the road amid a thousand shrubs. "Isn't it enchanting? Uncle James copied it from an Elizabethan cottage in England. Do say it is perfectly sweet. They all do. I wish it was mine. It might be too, if—" she broke off, and ran down the hill, blushing like the mid-Victorian maiden she aped.

The track continued alongside a hedge which served as a boundary for one side of the Dower House garden, and from thence to the road via a stile. Ursula Mulqueen waited for me on the top step.

"I love running, don't you?" she asked breathlessly.

"Sometimes," I replied shortly. I was in no mood to be challenged to a race to the gate of the Dower House. My companion was just as likely to offer it. I felt I was being led up the garden path both literally and metaphorically, and tried to stem the girlish prattle.

"See here, Miss Mulqueen. If what you say is correct and your uncle has no intention of selling this house, there is not much point in your wasting your time taking me over it."

"Oh, but you must see it," she insisted. "Uncle James doesn't often permit people through the Dower."

I said rather tartly: "I suppose it doesn't matter wasting my time."

Ursula Mulqueen widened her ingenuous stare.

"But you wouldn't be, dear Mrs Matheson. I can assure you that everyone who has seen it has come away quite thrilled. I remember a leading city architect describing it to Mother as an architect's dream come to life. Come along in."

"There are such things as nightmares," I murmured, following.

The interior of the Dower House was as pretentious and artificial as its name and my first glimpse of it had promised. All the more so because of its newness and unlived-in atmosphere. At least Holland Hall had had some years in which to lose its raw appearance. There were black beams and diamond-paned casement windows galore. The attempt at an Elizabethan aura clashed absurdly with various up-to-the-minute fittings.

I moved around the house, mentally adjusting our modern furniture within this Elizabethan solecism. I still had hopes, despite Ursula Mulqueen's parroted opinion on the matter, that Uncle James and I would do business together.

"The garden is in remarkably good order." I was surveying the terraced slope and row of golden poplars from the room I had visualized as John's study.

"It is mostly my father's work," Ursula Mulqueen told me. "Gardening is his hobby when he is not managing the home farm for Uncle James. He and Ames are always planning new landscapes. Not that Ames gets much time either."

"I should think that in running a big place like the Hall no one would have any free time."

"We all have our own little jobs to do," she replied tritely.

"What do you do?" I asked, before I could stop myself.

"I help Mother. Arrange the flowers and things like that. I am always busy."

"Incredible!" I murmured. "I didn't believe there was such a person left. Don't you ever want to get out into the big world? Carve yourself a career or do something?"

"Uncle James says that the only career for a woman in our station of life is marriage," Ursula Mulqueen stated in all seriousness.

"But how are you to achieve that sublime state if you don't get out?"

"Uncle James arranges everything. He always does. He has remarkable executive powers. I have heard Mother say so."

"He seems to be a remarkable man," I said, losing interest. The girl hadn't an original idea in her head. Every word she spoke seemed to be quoted from someone else.

I followed my guide back to the Hall, lending but half an ear to her prattle on the manifold remarkable qualities of her Uncle James.

Perhaps my slight attention was enough to absorb what Ursula Mulqueen told me that late afternoon last autumn. I was to hear and form many opinions on the character of James Holland, but Ursula's reading of him as a romantic figure has stuck in my mind to this day. She may have been sincere when she described him as such. I cannot yet be sure. The girl was and still is a complete enigma to me.

As far as I can remember, separating the facts from the loquacious mist in which Ursula Mulqueen shrouded her remarks, it was James Holland's own uncle who first settled in Australia. Like some of the other piratical pioneers of his time, he obtained vast areas of property for the proverbial song. These he bequeathed to his nephew and heir together with his own ruthlessness and sublime snobbery. I gathered, from certain reverent hints Ursula let drop, that the family was descended from a famous English house. It was considered an established fact that the cynical, brilliant Charles James Fox held an important place in the family tree.

James Holland's way of life was based on the ambition to establish a class parallel to, if not the same as, the landed gentry of the home country. Hence the size of Holland Hall, out of all proportion to his needs and those who lived with him. The lodge and the crouching lions on the stone pillars flanking the gates were a typical manifestation of his ambition. Then there was the picture gallery in the house itself, containing some very bad specimens of portrait painting. I learned later that ironically enough the only picture worth looking at was a small water-colour of an Australian bush scene. There had also been some attempts to form a local hunt, but without success. The foxes which had been imported for this pastime now raided the poultry farm, much to the disgust of Ursula's father.

Ursula's story sounded absurd to me. Nevertheless it was quite true. James Holland had both the money and the influence with which to indulge his whims. Everything was on his side but one important factor. And that was time.

When Holland Hall was built as a pseudo-country residence, it had not been reckoned on the city spreading into such far-reaching suburbs. Bit by bit the distance between the Hall and town was being bridged by small, modern houses. Whether Mr Holland liked it or not Middleburn was just another suburb of Melbourne, in spite of its isolation and air of a country village.

So far James Holland had managed to keep Middleburn at bay. He owned acres of land on either side and opposite the Hall. By dint of turning part of these into public golf links and opening his artificial wood to the public at certain times for charitable purposes, he had managed to block the local Council's demands that he should sell some of it. The vast open paddocks that isolated the Hall had been given over to pasture for cows (he owned the local dairy) and sheep from some of his drought-stricken properties in the north.

In Middleburn itself, he was landlord to the greater percentage of the shops and such houses as were not privately owned. Even the tradesmen bought their supplies from the home farm which was situated another mile along the road. Thus Mr Holland held a tight grip on the village and its inhabitants. He was the Squire. They were his tenants.

V

It was growing quite dark in the wood; and late, for I could feel that bite in the air which came as soon as the sun touched the horizon. Through the trees I caught a glimpse now and then of the white tower of the Hall. A splendid view of the whole countryside could be obtained from it, as I discovered later. It was an ideal position from which to follow a person's movements around the estate.

The tower room suddenly flashed into light and was as abruptly darkened, as though someone had pressed the switch and then realized that they could be seen through the swiftly falling dusk for miles around.

I poked Ursula Mulqueen in the back.

"Did you see the light in the tower? Look! There it is again."

"How extraordinary!" exclaimed my companion. "It makes the tower look like a lighthouse; as if it was signalling."

I cast a sharp glance in Ursula's direction, but her face was now only a white blur in the gloom. She had taken the words right out of my mouth.

Ursula went on a shade too quickly: "Are you going back to town by train? I'll look up the timetable for you when we get in."

Keeping one eye on the tower for any repetition of the signalling, I picked my way carefully along the flagged walk to the conservatory.

We entered the front hall from behind the stairs just as a woman dressed in trailing black lace was descending. She paused, leaning over the bannister.

"Is that you, Ursie? Where have you been? I have been looking all over the house for you."

The voice was fond, playful, but I did not like it. There was an underlying tone of peevishness.

Ursula went to the foot of the stairs. "Uncle James asked me to take Mrs Matheson over to the Dower House. I'm afraid poor Mrs Matheson has fallen in love with it. I feel so sorry for her. Did you want me for something, Mother?"

Mrs Mulqueen turned her smile in my direction. It was not reflected in her wide, bland eyes. I received a gracious nod which made me feel like the prospective housemaid once more.

"I'll take care of Mrs Matheson, dear. Run up and have your bath. I've laid out the white frock. I'll be up later to tie your sash nicely. The Quirks are dining, you know. And dear—"

"Yes, Mother?"

"Don't run off like that again, without telling me where you are going. I was quite worried."

Ursula paused on the same step as her mother. Watching them from the foot of the stairs, I glimpsed a certain challenge in her stance.

She said quietly: "I couldn't find you, Mother."

They stared at each other for a moment. Mrs Mulqueen turned aside, laughing gently.

"These young girls, Mrs Matheson," she said, throwing out her hands, "so independent! Come with me." She drew me along the hall. "So you liked the Dower. Enchanting place, isn't it? Quite a treat to see a house built in such good taste." She patted my arm. "You shouldn't have become so excited. I tell James he is quite cruel letting you young girls through it. But it really is frightfully amusing seeing you get thrilled with it and then James refusing to sell. You should hear James tell stories of the tearful interviews he has had. He has such a sense of humour."

"The same sense of fun boys have when they pull flies' wings off," I agreed, pausing with her outside the door of James Holland's study.

"Oh dear!" Mrs Mulqueen said. "I forgot Yvonne was with James. We will have to wait. It would never do to interrupt. Sit down, Mrs Matheson."

I did so, but Mrs Mulqueen stood as near to the study door as she could.

"Tell me all about yourself," she requested without interest. Voices rose and fell in the study. I could hear Yvonne Holland sobbing.

"I do wish dear Yvonne would learn to control herself. We Hollands know how to disguise our emotions. Lack of control is so ill-bred, don't you think so, Mrs Matheson? But of course poor Yvonne hasn't had a chance. Good breeding is innate, I always say."

I stood up.

"What are you going to do?" Mrs Mulqueen asked sharply.

"Nothing," I replied, and sat down again. "Couldn't you stop your brother bullying that young girl?"

"You mustn't worry about Yvonne. She just doesn't understand James. She has no idea how to handle him. Not like Ursie, now. So sweet and pliable. James just dotes on my little girl."

I sat helpless. Bits of incoherent conversation escaped. But only one sentence came clearly through the study door. Yvonne—on a high, hysterical note—sobbed out: "You child-murderer! I could kill you for it!"

There were some short ugly sounds and the sobbing terminated abruptly. I got up quickly. Mrs Mulqueen put her hand on my arm. When she smiled there was a sudden striking resemblance to her brother. The door of the study opened and Yvonne Holland rushed out, one hand across her face.

James Holland stood in the middle of the room. The heavy crimson hangings were drawn across the windows. A standard lamp was all that lighted the room.

"Come in, Mrs Matheson," he said, and went back to his desk. "Sit down. You need not stay, Elizabeth."

Mrs Mulqueen glanced along the hall before entering.

"James, why don't you send her away? She doesn't belong here. She never will be a Holland. Let her go."

Holland picked up a letter from his desk and scanned it without expression. "She was my son's wife. Her child is a Holland. One day he will take my place here. Yvonne has responsibilities. She must be taught to realize them." He put the letter down and looked at me. "You saw the Dower and like it, Mrs Matheson?"

"I think your house would be most suitable for us. I suppose you wouldn't consider—"

Mrs Mulqueen broke in with her soft laugh. It was an artificial sound, like an amateur on the stage. A series of descending "ha-has."

"I warned you not to become fond of the Dower," she said, wagging one finger at me. "My brother has no intention of selling it, have you, James?"

Holland spoke slowly without taking his eyes from the letter on his desk. "I'll let the Dower House to you, Mrs Matheson."

"Our idea is to buy a house, not to rent one," I said, and got to my feet.

Holland surveyed me with surprise. "You refuse my offer?"

"I do," I replied boldly. "Relations between landlord and tenant are always insecure. I wouldn't trust you, Mr Holland."

Mrs Mulqueen gasped.

"Well, really!" she began. Holland silenced her.

"You are a very forthright young woman," he observed. "Suppose I offer you an option of buying the Dower in—shall we say—six months' time?"

"James," Elizabeth Mulqueen said in a plaintive voice. He glanced at her, an ironic gleam in his eye.

"You wouldn't like to have the police for neighbours, Elizabeth? Or were you expecting me to give the Dower to you?"

"It is your house, James," Mrs Mulqueen answered brightly.

"I accept your offer," I said, adding with caution, "providing you put it in writing."

He scribbled on a sheet of paper and pushed it across the desk. "My solicitors' address. Your husband may contact them. Braithwaite will arrange the details of our agreement. Good night, Mrs Matheson."

A thought occurred to me. "Mr Cruikshank. Will I let him know of your decision?"

There was a slight pause.

"You need not concern yourself with Cruikshank," Holland said shortly. "Elizabeth, show Mrs Matheson out."

Although he did not get up from his desk I felt moved to say: "Thank you for your generosity, Mr Holland. You cannot know what this means to us. Good night."

I did not know then about the estate agent, Arthur Cruikshank. Even if I had, I doubt whether I would have cared.

I had found a house.

CHAPTER TWO

I

Mr Cruikshank had disappeared. He had walked out of Holland Hall, down the gravelled driveway, and vanished into thin air.

I did not hear of it until some time later. Inquiries as to his whereabouts were not started for several days after the actual disappearance. Cruikshank's sister, Maud, set the ball rolling. She went to the local police station and told Sergeant Billings that her brother had not been at the shop since late afternoon on a certain date. She had last seen him in the company of a smartly dressed young woman, who might be described as fair and rather tall, but who had no distinguishing marks except perhaps an unusually square jaw.

Sergeant Billings took down all her information in a notebook with a blunt pencil moistened by his tongue, and since Miss Cruikshank seemed calm enough and not at all upset by her brother's likely fate, offered no sympathy. He told her she would be notified as to police action during the course of the next few days. He then put in an official report to send to Russell Street Headquarters, where the matter reached John's ears. Not that he had anything to do with mere disappearances. Nothing less than a juicy murder could command his attention.

One of his colleagues at Russell Street, recalling that we had recently moved to Middleburn, brought the official report to him as a matter of interest. I do not know whether John let out then that I was the square-jawed young woman last seen with the estate agent, but he must have been unmercifully chaffed before the whole case was broken.

The way in which John passed on the information was typical of him. It was the night we were hanging the curtains in the study. I was standing back and debating whether or not to have a valance of figured chintz to match the side drapes when I caught his eyes fixed on me. I looked at him inquiringly.

"Yes, you have got one," he remarked meditatively. I was puzzled and glanced back at the curtains.

"No, don't turn away. Show me your chin again. Profile and then full face."

I moved my head obediently. "Yes, I would definitely say it was square. Has anyone remarked on it before?"

"Dozens. What on earth are you talking about?"

He went on musingly. "Fair hair. Tall. Do you dress smartly, my pet?"

"I try to. What is this?"

"Weight about ten stone?"

"Nine," I corrected with some indignation. "Why this police description? Am I wanted for something?"

John began to fill a pipe with an air of deliberation. He seemed amused.

"Yes and no. When I say yes—"

"You sound like my friend the estate agent," I interrupted. "I told you about him. He always looks at a question from both sides. Tedious when you are in a hurry for an answer."

"It's strange you should mention him," John said.

"And why, pray?"

"A report came in at Headquarters that he has disappeared."

"Has he?" I asked without much interest. "But what has he got to do with me?"

John's grin broadened considerably. "Only that he was last seen in the company of a young woman answering accurately to your description. You haven't been indulging in a spot of kidnapping, have you, Maggie?"

"Certainly not. I haven't seen the man since that day he took me to the Hall."

"Which is precisely the day and time he vanished."

"What!" I exclaimed incredulously. "If this is a joke, I think your idea of humour is feeble."

"It's no joke, I can assure you. Think of my career. Wife of C.I.D. man wanted for police interrogation. No good, Maggie."

"Then stop grinning like a gargoyle. Am I likely to be questioned?"

"The interrogation is about to commence," John said, taking up his position behind the desk. "I promised Billings, who is in charge here at Middleburn, I'd find out what you know. So you have nothing to fear."

"I'm not afraid," I said, eyeing him carefully withal. "Fire your questions. After all, you did it once before. And that was a case of murder, not kidnapping. Or am I supposed to have murdered Cruikshank?"

John winced a little. I knew I had touched a raw spot and sat down on his knee in penitence.

"That was mean," I admitted, tucking my head under his chin. "On with the questions."

John shifted my elbow out of his ribs and blew the top of my hair from his face.

"This is the first time I have cross-examined anyone sitting on my lap."

"I should hope that you have neither cross-examined nor done anything else," I retorted.

"Sit up, Maggie. It is a disadvantage not being able to see the witness's face."

"No fear. I'm comfortable as I am. What do you want to know?"

"This is not the way to conduct an inquiry," said John resignedly. "Just tell me how you came to be with Cruikshank, how and where you left him and at what time. As accurately as you can."

"You know how. He took me up to the Hall to see Mr Holland."

"Of course I know, but Sergeant Billings doesn't. You'd better pretend I'm him."

This struck me as funny.

"If you start giggling, Maggie, I'll push you off and make you sit opposite to me in proper questioning style."

I related all I did that afternoon with the estate agent and how I had left him alone with Mr Holland in the latter's study while Ursula Mulqueen took me over to the Dower.

"Just a minute," John interrupted. "Why didn't Cruikshank go with you? Isn't it customary for the agent to accompany the prospective tenant over a house?"

"He stopped to speak to Mr Holland."

"Did he stay of his own accord or was it at Mr Holland's request?"

"Mr Holland's, I fancy. He said something about wanting to have a word with him."

"How did Holland sound?"

I thought for a minute. "Curt. He seemed annoyed Cruikshank had not answered an earlier summons."

"What time was this?"

"Half-past four-ish. I noticed a tea tray on Mr Holland's desk. I must have been the best part of an hour with Ursula by the time we walked through the wood, looked at the house and returned. I remember catching a train from Middleburn about a quarter to six."

"About four-thirty," John nodded in approval. "And Cruikshank wasn't there when you got back?"

"No. Mr Holland was alone in the study. We met Ursula's mother in the passage. She took me along."

"Did Mr Holland make any comment about Cruikshank?"

Again I gave John's question some thought.

"I can't quite remember. I did ask if I should get in touch with Cruikshank to tell him about taking the house, but the Squire said: 'No. I'll fix it up with him; just see my solicitors.' I think that was all."

"Cruikshank didn't say where he was going after he left the Hall? Not waiting to see you was odd."

"So I thought at the time. Evidently the business was not to go through the agent at all. We pay a monthly cheque to Braithwaite, don't we?"

"Very odd," John said again, frowning. "I wonder why Holland took it out of the agent's hands."

"Perhaps things are getting tight and he can't afford a shilling in the pound to an agent," I suggested.

"You can guarantee Braithwaite doesn't do it for nothing. No, there's something unusual there. Who else was in the house when you left Cruikshank and Holland together?"

"Yvonne was. I presume Mrs Mulqueen was too. She came down from upstairs as Ursula and I came in. I don't know the domestic arrangements of the Hall, but I suppose someone was in the kitchen. There was going to be a dinner party that night."

"I'll suggest to Sergeant Billings to check up on them. What was your impression of Cruikshank when you left him? Was he frightened or ill-at-ease?"

I sat up with a jolt. "You're not thinking Mr Holland killed him and buried him in the cellar, are you?"

"Don't be silly," John said severely. "These are routine questions. You always ask how the vanished seemed when seen last. He might have lost his memory or something."

I sank back again. "Well, he certainly didn't appear frightened or embarrassed. On the way up, he was confident he could do something for us in regard to the Dower. I think Cruikshank considered himself master of the situation. But then, he seems the type of person who always does."

"That was definitely the last you saw of Cruikshank, Maggie?" John's voice was serious.

"You're not doubting my word, I hope," I said indignantly. "I'd like to get my hands on the person who dragged me into this."

"That should be easy. It was Miss Maud Cruikshank."

II

The oddest part of Mr Cruikshank's disappearance was the tardy way in which his sister went to the police. She maintained over and over again that Arthur was in the habit of going away for a couple of days at a time without any notice; although, as a rule, a note came in the mail explaining his absence and announcing his probable return. But as a letter did not come, and a quick search revealed that none of his clothes were missing, she became concerned.

I am repeating her statement word for word. Personally I didn't believe a word of it, and still don't. I think she guessed what was afoot even then and that continuous inquiries for Mr Cruikshank from customers at the shop goaded her into going to the police.

If Miss Cruikshank could describe my appearance so accurately, surely she must have recognized me that day I called into the shop. If she was so concerned about her brother, she would have commenced her own inquiries then and there. To this Miss Cruikshank replied that working had taken her mind off the subject. It was a feeble excuse. I was able to push my point by recalling a conversation between her and a customer wandering about the bookshelves in search of a light romance.

"*Desert Love!*" exclaimed this discriminating reader. "Have I read it, Miss Cruikshank?"

"I'll check up with your card, Mrs Bellamy."

"Please do. I seem to remember the name. About sheiks and slaves. Where is Mr Cruikshank? He would know whether I have had it."

Miss Cruikshank left me to run through a tray of index cards.

"He was called away for a few days. I expect him home any time now," she said, without looking up.

The Bellamy woman, whom I had been regarding with an absent-minded interest—I had seen her somewhere before—made a sound of impatience and reached down *Love in the Starlight*.

"So hard to find something I haven't read," she murmured.

I agreed amiably, and pointed out a scarcely marked copy of *The Good Companions* tucked away in a corner.

"It's fairly old, but it bears reading several times."

"Oh, *The Good Companions*. Yes, I saw the picture years ago. I got the book afterwards, of course, but it seemed so long that I— why, Maggie Byrnes! Fancy running into you after all this time."

A swift, all-enveloping glance took in my hair-do, clothes and figure.

"You remember me, of course. It must be four years—no, five. What are you doing in this part of the world? Our sweet little Middleburn. You are married, of course."

Another rapid look was shot over me.

"Very much so," I replied, recalling Mrs Bellamy's face. The use of superfluous phrases had placed her. She had worked in the Trunk Exchange for a while, as dunderhead a telephonist as anyone could hope to hear. In those days her name was Connie Rowe.

"Just wait a minute until Miss Cruikshank stamps this book, Maggie. We'll have a nice long chat while we shop. I've got Peter outside."

"And I've got Tony," I said, not to be outdone.

"Your son? How delightful! I am just dying to—yes, this one, please, Miss Cruikshank. No return. When will Mr Cruikshank be back? I want to see him most urgently; or rather my husband does."

"I expect him home tomorrow, Mrs Bellamy."

"That's what she said two days ago," Connie whispered, pushing me out the door. "I do believe he has gone into hiding or something. Harold is positively furious. Do you know the man has been systematically robbing us for years? Is this your little boy?"

She bent down in front of the pusher. Tony gave her that cruel speculative stare children do to strangers.

"My dear, the image of you, of course. Where is my Peter? Peter," she called. "Oh, there he is. At the butcher's shop as usual. Come here, you bad boy."

Peter proved to be not as I had anticipated, a small boy, but a cheeky black-and-white terrier. I had been fully prepared to return the compliment, and say how like he was to Connie.

I remarked rather weakly: "What a nice little dog."

"He's an angel," Connie announced, giving him a squeeze. "Such a comfort to me. But his nose will be out of joint soon, won't it, Peter boy? Poor little pet. You won't be too jealous, will you, darling? Now jump down and let Mummy Bellamy get on with her shopping. In here, Maggie. I want to pick up some sandwiches. Ham, of course. My dear, I positively crave for anything in the pork line. My own mother was just the same. Can I tie Peter to your pusher?"

"No," I said firmly, visualizing her beastly dog dragging Tony and pusher into the middle of High Street. "What about that post?"

"Yes, that will do. You are fussy, Maggie."

I followed her into the shop. A large parcel of sandwiches was passed over the counter.

"Not all for Mummy Bellamy," Connie coyly assured me. "It is my turn at the Community Centre today. Afternoon tea, you know. You must come with me."

I bought some bacon for breakfast and immediately regretted it, when Connie remarked in her high-pitched voice: "How frightfully coincidental!"

"My dear," she confided, as we left the delicatessen, "I've got so much to tell you, I hardly know where to begin. Where are you living, Maggie?"

"At a place called the Dower House. We are hoping to change the pretentious title after six months. At the moment it belongs to the Squire of Middleburn."

"The Squire? Oh, you mean Mr Holland, of course. Isn't he too awesome? Those black bars of eyebrows with that white hair. We all loathe him in Middleburn. The sooner he passes away the happier a lot of people will be. Fancy you getting the Dower! I heard he would never let it go, even after his son's accident. But," said Connie, pausing to take breath, "I don't know if I'd call you lucky, Maggie."

"I believe I am in these times," I replied, steering the pusher carefully to avoid Peter's jerking leash.

"Well, Maggie"—Connie spoke in that tone of voice people use when they are a little envious of another's possessions—"all I can say is that you've walked slap-bang into trouble. I hope you won't regret it."

"Why do you say that?" I asked quickly. I was sensitive to another's opinion regarding our choice of abode, although I could not say why. I think I must have been uneasy about our connection with Holland Hall from the start.

"I don't quite know," Connie confessed, after a moment's thought. "I just feel trouble, that's all. Harold says I am psychic. That household simply reeks of mystery. Such a collection of incompatibles, you know. But there! You're used to that sort of thing, aren't you, Maggie? Weren't you mixed up in that funny business at the Exchange a few years back?"

"Very little," I replied shortly, determined that Connie and everyone else would learn nothing about "that funny business" from me. It brought back too many bitter memories.

Connie stopped and eyed me for a minute. "I would love to know exactly—" she began.

I shook my head. "Nothing doing."

"And you married the policeman who solved the case! How terribly romantic. You must lead an exciting life."

"Quite humdrum," I assured her. "Am I really bidden to the Community Centre?"

Connie was easy to divert. "My dear, I insist. The other lasses will be thrilled to meet you. We are a frightfully enthusiastic organization. Lectures, art classes, dramatics. We foster a spirit of culture in Middleburn, you know. Such fun!"

"It sounds hilarious," I said, as Connie swept me along to a large hall set back from the street and surrounded by lawns and trees.

"Does the Squire own this too?" I asked, observing the letter H wrought in stone above the main door.

"Maggie, you can't turn round in Middleburn without bumping into Mr Holland. Sometimes it is positively terrifying. Don't say I didn't warn you if he comes to put pressure on you. I can see his idea, of course."

"What idea?"

"Wait and see," Connie said mysteriously. "Just remember I warned you. Now, are we ready? Leave Tony out here with the other children. He will be well looked after."

There was a considerable amount of noise issuing forth from the hall. Connie sailed in, nodding and smiling as she led me past rows of knitting women and up a short flight of steps to the stage. I faced a battery of critical feminine eyes as the chatter broke off abruptly. Connie made straight for the executives' table, dragging me by the hand.

"Brenda, I am most fearfully sorry for being late. I met an old friend. Mrs Gurney, Maggie," and I was introduced to the president of the Community Centre, who surveyed me with a sympathetic twinkle in her friendly gaze.

"Connie, must you?" I murmured, as she reached over and rang the handbell on the president's table.

"Girls," she announced to the room at large. "An asset to Middleburn. May I introduce Mrs—Maggie, what is your name again?"

"Matheson," I muttered, looking around for a way of escape. I noticed a girl sitting at the end of the official table. Her head was bent, but she looked familiar.

"Maggie, our secretary." I bowed to a stolid-looking woman in horn-rimmed glasses. She took them off, nodded and replaced them on the bridge of her nose. "And Mrs Holland at the end of the table."

Yvonne Holland was gazing at me intensely now. She looked smaller and thinner when seated. Her hand plucked at the buttons of her mustard tweed jacket.

"Brenda," Connie ran on. "Maggie must give us a lecture on crime. She knows such a lot about murders and things. Her husband, you know. I do think it most romantic to be married to a super-sleuth. Does he carry a gun, Maggie?"

Mrs Gurney said: "Connie, do make the tea. We are all dying of thirst. Sit down and relax, Mrs Matheson. We really are nice people."

"I felt like a Christian thrown to the lions," I declared, sitting angle-wise so that I could see Yvonne Holland. She had recognized me.

"Will you really give us a talk on crime?" Mrs Gurney asked, her eyes dancing.

"Certainly not."

"Such a pity. A lot of scope for murders here."

I said with feeling: "Connie never knew how close to death she was."

"Oh, dear!" Brenda Gurney ejaculated suddenly. "I'm afraid you're in for something."

"What now?" I asked in resignation.

"Our dramatic coach, Mrs Parkes. I saw Connie talking to her. Bear up. All for Middleburn culture, you know. Hullo, Marion, wherefore art thou?"

A stout female, clad in a sort of Grecian tunic, took up a position in front of me.

"Please don't abuse Shakespeare, Brenda," she admonished in a sonorous voice. "I find it in very poor taste. If you want to quote, make it quite clear you are doing so." She placed the palms of her hands firmly on the table. "Now, Mrs Matheson, can you act?"

I blinked up at the large-chinned face bending over me.

"I run the dramatic side of our organization," she explained, as Mrs Gurney laughingly left me in her clutches. "Every year we do either scenes from Shakespeare or a farce. It is Shakespeare's turn this year. You must be in it. I am so short of tall girls for the male parts."

"I don't think I'd be any good," I said, watching Yvonne Holland half-rise and then sit down again, as though she had changed her mind.

"Nonsense!" Mrs Parkes said vigorously. "With your background of drama you will be just the thing. Connie said you were a detective or something before you got married. All you have to do is to be perfectly natural in your rôle. As Shakespeare says, 'All the world's a stage.' Now what sort of part would you like?"

"A murderer," I said.

"A murderer? Now let me see. Yes, we are doing a scene from *Richard III.* I should be able to fit you in nicely. It is such a pleasure to find someone so enthusiastic. Not like dear Brenda. She was always making fun at rehearsals. President or no, I had to get her to resign from the dramatic society. It really caused quite—"

"Excuse me," I said, getting up. Yvonne Holland had slipped away from the official table; under cover of serving the afternoon tea, she was making for the back of the hall. I followed her. She sat down near the door, holding her cup aslant so that the tea spilled into the saucer, soaking one of Connie's ham sandwiches.

"I couldn't stand any more either," I told her, as I sat down beside her. "Is it always so grim?"

"I don't have to come often," she replied hesitantly. "Usually Mrs Mulqueen or Ursula does. But Mr Holland wanted me to come today. He is closing this hall," she went on jerkily, dropping her lashes over sudden tears. "I had to tell them. It was so awful standing up in front of them all. I'm sure they thought it was my fault."

"He gave you the unpleasant task of breaking the news on purpose?" I queried.

The girl nodded.

The handbell on the table was rung again and again and the stolid-looking woman in the horn-rimmed glasses stood up and started to rattle off a quantity of notices of future activities.

"Closing this place doesn't seem to have mattered much," I observed.

The secretary on the stage took off her glasses and peered down to where we were sitting. "If everyone kindly listened to the announcements maybe I wouldn't have to repeat myself." She replaced her glasses and went on with the notices.

"Let's get out of here," I suggested to Yvonne.

"I can't," she whispered back. "Mr Holland—"

"Rot," I said, pulling her up.

The horn-rimmed secretary paused again.

"She has just remembered she left the gas on," I explained, pushing Yvonne out the door.

"Spare me from women in bulk," I said, when safely outside.

We strolled over the grass together. Groups of children were playing among the garden seats under the trees. Tony was having toys snatched from him by a flaxen-haired little girl in a very short frock.

"Would you like to see my baby?" Yvonne asked shyly. "You didn't that day, did you? He is just over here."

"Who is that with the children? And why must she sit on the ground? She looks appalling."

"Miss Potts-Power," Yvonne answered, with a faint sparkle in her voice. "She is on the crèche committee. She loves children."

"And tells everyone so. I know the type."

I watched the dumpy girl on the lawn endeavouring to draw Tony onto her knee, one hand brushing back his hair in a disgusting fashion.

"What a darling little boy!" she cooed. "What is your name, my pet?"

The darling little boy smacked her hand away without ceremony and fled to my side.

"What is his name, Mrs Matheson?" Miss Potts-Power asked, advancing on her knees after him.

"Anthony John. I'm sorry he hit you, but he is rather shy. Not used to large gatherings, are you, Tony?"

I loosened the clutch on my leg. Tony retreated still further behind Baby Holland's pram. "He'll come round presently," I said. "Just leave him be."

"What a lovely name!" remarked Tony's pursuer idiotically. "Come here, Anthony, and we'll play gee-gees."

The horrible woman actually put the palms of her hands on the ground, presenting her fat behind invitingly. Tony, displaying a masterly sense of timing, dodged round the other side of the pram and back to the other children. Miss Potts-Power got up and tried desperately not to look hurt.

I felt it was for me to make up for Tony's lack of taste, and said hurriedly: "It is very good of you to play with the youngsters."

"Oh, but I love to," exclaimed Miss Potts-Power, trying to tidy her damp wisps of hair. "I simply adore children. It must be lovely to have a baby. If poor mother," she continued in a regretful tone, "wasn't an invalid and needed me, I would have got married and had dozens."

Yvonne took this statement seriously. She spoke in a low tense voice. "I wanted a lot of children too. If only—" She broke off and tried to hide her flushed face by bending over the baby. There was an awkward silence.

I was relieved to see Brenda Gurney coming across the lawn to meet us.

"Cowards, both of you," she declared pleasantly. "Yvonne, I am so sorry. We all understand. Most of us, anyway. I'm afraid Connie is after your blood. Here she is now."

Yvonne's hand went to the buttons of her jacket again.

Connie came up like a destroyer. "It is just too ridiculous for words. Yvonne, you must do something. What reason has Mr

Holland for closing the hall? Can you tell me that?"

"He didn't say, Connie," the girl stammered.

"You asked him, of course," Connie said scathingly. "Really, Yvonne, in an emergency like this you should assert yourself."

"Leave her alone," Mrs Gurney interposed good-naturedly. "Everything will turn out all right."

Connie swung to starboard. "It's all very well taking that attitude, Brenda, but I think you are to blame for Mr Holland's nastiness. Everyone could guess who you were taking off at Marion's auditions last week. That sugary little sneak—I know Ursula Mulqueen is related to you, Yvonne, and I'm sorry—must have told her mother."

"What did you do?" I asked, as Brenda Gurney listened to the tirade with an amused smile.

"Marion was playing up to Ursula Mulqueen, although she really is a good little actress. You'd be amazed. I couldn't stand the crawling, so when my turn came I gave an interpretation of her ladyship from the Hall among her villagers."

"Something will have to be done," Connie declared. She was becoming quite heated. "Something drastic." Her eye lighted on me.

"I must go," I said hurriedly, strapping Tony into his pusher. "I'll see you again some time, Connie. It has been a grand afternoon."

"My dear, so marvellous to have a distinguished detective living in this lawless district. Harold will be frightfully interested when I tell him. You'll be at Brenda's next week, of course. I'll see you then."

I was embarrassed and must have shown it. Mrs Gurney said in her tolerant, amused way: "Give me time, Connie. I haven't asked her yet. But you will come, won't you, Mrs Matheson? This day next week."

"I'd love to. Are you coming my way?" I asked Yvonne.

III

"Dear little things, aren't they?" I remarked, as we passed noisily through the village. Tony was tugging at his straps irritably and baby Holland kept up a continuous whimper in spite of his dummy.

The habitual scared-rabbit expression on Yvonne's face gave way to tenderness as she looked down at the pale little face of her son.

We began to climb up to Holland Hall. "You take Tony up the hill," I suggested. "I'll push your pram. What on earth possessed you to get such a heavy one?"

Her voice sounded bitter. "Mr Holland ordered it. It was the most expensive in the shop."

"You know," I remarked tentatively. "You shouldn't let those Hollands order your life for you all the time. Stand up for yourself a little."

She made no reply to this. She was staring down at Tony, who was very intrigued by the change of driver.

I went on, feeling my way carefully. "By the way, where is the local Health Centre? I haven't had Tony weighed for an age."

"In Mainbridge Road. It runs off from the street which goes down by the Post Office."

"Sounds fairly complicated. Perhaps you could come with me and show me the way. What day do you go?"

Yvonne replied stonily: "I don't go at all. Mr Holland doesn't like it."

"Why ever not? If you had a chat with the sister in charge it would probably make all the difference to this little fellow. Does he always cry like this?"

"No, only just lately. He's teething, Nurse says. She was my husband's nurse and knows a lot about babies. That is another reason why I don't visit the Health Centre." She finished rather defiantly, as though daring me to think her weak-willed.

"Your husband's nurse, eh? She must be fairly old."

"The Health Centre sister is not young."

"So you have been to the Health Centre," I said swiftly. "Why didn't you go back?"

"I've told you," she replied, becoming distressed. "Mr Holland doesn't like it. That one time I went there was a terrible row. I live in his house. I must do as he wishes."

"Even when it concerns your child's welfare? And talking about Jimmy, there is just one thing I have been wanting to do ever since I saw him."

I stopped the pram, jerking on the brake with my foot, and bent quickly. The dummy was lying slack in the child's mouth.

The pale lips did not close on to it as I gently unpinned the cord with which it was attached.

"Just this," I said, and threw the dummy with all my strength over the hedge into a fairway of the golf course.

Yvonne looked horrified. "You shouldn't have done that. Nurse will only get him another one. And it does quieten him."

"If she gets him another one it'll be your turn to play ball with it. Don't be a foolish girl. Dummies are senseless, unhealthy things. Now promise you'll take me to the Health Centre tomorrow. I'll call for you about three."

Yvonne glanced about her as though frightened someone might hear.

"Please don't come up to the house. Wait here at the gates."

"Then you'll come?"

"I may be able to slip out. Please don't be angry if I can't manage it. Thank you for wheeling the pram."

"Till tomorrow then?"

She nodded. I turned off smartly in case she changed her mind, and headed back to the village.

Middleburn had a neat little shopping centre devoid to date of any chain stores. I learned later that James Holland discouraged them. As he held mortgages over the majority of the shops, the entrance of any combine interest into the village would weaken his alarmingly big influence.

I established relations with a garrulous butcher and, by abrupt contrast, a taciturn grocer. The latter eyed me with suspicion when I followed up an explanation of our recent arrival in Middleburn by asking for sundry goods which were difficult to acquire. The fruiterer, however, greeted me by name. He dabbled in psychology, which had won him more custom than the other two greengrocers in High Street. He made it his business to learn the names and circumstances of newcomers to Middleburn. If he knew that the budget would not stand the largest apples, he whispered confidentially that the cheaper ones were a much better buy.

It seems ludicrous that such mundane matters should have been the cause of dragging me further into the web. And yet that is just what happened. If I had not been bent on consolidating my position with the tradespeople, I would never have chosen to cross the road at that particular moment. I would not have overheard those few words which were to make me waver in my determination to keep away from mysteries.

A big maroon car had slowed down in answer to a signal from the pavement. I paused on the road for a moment, waiting for it to park. The woman who had attracted the driver's attention pulled open the front door as I skirted the back of the car. I was sufficiently close to hear her say in a low, rapid voice: "If you don't do something very soon that child will die. It's murder!"

"I can do nothing," was the reply. "It is too dangerous. We can only wait."

The front wheels of Tony's pusher were on the pavement; the back ones and my feet were in the running water of the gutter. I gave the pusher a jerk which sent it up on the footpath and sauntered casually alongside the maroon car.

"Wait!" exclaimed the woman. "Don't you want to stop this horrible business?"

"Quiet," said the man urgently. "We will talk about it again. Get in."

I stopped fiddling with Tony's straps and glanced up. As the man leaned over to shut the door of the car his eyes met mine.

They looked puzzled for a moment, then troubled. He frowned, his hand moving over the dashboard uncertainly. The car started with a jolt. I watched it go down the street, driven by the unwelcome visitor I had seen bending over Yvonne Holland's baby at the Hall.

CHAPTER THREE

I

The telephone was ringing as I came in the gate of the Dower. I left Tony on the porch with a word of warning and hurried inside to answer it.

A pleasant masculine voice said: "Mrs Matheson? I have a message from your husband. He is delayed at the office and will not be home for dinner."

"Blast!" I said, thinking of the meal I had prepared. "Thanks very much."

"Just one moment, please," said the voice hurriedly.

"Yes?"

"Mr Holland sends his compliments. Will you and Inspector Matheson dine at the Hall next week?"

The invitation took my breath away. Partly because I had presumed the voice came from Russell Street.

"This is Ames speaking from the Hall," he announced, evidently guessing at my confusion. "You were out when Inspector Matheson rang. I promised to relay his message." The Dower House telephone was only an extension from the Hall.

Ames? The name was faintly familiar. Oh, yes, Mr Holland's general factotum; overseer, secretary, greenkeeper, butler and what have you. Ursula Mulqueen had told me about him. His father had served the Hollands in the same capacity until his retirement to the Lodge.

"Mr Holland wants us to dine with him," I repeated, playing for time.

"Yes, Mrs Matheson. Will Wednesday night suit you?"

I frowned at the wall.

"As far as I know now. But my husband is engaged on a case and might not be able to make it."

There was a pause before Ames spoke. "I will inform Mr Holland. I am sure he will understand. Cocktails are served at seven, Mrs Matheson." I heard the receiver being replaced.

I went back to the porch to bring Tony in for his meal. The phone rang again. Ames' voice was becoming familiar. This time he sounded apologetic.

"I forgot to mention, Mrs Matheson, that Mr Holland likes his guests to wear evening dress."

"We always do," I replied loftily, and took pleasure in ringing off first.

I moved about the house quickly. There was still a great deal of unpacking and arranging of furniture to be done. Ordinarily I would have welcomed the chance of John being out of the way to get it done. But that night I felt nervous. The odd creaks and reverberations, to which one becomes accustomed after a time, seemed unnatural and sinister to my ears. The silence was heavy. It made the noises sound muffled and furtive. A constant beat from the frogs in the creek and the hum of night insects reminded me of the isolated position of the Dower House. I kept Tony from bed for as long as his temper could stand it. His worn-out crying comforted me that lonely night, where it would have irritated me at another time.

In fact, I had the jitters so badly that I was compelled to put away the detective story I was reading at dinner. Even the radio was tuned into some gruesome play by Edgar Allan Poe. For a while I went bravely around the house, pulling down blinds and flooding the rooms with light. My dinner dishes were washed and dried with a clatter, but I did not open the kitchen door to put scraps in the garbage bin on the porch. An opossum in the roof, stirring before his midnight scampers, almost caused me to drop a stack of plates. I shook my fist at the ceiling, took a firm grip of myself and went into John's study to unpack a case of books.

It was this one small room, fourteen feet square, because it fitted the green carpet perfectly, which had reconciled John to the distance from town and the unreliable train service. The walls were lined with bookshelves and a gas fire had been neatly fitted opposite to the only sensible position to put a desk. This was in an alcove formed by windows facing three ways.

I crossed to them slowly and deliberately to draw the blinds, mindful that at least I had Tony for company. A mist had risen up from the creek at the back of the Dower property where the frogs still croaked incessantly. Somewhere above the mist the moon was shining, making the white trunks of the English trees in the wood slim and wraith-like, and illuminating the tower of the Hall. I forced myself to wait, watching it. I don't know why. Perhaps I was daring myself to be afraid if that mysterious light flashed from it again. I even counted up to twenty before I dropped the shade, and called myself a fool.

Kneeling beside the open case, I began to sort books. They were mainly technical tomes belonging to John, but there were a few novels of mine and a set of Shakespeare which had been a school prize. Turning over pages at random as I crouched there on the floor, something made me glance towards the door. It was closed against the draught, but I could have sworn a thread of cold air blew on my neck that I had not noticed before. Terrified, I watched the door handle, half expecting to see it slide around. I knew I was being absurd and tried to call lightly: "Is that you, darling?"

The heavy pressing silence dulled my words. Again I became conscious of the croaking of the frogs, monotonous and lonely.

"This will never do," I told myself severely, getting up from the floor and letting the lid of the case close with a bang.

I opened the door and went into the hall. At one end the porch light shining through the narrow windows flanking the front door made a pattern on the carpet. I watched it for a moment. It was quite still. At the far end of the passage a lamp was aglow just outside Tony's room.

He was breathing quietly. The nursery was full of the warmth and companionship of him. I leaned over the cot, wishing suddenly that he was twenty years older. It would have been good to remain

there with him, but I realized that once I gave in to this state of nerves I would never be happy alone again in the Dower House. Sounds and shadows became unheard and unheeded in John's solid, satisfying presence. I left Tony's room resolved to continue with the unpacking. With one hand on the doorknob, I shot a would-be careless glance down to the front door.

That glance developed into a fascinated stare. I stood clamped to the floor, the only moving thing about me an icy drop winding its way down my spine. The pattern on the carpet just inside the front door had altered. It was blurred by the shadow of a head and shoulders. I watched it, too frightened to move. A hand was passed slowly over the leadlight.

II

The doorbell rang briefly. Who would be calling on me at this hour? Whom did I know so well in Middleburn that they would call at all?

I approached a few paces, my eye falling on a stout walking stick in the hallstand. I gripped this more to gain in moral courage than with any other design and called firmly despite my knocking knees: "Who is it?"

My breath came quickly as I waited for a reply. "My name is Mulqueen," spoke a man's voice through the windows. "Is that Mrs Matheson? Can I come in?"

I ran down the remainder of the hall and took the chain off the door to admit the visitor. A short, ball-like man clad in a mackinaw jacket and a tweed cap stepped across the threshold. He had a pair of small twinkling eyes and a red tip to his nose.

"Hope I didn't frighten you," he shot at me. "Heard you were all alone and thought I'd pop in to see if everything was all right."

My relief made me garrulous.

"Not at all. Come into my husband's study. I didn't light a fire as I was by myself, but there is a gas jet. Here! Let me take your cap. And what about your jacket? It is so cold out. You might notice it more after the warm room."

The bright eyes regarded me shrewdly.

"Windy?"

I laughed. "Very. I read too many detective stories. In here. I have been trying to forget the strange noises by unpacking."

Ernest Mulqueen sat down on the edge of a chair and spread his hands to the fire. I found it hard to stifle a gasp at the sight of them.

He said: "Just as well you didn't see them before I introduced myself. Rabbits. I have a gin set in the wood for foxes. Go round this time every night to put the bunnies out of their agony. They will jump in, silly creatures." He scrubbed at his bloody hands with a still bloodier handkerchief. "Humane. You probably heard me."

I regarded him squeamishly. "I did hear some odd knocking coming from the direction of the wood. Do you—"

"That was me. The nearest tree. Instantaneous."

I made a mental resolve to pass by the wood in future. Ernest Mulqueen must have read my thoughts. He was a hearty, earthy little man, gifted with a keen perspicacity. Almost at once I wondered how he came to marry into the noble family of Holland, and still further how he begot a namby-pamby daughter like Ursula. She should have been a big-boned girl with useful hands: wholesome, not in the mid-Victorian sense, but rather like brown bread.

He reassured me regarding the results of his humaneness. "Quite off the beaten track. You won't see any muck."

"Gin?" I queried, puzzled.

"A trap," he explained. "I'm after that fox which is making a nuisance of itself on the poultry run. He's hiding out in the wood. Of all the crazy things the old man has ever done, importing a pair of foxes is the craziest. The only hunting people want to do round here is for houses." He broke off abruptly. "How do you like this house?"

"We were lucky to get it," I said carefully.

"Too right, you were! Never thought the old man would let it go out of the family, even after Jim's smash."

"What happened exactly?" I asked, tilting back my chair to reach the cigarettes on John's desk. I offered them to my visitor. "Not for me, thanks. I have a pipe if you don't mind the stink. Jim? No one seems to know. Took his plane up one fine day and it fell to bits, Jim with it. The old man was rather cut up." He drew on his pipe and said between puffs: "Tried his hardest to blame someone other than Jim. Apple of his eye, Jim was."

"Aren't all sons?" I said, rather sentimentally.

"Not like a Holland. You'd think they were the chosen people, the stuff that is spouted about ancestors and continuing the line. Suppose I shouldn't say that, the wife being one before I married her. But they do get your goat occasionally."

I could not think of any suitable comment to make so I let him ramble on. He was obviously finding relief in blowing off steam after breathing in the refined air of the Hall.

"Born and bred in the country, I was. The land is the only place for me. Can't stand this polite roguery that goes under the name of business. The old man would sell us all to make a shilling, and then turn round and gas about upholding the prestige of the family. What family, I ask you. He'll pop off sooner or later and Jim has already gone. There's only that snivelling brat of Yvonne's left, and he won't make the grade, I bet."

I started a little and my cigarette fell from my fingers. I bent to pick it up.

"Isn't Mrs Holland's son a strong child?"

"I dunno. Seems to me he's always bawling. I don't think they give the kid enough to eat. All these fancy ideas about vitamins. Lot of rot. Mind you, it's only just lately that he's got like that. He used to be a bonny little nipper."

"Perhaps Mrs Holland should take him to a doctor," I suggested, watching him closely.

"James doesn't believe in coddling the kid. There's some old witch in the house who used to be Jim's nurse. He swears by her."

"What does Yvonne say?"

Ernest Mulqueen knocked out his foul-smelling dottle.

"Nothing. It's what the old man says that goes. Maybe you'll find that out yourself one day."

He added with a trace of bitterness: "You can't fight him. He always wins. Look at me! I used to run my own place up the Riverina way. When I married the wife what happens? She develops a heart or something and must be near dear James. Ursie must be brought up right. My farm can be run along with the rest of his property. To cut a long story short, he collars my land, puts me down here at a miserable screw and gathers in the profits."

"Why don't you go back?"

My practical suggestion startled him. He muttered something about not leaving Ursie in the old man's clutches.

"Anyway, the wife wouldn't go now. You must have a woman on the farm. It never did suit her. Can't think sometimes why she married me. Taken by and large, I'm fairly content. Nothing to worry about and regular money coming in."

"But Ursula," I insisted. "Wouldn't she go back with you?"

"The wife has ideas for Ursie," he declared bluntly. "Anyway, it's too late. It's all one property now. The old man made it a legal arrangement. Got in old Braithwaite and I signed on the dotted line. Fool that I was!"

Mulqueen got up from his chair slowly, due more to reluctance to go into the cold air than physical tardiness. His actions and movements were always brisk.

"Well, I must toddle along. What time will hubby be home, Mrs Matheson?"

"I expect him any moment. Thank you for keeping me company. You saved me from becoming a gibbering idiot."

I led the way down the hall, switching on the lights as I passed. Ernest Mulqueen shrugged himself into his mackinaw.

"You don't want to be nervous. Very nice neighbourhood, you know."

"I do know. But it was the first night I had alone here. In future any bumps and bangs from the wood will make me feel safe. Mind the steps from the porch."

He turned back.

"Drat! Mind like a sieve. Had a message for you from the old man. He went away today on urgent business. At least, that is what that smooth-faced young feller told me. You are to use the golf course when you like, free, nixy and for nothing. I was to tell you."

"That is very nice of Mr Holland."

Mulqueen glanced at me for a moment. He was very shrewd, despite the bunglings over his farm. Perhaps they had taught him a never-to-be-forgotten lesson.

"Better do as he wishes," he advised. "I've always found it worth while to keep on his right side myself. And you do want to buy this place, don't you?"

I watched my caller out of the gate and was about to switch off the porch light when a taller and very familiar figure came out of the mist. The pair nearly collided. Mulqueen said good night, and turned back to wave at me in a mischievous manner. John's hand went to his hat in a half-hearted way of salute. He waited until Ernest Mulqueen had disappeared.

"So!" he began, advancing up the flagged path. "I've found you out at last. Damn! I've stubbed my toe again on these beastly stones. Why is there only one here and there? Couldn't they afford a complete path?"

"Elizabethan effect, darling, I daresay." I reached up to remove his hat, dropping a kiss on his nose in transit. "Aren't you rather late? Go into the study and I'll bring you some supper."

"Late! You brazen woman." John followed me to the kitchen.

"If you are scandalized at my caller, let me inform you that he saved your wife's reason tonight."

"He has achieved the impossible. What was the trouble?"

I stopped cutting bread and waved the knife around in a vague gesture. "Strange house. Stranger noises. Cheese toast?"

"Definitely cheese toast." He lighted the gas under the kettle and came back to sit on the edge of the table.

"You had the jitters?" He said seriously: "Now, look here, Maggie! Are you quite certain—"

"Absolutely," I interrupted hastily, and went on to tell him about Ernest Mulqueen.

I was living in the Dower on probation; dependent on Mr Holland's whims and favors on one side, while John, on the other, was not quite satisfied. I had to steer a careful course for the next few months and convince John that everything in the garden was lovely, while bowing and scraping to our landlord. It was like walking a tightrope; an old simile, but an apt one. One slip either side would mean disaster.

We carried the supper into the study.

John said, sniffing the air: "Plug! I wonder how the aristocratic Holland noses like that."

"Probably the poor man keeps it a secret. By the way, a royal command has been issued. Dinner next week at the Hall, and will we kindly dress. Can you make it?"

"Stiff shirt?" asked John incredulously.

"Indubitably. I said Wednesday and left a loophole for you, just in case you didn't feel equal to the strain. You could be working late, but I'd rather like you to meet them," I said carefully, curious as to what impression John had of the household the other side of the wood. Although his knowledge of it was superficial and his mind too highly disciplined to indulge in imaginative conjectures, some past experience might make him view the Hall ménage with misgiving.

John cocked an eyebrow at me. "Oho! And why, might I ask?" I met his look squarely, and replied without batting an eyelid.

"It does you good to get out and forget crime for a change."

"I suppose Wednesday will be as good as any other night. Any other feelers from the big man?"

"Why do you say that?" I asked curiously. "As a matter of fact, I have been given free run of the golf course. Do you know, I have an odd feeling that we are being used."

"And I have a feeling," mimicked John, "that you are right. Explain what you mean, please."

"I haven't a notion. Just a feminine shot in the dark. Why, as I have asked before, did you want to know about more feelers?"

"The equivalent of the feminine shot. I had a telephone call from Holland first thing this morning."

I glanced up too eagerly.

"You did? What did he want? You know, darling, I'm certain there's something fishy going on at the Hall. First of all, Cruikshank, and today I overheard—"

I shut my mouth firmly as a grin developed widely on his.

"Trapped, by Jupiter! Give a woman a little encouragement and she'll tell all. What was it you overheard?"

"Very clever! What did Holland want?"

"I can't tell you."

I raised one shoulder huffily.

"You see," John explained, "I hadn't arrived at the office when he rang."

"Very, very clever. Didn't you call him back?"

"Certainly not. I suffer from an inverted type of snobbery. Let him come to me. Now, what was it you were about to say?" John said conversationally.

"Nothing of great interest," I answered, determined not to be caught again. "You haven't inquired about Tony."

John continued to gaze at me. "If you are getting into mischief or anywhere near it, back we go to the flat. That is my first and last warning. All right, how is Tony?"

"Fine," I replied lamely. "Let me see. What happened today?" I passed over the events in my mind, blue-pencilling them severely, and thought of Connie Bellamy.

"I met a girl from the Exchange. She is married and lives out here. I was swept along to the local Community Centre to meet Middleburn society."

"Do I know her?"

"Connie Bellamy? No, she had left before your little sojourn at Central. A gasbag with a limited vocabulary. As a result, her conversation becomes rather monotonous. Husband Harold will be thrilled to know we are living in Middleburn. How is the case of the missing estate agent going?"

"In routine, as far as I know. I gave your dope to Billings. How you change from one subject to another, Maggie!"

"That's just where you're wrong," I said in triumph. "There is a definite follow-on from talking about Connie to Cruikshank. It might be of interest to Sergeant Billings."

"Well, what is it?"

"Connie Bellamy told me Cruikshank has been systematically robbing them for years." John took it quite calmly. "Sounds interesting. What did she mean exactly?"

"I couldn't say. I didn't ask her."

"I'll tell Billings. He may make something out of it. He still has Holland to interview. The old man is proving difficult."

"Mulqueen told me tonight he has gone away for a few days. Yvonne Holland will be relieved."

"You seem to know a great deal about the Hollands," was John's ominously casual comment.

III

But Yvonne was not at the gates of the Hall when I arrived, and it must have been after three then. Tony had been tiresome about getting dressed and had delayed us. I paused uncertainly at the foot of one of the grey stone pillars bearing a lion couchant. It might have been possible that she had gone on, not willing to be seen loitering from the house. But the road ran straight down from the Hall and there was no sign of her in the distance. I let Tony out of the pusher and decided to give her a few minutes' grace.

Once free of the straps Tony revelled in his unexpected freedom. I was trying to keep within the shadow of the lion, for I had no wish to be spied upon from the Hall. It gave you that feeling. The square squat tower seemed like an enormous eye which embraced all within its vision with a sinister contemplativeness. I made a half-hearted attempt to put Tony back into the pusher, but his immediate howls of protest were more likely to gain attention than his wandering inside the gate. Yvonne could not be much longer, so I let him stray to a threatened boundary.

It was another glorious autumn day. I moved round the pillar and propped myself up against it in the sun, closing my eyes against the glare.

Presently Tony let out a yelp. He came running up, one finger in his mouth and tears pouring with that amazing rapidity unequalled by any other than a child. When I knew he was hurt my concern at the noise he was creating vanished. I explored his finger carefully. A jagged thorn had torn the skin and imbedded itself. It looked very nasty and was quite capable of making itself unpleasant if action was not taken immediately. I held his fat wrist firmly palm up, pulling at the fast-disappearing head of the thorn.

"Hold still, my treasure," I adjured, but he kept jerking his hand away.

A voice spoke from behind me. "Could I be of assistance, Mrs Matheson?"

I glanced over my shoulder and then straightened up. It was Ames. The ubiquitous, versatile Ames. I recognized the smooth, courteous voice.

Ames advanced towards Tony and bent down.

"May I see? Perhaps my wife could fix it."

I studied him as he bent over Tony. He was long and firmly built with a well-shaped head. He appeared to be in his late thirties but was of the type who mature early and retain the same age for many years. That afternoon he wore khaki overalls and boots, for he had been working in the garden. I was to see Ames in many garbs. He dressed to each of the multitudinous jobs he handled and was sartorially perfect in each.

He straightened up. "Come into the Lodge, Mrs Matheson. I'll get some hot water and tweezers. We'll have that thorn out in no time."

"This is very kind of you," I said, following him to the tiny porch. The door of the Lodge opened directly into a living-room pleasant with sun-faded chintzes and flowers.

Two people sat there.

"Harriet," Ames introduced his wife, "this is Mrs Matheson."

"Haven't we met before?" I asked Mrs Ames. She turned her face full round and I saw the port-wine stain. "In Mr Cruikshank's shop, was it not?"

She nodded without speaking and turned her face to profile again.

"And my father, Mrs Matheson."

The white-haired, handsome man rose, slipping his unlit pipe into his pocket. "We heard the commotion. Has the little chap hurt himself badly?"

"A thorn," Ames explained. "Harriet, will you have a look at it, please?"

Mrs Ames rose and came across the room to Tony, keeping the scar turned away from me. Ames went away for the hot water.

"You have a professional touch," I told Harriet Ames pleasantly, watching her firm, unhurried hands.

A small boy came into the room bearing an enamel kidney dish with bandages and antiseptic on it.

"Put it on the table, Robin," Mrs Ames said in her toneless voice.

"This is your boy?" I glanced from mother to son. He had gone to stand by his grandfather's chair. The old man rested his hand on the dark curls. Robin was a beautiful child with a poise that would have shamed an adolescent.

Mrs Ames did not reply, but merely nodded again and held out her hand for the bowl of water as her husband came back into the room.

Tony, his attention taken up by this remarkable specimen of his own generation, allowed his finger to be bathed and dressed without a murmur. I saw a smile pass between the two little boys and drew my brows together, inexplicably disturbed.

"I believe Mr Holland has gone away," I said to Ames. "Does the arrangement still stand for Wednesday?"

"Mr Holland left instructions. I had a wire today saying he would be home in time. He was most insistent that Mr Matheson should be present."

"There is a complication when it comes to us both coming," I said, indicating Tony.

Mrs Ames said without looking up: "I will stay at the Dower on Wednesday night. You will be able to manage, Robert. I will give the staff their orders during the afternoon." She released Tony's hand and turned to tidy the tray. I got up.

"How will that arrangement suit you, Mrs Matheson?" Ames asked, following me to the door.

"Excellently. I will be happy to leave Tony in such good hands. Good-bye and thank you."

Old man Ames and Robin both bowed with a strange courtesy, but Mrs Ames did not look up until I was out of the Lodge. I saw her watching me as I passed under the windows, the sun striking full onto her ravaged face.

IV

Yvonne caught up with me when I was about half-way to the village. She had her baby propped up with pillows. His face in repose still had a thin, pinched look about it, but he seemed more contented than on the previous day. I pointed this out to her.

"Nurse Stone was terribly cross about the dummy," she announced. "She immediately rang through to the Lodge and told Mrs Ames to put one down on the shopping list."

In spite of my protestation to Yvonne, locating the Middleburn Health Centre was a simple task. It was merely a matter of following the prams.

It was a sunny brick building with a verandah built on two sides. Yvonne squeezed her pram into the last available place and lifted up the child carefully. Holding Tony by one hand, I waited for her as she collected oddments of clothing without which one never travels with a baby.

She preceded me into the L-shaped room. It was bright with gay curtains and posters illustrating the importance of the foundation foods. Already several mothers were waiting their turn for the scales.

A small room led from the main one. There the sister-in-charge sat interviewing each mother after her child was weighed.

"What is her name?" I asked Yvonne, watching her undress Jimmy across her knee. She found it awkward.

"Sister Heather. She's been here a long time. I believe she would have resigned long ago but for the shortage of fully trained staff. She loves the babies."

She arose and moved over to the weighing table. Jimmy let out a cry as the cold basket met his naked behind. Yvonne flushed up at once and cast an apologetic look around the room. She made some attempts to soothe the child by snapping her fingers while the nurse arranged the weights. The child's crying infected other members of the community, so much so that by the time I got up to go into Sister Heather's office the whole room was a roar. It was really rather funny, although Yvonne was a little distressed.

I pushed Tony into the room, turning back to close the door against the din.

"Talk about feeding time at the Zoo," I began. I stopped abruptly. Sister Heather had raised her head. The fountain-pen with which she had been writing slipped from her fingers. We stared at each other for a long moment in silence. A moment in which our eyes were held, puzzlement changing to recognition and on her part a startled look. Tony pulled up a chair for himself and clambered into it noisily.

Sister Heather was the first to recover her composure. She held out her hand, smiling. "How do you do? You're a newcomer, aren't you? Please sit down while I make out a form for you."

I murmured something inaudible and idiotic, pushing Tony off his chair and sitting down with him on my knee.

Sister Heather's gentle voice flowed on, asking particulars as to Tony's age, weight and diet. When I gave my address her hand hesitated in writing for a moment. The pause was barely noticeable and might only have been imagination on my part. It was incredible that this serene-looking woman was the one I had overheard talking of murder. For some reason the short strained sentences Sister Heather had uttered in the middle of High Street were something between us that was going to be ignored; on her side at any rate.

"We have only just moved into the Dower House," I said, watching her closely. She was drawing up a graph illustrating Tony's progress.

"So I heard," she replied smoothly. "You were lucky to find such a place. You must be in high favour with Mr Holland."

Somehow I didn't like the way Sister Heather said that. There was a faint hostility in her voice. I attacked again.

"By the way, Mr Holland's grandson was instrumental in bringing me here." I paused a moment. She did not look up.

"Indeed?"

"Mrs Holland offered me her escort. She doesn't come here often, I believe."

"I will be glad to see her baby again," Sister Heather said in the same non-committal manner. She drew out a tape measure and started to take Tony's head and chest measurements.

"I don't think that baby is well," I said bluntly. "You must do something." She looked at me over Tony's head. Her eyes were quite blank.

"Mr Holland exercises a considerable influence in this district," she informed me in an even tone. "If you wish to stand well in his favour you would be wise not to interfere with the members of his family."

I did not give up. "Not even if it is a matter of life and death, Sister?"

Her eyes flickered. She moved back to her side of the desk.

"I am afraid I don't understand you, Mrs Matheson." There was a note of finality in her voice. I sighed and got up.

"All right," I agreed. "Have it your own way. I'm to mind my own business, am I? But I do hope you will give that baby a good examination and some strong advice to his mother. Thanks very much for looking at Tony. I will be along again." I turned back from the door. "By the way, Sister, can you recommend the local doctor? I am anxious to have one close at hand."

My simple request had an amazing effect on Sister Heather. She looked confused and stammered slightly, losing the polite detachment with which she had greeted my attempt to force an open discussion on the Holland baby. After some hesitation she told me Dr Trefont was the local man's name. He held good degrees and had a postgraduate obstetrical record. He was well liked in confinement cases. Very good with children's diseases.

I took myself off to await Yvonne outside. She did not take long in Sister Heather's office, a fact that rather disturbed me.

"Well?" I said, as she put Jimmy back in the pram. "How did he go? What did Sister Heather say about him?"

"He's all right," she replied with a curtness wholly unlike her.

"How is his weight?" I persisted.

"He has lost a bit, but considering he's teething I'm not worrying."

The latter part of her statement was without doubt a lie. She was more than worried, she was scared.

"What's the matter?" I asked gently. "You look upset. Is it your baby?"

We walked along in silence for a moment. I waited patiently. Yvonne seemed undecided whether to speak.

"Oh, Mrs Matheson," she burst out presently. "She wants me to take Jimmy to that man."

"What man?"

"Doctor Trefont. I couldn't. Why should Jimmy want a doctor? He's well enough. But for his teeth he's—"

"Listen to me, my child," I broke in. "Don't put too much blame on teething. That's a very old one. Do as Sister Heather tells you. Go along to the medicine man."

She shook her head stubbornly. "I couldn't," she repeated. "Not to him. Mr Holland wouldn't hear of it."

"What's wrong with Trefont? I'm going to him myself."

Yvonne stopped her pram and gazed at me earnestly. "Don't, Mrs Matheson. Don't go to Dr Trefont." She spoke in dead seriousness.

I replied lightly: "You talk as though the man is an abortionist or something."

She flushed at my words, and changed the subject.

Yvonne's earnest request could not but affect me. I had marked too the note of hesitation even as the Health Centre sister had given the recommendation.

That night I rang my old doctor to ask him what he thought. He grunted, "Good idea," in reply to my careful explanation.

"Glad to get rid of you. Much too busy. Trefont? Nothing against him that I know of. Anyone who has gone through the university here must be all right. I'll fossick around and see if I can dig up any dirt. How's your brat? You needn't tell me. I'd forgotten you're no longer a patient of mine. Not interested now."

I rang off, grinning. Doctor Johnson was a dear old chap. If there was anything at all shady about Trefont, he would soon let me know.

On impulse I took up the phone again. It was connected in John's study and I leant against the edge of his desk as I dialled.

John heaved an ostentatious sigh. "Last one, darling. I won't be long. Hullo, is that you, Connie? Maggie speaking. How are you?"

I certainly gave the right cue. Connie held forth for some time on her various symptoms and ailments. I listened patiently for a time before I cut in.

"Quite so. I rang to find out the name of your doctor. Is he by any chance Trefont? He is? How do you like him? I'm thinking of going to him myself."

Connie liked him fairly well, but was not enthusiastic. He had been well recommended. "But he lacked polish if you know what I mean, Maggie. Of course—"

"No bedside manner. Is that it?"

It was, precisely. But a good doctor. Most of the girls around Middleburn went to him.

"Sounds as though he'll do. Thanks, Connie. By the way, what about you and—er—Harold dining with us one night?"

We arranged the date, and I rang off satisfied with my calling for the time being.

CHAPTER FOUR

I

The day of the dinner-party at the Hall dawned much the same as any other day. A feeling of pleasant anticipation was mine that morning. There were no grim forebodings or terrible premonitions. "Nobody knows what night will bring," or similar gloomy phrases, never entered my head.

Half-way through the morning Ames rang with the suggestion that I should squeeze in a game of golf before the Squire returned. Mrs Ames would come to the Dower in the afternoon. Mindful of Ernest Mulqueen's advice, I jumped at the offer.

Mrs Ames arrived a few minutes before the appointed hour. She wore the usual tweed coat with its big collar almost covering her face, and carried an attaché case. Robin was with her, one hand grasping a bunch of geraniums. Under his arm were a number of brightly coloured books. The flowers, it appeared, were for me, while the books were to form an overture to Tony.

I gave Mrs Ames a few instructions and slipped out unobtrusively.

The links were almost deserted. There was no one in the tiny office to take a green fee, so I moved off without delay. Greenkeepers have the habit of popping up at the eighteenth hole, just as you are congratulating yourself on getting a free game. I had a very brief run for my lack of payment that time. I approached the first green with stiff shots through lack of practice, and there was Ames seated on a diesel-driven mower on the other side of the pin. He dismissed my offer of payment with a word that Mr Holland would not like it, and cut off his engine to watch me drive off the second tee. It was not a very marvellous drive, but straight and true. I went down the slope, anxious to be away from his gaze. I knew he was as perfect a golfer as he was in his many other crafts.

About the fifth hole, when my muscles were starting to relax and the sound of a lark in the cloudless sky above was heightening my enjoyment, I stroked through another solitary female player. I was thoroughly delighting in one long unkind shot when I was hailed by name from a thicket where she had retired for safety.

As I approached I recognized a woman I had met at the Middleburn Community Centre—the one who adored children. She clapped her hands after my next stroke in earnest applause. I eyed her with a sinking feeling. My happy solitary game was going to be a thing of the past.

"Hello, Mrs Matheson. I'm so glad to see you. You do play well."

It was the only shot she had seen me make and that was a fluke.

"Miss—" I began gropingly.

"Potts-Power. But please call me Daisy. Everyone does. I'm quite a figure in Middleburn. A gay spinster amongst all you young-marrieds. Tell me, how is my little Anthony?"

I winced throughout this speech. "He is Mrs Ames' little Tony at the moment," I said, glancing backward in the vain hope that someone might be wanting to drive off.

"Isn't she a funny person? So hard to make friends with her. I suppose her poor face makes her shy. I do like to be friendly with everyone, don't you?"

I began to edge away.

"Wait until I play this ball," Miss Potts-Power begged. "We can go along together and have a nice chat. Unless you want to go ahead. I'm afraid I'm a bit slow."

"Not at all," I replied, feeling hemmed in.

"It's so much nicer playing twosome, don't you think?" asked Miss Potts-Power. I could not bring myself to even think of her as Daisy yet.

She bent down low and hacked at her ball. Incredibly it trickled onto the green.

"That just shows what the influence of a good player can do," she remarked fulsomely. I made no comment as I moved after my ball and took up a stance.

Miss Potts-Power chatted on in an unconcerned fashion behind me. Ames was giving her lessons. Didn't I think he was a frightfully nice man? So handsome and well-spoken. So utterly devoted to his wife and son, and to his poor old father, and, of course, the Hollands too. Indeed he was marvellous to everybody, even poor little her.

I made a swipe at my ball, hoping for the best.

"I don't often get the opportunity to play golf, you know. But Mother was having a nap and I just felt I had to get out. She always has a nap when we are going out at night. I'm sure you can't guess where we're going. I'll give you three chances."

I glowered at the distance separating my ball from the pin.

"The Zoo!" I suggested.

"'The Zoo'," she repeated blankly. "Oh, you're teasing me. All right, if you won't play—"

"I'm trying to," I muttered fiercely, following through the putt.

"—I'll tell you. It is such a coincidence, really. It's all over the village about Mr Holland's party. You can't keep anything secret in Middleburn. It is just as well Mrs Ames could mind Tony, because I was going to offer if she couldn't, you know, and I never break a promise, even though it means doing without some outing more pleasant."

I sank my ball at last and held the pin as Miss Potts-Power holed out in five or six putts. The last one ended on the tip of the hole. I gave it a surreptitious nudge with my toe to help it on its way.

"Mother and I have been invited to dinner at Holland Hall. There now, aren't you surprised?"

"Very!" I said, knowing my cue. "But why should I be?"

"How silly of me! Of course you haven't been here long enough to know. And actually it was Ames who issued the invitation, so it mightn't count for anything."

"You are holding me in suspense," I said, speculating on the best way to cross the creek half-way down the sixth fairway. A discreet stroke to land just this side or a bold bid in the hope it might come off?

"You always lose a ball here," Miss Potts-Power said happily. "Ames must find dozens in that creek."

"He won't find any of mine," I said, playing the careful game. "You were saying about tonight?"

"Tonight? Oh, yes. So odd of Mr Holland. You see, he and mother haven't spoken to each other for years." She paused for effect.

I made some fitting sound of incredulity.

"What do you make of it, Mrs Matheson? You are a bit of a detective, I believe."

I slammed my wood into the bag with unnecessary force.

Blast Connie and her prattling!

"On the face of it I should say the quarrel, if such it was, was going to be forgotten at last."

"As a matter of fact," Miss Potts-Power confessed, "I don't know if there was any actual quarrel. You see, mother has never spoken of it."

"In that case," I suggested, "it would be better not to waste our time with idle speculation. I wonder if you'd think me terribly rude if I went on. I'm anxious to get back to Tony."

"Of course not," she said, looking hurt. "Anyway, I'll see you tonight. Maybe we can have a nice long chat then."

I finished the fifteenth hole and paused to add up my card. The result was not too startling; in fact, low enough to make the playing of another three holes interesting. A mist hung low over the creek again. I glanced up at the sky. It had become overcast with a thin layer of cloud.

I gave an undecided look at my watch, shrugged and climbed on to the next tee. I played the next two holes well and felt fully justified in stealing time. This self-satisfaction vanished when I lost a ball second stroke off the last fairway. The mist was creeping up steadily. Combined with the fading daylight, I was forced to abandon the search in disgust.

I took a mental photograph of the approximate position of the ball, determined to try the search again the following day. Golf balls were too hard to come by to go losing them through sheer stupidity.

II

It was after six when I turned into the gateway of the Dower. Tony was having tea in the kitchen with his new friend. Some lively and completely unintelligible conversation was going on between them. Mrs Ames sat between them, her head bent over some intricate fancywork. She looked up as I burst in, anxious to see Tony after what now seemed a long separation.

"I hope you had a pleasant game," she remarked, bending her head again swiftly.

"Very pleasant, thank you. Tony, my lamb, not all that much in your mouth."

Robin had finished his tea. He slipped from his chair, wiping a perfectly clean face on an equally spotless feeder. Mrs Ames came up behind him to untie it, while I poured more milk for Tony.

"Now remember, Robin," I heard her say in a low tone. "Go home by the road and be very careful."

"Are you sending Robin home by himself?" I asked, swinging round in surprise. It was nearly pitch-dark outside with that nasty mist coming up. Although the child seemed highly intelligent, he was not much more than a baby.

"Let him play with Tony while I get changed," I suggested. "I'll take him on my way to the Hall."

She accepted my offer without hesitation. I caught the merest hint of a smile on her averted face and felt warmed by it. You would hate to think that a woman who had been looking after your child as competently as she seemed to have looked after Tony and to whom you felt indebted was incapable of any response.

The two children delighted in the unexpected prolongation and spent the time rushing madly up and down the passage. Their shrieks of delight at this energetic and purposeless form of entertainment came to me as I took a leisurely bath and changed into a dinner dress. It was fun getting into a long skirt once again. I topped off the black crepe with a candy-striped jacket, and went to the mirror.

I took a satisfied look at my reflection from every possible angle and then a dissatisfied one at the bedroom clock. John was cutting it fine. I laid out his clothes in a dutiful fashion, and leaving the bedroom light aglow, went down the passage to the lounge-room, switching on lights as I went.

Tony rushed headlong to meet me. I snatched him up for a minute. Mrs Ames had bathed him before tea and put him into striped pyjamas and a scarlet dressing-gown. He wriggled away and tore down the passage after Robin.

Smell when allied to instinct becomes a highly acute sense. I could always tell when someone strange had been in my house. I had felt that as soon as I had returned from golf. Even if I hadn't known Mrs Ames and Robin were in the house, that sense would still have been mine. It was very strong as I entered the lounge-room. I smiled a little to myself. Not that I minded Mrs Ames using my sitting-room, but it did not seem quite in accordance with my conception of her. I wondered if she had inspected every room in the Dower. I could find out from Tony if I cared to pump a child in such a futile cause.

John came in just then. I was in the hall as soon as I heard his step on the flagged path. I hurried him off to change, and sat down to glance through the evening paper he had brought home.

There was a small oblong box lying alongside the paper. I opened it with the lack of conscience which wives seem to develop after a few years of married life. A dainty little corsage was inside. I pinned it onto the lapel of my jacket feeling abominably sentimental.

John came back presently, slipping cigarettes into his case. "Why is it," he demanded in a resigned fashion, "women always mess up a newspaper?"

He started to clear up the sheets on the floor while I sat clinging to one, my eyes glued on an item in the personal column.

"Did you see this?" I asked.

"See what? By the way, you might wait until I give you gifts before you thank me for them."

"Sorry, but I was overwhelmed. Have a look at this."

He read above my pointing finger. I looked into his face to see his reaction. He smiled round at me gently and said: "Are you ready, Mrs Matheson? May I offer you my arm?"

I put the paper down. "You knew about it," I accused him, rising and slipping a fur cape over my shoulders.

"Detectives always read the personal column. You never know what you may pick up."

"Well, what do you think about it?" I asked, goaded.

"It is certainly an original way to ask anyone to dinner. Tell me, should I go and say something polite to the nursemaid?"

"No, but you could slip her the fee she expects and is entitled to. We are escorting young Robin home too. Find him while I tuck Tony in."

My question had been gracefully but firmly evaded. John did not intend to discuss the item in the paper. I wondered if it was because I had been reticent about affairs at the Hall and he was piqued, or whether his attitude was becoming official. His remark was a fine example of understatement. To invite a man to dinner through the medium of the personal column was in itself odd, but when one knew that the proposed guest had disappeared in suspicious circumstances several days earlier the situation was even more out of the way.

"Will he be able to get himself to bed?" I asked Mrs Ames as Robin presented his hand in an enchanting fashion. His little fingers curled into mine without any shyness.

Mrs Ames watched him, answering my question with a nod.

"I hope you won't be lonely here by yourself," I persevered, trying to break through Harriet Ames' reserve.

"No, I won't be lonely," she replied, waiting for me to go.

She stood at the end of the hall as John opened the front door.

"Good night," I called, raising one hand.

"Don't try so hard, Maggie," John said, pulling the door to.

"Hullo. Who's this?"

The gate of the Dower had opened, and a female figure picked its way over the flags.

"Why, Miss Cruikshank! Good evening." I was surprised.

Miss Potts-Power had declared the Squire's party was all over the village. "I'm afraid we are just on our way out."

"Oh, dear!" Miss Cruikshank said. "I must be too early. She did say seven. The clock in the shop must have gained."

John had sized up the situation. He inserted his key in the door and swung it open. I caught a glimpse of Harriet Ames still standing at the end of the hall.

"A caller for you," John said pleasantly. He gently pushed Miss Cruikshank inside and shut the door again.

"But why didn't she say she had asked someone to keep her company," I exclaimed. "I would not have minded."

"Mrs Ames does not waste her breath in superfluous explanations. You asked if she would be lonely and she said no. Reason why would have transpired."

We followed the road round the curve to the entrance gates of the Hall, Robin still holding my hand in his engaging way. Further discussion on his mother's supreme reticence was inadvisable. His fingers moved slightly at the mention of her name.

Light shone from the unshaded windows of the Lodge. We could see inside the cosy living room. Robin's grandfather sat opposite another man at a table drawn up in front of the fire. One hand was poised over the chess pieces set out between them. He heard the steps on the stone porch and looked up. With a word to his companion he rose to his feet and disappeared out of vision. Robin loosened his hand and went forward eagerly as his grandfather appeared.

Old man Ames was as courteous as his son, but his manner held more warmth and sincerity. His attitude never conveyed the impression of a superficial correctitude as Robert Ames' did. He thanked us for bringing Robin home and seemed quite prepared to chat for a while had not John drawn my attention to the time.

The porch light was left aglow as we went up the drive, but this was soon lost to view, smothered by the developing fog. The poplars growing on either side of the drive seemed more closely knit by night. It was as though we were walking through a deep tunnel.

I made one or two rhetorical remarks to John, but he grunted, and did not seem disposed to talk. I had lost some of my exhilaration too. It had changed into a nervous excitement. That silent walk in the darkness and fog did not inspire gaiety. On the other hand there was an anticipatory thrill about it, as if the stillness and gloom were a prelude to feverish activity.

But even through the darkness I saw, or else my imagination sketched, the vague outline of the square white tower of the Hall looking down on us as we approached.

I began to be foolish and glance over my shoulder. But my imagination had not gone beyond the bounds of reality.

"Mat," I said suddenly, using an old nickname in my fright. John pulled me gently into the shade of the poplars. He seemed conscious of another presence too, and pressed my arm warningly. We stood there for one minute, two. Presently a shadow moved on the far side of the poplars. It moved quickly and quietly in the direction of the house. There was a slight brushing of the leafless branches. Except for that sound I might have imagined the dim form. But there was no breeze to make those trees move.

"Just another guest," John said at last. I pulled myself together.

"It only remains for there to be thirteen guests and we go home."

Even as I spoke flippantly in the endeavour to capture my first mood, something else happened. The light in the tower of the Hall began again to flash on and off. I pulled John along hurriedly. If we got near to the house there would be a good chance of seeing who was in the tower. We came into the open sweep of gravel below the terrace. The light had ceased to flicker. It shone steadily down, illuminating the marble pond in the centre of the oval. I scanned the windows of the tower keenly, but there was no one to be seen.

John followed my gaze. "A form of red carpet, I presume," he suggested.

"Quite likely," I replied.

The house was now brilliant with light. The front door stood wide open in spite of the inclement night. Music sounded—a sweet, hackneyed Strauss waltz, hard to give title to on account of the underlying similarity of many three-four time compositions, but nevertheless nostalgic and poignant. Somehow Strauss sounded quite at home in this strange house; as though the Hall belonged to the same era. The music conveyed the impression of corruption and tragedy beneath its gay polished exterior that must have existed in the Vienna of the Archduke Rudolph and his little Marie. That lilting melody was the leitmotif of the Holland case.

Ames, a picture of sartorial adaptability as usual, appeared as soon as we put foot on the top step. His role on this particular occasion, however, was rather confused. He seemed more a master of ceremonies than a butler. He took John's coat, suggesting I retain my fur.

"Some ladies find the house a trifle draughty."

His manner was perfect, but just the same I let slip my cape into his hands. He went on to say, without even blinking at my childish behaviour, "I regret that Mr Holland has not yet come in. He is expected at any moment. Will you come this way, please?"

He ushered us into the drawing-room, an apartment heavy with crimson and massive with mahogany. The Strauss waltz came from a Panatrope situated on the far side of the room. Daisy Potts-Power, dressed in shapeless draperies of flowered voile, was standing beside it. One hand hovered over the needle as the record neared completion, the other held back the loose sleeve which threatened to become entwined in the mechanism. Before I had time to greet her, a very deep voice spoke from behind the door.

"And again. Play it again, girl." I swung round. An elderly woman of immense, almost revolting girth was seated in a wheelchair half hidden by the door. She was attired in a garment which might have been a remnant from the hangings at the windows, and flashed a quantity of diamonds in dirty settings on her balloon-like fingers. These lay loosely on her lap. The grotesque immobile body was rendered all the more conspicuous because of the eyes that darted to and fro in their yellowing balls.

She spoke in her deep voice without hesitation. "I always choose this position. You can catch people without their party faces on."

Ames coughed. It was that deprecatory sound which is always associated with fictional butlers.

"Be quiet, Ames," said the crimson-velvet woman as he began to make introductions. She surveyed John with a basilisk eye. "So this is our detective! Well, young man, show me how good you are. What is my name and who am I?"

I had disliked the old woman on sight. Now I loathed her. I stepped in front of John and said coolly: "I also consider myself a detective. I'll show you I can be quite good too. Your name is Mrs Potts-Power and you are the unofficial first lady of Middleburn."

She was immensely pleased and a spasm indicative of delight spread throughout the heavy body.

"Splendid! Give me some more. Come here and sit by me."

I felt I could afford to punish the old woman. I shook my head. "Presently. I want to say good evening to your daughter." Ames had already introduced John to Daisy and left the room. Mrs Potts-Power clapped her hands like an Eastern potentate. Daisy came up on the instant.

"Mrs Matheson wants to say good evening to you."

"Oh—er—good night," Daisy said with a nervous giggle. It was clear enough now that she lived in awe of the tyrannical old woman. This talk of staying at home to care for mother was just a product of her hungry nature.

I said: "I think I will get my cape. There is quite a draught in this room."

As I left the drawing-room Mrs Potts-Power bellowed: "How long do we have to stay here before one of the Hollands puts in an appearance? I want my dinner."

The hall was still deserted when I came out of the powder room. I wandered along, pausing with critical eyes in front of one or two of the massive and gloomy oil paintings on the walls. A small telephone switchboard caught my attention. It stood in the deep shadow of the stairs opposite the double doors of the drawing-room. I was examining it casually when a smooth voice spoke behind me.

"Do you wish to make a call, Mrs Matheson? The line is engaged at the moment."

I turned swiftly. Ames was standing before the entrance to the drawing-room, a silver tray of drinks between his hands.

He waited, bland and impeccable, with his head tilted at just the right angle.

"Perhaps I should call the Dower," I suggested.

Ames' eyes went to the board again. "The extension is engaged also. I will try it for you presently." He moved slightly aside to let me pass ahead of him.

"I'll wait," I told him. "I know how to operate the board."

He inclined his head still further and went into the drawing-room. I leaned against the stairs and studied a gory painting of dead game. There was a brace of hares, blood bright upon their heads. They lay athwart a long-nosed gun, the redness staining the white cloth beneath. In the background leered a sharp-faced animal mask. A small window opened onto a darkling landscape.

My eyes were on the highlight of the painted gun barrel when reality and imagination seemed to coalesce. The sound as of a gunshot reverberated in the still deep mist outside the Hall. I heard it clearly, although it seemed far away in the night.

III

I hurried into the drawing-room. John met my anxious eyes with an inquiring look. I moved over to his side. Mrs Potts-Power and Daisy appeared unconcerned. The old woman was leaning back in her wheelchair, thick wrinkled lids half-hiding her restless eyes. Daisy was replaying the Strauss waltz. Then the sound occurred again. This time it was further away and not quite as full-bodied. Mrs Potts-Power opened her eyes wide and stirred irritably.

"Why must cars go backfiring just while I am enjoying the music?" she asked.

"Sherry, Maggie?" John said in my ear. Ames was bending the tray down towards me. I took a glass carefully. My hands were not quite steady. When Ames went out of the room for a moment I downed the sherry in one swallow.

"Bar-room manners," John commented. "What's the matter?"

"I thought the first one sounded like a gunshot. Silly?"

"Very silly."

Daisy raised her voice from across the room. "Such lovely sherry. I do think it is a most romantic beverage, don't you, Mrs Matheson?"

Mrs Potts-Power snorted. "Don't be a fool, girl. Ames, find me some whisky. I can't abide this wash."

"Now, Mother, please. You know what the doctor said about spirits."

"Daisy will pour the soda for me," said the old woman, grinning. "You heard what I said, Ames."

"Yes, madam." He came over towards me. "Mrs Ames has just called from the Dower. Everything is all right."

"Thank you, Ames."

"At last!" said Mrs Potts-Power rudely as Yvonne Holland came into the room, followed by a mild-looking young man. She wore a dinner-dress made of fine crimson wool and looked pretty but painfully thin. Her nervous hands plucked and smoothed the draped basque as she stammered apologies to Mrs Potts-Power.

The old woman let her go after she had had her fun, and sat ready to pounce on the next person who entered.

Yvonne saw me and led the young man over to be introduced. His name was Braithwaite. I drew my brows together when I heard it.

He saw the motion and said: "We had some correspondence over the Dower House, Mrs Matheson."

"Of course. How clever of you to guess I was trying to place you. I dislike a familiar name to elude me." He was one of Mr Holland's solicitors.

I introduced John and we chatted together for a while. Now and then Yvonne threw a glance in our direction. Daisy had claimed her attention, and was talking brightly about the weather.

Elizabeth Mulqueen entered a pace or two ahead of her daughter. Her studied entrance was upset by Mrs Potts-Power addressing her from behind the door and making her jump. She changed the sudden jerk into a graceful about-turn with praiseworthy aplomb.

"Dear Marguerite!" Mrs Mulqueen said sweetly. "How lovely to see you within these portals again. Do you remember my little girlie?"

Ursula was drawn forward. Beyond her mother's pink lace figure, I saw that she was wearing a frock patterned with rosebuds and a string of seed pearls.

Mrs Potts-Power looked at the muslin frills and the bow in the hair with an unkind eye. "As well as the day she was born nearly twenty-five years ago. Tell me, Elizabeth, where is James?"

Mrs Mulqueen threw a vague glance around the room. It took me in with a slight look of recognition. Ursula had already shown her pink gums in my direction.

"Isn't he down yet? I heard him moving around in his dressing-room some time ago."

"No, he isn't, and I want my dinner. You are all late."

Mrs Mulqueen left her talking and continued around the circle like a royal hostess. It was a pity, as Mrs Potts-Power declared loudly, that she had not put in her appearance earlier.

Ursula moved towards me. We exchanged a few conventional phrases. Presently she claimed young Braithwaite's attention. Again I observed young Yvonne Holland's glances in Alan Braithwaite's direction. A slightly clouded look came into her blue eyes when Ursula smiled at her sweetly.

Ernest Mulqueen entered in a surreptitious way. His could have been made a perfect entry had he been the type to wish it so. He appeared anxious not to draw attention to himself. I waved to him cheerily as to an old friend. Had he not borne me company during that first strange night at the Dower? I was surprised and more than a little embarrassed when he returned my wave with a blank stare. I dropped my hand and found John grinning at me.

Ames came to the doorway and announced dinner.

"Where is James?" Elizabeth Mulqueen asked in exasperation. "Ames, go up to his room and tell him we are all waiting."

Mrs Potts-Power rapped her daughter on the hand with her be-ringed knuckles. It was a signal to start pushing the wheelchair.

"I don't care where James is. I was invited here for dinner and I intend to have it."

I whispered to Yvonne as we passed through to the dining-room. "How is your baby? Might I see him later?"

"Certainly. I'll take you up to the nursery before coffee."

I said: "Mr Braithwaite seems a nice person. We resumed our acquaintance capitally." She flushed and glanced at me suspiciously. I retreated before she gave herself away any further.

That dinner was one of the most extraordinary affairs I have ever attended. To begin with, there was no host sitting at the top of the table. Ames had come back with the news that Mrs Mulqueen must have been mistaken. Mr Holland had not yet arrived. He had left a message previously that the dinner was to start punctually, even if he was not there.

"We don't even know why James has been gone for the last few days," Elizabeth Mulqueen said across the table to Mrs Potts-Power. "Do we, Ames?"

She invited his corroboration as he leaned down to pour wine into her glass. It must have been rather disconcerting for Ames to be addressed when playing his role of butler. But he replied without flickering an eyelash.

"No, madam."

"The only word we have had is a telegram from some outlandish spot saying he would be home tonight at seven," Mrs Mulqueen complained.

A second extraordinary thing about the dinner was an empty chair beside me with a place set opposite it. During the fish course it dawned on me who should have been sitting there. Once James Holland issued his royal command the guest should automatically be present, irrespective of whether he was dead, ill, or had lost his memory; one of which three misfortunes might be Mr Cruikshank's excuse.

The table was fairly quiet. Conversation was not particularly brilliant when it did take place. John was doing his best with Ursula Mulqueen, but he was somewhat frustrated by the latter's obvious desire to monopolize Alan Braithwaite to the exclusion of Yvonne, who sat on his other hand.

Ernest Mulqueen appeared completely crushed either by his stiff shirt or the company, and spoke little. He picked at the excellent dinner Mr Holland had provided to make up for his likely absence.

I would have expected Ernie to be a hearty eater and a boisterous table-talker. Elizabeth Mulqueen sat on his right. She had ignored him from the time he had entered the drawing-room, and addressed most of her remarks to old Mrs Potts-Power. The latter was shovelling food down and not even bothering to reply to the smooth sweet talk.

The only thing outside her plate that she noticed was Daisy, who tried to remonstrate with her about either the amount, type or speed of dispatch of the food. She rapped her daughter's hand in a gesture which must have been familiar to Daisy. I would have rubbed the old lady's nose all over her face for humiliating me so.

"What an ill-assorted group of people we are," I thought absently. Then the idea came to me that quite possibly we were all part of some scheme of our absent host's. I glanced round again at my uncongenial table companions and felt an impotent rage spring up within me.

John and I, as newcomers, were included in the dinner party so as to feel the weight of James Holland's would-be omniscience. Or so I reasoned. The fact that he had failed to appear at the head of his own table held, without doubt, some significance. We were to be impressed by Elizabeth Mulqueen, cowed by old Mrs Potts-Power, and rendered pliable by both operations in time for Holland to mould us to his own purpose and satisfaction.

As for the other members of the party, it was easy to see what would happen. The meal was heavy and rich, the atmosphere brittle with tension caused by uncongeniality. It would be a moot point whether impaired digestions would start the squabbling or the squabbling would be the cause of the dyspepsia. Either way friction was inevitable. And that, I reasoned again, was exactly James Holland's aim.

Mrs Potts-Power belched long, loudly and with complete unashamedness. John's eyes twinkled at me over the table. He had no intention of being awed or cowed by these people. I grinned back, raising my table napkin as I saw Ursula Mulqueen's eyes on me. Even while she was trying to trap Alan Braithwaite into conversation she seemed to keep everyone under observation.

Yvonne drew me aside quietly as we left the dining-room. Instead of following the other women into the drawing-room we went upstairs together. Not until we were well out of earshot of the ground floor did she venture a remark.

"Nurse Stone may have gone downstairs to help the kitchen staff. Her room opens into the nursery." The remark would have puzzled me had I pondered on it. She spoke in her usual nervous way.

"Which is Mr Holland's room?" I asked, full of lively curiosity. The house and furnishings were magnificent even in their garishness. It was pointed out to me along with her own and Ursula's. Elizabeth and Ernest Mulqueen had their individual apartments in the east wing of the ground floor.

Yvonne knocked on the door almost opposite her own. A tentative, timid tap with her finger-tips. There was a slight pause before her knock was answered. I heard the creak of a bed and a few hurried movements, then the door was opened.

Nurse Stone was another figure in James Holland's interpretation of squirearchy—in appearance at least. She was fat, rosy-cheeked, grey-haired. A typical story-book English nanny. Her smile, I came to learn, was a permanent fixture. It didn't deceive me even then. I had caught an odour of gin on her breath. We had interrupted Nurse Stone's relaxation with a bottle.

Yvonne's plea to see Jimmy, for such indeed it was, was foiled by a battery of smiles and a warm full voice protesting between "little pets" and "poor lambs" that he had just that minute popped off to sleep.

"But Mrs Matheson is so anxious to see him," Yvonne begged. "Can't we, for just one moment?" The woman's face changed. She did not lose the false smile, but a look of hostility came into her eyes as she glanced at me.

"So you're Mrs Matheson," she said with a certain significance in her voice. "No, I'm sorry, Mrs Jim, but you can't go in. Do you want to disturb him? You might frighten him if he awakened."

"Surely, his own mother—" I began mildly.

She shot me another glance. There was unveiled enmity in it now. I was quite prepared to stay and open battle. Unfortunately, my ally was for retreat. She drew me away from the room, apologizing for disturbing Nurse Stone.

"Mr Holland thinks very highly of her," Yvonne said. Her words were simple yet wholly explanatory.

I walked along the passage a few steps and then retraced them softly and swiftly. Yvonne stopped and gaped. I bent one ear to the door of Nurse Stone's room. There was a chink of glass against glass, another creak of the bed and a loud sigh. I nodded to myself.

"What is it?" Yvonne whispered.

"Isn't there another entrance into the nursery?" I asked softly.

"We could get in through the bathroom. The door may be unlocked."

"This one?" I asked, pointing. Yvonne nodded. We opened it carefully in case of squeaks. The door connecting to the nursery was slightly ajar.

"Put on the bathroom light," I told Yvonne. "It would be awful if we did wake him."

The child slept on his side with a dummy lying slackly in his mouth. In the dim glow from the bathroom I saw his little cheek was hectically flushed and put one finger carefully into the limp hand. It was slightly damp to feel. His temperature seemed normal. I raised my head and sniffed the air. It was close and stale. The blind was drawn over the window. When I raised it I saw the window was shut.

"For Heaven's sake," I whispered to Yvonne savagely. "The child is sleeping in a closed room. No wonder he is flushed, breathing stale air all the time. Did you know of this?" I slid the window up, drawing back the curtain. The fresh sweet air flowed in like a stream. The baby stirred and whimpered a little. We backed hastily out of the room, but not before I had pulled that beastly dummy from his mouth, confiscating both it and the jar of comforter smear which stood on the table beside the cot.

We arrived back into the drawing-room as the party was being divided up for solo. The after-dinner male session had not lasted long. I was not surprised. Ernest Mulqueen, young Braithwaite and John would not be my idea of a convivial trio. Although John and the solicitor might have something in common insofar as both had been at the university about the same time, you could not blend shop talk with Ernest Mulqueen's observations on gins and farming. Cruikshank, had it been possible or advisable for him to attend, would scarcely have made the party any more exciting.

Tempers became frayed during the card game. At my table Mrs Potts-Power picked continually at Daisy, who was a shocking player but held good cards and could not help but win—chiefly her mother's money, too. Mrs Potts-Power was a bad loser. She considered even the turn-up had a grudge against her. Elizabeth Mulqueen interrupted the game constantly by inventing small absurd errands for Ernest to run whenever he was sitting out. He became exasperated after a while and suggested, red in the face, that she fetch her handkerchief when her turn out arrived.

I swivelled round in my chair to watch John, who was at the other table playing a tricky misère. Daisy had under-called her hand in a solo. If she didn't walk it in with ten tricks, it wouldn't be the fault of her outrageous luck. The hand would not be interesting.

John made his misere through one or two awful blunders on Yvonne's part. Ursula, after the hand had finished, asked in her sweet girlish way why she had done such and such. Her manner was perfectly innocent, but it had the effect of making Yvonne both defiant and guilty. Alan Braithwaite intervened with legal tact, declaring that with such a big hand as his he couldn't see how John could have failed to make his misère. Ursula gave her tinkling laugh at this.

"You're not like poor Jim, Alan. He always pointed out Yvonne's mistakes to her. He said it was the only way to learn, didn't he, darling?"

Yvonne, who sat facing me, dropped her lids over sudden tears of distress. Young Braithwaite glanced from one girl to the other unhappily. Ursula was wearing her sweetest smile, as she cut the pack to John. He dealt a fresh hand without comment.

And so the party went on until the bickering developed near to quarrelling and the veiled barbs to open insults. Still James Holland did not appear. Ames hovered in and out, smooth with regrets, filling glasses, emptying ashtrays and adjusting cushions behind the ladies. If I had not seen Mrs Potts-Power hurl hers to the ground first I would have done the same. By the end of the evening everyone wore a look of hostility or malice. It developed into downright hatred when Elizabeth Mulqueen overheard me absently murmuring polite and untruthful phrases to Ames at the front door. I don't know how I came to pass her by, but Ames did seem to be the proper person to thank in James Holland's absence.

CHAPTER FIVE

I

The Dower House telephone rang in the early hours of the following morning. I was having a nightmare. One of those ghastly dreams which have neither form nor sense but are terrifying withal. Even the telephone bell was part of it until it penetrated my consciousness. It was not the continuous sound of an automatic impulse, for it came from the Hall, operated by whoever answered the call there.

I slid out of bed on the instant, feeling inexplicably disturbed. It would have been easy to pretend not to hear it and let the ringing awaken John. But somehow I did not. I wanted to get to that phone and hear whatever news it could tell me.

The clock in the dining-room was striking as I passed on the way to the study. I put my head in the door, switching on the light. It was half-past three. Something had prompted me to check the time. I spoke without thinking, all my good telephonic manners forgotten.

"Who is it?"

There was a pause before a slow voice that I came to know well asked to speak to John. The caller used his full official title.

The voice was so prosaic and monotonous that I lost part of my nervousness.

"He's asleep," I informed him tartly. "It's half-past three, you know. Can I give him a message at some more Christian hour?"

"No, that would not do. Must speak to the Inspector. Very important."

"What is it, Maggie?" asked John from behind me. He stood there, very large and solid, tying the sash of his dressing-gown. His hair was tousled but his face bore no trace of sleep. It was firm and his eyes were alert.

"For you," I said. "I think it's Russell Street."

I handed him the receiver. Suddenly a tremor passed through my body. John saw me tremble and gripped one arm around my shoulders as he spoke into the receiver. I dropped my head against his arm in the hope of hearing both sides of the conversation.

When he said: "Yes, Billings?" the disturbed feeling returned. I knew Sergeant Billings was in charge of Middleburn police station. He did most of the talking, but it was unintelligible to me. The grip around my shoulders tightened almost unbearably. I glanced up into John's face. It was blank and very, very official. I had seen that look before. Something pretty big had turned up.

"I'll be at the gates in ten minutes. Get a doctor."

"John," I said in a whisper.

John made as if to hang up. On impulse he put the receiver back to his ear. I watched him wonderingly. Then he gave the instrument to me with an inquiring lift of his brow. I heard it too—an unmistakable sound of breathing.

I gave John a slight push out of the way and rang back on the line. It was an excellent form of punishment. A direct ring in the ear is very unpleasant. John grinned broadly before his face returned to its official look. I followed him back to the bedroom, running to keep up with his speedy purposeful steps.

"Local?" I asked. Wives of policemen do not show too much curiosity. They would only get snubbed for their pains. John nodded. He started to dress. I watched him anxiously.

"Has Cruikshank been found?"

"Cruikshank?" He spoke the name absently as though it struck a faint chord. He paused in the act of pulling on his shoe. I held the other ready for him. He stared straight into my eyes.

"Maggie. That shot you say you heard. What time did it happen?" John's voice was imperative.

Without wanting to know the reason for his question, I thought quickly, one hand to my head.

"After seven. We arrived on time, don't you remember? You pointed that out. I was only in the drawing-room for a few minutes. I went to get my cape."

"About seven-ten, to allow a margin. Thanks."

He got up and found a muffler to wind around his neck. It would be cold out in that mist. It was becoming thicker at midnight when we returned from Holland Hall and that horrid dinner party. I waited for John to speak, my eyes on his face. For a moment it did not seem as though he was going to tell me. Then he did, abruptly. Another slow tremor took possession of me.

"Maggie darling! Something pretty ghastly has happened. You've been in this sort of thing before. Do you think you can stand it? It will mean some beastly memories of yours dug up again."

"Murder?" I mouthed the word. John took my shoulders in his hands. "Not that baby?"

He looked puzzled for a moment but brushed it off. He shelved my impulsive remark in a corner of his mind to be dealt with later.

"Mr Holland has been found shot dead in the grounds of the Hall." His eyes scanned my face curiously, but my only reaction was complete astonishment.

"The Squire!" I exclaimed, heedless of what I was saying in my surprise. "It seems impossible. Why, he—"

"I must go," John interrupted. "Billings will be waiting for me. Prepare some coffee and then go back to bed like a good girl."

"How long will you be?" I asked, trying to keep the nervous note out of my voice. The idea of being left alone in the house again and this time with a murderer across the way did not fill me with a sense of security. Even had I known then that my welfare was of immediate concern to the murderer, I doubt whether I would have been less nervous.

"As quick as I can. You'll be all right. There will probably be one of our men patrolling the road for the rest of the night."

I saw him out quickly. I was not prepared to stand in a lighted doorway for all and sundry to see I was alone in the house. The coffee took but a minute to prepare. I dallied over it, trying to spin out the time. Sleep was going to be impossible. I took a cup along to the study and lit the gas fire, using the same match for a cigarette. But drinking coffee and smoking took up only a little more time. I gazed at the clock and the asbestos bars of the fire alternately. An hour passed, and at last something happened.

The sound of a car drawing up outside the house jerked me to my feet. I switched off the study light and drew aside the curtains at the window cautiously. The dark bulk of the car was out of my line of vision, but I could see two long arms of light shining through the mist. I opened the window an inch and bent my head to listen, the wet air pressing against the side of my face.

Two figures slipped by me on the other side of the hawthorn hedge dividing the Dower land from that of the Hall. I caught a glimpse of white coats and a stretcher through the thicket. The figures disappeared along the track into the wood.

Weary and chilled, I waited there for what seemed another hour before a little cavalcade came slowly down the path. The body of our late host and landlord passed me on its way to the ambulance.

I shut the window and hurried down the passage to the kitchen. Body in ambulance meant body on the way to the morgue and post-mortem and John's work finished for the moment. It was not his habit to go searching for clues in the dark. A picket and a man on guard were all that were necessary until daylight.

John's key was in the door as I came down the passage with a tray in my hands. He was not alone. Two men were with him, and I recognized one with interest.

John's frown deepened as he saw me. "Still up, Maggie? Doctor Trefont, my wife. And Sergeant Billings, Maggie."

"How do you do," I said demurely to the doctor. But Trefont was more than my match. He said: "I know you well by sight. We have nearly met before, have we not, Mrs Matheson?"

"Twice," I agreed, not to be outdone. "On the terrace at the Hall and in Middleburn High Street. Shall I get more coffee, John?"

He had been listening to the interchange with a still deeper frown. I did not care for the "wait until I talk to you afterwards" look, and tried to merge myself into the background.

I hovered around the three men, pouring coffee and attracting their attention to a plate of sandwiches in ministering angel fashion. My ears were constantly pricked and I kept one eye on the doctor. His position in the case was going to be interesting. He had had some connection with the Hall prior to Mr Holland's death, and yet here he was working for the police.

John was behind his desk making a few notes. On one side of the fire Sergeant Billings sat upright, his enormous hands placed on his huge knees. The doctor lounged at his ease opposite, balancing his coffee cup on the arm of the chair. I was stupid not to have guessed his profession that first day at the Hall. All medicos seem stamped with the same casual independent air. John asked his subordinate a few questions first. They were ordinary routine affairs but the answers Billings gave were somewhat surprising, at least to my mind. For example, when asked at what time and by whom the body was found, Billings was unable to say. His speech became slower and a bit incoherent as he tried to explain.

According to Billings, he had been awakened by the telephone at about 3 a.m. A man's voice speaking in a quick, muffled manner, obviously disguised, told him that the dead body of Mr James Holland of Holland Hall, Middleburn, was lying on the track which cut through the wood. After giving this information the man rang off. At first the sergeant was inclined either to doubt his own hearing or else the sanity of the caller. There had never been anything worse than a few robberies in Middleburn during all the years in which he had served the district. And somehow saying it was Mr Holland—well, you know—it was rather hard to take in, him being such a figure and a force in these parts. Billings recovered his aplomb enough to get on to the mechanic at the local automatic exchange and order him to trace the call. "And did he?" John interrupted, whose patience with the sergeant was something I opened my eyes at.

He did. The call originated from a public telephone outside the Middleburn Post Office. Billings hurried out of the house—his was a resident police station situated in High Street—but he was about a quarter of an hour too late to see anyone suspicious lurking, as he termed it.

He went back to the house to dress. But only partially, I thought, catching a glimpse of striped winceyette under his uniform. Then he bethought himself of John. At this point, Sergeant Billings rolled a bulbous blue eye in my direction, as if it was my cue to carry on the story. I merely poured him out some more coffee.

To me, Sergeant Billings appeared little more than a bucolic oaf. That was why I marvelled at John's attention to his story. Later I discovered that Sergeant Billings' stripes were not unmerited and that his slow but painstaking investigations under expert direction contributed largely to the success of the case.

John turned to Doctor Trefont. He still sat at his ease and seemed agreeable to spending the rest of the night in front of our gas fire. John wanted an off-the-record account of death, a first impression of medical findings. Doctor Trefont's reply was even a greater surprise than Billings' story.

"Suicide," he said, without looking at John and while casually blowing smoke rings.

I nearly said "rubbish" aloud.

John's face did not show disgust or disappointment. He was never anxious for crime to come knocking at his door. The doctor screwed his head round to look at John, throwing me an amused glance in transit. As though he had guessed at my scepticism.

"That was my first unprejudiced impression," he elaborated.

"A post-mortem and a few police inquiries will no doubt cast doubts on it. But if a man is found shot through the head at close quarters with a gun in his hand, what else can I say?"

"You doubt your own medical findings, then, Doctor," John said pleasantly.

"I do. From the little I knew of, but the amount I heard about the late Mr Holland, suicide would be the last crime he would commit. Unless of course he had some deep far-flung plan to execute which necessitated his own removal. The man had a genius for running things his own way in this part of the world."

"That means enemies," John nodded. "Do you know of any?"

The doctor replied dryly: "Dozens, if by enemies you mean those who resented his high-handed behaviour. But I don't know of anyone who could be considered a worthy opponent—on the same social plane, as it were. However, when a man as feared and disliked as Holland is found shot dead, one can't help thinking that there might have been such an enemy."

There was a pause before John asked: "You say you knew Mr Holland only slightly? Who was his medical attendant?"

"He didn't have one. His health was remarkably robust."

"What about the rest of the family? Are they all so hardy?"

"I believe Mrs Ernest Mulqueen is considered a goldmine in Collins Street. I never attended her myself."

"Did you ever attend any other member of the household?" The doctor's attention was on the third cigarette he was rolling. "Occasionally members of the staff came to my surgery with minor cuts and ailments."

John dropped the subject at this point. I could have shaken him, but dared not interfere in any way. Surely he could sense the doctor's reluctance to speak about his medical dealings with the Hollands. The little he admitted had to be dragged out of him and he had skilfully avoided prevarication. No mention had been made of Yvonne and the baby. I was certain from what I had seen and overheard, and from hints dropped by Yvonne, that he had had some professional interest in her and the child. If John was not going to find out the nature of that interest, I was.

Beyond saying "I wish you'd gone to bed" in a worried voice, John did not reproach me further after the two men had left. I think he was glad I had been there, even if it was only to pour the coffee.

"It hardly seems worthwhile going back to bed," I commented, yawning at the clock. "Why can't murderers commit their crimes in office hours? It is as bad as being married to a doctor. Do you go to the office today or can you sleep in?"

"I must go in. I'll have to put in a report at once. It is not conclusive that owing to propinquity I will be placed in charge of this case." We went back to bed in silence. I was nearly asleep when John's voice spoke drowsily.

"There are a few questions I must ask you later, Maggie."

I started to snore gently.

II

Daylight brought Tony out of his cot. He ran wildly around the house, full of overpowering vitality which we both regarded with dull amazement. John went off immediately after breakfast, extracting a promise from me to get some rest when Tommy went down for his noonday nap.

Not long after he had gone, the telephone rang. I went to it with a frown. The extension line from the Hall which hitherto I had regarded as a necessary nuisance now appeared more in the light of a sinister connection between the two houses.

It was Yvonne, more nervous and rattled than ever.

Could I—would I please come over as soon as convenient. She felt she had no one to turn to. And I seemed—well, so practical.

Shuddering at the epithet, I said yes, certainly. I had intended coming tomorrow, not wishing to intrude on their private sorrow.

A rather hysterical sound greeted this conventional phrase and she rang off.

I went round the house with Tony at my heels. By emptying ashtrays from the study I was reminded of Doctor Trefont. Laying down my duster, I picked up the telephone from John's desk.

Ames answered my ring. His voice was grave and subdued as became a bereaved employee.

"Very, very shocking," was the smooth reply to yet another conventional phrase.

I waited for a few seconds, allowing time for Ames to switch the Dower extension onto the exchange line.

I was about to dial out my number when a voice broke in.

"Put me through to Mrs Matheson at the Dower House, please, Ames."

"Ames—" I said sharply. "Haven't you given me the line? Why is one extension key still open?"

"I'm sorry, Mrs Matheson. Mrs Mulqueen wishes to speak to you."

"What is it, Mrs Mulqueen?" I asked ungraciously. She started on a monologue which was much the same as Yvonne's insofar as an urgent desire to see me was expressed; the plea about not having anyone to turn to also was employed. But where Yvonne had seemed genuinely upset, I was persuaded that Elizabeth Mulqueen had some definite reason for wishing me to call.

"I will be over presently," I told her. "Now may I have the line, please?"

After arranging a time with Dr Trefont for that afternoon, I paused to gaze out of the study window. It was a perfect day, fine, crisp, clean. Tony clambered up onto the window seat beside me. I brushed his yellow hair to and fro, addressing him absently.

"The wood looks so serene by sunlight. Too placid and perfect a place to shelter violence. Yet only a few hours ago I was crouching here cold and fearful of what would be located in its very heart."

"Bang!" said Tony suddenly, with uncanny appropriateness.

"The result of a bang," I agreed. "A large, horrid bang."

Sergeant Billings with another man in uniform passed along the path below. I put my head out of the window.

"Hullo, Sergeant. Whither away?"

The two men stopped and peered through the hedge. I had the advantage, as they stood in the full sunlight.

"Good morning, Mrs Matheson. The Inspector asked us to look at the picket we fixed up last night."

"Is he in charge of the case, then?" I asked, not knowing whether to feel pleased or apprehensive. "Where is he?"

"At the Hall."

"I was just going over to pay my condolences. May I come through the wood and visit the scene of the crime? I promise not to trample on any clues."

I was taking a mean advantage of Sergeant Billings. In the normal course of events he would have refused, but as I was the wife of his superior officer he did not like to.

"By the way, Sergeant, is it murder or suicide? What was the result of the post-mortem?"

He replied guardedly: "Muchly what the doctor said. The shot could have been fired by Mr Holland himself. The gun was found near his right hand."

I shut my eyes for a minute. "Yes. He was right-handed. No fatal mistake on the murderer's part there."

"Murder or suicide, every avenue is being explored," said Sergeant Billings primly as he moved off.

Mr Holland's body had been found almost in the centre of the path, half-way between the two houses. Hand in hand with Tony, I arrived at the place, which was segregated by means of stakes joined together by rope. Sergeant Billings and his constable were scavenging around just outside this area. They seemed to be so busy stirring up the blanket of fallen leaves that I went on almost immediately. I was interested to know what John had sent them to find.

At the other end of the path I came on Ernest Mulqueen, clad in his mackinaw and tweed cap. He was wandering along with his eyes on the ground, and started violently when I spoke his name.

At once I was struck by his changed appearance. Like most tubby, rosy little men when dealt a severe shock, he had become pale and flabby-looking. Indeed he appeared so undone that I made an effort to brace him.

"I meant to cut you dead the next time we met," I informed him, "out of revenge for what you did last night."

For a moment my words might have been calamitous for the unnerving effect they had on Ernest Mulqueen. Then it penetrated that I was teasing him, and he tried to force a wobbly smile. It was a poor effort, barely touching the deep lines either side of his mouth which must have been caused by years of grins.

"You ignored me when you came in before dinner," I explained, helping him out. I was beginning to regard him in a new light. Murder or suicide, every avenue is being explored, Sergeant Billings had said. Ernest Mulqueen appeared to be one of these avenues. A man could not change overnight like he had without having something on his mind.

"Your hair was done differently," he tried to defend himself.

"No go. I always wear the same style for months on end."

I felt like someone staring through a magnifying glass at a moth on the end of a pin. And yet I could not stop myself.

"To tell you the truth," he said, in a bad attempt at sounding confidential, "you looked so smart and dressed up that I was scared to speak to you."

"Flattery can't help you," I said, shaking my head. "Confess now. You either wanted to snub me or else you had something on your mind."

My words were daring under the circumstances, in spite of a light tone. I felt a little frightened after I had spoken: colour flowed into Ernest Mulqueen's face. It was not his original ruddy colour but a flush of temper. He half raised a clenched fist.

"If it was anything on my mind that concerned you or your policeman husband, I would have told you," he snarled. He turned away quickly, plunging straight into the wood away from the path.

III

As I was skirting the Hall to the terrace a window opened in the east wing. Elizabeth Mulqueen put out her head.

"I have been watching for you," she called, beckoning imperiously. "Come in through the conservatory and along to my sitting-room."

"Where can I locate Mrs Holland? She rang first."

Elizabeth Mulqueen said something vague about Yvonne lying down and that I could see her presently. She shut the window before I could protest further.

I was interested to find out why Mrs Mulqueen desired my company so suddenly. It was with this desire and not in the spirit of meekness that I followed the directions to her sitting-room. If she only wanted someone to listen to her reactions and emotions at hearing of her brother's death, I doubted whether I would fit the bill.

I was beginning to think this was the reason for the summons, when she introduced a subject so casually that some sense that had been with me that horrid time at Central sprang to the fore.

I was told that neither Ernest nor Ursula had shown the proper sympathy and consideration. Of course, Ernest could not be expected to have the finer feelings of a Holland, but she had tried to bring Ursula up so carefully. After all it was her own brother who had committed suicide—

"Just a minute," I broke in. "Who told you it was suicide?"

Mrs Mulqueen opened her eyes at that. "Why, of course it was suicide. You don't think it was an accident, do you?"

"No, I don't," I said bluntly. "I think it was murder."

She manifested terrible shock. It was far too histrionic to be genuine.

"But who?" she wailed, pressing her fingers to her forehead. "Who would want to murder poor James? I just can't believe it. I won't believe it."

"Then why should poor James want to commit suicide? I only met him once, but he seemed the last person in the world who would take his own life."

"I don't believe it," Elizabeth Mulqueen repeated, throwing back her head. "James has never been the same since my nephew was killed. His only son. So very tragic. James has had a life with many disappointments and much unhappiness. I think Jim's death was the last straw. My poor, poor brother." She averted her face and dabbed at her eyes ostentatiously.

"That happened nearly eighteen months ago," I pointed out. "Do you think he would have brooded on suicide for all that time, and then done the deed on the very night he was giving a dinner party? Furthermore, I can't see him committing suicide in the middle of the wood on a damp cold night. What was he doing there? Where had he been?"

Mrs Mulqueen remained silent. I released my grip of Tony's jumper and let him stray around the over-furnished room.

Presently my hostess, completely ignoring my two questions, leaned forward to pat my hand.

"You've cheered me up considerably," she said on a sigh. "I knew I was right asking you to come. You've been very kind."

I was trying to recall what words of consolation I had uttered, when she said: "By the way, being the wife of the officer in charge of the inquiry into my brother's death, I suppose you have his ear and are able to assist in a lot of ways. You've worked together before, so I've been told."

I made no reply. Any reference to the circumstances under which John and I had met always made me tongue-tied, and in the face of Mrs Mulqueen's wagging finger to boot, there seemed nothing to say.

"I am sure," she went on, "there must be a lot of tedious detail which has nothing whatsoever to do with the result of such an inquiry. Red herrings, if you follow my meaning. I think I might be doing your husband a good turn if you will tell him that I must have made a mistake last night. I only imagined hearing my brother in his room. You know how it is. You expect to hear things and think they take place. You see, the light was on in James' room. I supposed that he must have returned and was there. Silly how we women always leap to conclusions. So you will tell your husband, won't you?"

"If you like," I said slowly. I had been following Tony's progress round the room with my eyes when a thought occurred to me.

"Just tell me one thing, Mrs Mulqueen. What were you doing on the floor above when your suite is down here in the east wing?"

She answered without a blink. "I went up to the tower to switch on the light. It throws out such a radiance. I knew James liked it being on when he gave a party."

"Is there anything wrong with the switch?" I asked. "Anything that would make it flicker on and off?"

She got up from her chair suddenly.

"Now, little boy, don't touch my pretty pictures."

I grabbed Tony's hand and moved to the door. "That reminds me of another matter, Mrs Mulqueen," I said pleasantly. "Since I am behaving so inquisitively, may I know why you keep that picture hanging face to the wall?"

"What picture? Oh, that is a photograph of James's wife. She died. Keeping the photograph so is just my little way of mourning her. I was very fond of Olivia, very fond indeed. It is sad to think they are both gone and I am left, the last Holland."

I left her to reflect on her solitary state. She seemed to have forgotten the existence of the youngest Holland, frail though it might be. Ames was at the foot of the stairs as I came along the passage.

"Mrs Mulqueen told me to come in through the conservatory door," I told him, feeling some explanation was due—the effect Ames always had on me. "Mrs Holland is in her room, I suppose?"

"Just one minute, Mrs Matheson."

He spoke urgently, with one hand outstretched. I glanced at it with raised brows. Ames dropped it, looking foolish.

"I want to tell you something," he said.

"What is it?" I asked with curiosity.

He was shaken out of his habitual suaveness. Ames lowered his voice, glancing down the long passage.

"Mrs Matheson, Mr Holland did not commit suicide. I know everything points that way, but I knew the late Mr Holland too well. He would never have killed himself. I—" He threw another glance over his shoulder. "It may sound presumptuous, but I was very attached to the late Mr Holland. I can't let his death go unavenged."

"That's all right, Ames. I don't think anyone else thinks it either, excepting perhaps Mrs Mulqueen. But why tell me this?"

"I thought perhaps you may be able to persuade your husband. He is in charge of the inquiry. I can prove Mr Holland didn't do it himself."

"Well, if you can prove it, what are you worrying about? What's your proof?"

"I don't know if you can count it as evidence yet, but a revolver was stolen from the study some time ago. Mr Holland complained of the loss and asked me to look into the matter for him."

I put one foot on the first step to brace myself against Tony, who was dragging at my hand. "Have you told my husband that?" I asked Ames.

"No, not yet. You see, the police have come across a letter which might help the suicide theory. If I told them about the missing gun, they might think it clinches the matter. But if you told Inspector Matheson it might be very different."

I looked Ames over frowningly. He dropped his eyes to Tony.

"All right," I said. "I'll tell him."

He thanked me. In order to show his appreciation, he relieved me of Tony's fidgetings by suggesting that he should go down to the Lodge to play with Robin for a while. Thus Ames and I became somewhat involved in the matter of gratitude. Tony's enlivening presence was not exactly suitable on a visit of condolence.

I went upstairs wondering how many more times I was to act as a liaison officer between suspects and police. Elizabeth Mulqueen's story might be as thin as paper, but Ames' had a ring of sincerity to it.

Yvonne was lying on her bed in a darkened room. Even in the dim light her face looked ghastly. I sat down in a chair near the bed, begging her not to get up. I felt awkward and ill-at-ease as she remained silent. I did not know what was expected of me. You can't go sympathizing with anyone losing a father-in-law they both feared and disliked, and at whose demise the only emotion experienced must be one of relief.

Presently, without looking at me, Yvonne said in a low tense voice: "Your husband thinks it is suicide, doesn't he? He must. Anything else is out of the question."

I was becoming very tired of being expected to use my influence and said so.

"Don't tell me you invited me here to enlist my sympathy on that account. I don't know what my husband thinks, but I do know nothing I can do or say will change his sense of duty and justice. Just get that into your head right at the start."

I got up. If that was all Yvonne wanted I was prepared to leave.

She put out a hand. "Don't go. Please stay for a moment, Mrs Matheson. I'm so upset and bewildered. I think I'm going mad. I don't know what I'm saying."

I sat down again, ashamed of my sudden outburst. Yvonne had not merited it wholly. It was the result of slow reaction on my part to Elizabeth Mulqueen's innuendoes.

"How is the infant?" I asked to break the tension. "He is likely to be an important person now, is he not?"

"If you mean the money," Yvonne replied with bitterness, "I suppose he is."

I went on gently. "You know, now Mr Holland is dead, you must exert yourself. Get Jimmy away from here. I would put him into a good children's hospital for a week or two to fix his diet and to build him up. What about it?"

She nodded listlessly.

"I am extremely puzzled about your late father-in-law," I went on. "He seemed anxious that the male line of Hollands should continue, and yet—"

I paused. She glanced at me expectantly.

"What do you mean?"

I threw out my hands, a little embarrassed.

"I have to confess I overheard you and Mr Holland quarrelling. The day I called about the Dower House, do you remember? There was a certain accusation you hurled at him." Yvonne raised herself abruptly. "What do you mean? What did you overhear?"

I eyed her uneasily. She was panting slightly.

"Why," I asked slowly, "did you accuse Mr Holland of child murder? Why should he want to murder his own grandchild?"

She fell back against the pillows with closed eyes.

"Yvonne!" I said in an urgent voice.

Yvonne opened her eyes and gave a twisted smile, quite without mirth. "Don't worry. I haven't fainted." She turned her head towards the window and seemed to forget me.

"What did you mean by that outburst?" I demanded. "Why did you say 'I could kill you for it'?"

"Did I say that?" she asked, in a whisper still. "I don't remember. Did I really say that?"

I returned her gaze steadily.

A knock came at the door. I went to answer it.

"Please," said Yvonne in a soft tone, "if that is Ursula, don't let her in. I don't think I can bear it now."

It was Nurse Stone. She gave me the same look of scarcely veiled hostility I had earned the previous night. But I thought I detected a certain fawning quality in her tone, no doubt due to John's position again.

"The police want to interview me. Will you tell Mrs Holland to listen for Baby?" She made an attempt to peer around the door, which I frustrated.

Yvonne was struggling off the bed. "I must go downstairs. He is on the terrace in the sun."

"Stay where you are," I ordered. "I'll go and see if he is all right and get one of the maids to listen for him. They'll tell you if you're wanted."

IV

The child was sleeping peacefully. I tucked his hand under the blanket and watched him frowningly. Hitherto I had considered that the baby was, as it were, *in medias res,* but now it appeared he was *inter alia,* and that a bigger and much deeper game was being played.

A familiar voice called my name. I wandered along the terrace to the study window.

"Can I come in?" I asked, bending double under the French window as I spoke.

"What are you doing here?" John demanded, getting up from the big mahogany desk.

"I came in answer to a royal summons. The brat is playing at the Lodge." I wandered over to James Holland's desk. John had been going through it.

"What a rotten game yours is," I remarked, indicating the piles of papers which included letters.

"You become hardened to it," John replied briefly. "Maggie, did we ever receive a letter from Holland?"

"I don't think so. I never saw one."

John took my handbag from my grasp, extracted the hand mirror and held it in front of the blotting-pad from the desk. "Holland blotted an envelope addressed to me. Why didn't I receive it?"

"Perhaps he forgot to post it," I suggested, "or decided not to send it." John frowned at the pad and then put it aside. He ran both hands through his hair in a tired fashion. "Are you tossing to decide whether it is murder or suicide?" I asked.

He grinned ruefully. "It looks like coming to that. Certain facts are hard to get away from. Take a look at that, for example."

I picked up the letter. It bore the inscription of a well-known firm of private detectives. Messrs. Dawson & Heeps regretted very much that they had nothing further to report on the inquiry into the death of James Alexander Holland who crashed in his plane in the north of Victoria eighteen months ago. The letter suggested politely but firmly that Mr Holland was wasting his time in trying to bring about any other decision but that of accidental death.

"Did the Squire think there was dirty work done?" I asked, passing back the letter.

"Evidently. But look what an excuse this is for suicide, Maggie. For eighteen months old man Holland has been hanging on, trying to make someone pay for the death of his son. Then Dawson & Heeps tell him to snap out of it, it was an accident. The boy had come to the end of his allotted span and you can't argue with the Almighty about the justice of it."

"That's all very well," I objected. "But why doesn't he shoot himself immediately on receipt of this letter? Why go off on some trip, arrange a dinner party and keep his suicide for that moment? Where had he been?"

John put the letter back on its pile.

"Nobody seems to know exactly where James Holland went. Not even Ames."

"What about the telegram Ames received? Where was it lodged?"

"Some obscure little country town out of Bendigo."

"Can't Ames tell you why the Squire left Middleburn? I thought he was conversant with all Holland's business."

"He has no idea," John said, seating himself at the desk. "I have someone trying to trace Holland's movements, but it is a hell of a job."

"So it is going to be suicide," I said, sitting down on the arm of a chair. "Well, that should fit in with everyone's wishes, except perhaps Ames," I added as an afterthought.

John looked up quickly. "What's that?"

I told him about my conversation with Elizabeth Mulqueen, Ames and Yvonne, omitting the part about the baby. With his new official standing John could and would order me offstage if he considered my concern for Jimmy was involving me in the affairs of the Hall. However, he was more interested in the missing gun Ames spoke about than any tell-tale break in my story.

"Ames said Mr Holland complained of the loss? That's odd, if the man meant to use it on himself." There was a pause. John stared in front of him, frowning again.

"When do you want lunch?" I asked presently.

He looked up, his face clearing.

"Now," he grinned, "but unfortunately I can't come yet. Young Braithwaite is coming out from town with the will. Don't wait for me. I may be able to scrounge something here." Billings appeared at the window. He saw us together, backed a step and coughed.

"Come in, Sergeant," John called. "Did you find it?"

Billings stepped over the sill.

"Not a trace, sir. Are you sure we are looking for the right thing?" I glanced from one man to the other with raised brows. Observing my mystification, John grinned again.

"What are you talking about?" I demanded. There were times when I knew I was allowed to ask questions.

"We don't know ourselves. There was a note in the post-mortem report about a wound in the right leg of the body just above the instep. The trousers Mr Holland wore were torn at that place. I sent Sergeant Billings out this morning to look for barbed wire with traces of the material adhering. He reports no luck."

"Look here!" I protested. "I thought you inferred this was going to be suicide. Why all these careful investigations?"

"Just routine," John replied airily. "We now await the will. Further light might be thrown on this question of murder or suicide. Money, and there must have been quite an amount of it, always talks. In this instance I hope it will speak long and loudly."

"I had better go," I said, getting up. "Tony will be wanting his dinner and his sleep. Do I expect you when I see you? Steak and kidney pie and the remains of the day before yesterday's sweet for dinner."

"It will make me rush home madly at six o'clock," John promised, as I nodded good-bye to Sergeant Billings.

Ursula Mulqueen was strolling leisurely down the drive in the direction of the gates. It was only my knowledge of the time which caused me to catch up with her. I had intended passing on after a brief word.

"Oh, Mrs Matheson!" she said, opening her eyes and mouth wide. "Isn't it perfectly dreadful about poor dear Uncle. To think that we were all sitting down to dinner waiting for him last night and he was lying out there in the wood alone. It pains me to think of him being by himself at such a time, without anyone to help him on his journey."

"As far as I can see someone did help him on his journey," I told her with brutal frankness.

The shocked and sad expression changed immediately to horror. Her face mirrored exactly the transition that had taken place on her mother's.

"Surely," she protested, "your husband doesn't think someone deliberately killed Uncle James! Who would want to do that? What reason could they have?"

My mind fled back to something John had once told me. Even motives for murder can be arranged into tabular form.

"Either someone who was frightened of him or jealous or else money was involved. In your Uncle James' case I'm inclined to think there might have been two reasons. Fear and money."

"I was never frightened of him," Ursula remarked inconsequentially, but with deadly aim. "Not like poor dear Yvonne. By the way, little Jimmy will be the owner of Holland Hall now, will he not?"

"How should I know?" I asked, recognizing a figure coming through the gates. "I see Mr Braithwaite approaching. Why don't you ask him? He is to bring a copy of the will to show the police."

Ursula left me at once. I watched her well-shaped legs flash up and down under the unattractive dress.

She drew the young solicitor off the drive into the garden, one hand on his arm. She must have known Alan Braithwaite was coming and was pacing the drive waiting to meet him. I shrugged disinterestedly and continued on my way.

Old man Ames was sitting on the porch sunning himself. I thought he looked dejected. His head was leaning on one hand as though he was deep in memories. It suddenly occurred to me that of all those living in and connected with the Hall, he was the one most likely to feel a sense of loss at James Holland's death, and to grieve sincerely.

There was no sign of Mrs Ames. Anxious to be on my way I called to him to convey my thanks for letting Tony play at the Lodge. Ames rose and came over to the railing. When I looked into his handsome face, I said what I should have said to each member of the Holland household I had seen and yet could not say. For Ames the words came spontaneously.

"I am so sorry. So very sorry."

He looked down at me in silence for a moment before he spoke. Somehow the words he quoted in reply did not jar my sympathetic mood. That line or two from the dying King Arthur's speech, unspoiled by further comment, seemed more appropriate than the most eloquent panegyric.

CHAPTER SIX

I

As he finished with each patient, Doctor Trefont came to the door connecting the surgery with the waiting-room to usher in a fresh one. Presently my turn came. I pulled Tony along with me. He was as nervous as a horse running a maiden race in that scrubbed and chromium environment, with the odour of antiseptic heavy in the air.

Doctor Trefont might never have seen me before for all the signs of recognition he gave. He put his blunt-fingered hand on Tony's head for a brief moment before going round to his side of the desk. He selected a card and spoke without raising his eyes from his pen.

"Your name, please?"

"Matheson," I snapped, annoyed at the pretence.

He looked up at me with his mild gaze. "I want your full name," he said gently.

"This is not exactly a professional visit," I confessed. "I thought it a good notion since we propose settling in this district to make myself known to a Middleburn doctor."

He accepted this with a friendly nod. I watched him carefully over Tony's head. "You were recommended by Mrs Bellamy. Sister Heather at the Health Centre also told me to come to you."

He inclined his head without speaking.

I went on deliberately. "I went there one day with Mrs Yvonne Holland."

"So I learned from Sister Heather," said the doctor calmly. "You ran a great risk of earning the displeasure of Mr Holland."

"Doctor," I said, trying to hold his eyes. "Why is the attitude at the Hall so hostile towards you and Sister Heather? Mrs Holland almost begged me not to come here. Have you ever attended her?"

He looked at me in an odd, almost quizzical way. "If I said no, it would be the truth. But you wouldn't believe it, would you? You would keep on ferreting around until you found some reason for that animosity you say the family at the Hall have for me. Let me give you some advice, Mrs Matheson, as an ordinary person as well as your doctor. It is never wise to become too curious about things outside the law. Leave it to your husband and the men of his profession." He dropped his gaze and made some notes on the card under his hand.

"I agree with what you say," I replied, trying to maintain the conversation on the same lines, "but unfortunately there are certain factors which place me in an awkward position. I consider that I have in my possession more information than the police have."

"You should give this information to Inspector Matheson," Doctor Trefont said, continuing with his spasmodic writing.

I put my head on one side to look at him speculatively.

"I wonder. I think it is rather brave of you to make that suggestion. I can't tell my husband because any proof I have which involves me even slightly with the Hall will mean expulsion from Middleburn and a house to which I am becoming rather attached, in spite of its bizarre appearance. If you knew the miles I walked to find that house, you would understand."

I got up and said without hope: "I suppose you wouldn't like to save me the trouble of ferreting, as you call it?"

"Certainly not," Doctor Trefont replied in a perfectly amiable voice. "If you will persist in this foolishness my only wish is that you will find a red herring or two to keep you occupied and out of mischief."

"I see your point," I replied, grinning. "But it would save a lot of time if you could tell what you were doing on the terrace of the Hall that first day I saw you; why Mr Holland and Yvonne vied with each other belabouring you with their tongues; and what Sister Heather meant when she got into your car in High Street."

He frowned in a startled way. I pressed home the attack.

"You know," I said conversationally, "when anyone uses the word 'murder' I always prick up my ears. I think most people would be inclined to. You should warn Sister Heather to be more discreet."

The worried look on Doctor Trefont's face, followed up by this Parthian shot, should have provided an excellent exit.

Unfortunately, my departure was spoiled by Tony's sudden and tenacious interest in the sterilizer near the door.

Doctor Trefont followed me to the door.

"I will see you again," I told him, "with my ferret. Good-bye, Doctor Trefont." The door was closed behind me with more than necessary force.

I wheeled Tony down the surgery path, and headed towards the village, deep in thought. So often murder mysteries have been compared with jigsaw puzzles. The comparison has become tedious, but James Holland's death and the tangled web of reticence and mystery which I found at the Hall and in Middleburn itself were a perfect example of one.

There was some connection between all the pieces I had picked up and examined, but it was easy to forget the importance of one when overwhelmed with the sudden significance of another. Which was precisely what happened, as I walked along the High Street through the shopping centre.

My mind was filled with the presence of Doctor Trefont and Sister Heather when I entered the Middleburn library, estate and many other agencies, and dry-cleaning establishment. And there waiting to serve me, dressed in his shirtsleeves and sateen apron, was Mr Cruikshank.

II

I had expected Cruikshank to be found skulking in the bush country outside Middleburn or wandering in another suburb with a lost memory. I might have been less surprised had he been found dead in suspicious circumstances. But I certainly did not expect to find him exactly as I did that first day in Middleburn; not only alive and well and in his own setting, but with his manner having undergone no change whatsoever. Just as though he had never disappeared.

I managed to move my tongue about at last and to ask if my parcel had come in.

"Maud!" Cruikshank called, ignoring my glassy stare. "Mrs Matheson's grey flannels. And how are you liking the Dower House, Mrs Matheson? Settling in all right?"

The man's effrontery was astounding.

Cruikshank continued: "Such a sad, sad affair at the Hall. Poor Mr Holland. Middleburn won't be the same without him. Shocking to go like that."

He passed his head to and fro, tut-tutting. His words gave no indication whether he favoured the theory of suicide or murder.

"I heard about it this morning when I got back," he continued. "It almost bowled me over, as the saying goes. I have been out of Middleburn for a few days visiting an aged aunt of ours. You may have noticed me gone."

Cruikshank held me fascinated. It was just like listening to a radio play and wondering how the situation would be saved. In spite of my bewilderment, some shrewd instinct told me that this was going to be the story he wanted to reach the ears of the police before they came to him. It was a stroke of luck that I had walked into his shop that afternoon.

Cruikshank continued: "I understand that before last night's tragic affair I had been the talk of Middleburn." He smiled indulgently at his sister, who had brought in "my grey flannels."

"Foolish girl! And all because I did not wish to cause her any anxiety, Mrs Matheson."

Miss Cruikshank had been coached in her cues.

"You nearly had me demented, Arthur, going off and leaving no word. Naturally I went to the police. Who wouldn't, Mrs Matheson?"

I had got over the first paralysing surprise, through the gullible stage, and was now feeling annoyed at their childish playacting.

"Who wouldn't, indeed," I agreed with heavy sarcasm. "But why didn't you tell your sister where you were going, Mr Cruikshank?"

He patted Miss Cruikshank's hand in a nauseating fashion.

"It was like this, Mrs Matheson. My sister is very attached to our aunt. If Maud knew she was ill and wanted to see me, she would worry herself sick. I thought it best to slip off without a word. Mind you, I never anticipated being so long away. I did send a telegram, but Maud said she never received it. The post office system leaves much to be desired, don't you think, Mrs Matheson?"

"No," I said flatly, refusing to play their type of ball.

He passed over my interruption and reiterated about their aunt and her illness and Maud's unnecessary anxiety. It was pure padding. I cut it short by asking him if he had reported his presence to Sergeant Billings at the Middleburn Police Station.

He hadn't—not yet. The shop was in a turmoil. He had been so busy all day. Maud had let things go. She had been so worried.

I indicated the handset at the end of the counter.

"I suggest you ring the station now. It should only take about thirty seconds to make the call. If you pass me the telephone book I will look up the number."

Cruikshank was nonplussed. A certain venomous look came into his eye, such as one sees in a cornered rat. After a moment's hesitation he removed the receiver.

"Oh, dear," said Maud in a frightened voice as he dialled the number.

While he was speaking to Sergeant Billings I checked Connie Bellamy's address. There was something I wanted to follow up in connection with Cruikshank. "Better for the police to hear it direct," I said sweetly from the doorway. "I never was good at telling a secondhand story."

Connie Bellamy was sharing a cane couch with her dog in the garden. She waved as I approached, but did not get up.

"Such an effort," she excused herself in a satisfied way.

I replied dampingly, "Perhaps you are not getting enough exercise. That might be fat you're putting on, lying about like this."

"Nonsense, Maggie. I take exercise, of course. One mile before breakfast is worth ten after breakfast. Peter goes with me to keep me company, don't you, my angel? You look after mummy and see that she doesn't come to any harm." She raised her head from this idiotic prattle. "This lying about, as you call it, is another way of absorbing vitamin D. The sun, you know. Do you study your diet and see that it is well-balanced, Maggie?"

"I suppose so. When I have time."

"You don't seem very concerned. I do think it is all frightfully interesting."

"Let it go! I didn't come here to talk vitamins, but to tell you your friend Cruikshank has now done the re-appearing act."

Her glance suddenly avoided mine. "How odd of the man. Where had he been?"

"Visiting a sick aunt, so he told me," I replied, watching her closely. "I came to tell you because you expressed an urgent desire to see him. Why do you?"

"I didn't say that," Connie denied, still dodging my eye.

"You said your husband did," I said impatiently. "I was speaking in a general sense. What did you mean when you said Cruikshank has been systematically robbing you for years."

Connie adopted the playful style to combat my interrogations. She wagged one finger at me. "The same old Maggie. Always wanting to know what is going on. Of course, being married to a policeman has made you worse. I am sure your husband must have some very interesting stories to tell about crime. I am looking forward to meeting him."

I grinned at her. "Don't try and change the subject, Connie. Being a policeman's wife has made me suspicious of anyone trying to turn questions into questions."

"I'm sure I wasn't," she protested.

"All right," I said promptly. "Prove it. Tell me in what way Cruikshank has been robbing you. Has he been charging you more rent than he should?"

She looked affronted. "This house is our own. Harold would never pay rent to anyone. He doesn't hold with it."

"I thought it was, but I had to get you started. If the house is yours what connection have you with the local estate agent?"

"None at all," Connie retorted. "I do wish you would stop this questioning, Maggie. You're making my head ache."

"I will, as soon as you've told me what I want to know," I replied cheerfully. "It is good training for developing your powers of endurance."

"I refuse to discuss the subject," Connie snapped. "It is none of your business and Harold said—"

"Oho," I said, as she stopped short. "So Harold told you to shut up, did he? I wonder why."

"Because," Connie blurted out, "it is best to be very careful at this time. We don't want to become involved with the Hall. Harold was most upset when I told him what I said to you. Most unreasonable of him, of course, when he more or less inferred your husband might be able to help us—" She broke off again with one hand at her mouth. "Oh, damn you, Maggie. What do you mean by worming it out of me this way!"

"I suggest you go on," I threatened. "It would be better if I could tell John the whole story, not half. He might start brooding on all sorts of things which might involve you properly."

Connie looked a little frightened. "Maggie, you won't tell him! I do think you are awful treating me like this when I am in a delicate condition."

"Think how painful it is for me. But I'll stop, just for your sake. Perhaps you will be able to persuade Harold to have a talk with John when you come to dinner. From a policeman's wife, you might pass on the idea to him. By the way, how did you come to buy this house? It is really very nice, Connie."

"Do you like it?" she asked, pleased and diverted. "Hasn't Harold made the garden lovely? Of course, our bad boy Peter tries to wreck it. We bought the house under a scheme old Mr Holland ran. I believe he built this whole block."

I glanced at her quickly. Connie had let fall something that all my questioning and bullying had not surprised. What was better still, she was not conscious of it.

"Will you stay to tea?" Connie asked, pushing Peter to the ground.

"I'd love it. Providing," I added guardedly, "it won't be a glass of milk and cheese sandwiches. I refuse to be stuffed with calcium."

After tea Connie decided perhaps she did need more exercise and walked as far as the High Street with me. Half-way up the hill we passed the Potts Power residence. Daisy was watering the front garden, waving the hose around in three-four time to the sound of music from inside. Connie called a greeting and remarked how dry it was this autumn. Daisy replied in kind and then caught sight of me. She ran over to the fence. I glanced surreptitiously at my watch. The steak and kidney pie would have to cook itself if she chatted for long.

"Of course, you met Miss Potts-Power at the Community Centre, didn't you, Maggie?"

Before I had time to speak, Daisy said: "Oh, I feel Maggie and I are old friends. Wasn't it dreadful last night, Maggie? Fancy us all together like that! I said to mother when I heard the news, Maggie must be feeling dreadful. This is the second time she has come up against murder."

I flinched every time she spoke my name but found her last sentence interesting enough to overcome a desire to hit her on the head.

"So you think it was murder, do you?"

"Mother says it was. And she is always right. James Holland wouldn't have the humility to kill himself. Those were her very words. But it is dreadful, isn't it? We knew him so well."

"I thought you said he and your mother had quarrelled and hadn't spoken for years."

"Did I?" she queried vaguely. "But what is time, Maggie? Mother admired and respected him, I am sure."

"Time will mean dinner won't be ready for my husband if I don't push off," I said, directing another glance at my watch.

"Oh, just one minute, Maggie," Daisy almost begged. Her attitude of semi-adoration both embarrassed and annoyed me. "I called on you earlier this afternoon, but you were out. I thought you might like someone understanding near you at this time."

"Mr Holland was no relation of mine," I said, surprised.

"I know that, Maggie. But you see Connie was telling me all

about that time at the Telephone Exchange, and I thought it might bring back horrid memories."

Her words irritated me not only by the interference they interpreted, but because they were almost identical with John's. She made them sound a little ridiculous.

"Mrs Bellamy had left the Exchange before that affair started," I said, shooting an annihilating glance at Connie. "She can't know more than the newspapers published."

"Please, please don't be angry, Maggie," Daisy implored. "It wasn't only that. You see, I was afraid I'd given you the wrong impression about mother and Mr Holland. I mean they had never really quarrelled about anything specific. Now Mr Holland is dead it would be dreadful if the wrong impression reached the police and mother became involved."

So Daisy was just like the rest of them: all fearful of being involved. The very word had become a common denominator.

All were out to use me as a buffer between their uneasy consciences and John.

"I don't think you need worry even if it does reach the police," I told her. "When the shot that killed Mr Holland was fired, you and your mother were both in the presence of the very man who is now in charge of the case. Another matter—how was your mother to execute a plan of murder to look like suicide when she is confined to a wheelchair?"

Daisy's mouth fell open slightly.

"Oh," she said, and flushed all over her plain round face. "Of course. She couldn't, could she? She can't get out of her wheelchair. How stupid I am. Good-bye, Maggie, good-bye, Connie." She turned and fled indoors.

Connie and I proceeded up the hill.

"She can get out of her wheelchair," Connie said suddenly.

"Mrs Potts-Power? How do you know?"

"Well, I haven't actually seen her," Connie replied with newly acquired caution. "But one day when I was passing I saw the wheelchair in an obscure corner of the garden. It was empty."

"That's nothing. She could have been lying down inside."

"Someone was playing the gramophone," Connie insisted. "It wasn't Daisy. She went into town that day. I can't remember the name of the record, but it was one of those waltz tunes Mrs Potts-Power is always playing. It went like this."

"Strauss will turn in his grave," I commented.

"I think the old lady was left in the garden and she decided that while Daisy was out of the way she'd try out her legs. She always struck me as a hypocritical old tyrant. I only hope Daisy finds her out soon and leaves her flat."

"There might be a dozen explanations of that empty wheelchair. I wouldn't go round saying too much about it. A murder has taken place, you know. And in spite of Daisy's assurances to the contrary there must have been something in the quarrel between her mother and Mr Holland."

"Was he really murdered, Maggie?" Connie asked on the instant. "I heard so many rumours today."

"You don't want to listen to rumours. An inquest will probably be held within the next few days."

"But what is your own private opinion? With your experience you should know."

"Connie," I said with force, "if you refer once again to my past, this happy friendship, the threads of which we are picking up, will end. I am not in a position to give an opinion even if I wanted to."

This was not exactly true, as I was already convinced that, in spite of any evidence to the contrary, James Holland was murdered. But with John in charge of investigations my position was a delicate one. The fact that we lived in the same district and were neighbours to where the crime had taken place meant watching my step. It would not do to show a tendency for one side or the other.

III

The steak and kidney pie had plenty of time in which to brown nicely, as six o'clock struck and John did not come in. I bathed and fed Tony and let him roam round the house in pyjamas while I went into the study to call up the Hall to find out how much longer John would be.

I looked out the window to the square tower of the Hall rising above the trees as I spoke to Ames.

The Inspector had left. He should be at the Dower House any minute. I heard John's step in the hall and Tony's whoop of delight.

"He is here now. Thank you, Ames."

"Just one moment, Mrs Matheson."

There was a message for me. Would I please ring the following number. It sounded familiar. I asked Ames for the line at once.

John came in with Tony on his shoulder.

"I won't be a minute," I promised. "Dinner is ready. Put the boy into bed, will you?"

I did not want John to overhear even my side of the telephone conversation. This trail was my own particular baby; which, all things considered, was rather an apt metaphor.

Doctor Johnson came to the phone after a short wait. He grumbled at me for interrupting his dinner. "This is the same time you chose to have your brat, Maggie. Don't make a habit of it."

"Sorry, but I was interested to learn you rang me. What news?"

"Not much. It all depends on the interpretation you can put on it. Have you been to Trefont yet?"

"I did today. Would you think me frightfully silly if I asked you not to mention names?"

"Is the line tapped? You're living in a queer part of the world if what the papers say is true. Afraid I'll have to say names if you want the news."

I paused a minute, straining my ears to catch the slightest sound on the wire.

"All right. Go ahead. What is it?"

"The man you saw today—"

"Doctor Trefont?"

"Damn it, I thought you said to be discreet. All I have to report is that he was anaesthetist to Barry Clowes at one time."

"What does that mean?" I asked, perplexed. "Who and what is Barry Clowes?"

"Big Collins Street gynaecologist. Also a big-time abortionist. That is the only dirt I can dig up against Trefont. He is no longer associated with him. His professional record may be as pure as snow now."

There was a pause as I frowned over this information. Doctor Johnson's voice said peevishly, "Can I go back to my steak and kidney pie, please?"

"Certainly. I am anxious to start my own. Thanks a lot, Doc, for the information. I'll let you know if it comes in useful. Good-bye."

John put his head in the door as I put down the receiver.

"Are you coming, Maggie? The brat won't lie down."

We settled Tony with a combination of threats and cajolement and went down to the dining-room.

John was looking pale and very tired. He went through the usual lassitude with every case he handled. On the job he was keen, alert and untiring, but once at home he seemed to sag completely, and to depend on me for a renewal of spirits. I did what I could by keeping the conversation frothy and the menu attractive. It might have surprised Connie to learn how I studied the chart with a view to increasing vitality-giving foods.

Adopting a high-handed manner that went over well with Tony, I sent John into the lounge-room to light a fire and relax. Presently I took along a tray of coffee, prepared for a cosy domestic evening, only to find the lounge-room dark and chill. John was seated at his desk in the study.

"I might have known," I said resignedly, setting down the tray and going over to light the gas fire. "Can't you relax just for tonight?"

"With the inquest tomorrow?" he asked irritably. "Do you know what will happen if I can't find some scrap of a clue, some tiny particle of evidence amongst all this?" He indicated the spread of papers on the desk. "Suicide whilst of unsound mind! Maggie, it was not suicide. A very clever person planned this. Is that person cleverer than the police, than I?"

"No," I said promptly. "You'll find your clue. Just take it easily."

"With every pointer heading towards the wrong verdict? I wouldn't admit it to anyone else but you, but I'm feeling rattled." He got up restlessly and went over to the window.

"What about the will?" I asked, dropping a lemon ring into John's cup. On a case, he liked his coffee very black. "What happened with Braithwaite?"

His face lightened for a moment. "I feel sorry for that poor fellow. He is having trouble with the ladies. I had to prise him free from the Mulqueen girl and Mrs Holland before I could get any sense out of him."

"I met Ursula lying in wait for him as I left. I didn't know Yvonne was doing the same. She had been lying down in her room. Where is all the money going?"

"That's the trouble," John said gloomily. "You could say the will was rather unusual and enough to inspire half a dozen motives, but you can hardly suspect an infant of getting out of his cot and shooting his own grandfather, can you?"

"Yvonne's son is the heir, is he? I'm not surprised. I doubt if anyone else will be. The old man set great store by the family name. Anything else of interest?"

"They all get their share, even the servants. Yvonne Holland has a sort of trust fund which reverts to the estate if she marries again. She and the Mulqueens are to manage the estate in conjunction with Ames until the youngster reaches twenty-one."

I frowned. "That's bad. It looks as if they will all stay on at the Hall together. I suppose they could hardly do anything else just now. The housing problem, of which we knew so much."

"There was one item in the will which may be of interest to you. The old man evidently decided that when he died there would be no need for a Dower House. This place is to be separated from the rest of the estate and sold. Braithwaite seemed to think there would be nothing in the way of our buying it."

I got up in my excitement. "Why, that's marvellous! Now we can change the name to something sensible." Suddenly a thought struck me, and I said in mock seriousness: "I hope you don't think I knew of that clause and killed the Squire myself."

He grinned back. "No, I don't. But I bet, providing we can make it murder and not suicide, that some busybodies will pass that suggestion around."

"In that case," I said lightly, "I had better start finding the real killer myself."

John shot me a sharp glance. "Maggie, if you worry me, I won't buy the house. I think I'll hold over arrangements with Braithwaite until this case is wound up."

I came round to his chair. "Why, Inspector Matheson! That's blackmail."

"It'll be murder if you get in my hair over this business. It's no use giving me innocent looks. I know you're playing some foolish underhand game. When are you going to tell me what you know?"

"When you hand over the title deeds of the house," I said, with my sweetest smile.

"A deadlock. All right, my girl! You have my warning. Step on my corns or Sergeant Billings' and out we go."

"Talking about Sergeant Billings, did he tell you Cruikshank is back under his sateen apron once more?"

"He did. He was going to see Cruikshank sometime this evening."

"Doesn't the missing gun help at all?" I asked presently, as John kept turning over the same piece of paper.

"I talked with Ames about it. He was quite insistent that the Squire complained of its loss. But Holland might have mislaid it himself through forgetfulness. Or he may have mentioned it first in case Ames noticed its absence. If a man really sets out to commit suicide he doesn't want to be frustrated half-way. The faithful steward might have suspected something. No, Maggie, there are only two things I can find in all this mess. The first might be so coincidental that it signifies nothing. The other, though more concrete, has me quite puzzled."

"What are they?" I lighted two cigarettes and passed one over to John.

"The first is the time of the shot. And here we could make a supplementary note. You were standing in the passage when you heard a sound which you immediately guessed was a gunshot. How did it happen I passed off that same sound and a subsequent one as a car backfiring?"

"The front door was open," I reminded him.

"Hmm. Yes, I suppose that was it," John sounded dubious. "However, to get back to the time factor. Don't you regard it as curious that at that particular time not one member of the household was present in the room? I think it must have been about ten minutes later before any of them came in."

I frowned at the tip of my cigarette. "You mean that if it is murder, quite a few people who might be found wanting the Squire out of this world will have to start looking for alibis."

"You are still presupposing murder, Maggie. What I am driving at is this: it was unnatural for not one of the Hollands to be present to receive guests."

"They probably thought the Squire was there. The Hall is a ranch of a place, and no one seemed eager to be in his company for long. Remember Mrs Mulqueen sent Ames up to the Squire's room. She thought she had heard him moving about."

"And yet this morning she informs you that she was mistaken. I wonder why."

I hesitated a minute. "I think she wanted to draw attention away from the fact that she was on that floor. Her own rooms are on the ground floor in the east wing. I don't know what her game is, but she knows something about that flickering light we saw in the tower."

"You mean she used the tower as a means of signalling to someone?"

"Well, it looks like it."

"What stupid nonsense!" John said, irritable again. "Time enough to go into that if and when we establish the murder theory. The other point I was going to mention is the mark on one of Holland's ankles. The post-mortem report was delightfully vague—suggested it was caused by barbed wire."

"That's quite possible. The wood is divided from the road by a barbed-wire fence. He might have got through the fence and caught his leg."

John shook his head in a dissatisfied way. "Have you found out who reported the body?" I asked, still trying to make helpful suggestions.

"No. But that's nothing, People don't like being involved with bodies, especially with those of well-known persons. Anonymous reports are not uncommon at Russell Street."

I sighed and thought again. A silence fell, to be broken when John said: "By the way, Maggie, I meant to ask you before. What did you mean—"

"Hush," I interrupted hastily and got to my feet. "Was that Tony calling?"

"I didn't hear him."

"I'll go and have a peep at him."

I got out of the room quickly, closing the door behind me. If I stayed out long enough John would get on with his notes and shelve what he wanted to ask. Tony was sleeping deeply as I had expected, but I wasted time straightening his bedclothes and dawdled back to the study. John must be given ample opportunity to defer any leading questions.

Then quite suddenly I was overcome by that uncanny sensation that all this had happened before. The circumstances and my actions were vaguely familiar. At first I thought the feeling might be connected with some hitherto unremembered dream. Then I saw the shadow against the leadlight of the front door and hurried forward. During the evening a banging noise had sounded from the wood now and then. Ernest Mulqueen was still putting his rabbits out of their misery.

But it was not Ernest who stood on the porch that night. It was Elizabeth, his wife. I was taken aback at seeing her, and my first instinctive thought was "Now, what does she want?"

"Mrs Matheson, how nice to find you in," Mrs Mulqueen said, extending a gracious hand. "I was out for a little stroll. I simply had to get out of the house. So many memories of poor James."

I cast her a close look. She wore a musquash coat slung across her shoulders, the arms hanging loose. The low V of her black dress held a diamond clip. With her fading hair hidden by a chiffon turban of scarlet that matched her lips and nails, she looked twenty years younger.

I took her down to the study, grateful for her presence insofar as I was cold and John could hardly start questioning me now.

After its first look of irritation, John's face settled into a polite mask. He hated having his thread of thought interrupted. Mrs Mulqueen kept up a patter about poor dear James that told nothing and committed herself not at all. John did not use her unexpected visit to any advantage. I don't think he was interested yet. His one idea was to find that clue to fix the inquest decision the following day.

In fact, no one was very interested, either in each other or in the conversation that we all pushed along. I noticed Mrs Mulqueen glance at the clock once or twice, and about ten times that number at the tiny jewelled watch on her wrist. A hectic flush grew up gradually under her skilfully tinted cheeks.

After some time she leapt up right in the middle of a sentence and said: "I really must go now. They will be wondering what has become of me at home. Please don't get up, Mr Matheson. Or should I say Inspector?"

John held open the door.

"Not yet, anyway," he said, very pleasantly. I glanced at him sharply, but Mrs Mulqueen did not seem to take in the significance of his remark.

We both followed her down the hall to the front door. She thanked us for cheering her up and making her forget poor dear James for a while. I wondered again how we had done this, and murmured some conventional reply.

We watched her to the curve in the flagged path before John closed the door. The gate clicked as I turned off the porch light. John gave me a heavy look and went back to the study.

"Sorry, darling," I said, following him.

"The trouble with you, Maggie," he informed me, "is you don't know when to stall people off. You'd let them talk and pour out their troubles, imaginary and otherwise, until the cows come home."

"That's your own system, my boy," I retorted. "I learnt it from you. Let them talk. You'll soon find out what they are hiding. Those were your own sage words. What's the matter?"

John had cocked his head on one side and raised a hand for silence. I listened in the stillness of the room. The night sounds were very clear. I made a vague decision to inquire some time what exactly went to make up those sounds. The only one I could recognize was a rhythmical throb from the frogs in the creek at the bottom of the garden.

"What are you listening to?" I asked.

"Nothing," John said with a grin. "It was a 'lack of' I was trying to hear. There has been some occasional banging going on in the wood, but it has stopped now for some time. I am curious to know what it was."

"Easily explained," I said airily, and went on to tell him about Ernest Mulqueen and the gin set in the wood.

"Just a minute," John interrupted. "Wasn't that it again?"

I listened again for a moment or two. I opened my mouth to pass an inane remark about hearing things, when a sound did happen. It froze me to my chair, but my eyes darted to John's face. A woman started to scream shrilly. A short sharp sound that ended before it should have—as though it was stifled before conclusion.

IV

John moved at once. "I'm going out. Stay here, Maggie. Ring Billings to come over at once."

I wanted to say "Don't go," or to beg to go with him.

He said over his shoulder, reading my thoughts: "You can't leave Tony here by himself."

I had the calling line at the Hall almost before the front door banged. John's footsteps running along the path the other side of the hedge came to my ears, at the same time as Sergeant Billings' slow voice. I told him briefly that Inspector Matheson had gone up to the wood and wanted the Sergeant to join him.

I felt a vague admiration not unmixed with surprise when Sergeant Billings said he would come at once without further questions. The receiver was banged down in my ear. There was nothing more I could do but sit about and wonder how long John would be and what he would find up there in the wood.

In the hurry and scramble I had noticed him open a drawer in his desk and pull out a torch. I went over to the window and pulled back the curtain, straining my eyes to catch a glimpse of light amongst the darkness of the trees.

Suddenly I thought I saw a figure slipping out of the thicket onto the path above the house. It was no more than a lighter shadow against all that darkness. On impulse I hurried down the passage to the front door and out onto the porch. The figure had broken away from the track again. I hastened down the flagged path to the front gate, just in time to see the someone having difficulty in getting through the fence fifty yards down the road. The figure hugged the shadows until it went beyond the vision of my straining eyes.

I stayed at the gate, thinking hard. Sergeant Billings' bicycle lamp came weaving its way along the road. He jumped off just where the hedge joined the road and did not see me.

I called his name urgently. He glanced around at once.

"Here," I called. "At the gate. It is Mrs Matheson."

He came up, the bicycle lamp in his hand.

"Where is the Inspector?" he asked.

"Somewhere up in the wood," I replied, shading my eyes against the light he flashed on me. "Tell me quickly, did you see anyone on the road as you came along?"

He shook his head, anxious to join John. I did not detain him and went slowly back to the study. Mechanically I picked up a cigarette and John's automatic lighter that lay on the desk. But I did not light the cigarette. I dropped it extravagantly to the floor, and slipping the lighter into the pocket of my jacket made for the front door again. This time I locked it after me with a vague prayer for Tony's well-being and the comforting reflection that this new impulse would only take me a short time and not far from the house.

Outside, the road was deserted. I hurried along to a certain point. There I flicked the lighter, thankful for the still autumn night and promising to buy a torch the following day for my exclusive use. Bending double on the grassy bank alongside the road, I ran the tiny flame carefully along the middle strand of the barbed wire.

Presently there was a small hiss and my own breath blew out the flame in excitement. I stood upright and flicked the tiny wheel again, cursing my suddenly clumsy fingers. Holding the flame steady, I bent down again and found what I was looking for. Twisted in the jagged wire and hardly visible even to me, who knew what to look for, were half a dozen short silvery hairs. The flame had singed a couple, but I recognized them beyond any doubt as belonging to the fur coat Elizabeth Mulqueen had worn that evening.

I pulled out my handkerchief and tied it round the wire. I wasn't going to risk missing John's commendation.

I got back to the house just in time. John and Sergeant Billings came down the path. They were not alone. Between them they supported a man who dragged his feet as though he was drunk.

John saw me waiting on the porch. "Get some water and a sponge, Maggie, please. And see if there is some brandy in the house."

Filled with curiosity at the turn of events, I hurried down to the kitchen. When I came back with a bowl of water and the remains of the Christmas pudding brandy, I found the strange man laid out on my lounge-room couch. He was conscious but dazed, and bled from a cut in one corner of his mouth. I could see he was making a desperate attempt to gather his wits together, and felt rather sorry for him. He was not much more than thirty and was quite good-looking in a bucolic sort of way.

I handed John a towel wrung out in cold water and watched his ministrations in silence.

"Sticking plaster, Maggie?"

I made for the medicine chest in the bathroom.

When I came back into the room, I heard Sergeant Billings say in a quiet tone: "It's him, sir. I could swear to it. Hearing him in the dark like that brought it all back to me."

John did not reply. He cut off a strip of adhesive tape and clapped it skilfully over the cut. Then he got to his feet and went over to the tray. He poured out a small quantity of brandy and gave it to the stranger to drink.

It was never John's way to heckle anyone when he was down, even in execution of his duty. I considered that admirable trait one of the main factors contributing to his successful career. He worked with his brain, not merely relying on circumstances. He gave the stranger time to pull himself together before he spoke. He asked his name and what had happened to him out there in the wood.

The stranger replied to the first question after some hesitation: "Nugent Parsons." Almost as though he was speculating on a false name.

However, no one could possibly think of a name like Nugent on the spur of the moment. But as to how he was injured and what he was doing in the wood, he remained obstinately silent.

Then John sprang his surprise, or rather Sergeant Billings'.

I told him afterwards it was mean of him to steal the Sergeant's thunder.

He asked in a clipped, clear voice: "Was it not you who rang the Middleburn police station early this morning to report the dead body of James Holland?"

CHAPTER SEVEN

I

Nugent Parsons nearly fainted under the sudden verbal attack. The strip of plaster became one with his face. I still felt sorry for him, although I appreciated John having his job to do. It was rather like eating your Christmas turkey, but refusing to see it killed. Parsons had been so much caught on the hop, as it were, that his obvious agitation could be interpreted only one way.

John said: "You were in the wood adjoining Holland Hall last night. Why?"

Parsons realized the way out of this predicament was not silence. It was too serious to remain silent. The consequences would be damning. On the other hand the explanation he gave was just as bad. Considering murder was the subject around which the discussion revolved, it was very poor. To say lamely that he had been for a walk and had accidentally stumbled on the body did not have much force about it.

"The wood is private property," John said. "Is it your custom to take a walk through other people's estates?"

Nugent Parsons replied swiftly to this. "I am employed at the home farm. There is no fence separating it from the rest of the property."

"Where exactly did this walk of yours begin and what route did it follow?" There was a sceptical note in John's voice.

Parsons hesitated too long before he answered: "I walked from the men's quarters along the road and then cut round the other side of the Hall through the wood back again."

"What time was that?"

"About seven, I think. It may have been some minutes after. I went as soon as I finished my evening meal."

I glanced at John quickly, wondering if he was thinking of the shadow we had seen slipping through the trees as we had gone along the drive. But he was after another point.

"That means you must have found Mr Holland's body very soon after the shot. Why didn't you advise the police at once?"

Parsons was caught badly. He stammered something about not wishing to get mixed up in anything. As John had told me this reluctance was often his experience, he could not but let it go.

"As the sound of the shot must have come from the wood, how does it happen you continued your walk in that direction? You might have guessed something was wrong. I gather you would rather dodge trouble."

A slightly bewildered look came over Parsons' face. He said with difficulty: "I didn't know it was a shot. I did hear a car backfiring. It didn't occur to me it was an explosion from a gun."

I frowned a little at this statement.

"You say you cut along the other side of the Hall, Mr Parsons. Do you mean outside the boundary fence or within it?"

"There is a path following the drive the other side of the poplars. It branches off and goes behind the house." John threw me a quick look as though to say: "Here is the question you want asked."

"Did you see anyone going along the drive?"

Parsons said "No" in a careful voice. There was almost a triumphant sound about it as if he was congratulating himself on being able to answer openly and truthfully.

"Or anyone on the same path as you used?" John asked. He was clever. He read Parsons' mind like a book.

He said "No" again. But this time his voice wavered.

John pounced on it. "You are not certain. You might have seen someone?" Parsons thought for a moment. He was weighing the pros and cons of something.

Presently, without raising his eyes, he said: "While I was waiting just beyond the Lodge, I thought I saw someone moving along the path some distance ahead. Of course it may have been a trick of the shadows, but I got the impression it was someone I knew. Mr Mulqueen from the Hall."

John took this without expression. I had detected a faintly malicious undertone in Parsons' voice, and thought I knew the reason why. It was a rather astounding reason, but one that had occurred to me when I first clapped eyes on Nugent Parsons. I made a *moue* of distaste to myself.

If Parsons had intended anything malicious in his statement it only repercussed on himself. Beyond directing Sergeant Billings to make a note of the possibility of the person being Ernest Mulqueen, John ignored it.

"Why were you waiting near the Lodge? Had you arranged to meet someone there?"

Parsons stammered badly again. "No, of course not. I wasn't waiting for anything—anyone. I paused—to light a cigarette. It couldn't have been more than a minute before I saw Mr Mulqueen. Then I moved off at once."

"You did not want him to see you? Is that correct?"

"Yes—no. I mean—I didn't care whether he did or didn't." Parsons' hands were shaking and he dropped his eyes again. "Can't all this wait until the morning? I don't feel quite up to things at the moment."

"I can understand that," John agreed smoothly, his eyes on the discoloured patch growing at Parsons' mouth. "How did you come by that? It looks to me like a blow from someone's fist."

Parsons put his hand up to cover his face in a self-conscious manner.

"I—I ran into a tree in the dark," he muttered.

"When you were taking a walk as you did last night?" John queried in an abominable voice. "You seem to make these nocturnal strolls a habit, Mr Parsons. What I can't understand is your lack of sensibility in taking the same route after finding a corpse the previous night."

Parsons made no answer. There was nothing he could say in the face of such heavy sarcasm.

John continued: "You also seem to be rather hard of hearing. You are doubtful about hearing the gunshot last night."

"Tell me, was a woman's scream in the wood tonight also inaudible to you?" Parsons raised his eyes and stared defiantly: "I didn't hear a woman scream."

John held his gaze for a moment or two and then turned away, shrugging.

"You can go home, if you like," he suggested. His manner conveyed that the interview had not been of much use to him. It was not worth continuing.

Parsons got to his feet. He looked at me awkwardly. He could hardly thank me for my hospitality when John had used his presence to more advantage than was proper in a host.

And he hadn't finished yet. Parsons was at the door with Sergeant Billings at his heels when John said over his shoulder: "Before you go, Mr Parsons, will you tell me exactly how you found Mr Holland?"

John had his head turned away from the two men. Only I could see his face. I thought he looked strained, and watched him anxiously.

Parsons replied, almost mechanically: "I was walking along the track through the wood when I came on the figure of a man lying on his back in the middle of the path. I might have tripped over him but for the fact that I had a torch with me. I flashed it on the face and recognized Mr James Holland from the Hall. He had a wound in his head. In his right hand he held a gun."

John interrupted without turning round. "You say you found him lying on his back. In what position were the legs? Were they drawn up or extended?"

Parsons glanced at Sergeant Billings. He feared some trap. "I swear I did not touch him. I was only there for a minute. There was nothing I could do. He was dead. His hand was almost cold."

"Answer my question," John said wearily. "In what position were the legs?"

"Extended, I think. I was rather upset. I did not notice much."

John's face reflected the weary note in his voice. "You may go," he repeated. "You too, Sergeant. There will be nothing further tonight. Good night."

He made no move to see them off the premises. In my uncertain role of hostess I had no wish to speed the parting guest with any other excuse than to make certain that the front door was locked after them.

Parsons made his departure hastily. I watched him pass along the fence on his way to the farm buildings further up the road. Sergeant Billings glanced down at my detaining hand in embarrassment. I loosened my grip on his sleeve, grinning.

"Forward woman, aren't I, Sergeant? I want you to do something for me. A few yards along the road you'll find a handkerchief of mine tied to the fence. You've got a flashlight on your bicycle, haven't you? Inspect what you find underneath the handkerchief very carefully. You'll probably find it of some interest. Good night."

II

I went back to the lounge-room. John looked up at me with a wry smile.

"Nothing?" I asked.

"A few points, but not what I want for the moment. I'm worried about that inquest, Maggie. If we miss out on that it will mean a hell of a job."

"You'll find a clue," I said hopefully. I sat down opposite. "Are you in the irritating position of guessing all about our new friend Nugent, or can I suggest a few things that may enlighten you?"

"I have a fair idea. But give me your view of the situation. What did you make of Nugent Parsons?"

"He's very good-looking," I said reflectively. John sighed ostentatiously. "But in rather a weak way," I went on, unruffled. "It would be easy to make an impression on him. As a matter of fact I felt a bit sorry for him."

"Well?" said John.

"Odd, don't you think, how the Mulqueen woman popped in tonight all painted up like a Jezebel? She seemed to be waiting for a certain time and then popped out again. It wasn't long after that we heard a woman's scream. Also very soon after, Ernest Mulqueen finished off his last rabbit and made tracks for home."

John frowned. "Young Parsons and that old hag?"

"Not so old," I protested. "And you must admit she looked rather snappy tonight. She's just at that age, you know. She looks the type who would carry on an intrigue just for the excitement and thrill of it. Disgusting what we women come to, isn't it?"

John mumbled something like "Damned fool."

"It looks as though Ernest surprised them. She came rushing out of the wood just after you left, leaving some evidence on the barbed-wire fence in her hurry. I told Sergeant Billings to collect it. Did I do right?"

John nodded briefly and approvingly. "What else can my clever wife tell me?"

"Not much. Except it is obvious Nugent Parsons doesn't like Ernest Mulqueen. Suspicious shadows develop into him under the slightest pressure of Nugent's imagination. I wonder if it was he or Ernest we saw last night. Funny the way they were both slinking."

"I consider it funnier that Parsons can't take in a gunshot when he hears one," John said with irritation. "A farm worker must know something about firearms."

"Yes," I agreed. "He seemed quite sincere about it too." John made no comment. He brought out his pipe and filled it mechanically, his eyes fixed on a point beyond me.

I said presently: "Will I be interrupting a train of thought if I give you my idea why Parsons was waiting in the Hall grounds?"

John brought his gaze to meet mine. "Eh? No, not at all. Go on."

"You don't sound a bit interested," I complained. "My theory is that he was waiting for a signal from Elizabeth Mulqueen. Remember the tower light? It must have meant that she couldn't meet him that night but would keep the tryst the following one. What do you think?"

"Quite feasible."

It was my turn to sigh. "You know, you are not a bit interested in what I'm saying. Had you guessed it all before?"

"Parts, anyway. You have been filling in the gaps admirably." He got to his feet. "I think I'll turn in, Maggie. Do you mind?"

"Of course not. I'm glad you're not going to sit up all night turning over bits of paper, searching for your missing clue."

John pulled me to my feet, and slid his hands up to my shoulders.

"Do you know," he said with a half smile. "I've got a hunch that clue is going to turn up any minute. There is something you said at the back of my mind that I just can't quite catch. But it will come."

I felt suddenly happy. "Tell me when it does."

He shook me slightly. "If you didn't chatter so much you wouldn't wrap up bits of important evidence so thickly. I have got to undo all the covering to get to them."

I thumped his chest with my closed fist. "Brute. You're taking away a nice comfortable feeling of smugness. In future I won't say a word."

"That would be foolish," he said in all seriousness. And so I was made happy again.

It is one thing to be complimented on being an excellent helpmate, but a very different matter to be awakened from a deep sleep in the early hours of the morning and have the compliment endorsed.

At first I thought John was crazy. He kept saying: "Rabbits, Maggie," until I was sufficiently awake to realize that he was not talking in his sleep. I struggled to understand his meaning.

"Wake up, darling. I want to tell you what a wonderful woman you are."

I rolled over, taking in the luminous face of the clock in transit.

"Must you, at this hour?" I asked resignedly. "Why rabbits?"

John said, enunciating clearly as though I was hard of hearing: "The inquest. Remember? The Holland inquest. I have found that clue. Only it's not a clue. It is something much better."

I was wide awake at once. "What is it? Quickly, tell me."

"The wound in Holland's leg. It had me puzzled. It wasn't caused by barbed wire. He caught his foot in a trap. Ernest Mulqueen's gin."

There was silence for a moment while I digested this triumphant statement.

"I think I'll go and work on the idea," John said. "Go back to sleep, Maggie. You've done your part."

I protested. I wanted to get up and stay with him, to discuss every possible angle of this new situation. For once John played the heavy husband and ordered me to stay where I was.

"I won't be able to go back to sleep," I stated definitely, submitting to being tucked in like a baby. But I could not stay awake even out of cussedness. John did not come back to bed again. He worked until Tony awoke, and further concentration was impossible. Then he brought a tray of tea into the bedroom, rousing me with aggressive heartiness. I gave Tony a biscuit to dip into my cup and said: "Did the clue work out all right?"

"Amazing possibilities." The weary, strained look of the previous night had gone. In spite of his lack of sleep and growth of beard, John looked fresh and alert. "You remember I asked Parsons if he had touched the body? The straightened legs did not look right. A man does not fall under a gunshot in that position."

"You mean the gin was employed to waylay the Squire, and that when the killer removed it, he forgot to place the legs in a natural position?"

"Precisely," John nodded. "And it is just that mistake backed up by the evidence of the gin that will make all the difference to the coroner's finding. It could even mean an early arrest," he added thoughtfully.

III

That afternoon was the date of Brenda Gurney's tea party, and I found myself regretting having accepted the invitation. It seemed an age since that day Connie Bellamy introduced me to the Middleburn Community Centre, although different members had called me in the ensuing week, particularly after James Holland's death.

I visualized myself parrying questions the whole afternoon, and becoming worn and bored. Such an anticipation was quite wrong, for at Brenda Gurney's party I found another piece of the jigsaw. It started as a suspicion and ended up a fact that had a great deal of significance in the case.

Again the day was blue and golden, making the tinted foliage of the wood an even more lovely sight than the green springing leaves I see now. The days were almost monotonous in their perfection. Clear, cold mornings with the sun strengthening to a summer's warmth. Then towards the end of the day a mist would rise from the creek. Even perfection becomes dreary. It was hard to conceive violent emotions being stirred in the midst of such peace. Perhaps the contrast of nature at fall and battling human nature made crime seem all the more horrible.

The village was almost empty of shoppers. The middle of the week seemed the recognized time for tea parties. I noticed that the Post Office clock registered a time too early to make my presence welcome in a home where several children had to be washed and dressed ready for guests. A notion occurred to me suddenly and I went into the Post Office.

The postmaster was a cheery individual who sat for the greater part of the day on a high stool behind the counter. A crutch was propped close by, but his extraordinarily long arms barely necessitated him using it to support his tucked-up trouser leg. Stamps, forms and telephones all lay within his reach.

He knew me. Ever since James Holland's death his interest, like so many others, had increased. I had no difficulty in obtaining my request, even though it meant him getting off his stool and rummaging through files under the counter. I wanted a list of wires or any other messages he knew of that were sent to Mr Holland when he was away.

"Here we are, Mrs Holmes," he said, hauling himself back to his position and flicking through a folder. " 'Fraid there's not much. Wait a bit, though. Mr Ames sent a couple. 'Can't locate Cruikshank for the dinner. What shall I do?' The old bloke wired back, 'Find him.' Like him, that was, Mrs Poirot. Real boss-cocky like."

"Anything else?" I asked.

"Another from Mr Ames. 'Have inserted notice in paper for Cruikshank. No answer as yet.'"

"Did Mr Holland reply to that one?"

"Not through this office. All I have now is a message saying when he would be home. I phoned it to the Hall, but they said don't bother about a written copy. Here it is still."

"You rang the wire through," I said quickly, picking up the slip he slid across to me and giving it a brief glance. "Who took it at the Hall?"

"Dunno, I'm sorry to say. Except it was a woman's voice. Can you make anything of that, Mrs Chan?"

"I might. Thanks for the co-operation. Good-bye, Doctor Watson."

"Hey, wait a minute," called the postmaster, grinning at my riposte. "You don't want one from your husband, do you?"

"I never finesse against my partner," I said from the doorway.

Brenda Gurney's party was very much the same as the numerous other afternoon teas I subsequently attended in Middleburn. The same set of young matrons was present and the conversation turned as usual to confinements and children generally. It was quite the thing to give an account of one's accouchements in intimate and minute detail. Each member of the party waited impatiently until she could relate her experiences, which were by far the most interesting.

I was surprised to note Yvonne Holland among those present. Whatever her feelings for her late father-in-law were, and I was not one to advocate respect for someone dead for whom one felt not the slightest liking in life, it would have been advisable for her to obey convention and stay away from any form of parties, however innocuous.

Several shocked glances were directed towards her during the afternoon. Brenda, easy-going, did not give a damn as long as Yvonne enjoyed herself. For myself, I was more interested than disapproving. Yvonne's attitude intrigued me. She had thrown off the chains of convention which had bound her to the Hall. Ill-timed as it was, I was glad to see she still had some courage left. But the carefree look about Yvonne smacked of defiance. I watched her carefully as she chattered and laughed a great deal. She gave herself away by the old habit of plucking at her belt as though it was too tight around the waist. The girl was absurdly slim to have produced a baby at all. Her hip bones stood out like two points through the sheer wool of her blue frock. It seemed to fall in a perfectly flat surface from neck to waist. She greeted me in gay bantering fashion which gave the impression we were old friends who could afford to be rude to each other.

"How is Jimmy?" I asked, when conversation had ceased to be general and the crowd broke up into discussion groups.

"Much better," she replied eagerly. "He seems to have picked up considerably during the last day or two. I am taking him down to the Health Centre tomorrow. I'm sure he has put on weight."

I said feebly: "Why, that's grand."

She had broken loose with a vengeance.

Yvonne went on: "Now that he's such an important person I think it is time he received more attention. Health Centres are very helpful, don't you think so?"

"Rather," I agreed in a faint voice. Her sudden vigour was almost overwhelming. "Why don't you take him straight to a doctor to give him a thorough overhaul?"

"I would, if I knew of someone suitable. You see, I never had a doctor except when Jimmy was born—I couldn't bear to go to the local man."

"Doctor Trefont?" I felt my way cautiously. "From all accounts he seems to be quite adequate."

Yvonne shook her head obstinately. She was perfectly willing to take the baby to Sister Heather but not to Doctor Trefont.

"What about the doctor who attended your confinement?" I suggested.

"He only handles obstetrics. He's a gynaecologist. A Collins Street man," she added, not without pride. It is amazing how more importance is added to one's case by saying that.

But Yvonne had not added her story to the harrowing collection. The omission puzzled me. I asked her the specialist's name.

At first her answer meant no more to me than fingers on a familiar chord. Barry Clowes. Where had I heard that name before? Barry— Then I remembered. I glanced at Yvonne a shade too quickly. Her eyes became suddenly wary as though she had spoken indiscreetly.

I said carelessly: "Quite a big shot, I believe. I was told he always employed his own anaesthetist. Am I right?"

Yvonne replied with some reluctance. "I had a special anaesthetist when Jimmy was born. Doctor Clowes always gives his patients the best attention. He believes in care before and after the birth."

"So I was told," I repeated significantly. Again Yvonne threw me that wary look.

"Was Doctor Trefont your anaesthetist?" I challenged her. I tried to hold her eyes and will her to answer. There was a pause. Then Yvonne dropped her gaze and quite deliberately upset her teacup over the arm of her chair. She jumped up dabbing at the tapestry. Our hostess came up leisurely.

"Oh, Brenda, I am sorry," Yvonne cried. "I can't think how I was so clumsy."

"Don't worry about it. I'll send one of the kids to get a cloth and mop it up. Let me get you another cup of tea."

"I really think," Yvonne said, with a guile that astounded me, "that I had better sit over there near the tea-table. I will be less likely to make a mess." She took up a position in the middle of a chattering group where intimate conversation of the type I wanted with Yvonne was impossible.

"How did it happen?" Brenda murmured. "I hate to suggest it of one of my guests, but I thought it was done on purpose. I just happened to be glancing this way. What do you think?"

"I won't commit myself," I said, smiling.

Brenda continued with her mopping. "You know, we were hoping you would be able to entertain us this afternoon. But Yvonne turned up and no one likes to mention the subject."

"Thank heaven for Yvonne," I replied, half-laughingly, half in earnest.

"I daresay, but we are bursting for the inside story. She's changed, don't you think?"

"Yvonne? Her present mood is unfamiliar to me. I doubt if she could change much underneath."

"She's a sweet little thing, but I think she was foolish coming today. She'll get herself talked about."

"I'm sure she has already," I said, nodding my head around the room.

Brenda sighed. "Yes, we're awful cats. But it does save life from becoming too monotonous. Have you heard the latest about her cousin-in-law?"

I started to work this out.

"Ursula Mulqueen," Mrs Gurney elucidated to save me trouble. "You must know her. Her clothes are appalling. That's the funny part."

"Is it?" I asked, wondering if I was becoming slow on the uptake.

"My conversation is always disjointed," my hostess said with a swift smile. "My husband says I lack mental coordination. The Mulqueen girl. Someone told me they saw her the other day in the cocktail lounge at the Albany."

"She must have been an incongruous sight," I said, thinking of that smart rendezvous and cherchez-vous.

"But she wasn't. She was dressed-up fit to conquer. Make-up, an exotic hair-do, and a stream of orchids to boot. What do you make of it?"

"I wouldn't care to give an opinion," I replied, not without truth. The story was too fantastic.

"You disappoint me, Mrs Matheson. Don't you give anything away?"

"I learned discretion in a very hard school," I told her. "I wasn't always so cautious. Talking of discretion, don't you think it is time you stopped pretending to clean that chair? Some curious glances are being directed our way."

I was left isolated when she went. The first impression I made on the Middleburn tea circle had not been a favourable one. I was regarded with some trepidation, as though I might turn remarks to some sinister purpose connected with the police. It was not until the case was finalized that I became an accepted member of Middleburn society.

Brenda Gurney moved through the chattering groups to the radio. It had been playing softly ever since I arrived. She turned the dial round and round, saying disgustedly, "News session everywhere. I may as well switch it off."

I called out to her across the room: "No, please don't. I'd like to hear it."

There might be some news of the inquest. All day I had been thinking of John. How he was faring and whether he had been able to persuade the coroner to give a satisfactory decision.

No one knew what I had in mind, but my raised voice had the effect of silencing the talk. I was too interested in the news to worry about making myself conspicuous. I moved nearer to the radio in case the chatter started again, asking permission of my hostess to tune it louder. I had to wait until the overseas and national news were read before I got what I wanted. It was the first item of the local news. The desultory talk around me broke off abruptly as Middleburn was mentioned. The announcer's voice filled Brenda Gurney's room as though it was devoid of any others but myself.

"A verdict of murder by person or persons unknown was given. It has been officially announced that Mr Ernest Mulqueen, of Holland Hall, Middleburn, has been detained for further questioning."

One or two of the party made ejaculations of shocked surprise. All eyes were turned to Yvonne. She took it very well. The girl had something more in her besides a superficial breeding gained by association with the Squire. She made no remark and her face remained impassive. But the seriousness of the position must have struck her forcibly, as she made her farewells almost immediately.

I felt curiously allied to Yvonne at that moment when hostile eyes turned upon her. She had lost her precarious footing in the society where I had not yet gained one. Nothing out of the way could be tolerated by these girls, except perhaps Brenda Gurney. I bade them all a hurried good-bye and left them to discuss us in peace.

I made no attempt to overtake Yvonne. There was nothing to say. She might or might not be fond of Ernest. The relationship was remote and his character and way of living far removed from her own. Besides she had shown a desire to avoid me.

We proceeded along in an absurd fashion, Yvonne wheeling her pram about ten yards in front of my pusher, wherein Tony slept surfeited with afternoon tea. Strangely enough she did not seem to realize I was there. Turning in at the Hall gates she caught a glimpse and stopped, beckoning me on with an imperiousness worthy of a Holland. The news of her uncle's detention had not upset the new mood.

As soon as I was within speaking distance, she said: "Isn't it terrible? Poor Aunt Elizabeth! What am I to say to her?"

"Mr Mulqueen hasn't been arrested," I pointed out. "Anyway, not yet. You are talking as though the hangman's noose was already around his throat. Detaining someone for further questioning does not make it a cut-and-dried affair."

The slight look of fear which passed through her eyes puzzled me.

"It has to be proved he killed your father-in-law. That demands a motive. If Mr Mulqueen can produce an alibi for the time of the murder he hasn't a thing to worry about."

"You mean," Yvonne said in her old hesitant voice, "that now it has been established Mr Holland was killed intentionally, we will all have to prove alibis?"

"Quite likely," I agreed in a cheerful voice. "It depends on whom the police's fancy alights."

Yvonne had become quite pale. She had lost her champagne vivacity.

"Would you like me to come up to the Hall with you?" I offered in a fit of charity. "Your aunt might be in a bad way."

"Who? Aunt Elizabeth? Of course. My mind was wandering. I would appreciate it if you came."

"This is my second appearance in the role of comforter," I told Yvonne. We parked the children on the terrace and entered through the window into Mr Holland's study. Yvonne looked about her. There was a certain agitation in her manner which she was trying desperately to hide. I waited for her to lead the way to the Mulqueens' wing. She paused near the desk, her hand straying over the polished surface to the extension telephone.

I glanced at her with raised brows. She said jerkily: "You know the way to Aunt Elizabeth's room. I have an urgent call to make. I won't be long."

She waited until I left the room before she lifted the receiver. The indicator shutter fell in the tiny switchboard near the stairs as I passed, but the alarm had been turned off. No one would hear Yvonne's extension ringing. Shrugging slightly, I hurried forward and took up the receiver.

Yvonne's voice requested Ames to give her a city number. I dialled it out without speaking and waited to hear the impulse. It was answered almost immediately. I recognized the voice of an experienced telephonist as the name Braithwaite and Braithwaite was announced. Yvonne asked for Mr Alan Braithwaite. I closed the keys and placed the receiver back, eyeing the connected lines with hungry curiosity.

Something prompted me to glance around. It was not a guilty look, but I could feel someone's eyes on me. I looked upwards to the stairs. On the first landing Ursula Mulqueen stood, one hand on the banister.

I said hurriedly: "I called to see if I could do anything for your mother when the phone rang. No one seemed to be around so I answered it."

Ursula tripped down the stairs, her curls bobbing about her shoulders.

"That was very kind of you, Mrs Matheson. Poor, dear father. It is all so bewildering and frightening. Was there any message?"

I answered without thinking: "It wasn't an inward call. Yvonne wanted Alan Braithwaite's number."

A slight flicker crossed Ursula's face, as though she found it an effort to retain the sweet exterior.

"Mother says girls who chase men forfeit their respect," she declared aimlessly, as she led the way to Mrs Mulqueen's rooms. A murmur of voices came from the east wing. Then she said something which rather astounded me. The words were trite certainly, but her voice had changed from its usual high lilting cadence. It took on a deeper tone, with the smoothest hint of satire beneath.

"Mother always knows best, don't you agree, Mrs Matheson?" She widened the doorway of the sitting-room very quietly and stepped aside. She had planned and executed a neat little peepshow.

Nugent Parsons stood near the window. Mrs Mulqueen was in front of him, her hands resting on his shoulders.

"We can't go on like this," Parsons was saying. "You were foolish asking me to come here. The police—"

"But darling Nugent," Mrs Mulqueen cooed up at him. "You must be patient. Nothing need be changed. Don't spoil things by losing your head."

"Everything is changed," he almost shouted. "For a while it was fun for both of us, but murder!" Mrs Mulqueen said in an odd voice: "You're not trying to get away from me, are you?"

"Yes, yes. I want to leave the Hall. I don't want to have anything more to do with you. You—you are an old woman."

I glanced at Ursula Mulqueen. She was smiling.

Elizabeth Mulqueen slowly removed one of her hands. "You'll regret that," she said, and struck him full on the mouth. I slipped back into the passage as Nugent Parsons rushed out.

CHAPTER EIGHT

I

"Tell me about the inquest," I requested John, after dinner.

"Nothing much to tell. I was relieved at the coroner's finding."

"I'm sure you were. Why did you detain Ernest Mulqueen?"

John began to fill a pipe slowly, staring into the fire.

"I could make a case against him if I cared to. The man has no alibi for the time of the crime. Furthermore, we have a witness to say that he was as far from the house as the gates."

I snapped my fingers. "That much for Nugent Parsons' evidence. A prejudiced witness. What about all the others who lack alibis?"

John said ruefully: "I would be glad to find someone with a watertight alibi, if only to try and disprove it. So far the field is crowded with suspects. When the shot was fired, we were the only ones in the drawing-room."

"Not the only ones," I corrected. "Daisy and Mrs Potts-Power were there. How about those for watertight alibis?"

"Quite so, but unfortunately can't disbelieve my own eyes. Unless Mrs Potts-Power split herself into a dual personage and one part went off to commit the murder while the other stared at me rudely, I fail to see how to break her alibi. The same goes for the daughter and Ames."

"What exactly is Ames' position at the Hall?" I asked presently. "He seems rather an oddity to me. A jack-of-all-trades. It's a wonder he is content to be so. He fills so many jobs expertly."

John put his feet to the ground and rested his hands on either arm of the chair as though to rise. "If you are really interested in a few routine inquiries we have made, I'll get some papers from the study. They may or may not be relevant to the case."

"Go ahead. I am very interested."

He threw a warning look over his shoulder. "No more than a wifely interest in your husband's work, Maggie."

"Of course not," I said innocently. "Whatever can you be thinking about?"

John shook his fist and went out.

The telephone rang in the study, but it did not delay John long.

"Who was it?" I asked, when he came back with a file of papers.

"Braithwaite. He was dining at the Hall. He has something to tell me. He'll be over presently."

I avoided John's eye. "Perhaps you could ask him about buying the house. Don't you think it is time we started pushing things along? It would be terrible if the family sold it over our heads."

"They won't," John stated calmly. "I'm not doing anything until this case is finished. You are not going to get into mischief a second time. Certainly not now you're married to me."

I said on a sigh: "I can't think why I did. Marry you, I mean."

John swept my feet off the couch and sat down. "My money, darling, and my good looks. Very rarely do they go together. Do you or don't you want to have a look at these papers?"

I sat up beside him. "I do, Midas-Adonis. What's this one?" I unfolded a typewritten sheet of paper bearing the Russell Street letterhead.

"That," said John, "should answer your inquiries about Ames. It is a list of the salaries and wages paid to the Hall and farm employees. You might note the first amount, which is more than your husband makes every year."

I whistled at the figures opposite Ames' name. "Very nice. No wonder he was content to stay."

"Another reason why I wouldn't try breaking Ames' alibi. No man in his right senses would kill a goose that laid eggs as large and golden as Holland did."

"Supposing he was blackmailing the Squire. This amount might be partly hush money."

"An absurd suggestion, Maggie. It is in every book of rules that the blackmailer never wipes out his source of income."

"But if Ames got more out of Holland dead? Isn't he to run the estates?"

"In conjunction with two others and only until Yvonne's baby is old enough to assume office. His hands are more tied than if Holland was alive. You may dismiss the idea. It has already been gone into."

"I will, but with a parting shot. A lot might happen in twenty years, or whenever it is Jimmy arrives at his inheritance."

"Unfortunately we cannot await possibilities of the years to come. The job is in the present. To convict a murderer of the death of James Holland."

"Don't sound so pompous."

"As a matter of fact," John confessed, "I wasn't thinking as I spoke. Your remark reminded me of something I have been waiting to ask you for the last few days. I was recalling what it was."

"Hush," I said hastily, putting up one finger. "Was that the doorbell? Go and see if it is Alan Braithwaite."

"Maggie, my own dear," John said in a tired voice. "Never use the same gag twice. Last time Mrs Mulqueen filled the breach. Young Braithwaite is missing his cue. I certainly didn't hear the doorbell."

I started up only to be pulled down again. "Don't you think I had better go and see?"

"You needn't bother. If you want to be secretive, we'll let it pass. I may even know what I was going to ask you."

"Quite likely," I agreed in a demure voice, taking up the paper again. "Is there anything further to catch the eye on this salary sheet?"

"You might note your friend Parsons' name. Holland was quite a good boss to work for. I wouldn't have minded being in his employ. Even the pension he paid old man Ames is quite respectable. According to the will, that is to continue. Holland waxed biblical in writing the bequest. There must have been some sort of bond of affection or respect between them."

"I should say both. The old man seemed to be the only genuine mourner I could find at the Hall. All the others were busy looking after their own interests."

"You can't expect anyone who has been murdered to have many mourners, sincere ones, anyway. Even to those nearest and would-be dearest, Holland's manner of death must be a source of embarrassment. Read this letter. You will find it interesting."

I took a folded sheet of cream notepaper to which a long sheet of foolscap was attached. I separated them, glancing down the foolscap. It held a neat list of names and addresses with an amount opposite each one. There were two other money columns, containing much smaller figures. Each column had been added up, and the totals worked out in percentages for purpose of comparison.

"You won't make head or tail of that until you see the letter," John informed me kindly.

"Oh no? That's just where you are wrong. I have got quite a fair idea."

I read the letter without much surprise, noting the date. It was three days before my interview with Mr Holland about the Dower House. When I came to the neat unflourishing signature of Harold Bellamy I looked up.

"Gently abusive!" I commented. "No wonder poor Connie was hot and bothered. It looks as though Cruikshank has been making some money out of them and a lot of other poor guileless fools."

"We can only presume it was Cruikshank. He was Holland's agent. Very clever of him to charge just a fraction more in each case for repayment of interest and principal on the houses Holland sold on terms. It makes quite a respectable percentage. With luck he could continue his practice forever without being detected. The first column is the amount paid, the second the agent's fee which usually comes out of it, and the third is the actual fee Cruikshank helped himself to by dint of overcharging his clients. I wonder how your friend's husband tumbled to it."

"Is this the Squire's handwriting?" I asked, tapping the sheet with the back of one finger.

John nodded. "I found it in his desk. When I saw the name on the letter I thought it might be of interest. Especially after what you told me."

I said thoughtfully, "Holland must have faced Cruikshank with this that day I saw the Dower. Cruikshank did a bunk, thinking Middleburn would be too hot to hold him. How fortunate for him Holland was murdered."

"He can still be sued by the executors of the estate. No, Maggie, there is something more in Cruikshank's disappearance than that."

"Perhaps," I suggested, "he has nothing to fear from them, now the Squire is out of the way. It may be ages before they come round to this business." I handed back the foolscap and letter. "By then he might have covered his tracks or worked out a convincing story."

"We are letting Cruikshank alone for the moment," John said. "If he is mixed up in this business as I think he might be, he'll show his hand somewhere."

"Well, keep your eye on him," I advised. "I never did like the man. What is the next item of interest?"

John flipped over the odd sheets of papers balanced on his crossed knee. He picked out one.

"What are you frowning over?" I asked, resting my chin on his shoulder.

"A receipt from Doctor Trefont for professional services rendered to Mrs James Holland. He didn't mention that he had attended her. I hope it only slipped his mind. I don't like being lied to."

"May I see?" I asked, as casually as I could. The bill itself did not convey much, insofar as the term "professional services" had not been enlarged upon. My eyes went to the date. It verified my suspicions so perfectly that I felt inclined to doubt my own deductions. But it must be so. The information Doctor Johnson had given me and the strange contradiction of Yvonne and her father-in-law, allied to their hostility towards Doctor Trefont, all fitted in. The reluctance of both the doctor and Yvonne to discuss their relations was easily understood. Taken by itself, James Holland's violent opposition was puzzling. There could be only one explanation of that. Either Trefont had been a victim of overwhelming coercion or else he too had been a guileless fool. In either instance he must have re-belled after the dirty work was done, and Holland had not liked it.

John's voice roused me.

"What was that?" I asked. "I was in a trance."

"I merely inquired if you had lost interest in the proceedings, or whether you are too tired to continue. You have been staring at a receipt in a vacant manner for the past five minutes."

"Sorry," I said, giving up the paper. "I am still keen."

I would have to get hold of that receipt later. It was not essential in Yvonne's case, although she might remain obstinately silent no matter what proof was produced. But if I read the doctor aright, he would not budge an inch unless I had something with which to back up my accusations.

John slipped the papers onto my knee and got up. "We'll have to continue later. That sounds like Braithwaite now. Don't lose any of those papers. They might prove important."

II

I think John's warning was issued in a perfectly innocent manner, but I was glad he did not see me start guiltily. I picked over the small pile quickly. There was only a brief moment before Braithwaite would be admitted.

Thumbing through those documents was like looking up an en-cyclopedia. It was easy to become diverted and forget the original purpose. That happened to me then, when I came across something that almost wiped everything else from my head. At first I thought it belonged to an untouched part of the pattern. I did not realize then that I had already filled in the outlying pieces.

The new item on which my interest became focused was a very old letter. So old that it was dissolving along the edges where it had been folded. I read it as quickly as the fading writing permitted. Then John pushed open the door for Braithwaite to enter. Reluctantly I placed the frail sheet with the rest of the papers and assumed my hostess expression.

John said to me: "Have we any of that brandy left, Maggie? Don't get up. Just tell me where it is." I glanced quickly at Alan Braithwaite. He looked pale around the gills.

"In the cupboard above the kitchen sink. Come and sit down, Mr Braithwaite."

He chose the easy chair John had been using earlier in the evening, but sat bolt upright, grasping his briefcase as though it held the Koh-i-Noor diamond.

"I am sorry to appear so rattled, Mrs Matheson," he remarked, glancing towards the curtained windows, "but the fact is I have had rather an unnerving experience."

"They are locked," I said soothingly.

Alan Braithwaite grinned at me sheepishly. "Perfectly absurd of me. I must be lily-livered. But it was the sheer unexpectedness of it. It caught me unawares."

"What did?" I asked in a patient voice.

John came back into the room with a glass in his hand.

"We are getting used to this form of hospitality," he informed Braithwaite. "Down the hatch and you'll feel better. Someone tried to snatch his bag, Maggie."

"Did they?" I asked, interested. "They weren't very successful. What happened?"

Young Braithwaite tried to disguise a shudder as he finished off the drink.

"I came through the wood. I thought it might be quicker as I was delayed longer than I expected at the Hall. It was dark, of course, but I know the path fairly well. As a point of interest it happened at that same turn where Mr Holland was found. For a moment I thought I was going to be another victim. Absurd, you know, what you imagine might be your last thoughts. All in a flash. I wondered what the devil I had done to deserve this. But I don't think the footpad meant murder. Anyway, not this time."

Like all lawyers, you take a hell of a time to get to the point, I thought irritably.

"Someone stepped up in front of me and dealt me a terrific blow in the solar plexus, at the same time making a grab at my bag."

"I suppose," said John, "it would be a futile question to ask if you recognized the would-be bandit."

"I'm afraid so. It was dark in the wood, what with the trees and everything. I can't even tell you if he was big or small."

"Or male or female," I supplied.

Alan Braithwaite gave me a surprised look. "A man, of course. I hadn't thought of that."

"A solar plexus punch is a favourite of the gentle sex," I told him. He looked a bit shocked.

"Luckily," he went on, "I had the presence of mind to keep a firm grip on the handle of my case. After the first abortive attempt my assailant made off. It took me several minutes to regain my breath. I came along here at once." He looked at John doubtfully. "I had it in mind to ring the police, but I suppose telling you amounts much to the same thing."

"If you like you can ring Sergeant Billings from here. The telephone is in my study. As it is a local matter he would be the best person to advise. There is very little I could do beyond telling him myself."

Braithwaite was a shade disappointed at John's detached view of the matter.

"You consider," he ventured with legal restraint, "that my assailant was just an ordinary thief after money or similar valuables?"

"Until I know what you have in the case, I can't think otherwise," John answered, in a manner worthy of the best legal circles.

"Perhaps it is as well to keep things formal," Braithwaite said, after pondering on the matter. "I will report the attack to Middleburn police station."

"Show him where the phone is, Maggie. I must clear up these papers."

I gave John another sharp look at this remark. I almost believed that he did not trust me alone with those papers for any length of time.

I took Braithwaite along to the study and rang the Hall. Ames answered it and expressed regret that the outward line was in use.

"I'll wait on," I said, when he offered to call when the line was disengaged. "The line is busy," I told Braithwaite. Holding the earpiece, I sat down in the desk chair and dropped my elbow on the arm.

"Yvonne said the phone has hardly stopped ringing all day," Braithwaite told me. "Some people have very bad sense of timing. You would think that they would hold off for a while."

"Curious, I suppose," I offered. "You can't get away from human nature. How was Yvonne today?" I did not say that I had already seen her. I wanted to know if her sudden spurt of self-assurance had gone. Evidently it had not.

"Bearing up remarkably well. I was surprised at her good spirits. You know, Mrs Matheson, that will the old man made is a great piece of injustice. It is hardly fair to expect Yvonne not to marry again."

I watched him closely. "If she wants to, she shouldn't let the money stand in her way."

"That's just what I told her," Alan Braithwaite informed me in all innocence. "She had such a short time with Jim, and that ended tragically. Mr Holland should have made some allowance, irrespective of her future plans."

"He probably didn't like the idea of the Holland money going out of the family. Hullo—this sounds like it."

Ames' smooth voice sounded in my ear. I asked for the police station number and handed the receiver to Braithwaite. There did not seem any point in retiring discreetly as I knew what Braithwaite was going to say. The conversation was a short one. Billings must have become accustomed to odd occurrences taking place in his district. Braithwaite did not have to repeat himself once.

"The matter is going to be looked into," he said, handing me back the phone with a shrug. "My brief escapade sounds a bit feeble now."

Automatically I held the receiver to my ear before ringing off. "Just one moment," I said, listening closely.

It was there again. A soft sound of someone breathing, the slight noise of an open line in another place. I rang on the line quickly, hoping to catch the eavesdropper, and listened in again. In my own ear there came the reverberation of a similar ring. I jumped and slammed the receiver on its stand indignantly.

"Come along," I said, ignoring Alan Braithwaite's inquiring gaze. "John will be wondering what has become of you. You said you had something important to tell him."

He followed me along the passage. "It may or may not be pertinent, but it is something I will have to look into if your husband does not. I would have been over sooner, but I was delayed at the Hall. Funeral arrangements, you know. Mrs Mulqueen was rather trying about them. She insists upon a huge affair instead of a private one. A small show would be in much better taste under the circumstances. What do you think?"

"From what I knew of Mr Holland the more pomp and ceremony the better. Had he but known the manner of his death he would consider an elaborate funeral a form of challenge to his murderer. I may be dead, but you can't kill my memory, so to speak."

John looked up as we entered.

"All in order," I said. "I think Billings took it without a blink. Are you two going to talk in a way I will understand or would you prefer me to go?"

"I would hate to do you out of the fire, Mrs Matheson. No doubt, you have your husband's confidence in many matters. If he does not object I see no reason why you need not remain."

I removed myself into a quiet corner. I could see John was becoming irritated at the legal touch. Alan Braithwaite conveyed the impression that there was all night ahead in which to propound theories. Whereas I knew John was nearly tired to death, in spite of his look of alertness. I hoped Braithwaite's air of importance was justified.

John tried to bring him around to the point at once. "You say someone tried to snatch your briefcase. Is there something in it you wanted to show me?"

"There is. But first I want to tell you about Mr Ernest Mulqueen. I went along to see him late this afternoon as I told you I would. I thought he might like to see a lawyer. He didn't seem in the least perturbed by his position. Instead he bombarded me with questions concerning his late brother-in-law's will. In a word, he wanted to know what he got out of the estate. Odd thing for a man under suspicion of murder, don't you agree? Please don't think I am betraying the confidence of a client. I was assured in no uncertain terms that when the time came Ernest Mulqueen would need no assistance from a pansy tie-waving solicitor like myself."

I let out a spurt of laughter from my corner. It sounded like the forthright little man. "However," continued Braithwaite, "I was also assured of my welcome. I was just the man Mr Mulqueen wanted to see. And forthwith he put in a claim for some obscure farm in the Riverina, which he said was amalgamated with some of the other Holland estates. He wants the farm separated and handed back to him. I told Mr Mulqueen I would look into the matter. When I got back to the office I went through some files and found certain papers appertaining to this farm. They were certainly in Mulqueen's name. The point is, if the farm is his how does it happen that the property affairs were in Mr Holland's hands? Mrs Mulqueen supplied an answer to that question tonight. She remembers vaguely my late father drawing up some document and Mr Mulqueen signing over the farm to her brother and being paid a lump sum. But unless you have the receipt for that money and the agreement she thinks was signed, all trace of them has disappeared."

"I have got nothing," John answered slowly.

Braithwaite shrugged his shoulders. "Well, on paper the farm is still Mulqueen's unless those two documents turn up. I thought you might be interested to learn of it."

Alan Braithwaite opened his case and took out a green book bound with calfskin. He turned over the pages lightly.

"This is a record of the home farm and household accounts. A rather rough one, I am compelled to admit. Mr Holland was accustomed to keep it in his study as a check on outgoing and incoming monies. The accounts were neither accurate or foolproof, but they helped maintain some sort of cost of running expenses connected with the Hall. You handed it to me along with other papers when we cleared out the desk."

John glanced over it frowningly. "Actually it was found in Mr Holland's bedroom. I only gave it a cursory glance and then passed it on to you for further perusal."

Alan Braithwaite smiled a little grimly. "I perused it today and found this." He pointed one finger to the top of a page and turning the leaf indicated the next number.

I craned forward to catch his meaning.

John said without expression: "Two sheets have been torn out. That wipes out any audit that can be made. You say Mr Holland kept these accounts?"

"It was his book, but I notice entries have been made in several different handwritings."

"Can you recognize them?" John asked quickly.

"Mr Holland employed as his accountant whoever was nearest to hand at the time. Usually members of his family, although I detect Ames' writing in a few instances. Rather beastly, isn't it?"

I knew what he meant. One of the family had been cooking the accounts to his advantage and had torn out the sheets before the police got hold of the book.

"It is remarkable Mr Holland did not observe anything out of the way," John observed.

"I don't think he regarded the accounts book very seriously. He was very open-handed with household money, so I am told. He entertained quite a lot. The fact that he barely wrote in it himself shows that he did not worry too much whether it balanced or not."

"Then it will be pretty hard to tell how much was taken," John said. "Have you any idea at all?"

"Not the faintest. The difference between the totals on the now consecutive leaves is rather large, but that is neither here nor there. The dates covered by the missing pages were times when Mr Holland was spending freely in entertainment."

"If we can discover who made the entries for those dates we will know who stole the pages. Did you make any inquiries at the Hall tonight?"

"A few. I wanted to tell you about it first. No one seemed interested or concerned at my questions." There was a pause. John frowned heavily into the fire. I was glad Alan Braithwaite's call had not been for nothing.

Just then a footstep sounded on the flagged path outside the window. Our visitor jumped slightly, and grinned when he saw my eyes on him.

The footsteps walked across the narrow stone porch. There was a pause as the owner felt for the bell. I put aside my knitting and left the room. I did not mind answering unexpected rings when two men were in the house.

Ursula Mulqueen stood at the door. She looked strongly like her mother standing there in her dark dress with a coat over her shoulders. Her lips were not parted in their customary vacant smile. They were pressed together in a purposeful manner. The Mulqueens were developing a habit of calling at the Dower. Oddly enough Ursula's words were almost the identical ones her mother had used. She had been out for a stroll and—

"Mr Braithwaite is here," I told her in order to save time. I stepped aside to let her into the hall.

"Alan? Now I think of it he did mention he was coming over. Is he talking business with your husband?"

"He was. I think they have finished now."

"Perhaps he will escort me home if he has finished."

"Are you sure you won't stay?" I asked ironically.

Alan Braithwaite frowned slightly as Ursula went into the room. John's look of irritation returned. Ursula's eyes took them both in speculatively. She glanced at the open briefcase and the papers John had made into a pile on the mahogany coffee table.

She turned a pleading little-girl look on Braithwaite. "Could you possibly see me home as far as the gates, Alan? I had no idea I was so late."

To John she said: "Inspector, I have come to plead on father's behalf. I know he could not possibly have done this wicked deed. Even if he had I'm sure there was some good excuse for killing poor Uncle James. Perhaps he was dying of some incurable disease and begged father to do it."

Braithwaite muttered: "Don't be idiotic, Ursula. I'm sure Inspector Matheson realizes your good intentions, but you'll do your father more harm than good talking like that."

Ursula swung round. "What have I said?" she cried fearfully.

Alan Braithwaite got up. "I'll take you home, Ursula. Are you ready?" Evidently he considered it was the only way to shut her up.

I grinned at John after they had left. The irritated expression left his face.

"What beats me," he said ruefully, "is that neither of them nor anyone else at the Hall realizes that Ernest Mulqueen's detention is a very minor step and that they are all without alibis."

"The full significance struck Yvonne this afternoon. I was the one who disillusioned her. Hullo, young Braithwaite has left his precious account book."

"I told him to. I want to have another look at it. Are you coming to bed? I'm just about all in."

III

I was half-asleep when I remembered about Doctor Trefont's receipt. It broke me into full consciousness with a jerk, which communicated itself to John.

He asked at once: "Is anything the matter?" I lay back again, trying to sound sleepy. "Just dreaming. Sorry if I disturbed you."

He made no comment and presently his breathing became steadier and louder. I pondered on what I should do. There would be no sense in taking the receipt from the file. Ten to one it would be missed immediately. To take a copy of it would be better. I waited for a few more minutes and tried to get out of bed stealthily.

John spoke again through the darkness. "For Heaven's sake, Maggie, try and relax. Would you like an aspirin?"

I was grateful for the idea. "I'll go and get one."

John gave a loud resigned groan and heaved himself up. "Stay where you are. I'll get it for you."

So much for my plan to make use of his idea. John came back, switched on the bedside light and handed me two tablets with a glass of water. I looked at them in dismay. If I took both pills there would be little chance of staying awake long enough to allow John to settle down so as to sneak out of the room. I took one with a sip of water, placing the other on the bedside table.

"Take them both," advised my annoying husband. "I can never sleep if you are on edge all night. The room tingles with your tired nerves. They make a hideous noise."

"No, really," I protested. "One will send me off."

"Take it, girl. I want some rest."

He held my nose between two fingers, and as my mouth fell open dropped the aspirin on my tongue, following it up with the tumbler of water to my lips. "Talk about third degree methods," I spluttered.

John turned off the light. "Just be quiet and take deep relaxing breaths. You'll soon be asleep."

I said: "Thank you, darling," in a meek voice.

It would be tough going. I suddenly realized how warm and comfortable I was. I wanted to sink further and further into the softness and warmth. My eyelids fell down once or twice. I jerked them open again. With a great effort I turned my head towards the luminous dial of the clock. If I could keep my eyes on that tiny glow of light there might be a chance. The trouble was I had to wait for John to go deeply asleep. If I got up too soon there was a strong likelihood of him demanding, 'What the hell are you up to now, Maggie?' And in a sharper tone than before.

Then I bethought myself of a trick which had never failed me in the old days during the night shifts at the Exchange. Rousing myself by a supreme effort of will I rapped my head with my knuckles sharply three times. Then I gave in, turned over and fell asleep repeating: "I will wake up at three o'clock."

Heaven knows why I picked that particular hour. I suppose because I had heard somewhere that sleep is deepest at that time. There would be less chance of disturbing John again. Also, it would give the double dose of aspirin an opportunity to work off.

Sure enough I awoke at three o'clock. Actually the clock said five minutes past the hour. I felt absurdly gratified when I remembered John pointing it out as five minutes fast. I was quite wide awake. It was not as dark as I had expected. My eyes were able to pick out familiar objects of furniture. There was no mist across the sky that night, and the stars shone as bright and hard as diamonds in the casement frame of the bedroom window.

I turned my head in the direction of John's breathing. Surely he would not awaken now. I slid out of bed and felt for my dressing gown. If he did I would have to make a call from Tony the excuse. I stood perfectly still beside the bed waiting for indications of John's wakefulness and planning my route across the room to the bedroom door. It would be too silly if I bumped into something and woke him that way.

I proceeded carefully on tiptoe, so much so that I nearly overbalanced. I crept down the passage in the darkness, not daring to switch on a light. It wasn't worth risking any sort of glow which might bring my sleeping spouse hurrying to my side. It was amazing how still and lonely the house seemed away from him. I wasn't exactly nervous. That would have been absurd with John close at hand. But I felt a sense of loneliness which kept me on edge with my senses alert.

Half-way down the passage I felt for the open study door. My safest move would be to conduct my researches by torchlight. I strained my eyes against the darkness and fumbled carefully in the desk drawer. My fingers fell first on John's official revolver. It was a nasty shock. I had thought it was the torch. Although I knew it was unloaded, I did not care to handle a weapon which, with the addition of a small part, could cause death so quickly.

With the torch glowing red through my fingers I went further along to the lounge-room. After the chilliness of the passage, it was warm and just a little stuffy. I could smell the remains of my own cigarettes and even a hint of spirits from the tumbler Alan Braithwaite had left on the table. Besides these definable smells, there was that intangible something which I recognized when someone outside ourselves had been in the house.

I moved across the room to the table, absently lifting the tumbler to see if a wet ring-mark had been left on the polished surface. Leaving the torch alight beside it, I opened John's file and hurriedly went through the papers. The receipt was still there. I lifted it out, scanning it again more closely. Then my eyes fell beyond it onto the pile. I put the receipt aside and lifted up the creased letter which had caught my interest before John had brought Alan Braithwaite in that evening. I could barely see the writing in the dim light. Picking up the torch, I held it directly over the page, moving it along as I re-read the faded words. It had been the signature which had caught my eye. I had only heard that name spoken in connection with the Hollands once before. What was it Elizabeth Mulqueen had said? "Olivia—a sweet girl. She died a long time ago."

She must have died officially with the Hollands the day she wrote that letter I held in my hand.

I am leaving you, James. I am running away because I hate you for what you have made of me. Trained and moulded me, as you put it. Don't go to the trouble of coming after me to bring me back. The only wife you'd bring back would be dead. And you always did fear scandal. I am going to make some new life out of what little you have left of me.

I don't even care about Jim. My son? Yours, James. You took him from me right from the start. I only pray that when you try to mould him according to your will he might one day disillusion you, and that your own pretentious tyrannical life will crash into oblivion, for such is the revenge I would like. I hope to witness that day. You need not concern yourself. I am not running away with another man. If I could have found one I would have been glad because of the blow to your pride. But I have found a dear friend, a counsellor and a comforter. What is the use of explaining to you. You are too proud and hard to judge anyone except on the lowest principles.

I can't even bring myself to write 'good-bye,' James, because that is too fine a word to pass between us. No doubt you will arrange some story to circulate about my disappearance to soothe your pride and stop any scandal. I don't care much if you do, because people will know underneath what I am doing although they will be too afraid to say it to your face. Strangely enough now for the first time since I met and married you I am afraid no longer. Fear is a bad emotion to kindle, James. One day it might rise up and strike at you instead.

Don't forget what I said about coming after me. I would as soon die as live as your wife again.

Olivia

I whistled very softly. What a letter! What a skeleton in the Holland cupboard! I wondered if he did go after her and she committed suicide as she had promised. The letter had a strong-willed sound about it. And yet Olivia couldn't have been like that if she had allowed herself to be "moulded and trained."

Quite suddenly Yvonne's face appeared before my mental vision. When reading the letter, I had visualized the writer as someone after the style of Yvonne. A similar fit of defiance, such as Yvonne was manifesting at this moment, had prompted Holland's wife to write such a letter. She was no longer afraid of him. Yvonne was no longer afraid of her environment. The softest and most pliable of worms turns sooner or later.

There were several interesting points about the letter which deserved further consideration. But it was advisable to keep to schedule. I realized I was very cold. The fire was no longer a small heap of glowing embers, but grey and dead-looking. The sight made me want to hurry back to the companionship of John.

"I'll just copy out the receipt now and think about the letter tomorrow. John might have something to say about it."

Nocturnal manoeuvres never run smoothly and efficiently. I had neglected to provide myself with pencil and paper. That meant another trip to the study and more fumbling in the darkness. I was fast losing my enthusiasm. Only the knowledge that what I was about would be useful, not to say necessary, made me stifle a yawn and go creeping down the passage again to the study.

I shut the door as quietly as an oilless hinge would allow and sat down at John's desk. The torch-light was wearing thin. I flashed it once into a drawer to find a sheet of paper. It lit up John's revolver. Odd how the sight of that weapon did not have the effect of making me feel safe, but rather the reverse. I took out the receipt from the pocket of my dressing-gown in the dark and held a pen ready so as not to waste the battery of the torch. I was nearly through with the copy when the light died. I could remember it well enough in order to complete the copy, but I had to put the original receipt in its file on the lounge-room table.

I unscrewed the bottom of the torch and pulled out the battery, stroking it firmly with my fingers to encourage some flicker. The copy went into my pocket. I got up holding the receipt and the torch.

Those last few minutes seemed to be the longest and most tedious of the whole escapade. But there was nothing to be gained by hurrying. Even the completion of my objective did not warrant any risk of bringing John to the scene. The squeaky hinge on the study door still had the effect of making me stop and listen for some movement.

As I put my head out the door a cold draught blew along the passage. I was immediately alive to that current of air. It registered something in my mind. I stood quite still for one minute before I remembered. You felt that sweeping current of air in a house running north and south when a window or door was open to the outside.

Out in the passage I was not so aware of it. It was more noticeable when stepping into the draught from a closed room. I hoped I might be imagining things and set my teeth against a jumpy feeling in my throat. I slid one hand along the wall of the passage and proceeded cautiously back to the lounge-room.

I was a few paces away from the half-open door when something flashed in the hall mirror directly opposite. Not even my clenched teeth could stop the feeling that my heart was in my mouth. I knew what the draught sweeping down the passage meant. The front door was open. I stood against the wall paralysed with fear. It was enough to feel nervous and on edge creeping around your own house in the dark early hours of the morning, but it became sheer stark terror when you realized an intruder was doing the same.

I wanted desperately to shriek for John, but somehow I restrained myself. I remained there pressed against the wall, taut and dumb. I did not have to wait long. Suddenly a crash and a splintering of glass sounded between the silence and the heavy thumping of my heart. Almost following on the noise a figure I could sense rather than see glided swiftly out of the lounge-room door. There was just a tiny click and abruptly the current of air sweeping in from the front door was cut off.

The cessation galvanized me into belated action. I switched on the torch and went into the lounge-room. A quick sweep of light over the room from a strategic position in the doorway did not reveal any further intruders. On the floor of the coffee table were the remains of Alan Braithwaite's tumbler. Whoever the stranger was he must have shied off at the crash, thinking it would awaken the household.

I went over to the table and stared down at John's file. It was still open where I had left it. If the intruder was after something in it he must have knocked over the glass before commencing the search. I loosened my grip on the receipt I was still holding in my left hand and replaced it. The torch-light was almost gone. I had no desire to be left in the darkness.

I closed the file quickly and hurried out of the room and down the passage to John.

CHAPTER NINE

I

The following morning I might have dreamed it all. It seemed impossible that anyone should have the audacity and the means to enter our house by the front door while we lay sleeping within. I might have considered the episode as part of a dream but for the fact that my nightmares never take such a clear and reasonable form. Also, there were still the remains of the shattered tumbler lying about the mahogany table.

I got up as soon as daylight was hard and cold enough to make the house look prosaic and not the background for moments of terror. Armed with a brush and pan, I went into the lounge-room without hesitation. Much as I wanted to confide in John about our prowler, I did not want to be asked any awkward questions. Just what I was doing around the house at that hour and why had I not roused him? The shattered glass had to be removed at once. Apart from the risk of Tony cutting himself, Tony's curious father might wonder how it came to be broken.

I swept up the pieces and then opened the windows for clean, fresh air. John might feel the same instinct about a stranger in a room as I did. I had no qualms of conscience in suppressing the facts of my nocturnal adventure, although I was certain it belonged to some part of the mystery which permeated Holland Hall. John was quite capable of unravelling that mystery without any assistance from me.

I paused outside the lounge-room, brush and pan in one hand. Then I went along to the front door. I opened it slowly, watching the lock under my hand. As the draught swept down the passage the kitchen door banged in the distance. I shut it, then re-opened it again. I knew how the intruder had entered—through the front door.

By pressing a tiny lever on the lock it could be drawn back to stay, even while the ordinary latch fell into position. Once that was accomplished, entering the house was merely a matter of turning the door handle. The adjustment must have been made the previous evening. Any earlier and John or I would have detected it when using our latch keys.

The intruder was a matter of an alternative—either Ursula Mulqueen or Braithwaite the solicitor. Had I known last night that it was one of them, I would not have been so frightened. That was the mistake I continually made; not being afraid of anyone I knew. If I had recognized the murderer as an acquaintance, my feelings would probably have been the same.

It was one thing identifying the prowler but quite another to work out what they wanted so urgently from John's file that made it necessary to take such a risk. Whatever it was, there was no doubt the venture had been unsuccessful. The time between my departure from the lounge-room and the falling tumbler was not enough to have covered an entrance, search, discovery and flight.

My eyes fell on the old-fashioned bolt and chain hanging loosely half-way down the jamb. Hitherto I had not bothered to use it when John was home. I smiled grimly to myself. There would be no repetition of last night's episode. The Dower was my house and I intended to keep it inviolate.

When John was in the house things seemed much the same as usual. But I noticed a difference when he left for town to interrogate Ernest Mulqueen. Not even Tony's scamperings up and down the passage banished that nasty feeling you get after your home has been broken into. I stood it until after lunch, when Tony went down for a nap. Then the house took on a deathly quiet, the same as I had crept through in the chill early hours.

I could not walk out of the place and leave Tony. Certainly there was the radio with which to infuse some atmosphere of unconcern through the house, but that was in the lounge-room. I felt quite incapable of sitting there after the events of the previous night. I wandered around the house waiting for Tony to finish his sleep. The perverse child seemed to be taking longer than usual. Most of the time I spent in the bedroom, pottering around and tidying drawers. I could sense John's presence more keenly there than in any other room. Last night it had seemed like a haven. Once I went into the study with some wild idea of calling the Hall and trying to trick Ursula into giving herself away. I stopped myself in time. The person who broke the tumbler may have been Alan Braithwaite.

At last Tony woke up, quite unconcerned with the moments of distress I had put in while he slept peacefully. I bundled him into a coat and muffler to take him out for a walk.

"Under your own steam today, my son," I said firmly. "It will take longer, but that is the idea. I don't want to get back until it's time for Daddy to be home. I'll only get the jitters again."

He climbed hopefully into the pusher as I searched for a harness to guide his steps. I shook my head. He got out with a loud sigh.

We wandered down the road towards the village. I had no set plan for the excursion, when my eye fell on the golf course at the right of the road. I remembered the ball I had lost on the day of James Holland's murder. There wasn't a chance of finding it, but it gave me an objective.

I lifted Tony over the fence and then got through myself. The long strap fastened to the harness was twitched from my grasp as Tony ran off down the second fairway. I cast an anxious look around, but no one was playing.

Presently he stopped and turned, waiting for me to catch up. I knew better than to hurry. It would only set him off again. As I proceeded at the same pace, he squatted down on the grass, bending over something interestedly. I made a sudden spurt and put my foot firmly on the trailing lead.

Tony did not seem to mind losing his stolen freedom. He stood upright with the object of his interest grasped tightly in one hand.

"Show," I commanded, remembering other souvenirs. Against some protest I prised open his small fist.

"Good Heavens!" I said with mild surprise. "Maybe there's a chance of finding that ball of mine if you can pick up a thing like this." It was a baby's dummy.

"What an extraordinary thing to find on a golf course," I remarked, not recollecting that I had thrown it there myself. "Come along, fellah. We'll make for the eighteenth. You can try out your sharp eyes there."

I tried to persuade Tony to throw the dummy away, but he put it carefully into a pocket.

We cut across the fairways. Once or twice I had to lift Tony across a narrow creek. Luckily it was dry, as I slipped and half fell, much to the child's amusement. We climbed up the slope of the seventeenth fairway. Ames was mowing the green. I thought it advisable to explain my presence on the course minus clubs and plus child. Also, I was unsure of my position. The open invitation to use the course may have ceased now with Mr Holland's decease.

Ames was playing his cheery open-air role that day, conformable to the links. He was in an ideal setting. I stood off the green looking up to where he sat in the saddle of the machine, the sun on his handsome face. He listened to my explanations and refrained from saying immediately that I had not a hope in Hades of finding the ball. He spoke intelligently to Tony, who stared back with his eyes and mouth wide open, and finally rounded off the conversation smoothly by commenting on the dryness of the season and general drought conditions.

I made a half-hearted search for the ball, beating around the scrub with a stick. Tony followed suit. It was a new sort of game to him. After stopping his weapon on the shin for the third occasion, I considered it time to close the search. The fruit of my labours consisted of a very old ball indecently denuded of its outer covering. I was putting this in Tony's pocket when a hail came from the tee. We hurriedly withdrew into the shelter of the trees and waited for a female golfer to drive off. She might have saved her breath, as the ball trickled to rest a hundred yards from where we had stood. When I saw that the female golfer was Daisy Potts-Power, I hastily worked out a plan of retreat to avoid meeting her. She had not recognized us and I had no desire to be caught again. Or hadn't I? A notion came to me suddenly. Maybe Daisy would be useful. I waited until she took a number three to a low-lying ball. It came straight across the course to the rough without gaining the slightest ground towards the green. I marked its fall with my eye and strolled over to wait for her.

Daisy entered among the trees with bent head and eyes on the ground.

"Here!" I called, giving the ball a nudge with my shoe to send it onto a tuft of grass. It was a sure bet that she would hit a tree getting out, but I had made the lie a bit easier.

"Fancy seeing you here!" Daisy cried, with a wide delighted smile. She spoke as though our last place of meeting had been the other side of the globe. "Are you not playing? But of course not. How foolish of me."

"This fellow impedes my freedom a little. I can't haul him around the links."

"So you are out for a walk together instead," Daisy said in a sentimental voice. "What grand company he is for you! You must be great pals."

I glanced about for Tony. He was off the lead again and I did not want him to stray. Actually he was standing immediately behind me, staring at Daisy. The beastly dummy he had found was in his mouth. I pulled it out, uncorking a long continuous sound of protest.

"Disgusting child!"

I wanted to throw the dummy away but the howl rose to such a crescendo that, with a strong warning, I replaced it in Tony's pocket.

"How quaint of him!" Daisy said. "I noticed he had it in his mouth but I did not like to make any comment."

I said in a firm voice: "No child of mine ever has nor ever will have a dummy. Your ball is here right at my feet. What are you going to use?"

She chose a number eight at random, buffeting two trees and pulling down a shower of leaves around us. After the confetti had blown away, I saw that her ball, by some marvellous chance, had just made the edge of the fairway. We strolled towards it together.

"I suppose," I said tentatively, working on my notion, "that your mother is having her afternoon nap." The slightest encouragement made Daisy loquacious. That was why few people gave it.

"I left her tucked up snugly in her chair in the garden. She likes to see people passing, you know. Mother's really marvellous the way she puts up with her suffering. Her patience makes me feel my life is really worthwhile, devoting it to her. She may drop off for a doze if she becomes easy. If only people realized how remarkable she is."

This disjointed speech was meant to convey two things: Firstly, that Daisy held the upper hand over her mother. Also, that she could have done something with her life had she so desired. From my impression of mother and daughter together, neither was convincing.

"If she likes to watch people going by," I said, "she must like visitors. I'll take Tony down to bring some brightness into her life."

Daisy was inordinately pleased. "Would you really? That would be nice of you. I would come back with you, but I want to see Ames. He promised to show me some strokes. I do think he is an awfully nice man, don't you? A real gentleman."

"Rather," I agreed, thankful that she thought so. "I'd hate you to miss a lesson."

She laughed self-consciously. "I suppose you consider my game needs it."

There wasn't much I could say to that. Daisy was one of those players who would never learn golf. She was like those who lack card-sense. Either it is in you or it is not. The same with golf. I waved her on to the green, full of admiration for Ames, who preserved the role of a real gentleman when tutoring Daisy in golf. The lesson would keep her occupied until I learned from Mrs Potts-Power what I wanted to know.

II

The first information I gleaned was not from the old woman, but of her. The wheelchair was certainly in a secluded corner of the garden, but there was no mountainous, heavy-eyed occupant tucked cosily up therein.

So Connie Bellamy was right. I was not surprised. Rather I was embarrassed for the old woman's sake. It is not pleasant to be taken in deception. From the low open windows at the front of the house came the sounds of the Viennese waltz to which Mrs Potts-Power was so addicted. I was beginning to hate Strauss. He was associated forever in my mind with that dreadful dinner at Holland Hall.

The garden path passed directly alongside the windows. I could not resist glancing in. Mrs Potts-Power was there as I had guessed. She stared directly into my eyes. That basilisk gaze of hers held me for a moment.

She said calmly: "I wondered when you would come. You'll find the front door open."

There was something uncanny about the way she sat there waiting for me, and not at all put out of countenance. I refused to be intimidated, although a sense of nervousness was mine.

When I entered the room she repeated: "I have been expecting to see you. I knew you would come sooner or later. Sit down and don't let that child fidget. I don't like children."

My maternal hackles rose. Mrs Potts-Power regarded me with malicious amusement. I sat down abruptly. If you want something from somebody you have to dance to her tune, even a Strauss waltz.

She passed over a box of chocolates and candy. I selected one for Tony.

Mrs Potts-Power said: "Put it straight into his mouth. I can't abide sticky fingers."

"You know," I said pensively, "you remind me very much of the late Mr Holland. Were you related?"

"Both malignancy and benignity are prerogatives of old age," retorted Mrs Potts-Power. "James Holland and I chose the former."

"With so much in common," I asked, "why did you quarrel with him?"

"You are a very inquisitive young woman," she replied.

"So he said also. Since you recognize curiosity as part of my make-up, perhaps you will tell me how you come to be out of your wheelchair? Does Daisy know?"

She chuckled, a low wobbly sound from the depths of her large stomach.

"Quite likely she has guessed. But it suits her better to deceive herself. 'Poor mother! So dependent on me.' Does she talk like that to you?"

My expression must have indicated my disgust.

"Come, come, girl," Mrs Potts-Power said sharply. "Don't you agree she is better being deceived? She's far happier. And I like being waited upon and coddled. Sometimes she nearly drives me to distraction with her patience and submissiveness. As a matter of fact my heart is none too steady. It doesn't justify a wheelchair, but it justifies me a little."

"If you do nothing but sit around and eat, no wonder your heart is dicky," I said.

"What have you come to see me about?" Mrs Potts-Power asked, heaving her bulk out of the chair after three attempts.

She moved the needle of the Panatrope to the edge of the disc.

"I thought you knew," I retorted. "You said you've been expecting me."

Mrs Potts-Power grinned. "I have a fair idea. But I wouldn't like to give away more than you wanted."

"Why did you quarrel with James Holland? Why were you, for the first time in years, suddenly invited to a dinner party at the Hall?"

She answered me without reticence. "I wanted Jim to marry Daisy. James didn't like the idea. I think he was worried that my influence would be stronger than his. It would have been too," she added reflectively. "I could hold out longer than James even when we were young. That's why I didn't marry him myself. It must have been a matter of ten years since I was at the Hall. I was there the other night at his invitation. I had won again."

"Mr Holland won one round," I pointed out. "His son married Yvonne."

Mrs Potts-Power snorted. "Picked out for him just as James selected Olivia. Poor weak fools, the pair of them. James wanted women merely for breeding purposes. He realized women like me complicated matters. Olivia was the same as Yvonne. No relatives—no money. Just a young, foolish child who would submit herself mentally and physically to a stronger character." She finished spitefully: "I daresay, had he thought of it, James would have got rid of them somehow, after they had served their purpose."

"Quite the feudal lord," I murmured. "Fate intervened in both cases, did it not?"

The old lady gave me a sharp glance. "What do you mean?"

"Before the idea occurred to Mr Holland to rid himself of his wife, she did it for him. In Yvonne's case his plans were upset by his son's untimely death. He was indifferent to her presence when she was no longer Jim's wife."

"Who has been talking to you? Elizabeth? How did you know about Olivia?"

"Mrs Mulqueen has told me nothing. But there is a photograph of Olivia Holland in her room. The picture caught my eye because it is turned to the wall. I defined it as a token of disgrace and punishment. Then I came across a letter. Strange how we women cannot resist writing farewell letters. It would have done your heart good to read it, if you considered Olivia a poor, weak fool."

"I knew Olivia ran off, although James did not broadcast the fact. But you can't go visiting relatives for years, especially when it is known you have none. Was there a man?" Mrs Potts-Power smacked her lips over this old scandal.

"No, I don't think so. I am sorry to disappoint you. Although Olivia admitted in the letter that someone was helping her."

Mrs Potts-Power stuffed caramels one after another into her mouth to make up for the disappointment. "I'd like to know who it was. Olivia hadn't a friend in the world except those James had. And you wouldn't call them exactly friends. Unless it was—" She broke off and turned her wicked eyes towards me.

I watched them, deeming it wiser not to urge her on. She was capable of leaving her remark uncompleted out of sheer cussedness. Her eyes narrowed to gleaming slits and widened again slowly. They looked at me blandly. Mrs Potts-Power had guessed at the identity of Olivia's friend. But she wasn't going to talk.

"Mrs Potts-Power," I asked, "where is Olivia now?"

"She is dead," Mrs Potts-Power replied promptly. "There was a death notice in the paper years ago. I remember reading it."

"How many years?" I inquired, disappointed but persevering. "Who put the notice in? Not James Holland. Olivia had left him, remember."

The blank look settled on Mrs Potts-Power's face again. She was hiding some secret knowledge behind it. She became suddenly talkative.

"I don't know how long ago it was. Jim was quite young at the time. My husband had just died. I had my own troubles. It did occur to me James might marry again, just to get someone to rear Jim. That was before that nurse came."

"Where did Olivia Holland die?" I persisted.

Mrs Potts-Power thought, and presently recollected the name of the country town. It struck a familiar chord.

"Then there is no chance of Olivia being still alive, and better still, living somewhere in the vicinity of the Hall?" I watched the old woman's face carefully.

"You have been reading too many mystery novels, Mrs Detective Matheson. Things don't work out like that in real life."

III

I left Mrs Potts-Power, my mind dazed with new discoveries and their confusing issues of possibilities and probabilities. She followed me out the front door and settled herself in the wheelchair, casting me a wicked look as she tucked the crocheted rug around her knees.

Tony's steps were lagging as we climbed up the hill to High Street. I gave him an absent hand, automatically checking a stumble now and then. Two ideas were firmly fixed in my mind. Unfortunately both were difficult to develop. Olivia, the one to whom James Holland's death was likely to prove a source of satisfaction and a fulfilment of revenge, was dead. She was out of this world, so far as a notice in the death column could prove. Could she have arranged her own death, or did Holland furnish the notice in order to stop scandalous whispers?

The second matter was the town from which Olivia's death had been reported. That same town was recorded as the receiving station of the telegram Mr Holland sent to the Hall just before his murder. It was no strange coincidence but a hint of the Squire's business during his last days. Had he, after all those years, suddenly decided to trace his erring wife's steps and verify her death? Had he discovered something concerning her which caused him to bring together an ill-assorted table of dinner guests in order to make known such information?

There were so many questions to ask, so many answers that might serve. My brain whirled desperately. I was glad when a voice interrupted, calling my name.

Connie Bellamy came panting up the street. As she drew near I had a sudden sinking feeling. All thoughts of Holland Hall and its kindred complications vanished. I had asked the Bellamys to dine that night and I had forgotten all about the invitation!

Connie must have found me distrait as we walked along together. She held her chatter for a brief spell. I laughed at the look of deep understanding she directed on me. She had been asking about the case and imagined my mind was occupied with its intricacies. Whereas I was swiftly planning an impromptu dinner for my forgotten guests.

Passing through the village, I said: "I hope it won't put you off, but you'll have to watch me buying your dinner. I had rather a rotten night and didn't feel up to preparing more than a grill and salad."

Connie probably thought me a shocking housewife, but at least that was better than the truth. I came out of the butcher's shop and found her talking to Daisy Potts-Power.

"Hullo," I said. Daisy carried her golf bag slung over one shoulder with a professional air. "How did the lesson go?"

She was brighter than ever and excited. "Awfully well. I feel as though I might begin to play now. Ames was terribly patient with me."

I frowned at the name. It would be a shocking thing if Daisy made a fool of herself in that way.

"Look," she said. "Tony has that dummy in his mouth again. Isn't he just the cutest thing?"

I swung round, catching a swift movement of Tony's hand from his mouth to behind his back. He regarded me with a solemn eye which did not falter before my more-in-sorrow-than-in-anger look. I was not going to risk a scene right in the middle of the village, so I dragged Connie off. "How was Mother?" Daisy yelled after us, over two or three heads.

"Most enlightening!" I called back. "You might tell her I said so. You'll find her in the garden all tucked up cosily in her chair."

"Have you been calling on Mrs Potts-Power?" asked Connie curiously. "Did she ask you to?"

"Not exactly. It was more a matter of telepathy. I found her most entertaining, the old fraud."

"Was she out of her wheelchair?"

"She was. And moving around as energetically as her bulk would allow. She's only an invalid for Daisy's sake. At least, so she says. I decline to comment on the situation."

Connie lost some of her customary talkativeness as we drew near the Dower. I detected a certain nervousness in her manner and remembered the original purpose of this dinner party of mine. The cause of her distress was a matter to be discussed between her husband and mine. I thought it best not to interfere. In any case, it always took an age to explain a situation to Connie. She had been the slowest telephonist at Central.

I hurried Tony through his evening meal, slicing tomatoes and washing another lettuce at the same time. My head ached, a legacy from the broken night and the afternoon's concentration on crime. The sudden readjustment of dinner arrangements and the prospect of the evening ahead did not improve it.

Connie proved herself quite competent when her aimless talk was stilled. Together we managed to prepare an adequate meal, fairly attractively served.

I gave Tony a quick face-and-hands sponge and put him into pyjamas. I did not feel equal to fitting in a bath amongst a dozen other things. I dumped him in his cot with a picture book to await John's homecoming. He was confused at all the rush and bustle. It made him restless. Twice when I went in to see if he was all right he was out of bed and wandering around the nursery.

That *would* happen when I had guests! Usually Tony went straight off to sleep as soon as he was tucked down. But, in the perverse way children have, he chose to misbehave that night.

After dinner—the grill was slightly overdone—John drew Harold Bellamy into the study, closing the door behind him. Connie stared at it in a frightened way.

"There's nothing to worry about," I said briskly, "as long as he is quite frank. You see, John found out about Cruikshank's little game himself. Come and help me with these dishes."

Connie said, following me out: "There is a letter Harold wrote to Mr Holland. Oh, Maggie, I'm so scared."

"Don't be scared. The letter has already come to light. I've read it myself, so you can understand how little John thinks of it. Drat! Was that Tony again?"

It was, and the poor lamb must have been crying for some time. The conversation at dinner had prevented me from hearing him. I went into the nursery, switching on the light. He was lying on his side facing the wall, and crying softly in a way that made me feel a brute to neglect him for a couple of dinner guests. I felt even worse when I lifted him. He lay in my arms limply, not caring who it was. I felt his forehead and neck anxiously, but there was no fever. He looked a little pale to my super-critical gaze, but his small tongue was quite pink and healthy.

I tucked him up in his cot again, leaving the nursery door ajar and the light aglow in the passage. Connie had started the dishes with a vigour that spelled uneasiness.

"What is the trouble with Tony?" she asked absently.

I found an apron and tied it on. "Dunno. I never have understood children and I never will. If I do the drying we will be about equal. Or would you rather I washed now?"

"I don't care. Are they still in the study?"

"Who? Oh, the men. I suppose so. I didn't hear them come out. We'll go back to the lounge-room after clearing up."

Poor Connie! Just because her precious Harold had been misguided enough to write a letter concerning Cruikshank's activities to the Squire, she seemed to believe her whole life was in jeopardy. However, this attitude was dispelled when we passed the study door on our way to the fire. A burst of hearty unrestrained masculine laughter nearly broke down the closed door.

I raised my brows at Connie. "Sounds like a serious conference. Dare we interrupt?"

Connie looked indignant. "To think that I have been nearly worrying myself sick! I do think it is too bad. Of course, I knew that there was really nothing to be frightened about, but—" Connie's relief had unplugged her volubility again.

I put my head in the study door.

"We are just coming, Maggie," John said hastily. "Sorry we have been so long."

"If the fire has gone down, you'll have to go out and get some kindling. I rather hope it has." I delayed John for a moment, my hand on his arm.

Connie whispered to her husband as they went along to the lounge-room.

"Everything under control?" I asked.

"No more than we reasoned. It all depends on Cruikshank's part as to whether or not the unsullied name of Bellamy comes into the case. Can I go now, please? I'm cold and bored."

I nodded in sympathy. "At least he appreciated your weak stories. And Connie regards you with awe. What now?" I picked up the telephone in the middle of the ring, holding it away from my ear as the sound continued.

"Go easy," I requested loudly into the mouthpiece.

"Mrs Matheson?" asked a voice. "Is that you, Maggie?" Yvonne. She sounded more like her old self—frightened, timid and bewildered. I nodded to John to go.

"What is it? Is anything the matter?" I asked.

Her voice came over the line in an incoherent rush. "Oh, Maggie, he's sick again. I just went in—and nurse—I don't know what's the matter with her. She won't wake up. I don't know what to do."

I gathered that it was Jimmy who was ill. I also guessed at the reason why Nurse Stone would not wake up. She was dead tight.

"Could you come over, Maggie?" Yvonne begged. "Jimmy doesn't look at all well. I don't know what to do."

"Are you alone?" I asked.

"Aunt Elizabeth is out somewhere. At least I think so. She was not in her room when I called her. Ursula is here, but she doesn't know anything about babies. Please come." She sounded almost beseeching.

"All right," I said resignedly. "I'll be over as soon as I can."

I went into the lounge-room. John was coaxing the fire along with the bellows.

"Sorry, people. Do you think you can do without me for a quarter of an hour? Yvonne Holland's baby is sick, and she thinks Doctor Maggie might be able to do something. I am afraid her confidence is misplaced."

John's face dropped along with the bellows from his hand. "Get the card table set up," I said soothingly. "By the time you've sorted out chips and found cards, I'll be back."

I went to find a coat and a scarf for my head. The light was still on outside Tony's room. I crept in, moving the door so that a slit of light fell across his face. He still looked pale and heavy, and his mouth hung slightly open. He was breathing heavily. I regarded him anxiously for a few moments.

IV

It was owing to Tony's inexplicable ailment and the knowledge that I had left John with some boring people who were not his friends and were merely my acquaintances, that made me choose the path through the wood to the Hall. I was so wrapped up in my concern for haste that it did not occur to me to be nervous until I was actually entering the thickest part of the artificial spinney. Then it was too late to pander to my nervousness, and I kept on.

The wood was full of the noises of rustling leaves, insects and small creatures. One absurd thought became fixed in my head. What would happen if I came face-to-face with Ernest Mulqueen's fox? It must still be prowling around owing to its would-be trapper's detention. Did a fox attack human beings as well as poultry? Or was it a creature to be subdued like a dog? From the fox, my mind went to the gin which had been awaiting it. The trap, whose cruel teeth had grasped the Squire instead. John told me Ernest Mulqueen insisted that he had left the gin set away from the path. Following his directions, Sergeant Billings had located the gin and taken it to headquarters for a closer examination. Traces of cloth and human blood, both identified as James Holland's, had been found adhering to it.

I stepped cautiously along the path, my torchlight playing on the ground two feet ahead. I was moving slowly now, and it was hard to restrain hasty glances over my shoulder and sideways into the thickly growing trees. I dared not give way to nerves. I would only start rushing madly through the wood, screaming like an insane woman. It was the terrible quiet loneliness of the place which frightened me most. I felt completely isolated from the rest of the world.

The wood was an ideal place for a tryst, be it for love or some more evil purpose. No one would hear. The trees would smother light laughter or a sobbing cry for mercy. No sound could vibrate against the damp foliage above and the wet earth underfoot.

It would not occur to such as James Holland to feel apprehensive on his own property. Safe in his arrogance, born of the fear of others, it was unbelievable that a killer should be waiting for him in the darkness of the wood.

He did not carry a torch as I did. He knew the path well. Only too well. That was to the murderer's advantage. James Holland stepped confidently along the track and stumbled straight into the gin. What time was it? Was there no faint glimmer of light at all? Enough to enable the Squire to see a step ahead? The shot was fired just after seven. Seven had been the hour fixed for his arrival at Holland Hall.

I halted suddenly in the track. But it was not to glance fearfully over my shoulder or to play the torchlight on a suspicious bush. I was nearly through the wood now. I could see lights shining from the windows of the Hall. It was nothing physical that pulled me up with such a jerk, but a blinding discovery. A revelation that I wanted to communicate to John at once.

Yvonne Holland must have thought I was quite mad. I had been called to the Hall to act as a pillar of strength to the fond mother of an ailing child, and all I wanted was the nearest telephone to talk to my husband whom I had left only a short time before. She looked faintly hurt and almost offended when I asked: "By the way, how is Jimmy now?" It was not very important to me then that her baby was sick again. Anyway, mine was ill too. She wasn't the only anxious mother in Middleburn.

Jimmy seemed better. He had vomited a great deal, but now he was asleep. I was still wanted to give my opinion on his condition.

"As soon as I've made a phone call, like a good girl," I said coaxingly. "I'll only be a minute."

Yvonne manipulated two pegs on the switchboard and led the way upstairs.

"You can use the phone in my room," she told me. She was afraid I might go off and forget Jimmy altogether. "Come along to the nursery when you have finished. Nurse is still asleep. She just won't wake up. I have given up trying."

"Best let her sleep it off," I said absently, waiting for John to answer the extension. Yvonne gave me a puzzled look, and made as though to speak.

John's voice said: "Hullo," and I waved her off.

"Darling," I cooed, in an attempt to control the excitement in my voice. "Are you still cold and bored?"

"What the—Oh, it's you, Maggie."

"Who did you think it was?" I asked promptly.

"Never mind. I am no longer cold. The fire is now burning well, no thanks to the green wood you bought. But I am still very, very bored. Suppose you come home instead of wasting time in ringing—"

"Never a waste of time," I assured him. "Tell me, is there a great deal of difference between the sounds of a gunshot and a car backfiring?"

John's answer came slowly after a slight pause. "Not much, I should say. What are you after?"

I told him about the sudden flash of insight I had coming through the woods. "Maybe it was a backfire I heard. James Holland was due home at five, not seven. I saw the original telegram at the Post Office yesterday. Nothing like a visit to the scene of the crime to jog the memory."

John sounded a bit shaken by my nervelessness, and commanded me to return home by the road.

"What do you think might happen to me?" I asked.

"I don't know. But do as you are told like a good girl. If you don't, I'll consider it a form of treading on my corns. And you know the hold I have over you there."

I said plaintively: "I only wanted to be quicker for your sake. What do you think of the time business?"

"It sounds promising. I'll look into it."

I gave him my word to go back by the road and rang off.

Crossing the landing which separated Yvonne's room from the nursery, something compelled me to glance down into the darkness of the hall below. I no longer felt nervy and on edge from my trip through the wood. Contact with John had a sobering up effect. So it could not have been a result of an overheated imagination which made me see a shadowy figure glide along the wall. I leaned over the railing, straining my eyes.

"Mrs Mulqueen?" I called on impulse. The sound of my voice echoed along the passage. No one came forward to be illuminated in the faint glow of light immediately below. There was no reply to my inquiring tone.

There was a pedestal light on the bottom newel. I went down the stairs and tilted the shade so that half the length of the passage was illuminated. There was no one there. No door was moving along the passage. There was no sound: I tilted the shade in the opposite direction but with the same result. Then my eyes fell on the switchboard full in the glare of the unshaded light. I moved along to look at it more closely. There must have been someone in the hall.

The two pegs Yvonne had arranged had been placed back in their original positions.

I crept along the passage to the Mulqueen apartments. The door to the sitting room was slightly open, but the room was in complete darkness.

"Mrs Mulqueen?" I said again, this time almost in a whisper. There was no sound, but I still had a sense of being watched. I put my hand around the door feeling for the light. The room was quiet and empty like the passage behind. I shrugged and prepared to go back to Yvonne. I had neglected my original purpose badly. Any more delay and Yvonne would probably start looking for me.

I put my head in Mrs Mulqueen's door once again in order to switch out the light. My eyes fell on the frame which held the photograph of James Holland's erring wife. It was like a blank enigmatic face. It neither beckoned nor repulsed my sudden overwhelming curiosity as I moved across the room.

I had learned something of the character of Olivia Holland from three different sources: sister-in-law Elizabeth, her own farewell letter to the Squire, and lastly from Mrs Potts-Power.

They all pointed to a direct similarity to Yvonne. I turned the frame around gently, holding it in both hands. The face I looked into was totally different from the confused mental picture I had composed. Yvonne could be considered pretty. This face was startlingly beautiful. But I felt a sort of anticlimax because it did not coincide with my own conception. I put my head on one side and regarded it in a puzzled way.

Somehow it was familiar to me. I studied it bit by bit. Usually I can recall people by the shape of their legs and their walks; similarly others can place a person by the hands. Unfortunately the only part of Olivia's limbs open to the beholder was the tip of one foot, and that was clad in a dainty shoe. My eyes went over the portrait again. Unconsciously I memorized it, noting the shape of the ears revealed by the upswept hairstyle. Ears were my first emergency. I do not know why, but I was glad later when Olivia's only picture was stolen from Mrs Mulqueen's sitting-room. Still perplexed about the sense of familiarity Olivia's face gave me, I turned the picture back to the wall.

Before I had time to turn around the door behind closed sharply. It may have swung to in a sudden draught from the outside passage. I was inclined to imagine a human hand had closed it. No matter under what influence the door closed, it gave me a nasty fright. I was becoming very tired of chasing people through dark houses.

I opened the door, somewhat relieved to find it unlocked. It would never have done for Elizabeth Mulqueen to return and find me in her sitting-room. With firm purposeful footsteps I retraced the way to the foot of the stairs. The pedestal light was still on. I cast one glance up and down the hall and mounted the stairs.

"Is that Mrs Matheson?" asked an uncertain voice from above. It was Yvonne.

"Yes. I'm just coming. Sorry to be so long. I thought I heard Mrs Mulqueen and came down to see her."

Yvonne took me straight to the nursery, keeping one hand on my arm. After all, the invitation had been extended merely to see Jimmy. So far I had done nothing but wander around the Hall in the dark, looking for shadowy forms and listening for strange noises.

The child did not seem very bad to me. Like Tony, Jimmy looked heavy and pale. I asked Yvonne a few intimate questions which were answered satisfactorily.

"Let him sleep," I advised. "If he is not better in the morning, ring Sister Heather at the Health Centre. It may be some new bug that's around. Tony was a bit off-colour too."

Yvonne said, knitting her brows in anxiety: "I don't think it can be anything new. He's been like this before."

I looked at her quickly, frowning at this information. She did not observe my glance, as she was bending low over the child. I made certain Jimmy was getting plenty of fresh air and drew her outside. She lost the air of assurance she had adopted as she gave me the details of Jimmy's sudden relapse.

I made no comment to her wail: "And he had started to do so well. I can't think what could have happened. Do you think it is some sort of chill in the stomach?"

I soothed Yvonne's worries as quickly as she would allow. They were mainly reiteration and I was anxious to be gone. As we passed Nurse Stone's room, the unmistakable sound of alcoholic snoring issued forth.

The journey down the drive to the gates was as shadowy and fraught with horrid imaginings as the one through the wood. I kept my mind firmly fixed on John and the fire and the waiting game of solo. Despite these prosaic thoughts, I was glad to see a light from the Lodge shining through the trees. Only the road beyond spelled real security from Holland Hall and its evil influence. Outside the gates I could deal with matters in a practical manner freed from imagination.

Once I looked back towards the house, and regretted it as much as Lot's wife must have done. The light in the tower was on. It flickered once or twice before it became dark. With my head turned slightly towards the Hall, I foolishly kept on walking. That was how I did not observe the piece of thin cord that was stretched across the drive.

My fall was heavy because it was unexpected. The torch was jerked from my hand and rolled several feet along the gravel driveway. I did not know the obstacle was intentional until I crawled after the torch and became entangled in the string. When I did realize the significance, I became paralysed with fright.

The thought came clearly to me: "What do I know? What clue do I hold?"

I considered it was important to work this out before my assassin struck. But no one moved out of the shadows to advance relentlessly on my prostrate figure. Presently I struggled to my feet and, daring myself out of my terror, shone the torch in a circle about me. It lighted up nothing but the poplar trees of the drive.

My hour was not then. I was being warned, that was all. That cord stretched across my path was like an unsigned letter ordering me to stop prying or it would be the worse for me.

I limped down the drive, mindful of my promise to John. As far as I could see, a trip through the wood would have been less fraught with danger than this one down the drive. I skulked close to the poplars, playing the light every inch of the way.

As I neared the Lodge, my heart thumped hard again. A man's figure had slipped from the shadow of the tiny porch. I smothered the torch at once and pressed back against the poplars. The figure moved stealthily towards the gates. There the man paused and turned around.

I waited, shaken from the fall and sick with fear. He seemed to be facing the place where I stood.

A sudden light shone from an unshaded window of the Lodge. The man moved at once. But he was not quick enough. I had time in which to recognize him.

It was Cruikshank, the estate agent, who behaved so furtively. He turned down the road towards the village.

I waited for a few moments before I crept from my hiding place. I had no desire to draw Cruikshank's attention. But like him I glanced back up the drive. The light in the tower had started to flicker again.

CHAPTER TEN

I

I deemed it politic to withhold from John the full facts concerning my fall in the Holland drive. If he should read the same significance into the string across my path as I did, our departure from Middleburn would be imminent. Apart from possession of the Dower House, there were too many interesting matters that I wanted to pursue. An evacuation was out of the question.

I passed off the incident as lightly as a shaken appearance could allow. The brandy bottle, hitherto hardly touched from one Christmas to another, came into play again. It was badly punished those days. I doubt if there will be enough left to make the sauce this year. I went to bed as carefully as the rollicking floor would permit.

After that first warning nothing happened for a day or two. I avoided the Hall and its household out of sheer necessity. Tony's health had me more concerned than crime. He was not actually ill, but he wandered listlessly about the house, ignoring any persuasion on my part to play outside in his sandpit. I knew he was off-colour by the way he dogged my footsteps, and meals were periods of trial. He kept me busy concocting dishes to attract his wayward appetite.

John was occupied in town. Headquarters had released Ernest Mulqueen, and he was working on other aspects of the case. Beyond recalling to ring Yvonne to inquire after her son, I gave very little time to thinking of anyone else but Tony.

I came into contact with one of the members of the Holland household in the most unexpected place. It seemed to set the ball rolling again, and I became as thickly immersed in affairs as before. As a matter of fact, it nearly meant my undoing. I doubt even now if that second affair was more of a warning than an actual attempt to end my interference.

After an excursion into gardening one weekend, John discovered that he was minus a certain pair of clippers which meant success or failure to the pruning. Hitherto I had congratulated myself on not mislaying anything during our move from the flat to the Dower House. But now it seemed I was wrong. Later that day John also discovered the shoe last was missing. I suddenly recalled an unobtrusive cupboard at the flat which I may have overlooked. There was a chance that both articles, along with others not yet missed, might still be there.

The idea of a return visit to the flat intrigued me. It would be interesting to compare the two dwellings, and to slap myself on the back yet again at having found the Dower. I would find it in me to pity and even to patronize, in a perfectly nice way, our old neighbours and the new occupants of the flat. There might be a shortage of houses, but it just showed what could be accomplished if one really tried.

I never dreamed that our successor would be Ursula Mulqueen. It didn't occur to me even when she opened the front door to my ring. I thought that by some extraordinary coincidence she was visiting a friend there.

I said "Good Heavens!" in a faint voice when I saw her. It was Ursula all right. Even though she was barely recognizable. Apart from her clothes—she was wearing slacks and a battle jacket of chalk-striped grey flannel—her very expression had altered. Her face was made up in a tan shade and was offset by a high-piled coiffure. The habitual sweet smile had given place to a firm full mouth that tilted only at the corners when she wished to manifest amusement or pleasure as she did then.

I stared at Ursula with unconscious rudeness. She did not seem at all embarrassed at being discovered in her second personality. I had heard the rumour, of course. She probably considered it a matter of time before the whole of Middleburn verified that rumour. Perhaps she no longer cared now that James Holland was out of the way.

I followed up my first inadequate exclamation with a feeble: "Fancy meeting you here!" My astonishment sent a guarded look into her eyes, now deeply blue because of her mascaraed lashes. She imagined my remarkable deductive powers had led me to her lair.

"Why not?" she asked coolly. "The only way to get a place nowadays is to follow up other people's movements."

"You mean," I said, unable to believe my own ears, "that this is your flat? You took it over when we left?"

"Why not?" she repeated.

I wanted to ask: "Where on earth do you get the money to run this double life? How do you fit it in with the Hall?"

Instead I bottled my curiosity temporarily and stated the object of my visit.

"Certainly," Ursula said in her new clipped voice. "Is it that cupboard in the laundry? I found some odds and ends there. Come through."

I followed her. Really, the slacks outfit made her figure appear very trim. One would never have guessed it under her shapeless Middleburn clothes.

Quite brazenly she mentioned the village. "Won't those things be too heavy for you to carry? I'll bring them out to the Hall with me."

"What about you?"

"Oh, I'll find a car from someone."

I gaped at her. The whole layout had a nasty look about it. She dropped her eyes. "Would you care for some tea? I was just going to make it."

"Thank you, I would," I said promptly. Ursula wanted to talk. There was no mistaking the purpose of her invitation.

"What about your little boy? Orange juice? Milk?"

"A biscuit will do, thanks. It will keep him out of mischief. Please don't go to any trouble." She busied herself with a kettle and found cups and saucers. Presently she said casually: "I suppose you've realized by now where the money comes from."

"I think I have an idea," I replied.

She said fiercely: "You can't blame me for what I have done. Who wouldn't have taken the opportunity? You've seen what it is like at home!"

"Pretty grim," I agreed. I made a sketchy wave with my teaspoon. "But did you have to be quite so drastic? This sort of life will lead you into a packet of trouble."

Ursula gave me a slightly puzzled look before continuing a tirade at her upbringing and the life she was expected to lead. She broke off suddenly.

"Well! What's going to happen now?" she demanded.

"I'm sure I don't know,'" I replied, taken aback. "It is a trite phrase, but your life is your own to make."

"You don't know!" she repeated. "Hasn't Inspector Matheson given you an idea what he will do?"

I opened my mouth to speak and then shut it like a trap. My eyes narrowed. The notion that Ursula and I had been at cross-purposes occurred to me. I was only just in time. Another wrong word from me and Ursula would have realized I did not know what she was talking about. I continued to survey her silently.

She set her cup down sharply in her saucer. "Well?" she said. "Speak up. Is he going to send me to prison?"

I sought vainly for a noncommittal answer. One that would lead Ursula on until I had unravelled this confusing conversation.

"Not yet," I said, in a grave voice.

She gave a short laugh and got down from her perch on the kitchen table. The drawn-up trouser of her crooked leg fell back into its perfect crease.

"Why is he holding fire?" she asked over one shoulder. She took cigarettes from a drawer and lit one expertly. "Now that he knows about the money, why doesn't he go ahead and arrest me?"

"Oh, yes!" I said, with care. "The money. Perhaps he does not consider it as important as you might think. After all, it is essentially your uncle's death that he is investigating."

Ursula turned round and tried to speak lightly. "You mean he'll leave my embezzling games for that awful oaf Billings to deal with? I'm not sure I don't feel insulted."

"Why do you call it embezzling?" I asked brightly. "Isn't there a softer term you can use?"

Her mouth drew down at the corners. "I suppose I could say I was claiming my just rights. After all, the allowance Uncle made was quite inadequate. What I got out of cooking his books was never missed. At least," she added bitterly, "until your husband came snooping around."

I passed over the rudeness to John. I was getting a grip on the situation at last and did not wish to become sidetracked. So it had been Ursula who had been juggling the household accounts. In order to lead this double life, to have an escape from the life of pretence in Middleburn, she had helped herself to the petty cash.

I felt I owed her an apology. "You are too ready to believe the worst of people," I told myself severely. Embezzler was a sweeter name than the one I had been calling her for the past ten minutes.

If it was Ursula who had been stealing the money, it must have been Ursula who had crept into our house that night. I attacked from a tactical position.

"You know," I remarked, helping myself to one of her cigarettes, "you gave me a hell of a fright that night."

"Did I? I can't say I'm sorry. You shouldn't have been about at that hour. I thought I was safe until I broke that glass. After the row it made, I gave up my search for the ledger."

It was my turn to be puzzled. "Why did you want the ledger?" I asked her. "You had already removed the evidence."

A sudden change passed over Ursula's face. I had made a wrong move. We stared at one another in silence, each trying to outwit the other.

Ursula did not know about the pages torn from the ledger until I had foolishly let it fall. Someone else must have done it.

Ursula's eyes had dropped away from mine. She was planning a way out of the situation she had precipitated. I do not think she was interested in who was responsible for her protection. It was enough that John had no evidence against her.

I got up to go. I had done enough damage. It was too late to change the state of affairs. Retreat was the only move left. Ursula was running the water over the tea things, her back towards me.

"I'd better get home," I said awkwardly. "Will you still bring those tools out for me?"

A sniff and a nod answered me. I frowned. I remembered someone at the Middleburn Community Centre saying what a splendid actress Ursula was.

"Here!" I said feebly. "Don't do that. Everything will be all right."

She swung round, a handkerchief to her eyes. "Oh, Mrs Matheson," she burst out. "Do you really think so? I can't tell you what that means to me to hear you say so."

This sounded like the Ursula I knew. I frowned all the deeper.

"Please don't tell your husband," she begged. "I was just being silly today. Forget all about the affair, won't you? Promise me you will. I can't bear to bring disgrace on my parents."

"Well, he doesn't know anyone broke in the other night," I admitted unwisely. The scene was assuming such proportions that Tony became affected. His lip fell.

Ursula grabbed my hand. "You didn't tell him? Just to protect me? Oh! How can I ever thank you."

"I didn't tell him for my own reasons," I said. "To be quite frank I wasn't sure whether it was you or not. As for telling my husband that you are to blame for the unusual mistakes in the Hall account book, he'll probably find out for himself sooner or later. He has a nasty habit of getting to the bottom of things, big or little. And that I want you to interpret as a warning. The best bet is to be quite candid with the police."

II

I left her, wondering why I was good at giving such advice when I did not use it myself. Had I known then that my presence was no longer a safety to the murderer but a menace, it might have been different.

Unfortunately I did not take the killer's first warning to heart. I should have retired from the lists then. After the second warning something happened which involved Tony, and naturally I was in the game until the bitter end.

I worked without John's knowledge because I considered that my unconventional approach to the case might help bring things to a head more quickly, which indeed it did. Even the abortive attempt to remove me from this earthly sphere helped.

I owe to Connie Bellamy the privilege of being able to explain to those who are interested my particular part and reactions to the crime and other mysteries which took place in Middleburn. But I am afraid Connie is unconscious of her great deed even to this day.

On the evening of the day I went to the flat, Connie and I arranged to see a show together. Middleburn does not boast a theatre, but several are accessible by bus routes. One of these theatres is very popular with Middleburn inhabitants. So much so that the bus is always very crowded, carrying about five times the number its licence allows.

There were many familiar faces amongst our fellow picturegoers. I must have seen them in the village at some time. One or two I recognized and we exchanged nods. Ames and his wife were having a night out together. Also another member of the Hall household, Nurse Stone. Maud Cruikshank stepped on at the bus stop just outside the shop. She stared through me after favouring Connie with a wide ingratiating smile.

As the bus started off again a man came running towards it and made a flying leap for the step. It was Nugent Parsons. He chatted to the driver all the way over to Ashton. He glanced at me several times when he thought I was not looking. Once our eyes met and we both glanced away.

"Do you know that fellow?" Connie whispered.

"Only slightly. Do you?"

"Not to speak to. He is considered the village Lothario. I have heard a few stories about him. Nice looking, don't you think?"

It was quite a good show. I enjoyed what John scornfully terms "ersatz emotion" because it freed my mind from real and less pleasant matters. The only flaw in the evening's enjoyment was the fact that a corner of the screen was obscured by the head of the person in front. Not much, but just enough to keep me conscious that I was not deep in the heart of Texas, as the title insinuated. It was also enough to puzzle me why the head looked familiar.

At interval time the head turned around and the mild eyes of Doctor Trefont surveyed us.

"Why! Good evening, doctor," Connie said. "Are you enjoying the programme? I didn't know it was you in front there."

"Had I known it was you, Mrs Bellamy, I would have requested before that you refrain from tapping your foot out of time to the music. I am reserving the sharper rebuke planned."

"She will under one condition," I retorted, "and that is you will move your head about three inches to the left. You are spoiling my vision."

"After that exchange of fault-finding, and with the promise that we will do as we would be done by, permit me to buy you both some refreshment." Dr Trefont called to a boy with a tray.

Connie said: "I think ice-cream will be best for me, don't you, doctor?"

I wriggled, but the doctor answered her gravely. His gentle gaze met mine for a minute as the lights faded.

"This way," Connie urged, when we emerged from the theatre. "The bus won't be there yet, but we'll get a good position before the rest of the crowd."

The Middleburn bus stand was obscurely placed amongst the many others that circulated from Ashton. To make matters more difficult a misty drizzle had commenced.

We placed ourselves on the edge of the pavement. Very soon a large crowd was banked up behind us and we were forced almost to the gutter. With the press of humanity and the seeping rain, I found it an uncomfortable end to a night's enjoyment. I longed for bed.

Two women arrived and forced themselves into a position beside us. I threw them a hostile look, which did not have any effect as it was very dark. One started complaining in an endless whining tone about the lateness of the bus. I felt like screaming with exasperation. I turned to her and pointed out the illuminated clock on a nearby shop.

"Look!" I said acidly. "It is only five minutes past the hour. The bus is not due until eleven-ten."

Whereat she said "Oh!" in a disbelieving voice and turned her whining remarks to the weather. It certainly seemed more than five minutes before a pair of yellow eyes came through the gently falling rain. I had changed weight from one foot to the other and was yawning in boredom and weariness.

I was so tired and relieved to see the bus that even now I cannot quite work out how it happened. At the sight of the oncoming bus the enormous crowd, which seemed quite out of proportion to the size of the conveyance, surged forward like cattle. Chivalry and lady-like behaviour gave place to animal instincts. In that restless moment as the bus drew near, Connie was flung forward violently from her perch on the extreme edge of the pavement. I made a grab for her coat, but she slipped heavily onto the road.

It was a mad, horrible moment. I felt paralysed both bodily and mentally. I heard a short sharp scream from behind me in the crowd. The twin yellow eyes swerved quickly. The bus ran up on the opposite pavement and stopped with a jolt. There was a moment of complete immobility and quietness. Then the crowd pressed forward towards Connie, who was lying on the road.

I pushed my way towards her and said in a clear voice: "I was with that woman. Let me nearer, please."

They fell aside at once. I knelt down on the wet road. Connie's eyes were wide open but she did not move. When she saw me she began to weep with hysterical abandon. There was no blood anywhere, although a large bruise was spreading on one cheekbone. I ran my hands along her arms and was about to do the same to her legs when a familiar voice spoke through the crowd.

"Can I be of assistance? I am a doctor."

I jumped up at once. "It is Mrs Bellamy, Doctor Trefont. I think she is all right, but she has had a bad shaking."

"How did this happen?" he asked, on the road beside me.

I shook my head. "She must have slipped. The crowd was pressing forward just as the bus came. It was a wonder it didn't run her down."

Connie heard me through her hysterical sobbing. She said in a high-pitched voice: "Someone pushed me. I felt someone's hands on my back. I was pushed."

Doctor Trefont got up. "A case of shock, that's all," he said in an expressionless tone. "No bones broken. I'll take you both home, Mrs Matheson. Wait here until I bring my car round."

Two or three men struggled to bring Connie to her feet. They half led, half carried her to the corner where the local council had placed a seat uncomfortably open to the weather.

"OK," I said, dismissing them. "I'll be right now. Your bus is about to leave."

The crowd was piling onto the bus. There were many loud-voiced comments and much peering back at us. I supported Connie as best I could. Her apparently inexhaustible supply of tears flowed over me in competition with the rain. I was thankful when Doctor Trefont parked alongside and we pushed Connie onto the back seat. I was becoming tired of so much moisture.

Doctor Trefont said: "I'll take you along to my surgery and fix something up for Mrs Bellamy. It will ease the shock and make her sleep."

Connie's crying had eased. She spoke in a trembling voice.

"I was pushed," she repeated. "I was deliberately pushed."

Doctor Trefont gave me a swift frowning glance, which I returned. A cold hand seemed to close down all over me. Quite suddenly I was frightened.

Connie spoke again. "I might have been killed. Why should anyone want to push me under the bus?"

"Shut up," I said, in a crisp voice. She had been speaking in a calm wondering tone that I disliked even more than the hysteria. "Pull yourself together, Connie."

Connie fell silent, while I tried to shake off the feeling of that heavy cold hand. I had one horrible suspicion that was gradually forming into a reality. Two words in the form of a question burned in my brain. "Why Connie?"

Doctor Trefont drove on at a steady pace through the wet darkness, his eyes on the road. Why had Connie been pushed deliberately in the way of the oncoming bus? Had she imagined it? Was it just an accident brought on by the carelessness of the surging mob?

I shut my eyes tight in order to gain a mental recollection of the crowd at the bus stand. I had felt bodies but not hands. Certainly not two hands as Connie firmly avowed she had. Why had it been Connie? Why was it not I? A tremor was set in motion through my body.

Doctor Trefont said without turning his eyes from the road: "A sedative won't do you any harm either, Mrs Matheson."

I clenched my teeth. "I daresay it won't," I struggled to reply.

Across my mental vision streamed faces—familiar faces and ones I recognized. People who had travelled across to Ashton with us in the bus. They must all have been standing in the crowd behind us. Waiting, while Connie and I stood on the very edge of the wet pavement. As a shape in the dark and drizzle Connie might easily have been mistaken for me. It was all so horribly simple.

Connie spoke again. "It will be marked," she said in a hopeless voice. "My baby will be marked. And I have been so careful. Whatever will Harold say?"

Doctor Trefont laughed gently beside me.

"Don't be idiotic!" I said crossly.

Connie was offended, which was about the best thing that could have happened. Her unnatural silence broke up and she began to give cases where prenatal shocks had definitely left some weird mark on the child. I let her ramble on unchecked. By the time we arrived at the surgery she was barely in need of "a shot of something in case of trouble." Doctor Trefont swabbed her arm with cotton wool and turned to me, needle in hand. His brows were raised inquiringly.

"I don't think so," I said in a would-be light tone. "After all, I wasn't pushed under a bus."

He gave me a hard look as though he read a double entendre. It was not until he had dropped Connie at her gate that he made any direct remark concerning the accident. He spoke to me over his shoulder.

"I should hate Mrs Bellamy to lose her child. Do you think you can help by making her forget the affair? There may be serious repercussions. The next week or so will show."

I could not resist the opening Doctor Trefont had given me. I answered him deliberately. "I will do what I can. It is an odd role for you, is it not? This sudden concern for the unborn?"

The car was passing his home in the High Street as I spoke. He pulled it up with a jerk. In a moment's panic I thought he was going to throw me out and make me walk home alone for my impertinent remark. While not prepared to eat humble pie, I did not relish a solitary hike at that hour.

He sat very still in the driver's seat, the engine still running and with undecided hands on the wheel. Suddenly he threw his arm over the back of the seat and opened the door of the car.

"Come in to the surgery again," he ordered abruptly. I got out and followed him in with a hard-beating heart. I had a notion that the cards were about to be placed face up on the table.

III

In the clear white light of his office I expected to see his face angry, and was braced to meet it. I clutched my handbag tightly, mindful of the evidence it held which would substantiate my first clumsy remark.

Oddly enough, Doctor Trefont did not seem at all annoyed. His mild eyes were thoughtful, almost considering. He turned away and lit a small spirit stove which stood on a bracket in a corner of the room.

"Will you have some coffee?" he asked politely. "My housekeeper usually has it ready here in case I am called out at night."

I hesitated for a short moment. He noticed the pause, even though his back was turned.

"I am not that sort of killer, Mrs Matheson," he said.

I accepted his offer and sat down in the patient's chair opposite his desk.

"Morally," I spoke deliberately again, "there is no difference be-tween the extinction of life whether it be in embryo, or embodied in a seventy-year-old man."

Doctor Trefont nodded slowly. "Morally, you are quite correct. So you did follow me up. What did you discover?"

I drew the copy of the receipt out of my bag and passed it across the desk in silence. The doctor changed his spectacles and perused it carefully.

"Very damning," he said, raising his head at last and changing back his glasses. "For two reasons. You have caught me out in a lie—or shall we say an omission? You must recall Mrs Yvonne Holland's name never came into the conversation I had with your husband. I flatter myself I evaded the issue rather well. Secondly, my professional attendance in connection with Barry Clowes is likely to be looked upon with suspicion. Even so, I doubt if the Medical Association would dare question his part in any activity. You may be certain he has himself well covered. Who showed you the original of this receipt? Mrs Holland?"

"The police have it," I told him. "I warn you my husband is not too pleased with the way you, in your capacity as police doctor, deceived him. So far he does not place on it the same significance I have."

Doctor Trefont turned off the spirit stove and poured the steam-ing coffee into two large cups. "And what significance do you place on this innocent-looking piece of paper?"

I sipped the coffee and found it good.

"I have seen quite a deal of Yvonne Holland during the past few weeks. From my observation of her mental and physical condition and along with other circumstances, I have formed my own con-clusion. I believe that after her baby was born steps were taken by means of an operation whereby she would never have another child."

There was a long pause. I felt that my words were hanging in the room and repeating themselves like an echo.

Presently Doctor Trefont gave forth a heavy sigh.

"A hell of a business." His voice was sad and slow. "I wonder if you would believe me, Mrs Matheson, if I said that although I was the anaesthetist I knew nothing whatsoever about the operation?"

"I would find it hard," I replied.

"True, nevertheless. I was called in at the last minute to administer the anaesthetic. Once Barry Clowes started I guessed what he was about. But what could I do? Jump up and leave the patient half-doped and stalk out of the theatre in professional dudgeon? What would you have done?"

"I am not a doctor," I said. "Who authorized such an operation? Was it with Yvonne's consent? Was the operation her idea?"

"I am not sure," Doctor Trefont answered. "After the distressing business was over my first move was to call at the Hall and seek an interview with Mr Holland. I was not received over-courteously. There had already been a brush between us over a minor matter. When I accused him of tricking me into unethical behaviour I was ordered out of the house. I endeavoured to contact Mrs Holland, but I was met by a blank refusal to see me."

"And yet," I said, watching him closely—I had no desire to be a victim of a plausible explanation: "You went back to the Hall. You were there that day I went to see Mr Holland about the Dower House."

He chuckled into his cup. "Not a very welcome guest, was I? I was hoping to come and go unobserved. I have to admit that the sight of you peering around the side of the terrace rather unnerved me."

"You need not have worried. I thought you were some relative caught baby-talking. Why did you want to see the child and yet avoid Yvonne and the Squire?"

There was another long pause. Doctor Trefont eyed me again with that long considering look.

"Mrs Matheson,'" he began abruptly. "The game has not yet been played out. So far a murder has taken place at the Hall, but that, I am convinced, is only part of the game. That part is your husband's responsibility. Mine is in preserving life while I can."

"Was someone trying to do the Holland baby an injury?" I persisted.

Doctor Trefont was silent. I lifted the receipt in a significant manner. The doctor shrugged helplessly.

"When a patient talks to a doctor," he said, "it is an understood thing that the conversation will go no further. Now it is the other way round. I am asking you to treat what I am going to tell you as confidential."

I thought this over for a moment. "Surely the police are entitled to know."

"Not until I have proof. The game is too dangerous to go to the police without definite evidence. I am only telling you now because I consider that you are, somewhat unlawfully, entitled to an explanation. You have seen and overheard too much."

I took the rebuke meekly.

He continued: "When you saw me on the Hall terrace that day I was bending over the Holland child. Has it ever occurred to you what I was doing?"

"You straightened up and put something into your pocket. I did not see what it was."

He smiled faintly. "Since you did not see, I am almost inclined not to tell you. I was so sure you did. It was a small instrument used for taking a blood test. I wanted a sample of Baby Holland's blood."

"Why?" I asked, before I could stop myself.

"Mrs Matheson, your curiosity is insatiable. When it came to my ears that the Holland child's health was deteriorating rapidly I began to entertain certain suspicions. By diverse means, with which I will not detain you, I discovered that the child's diet was satisfactory, well-balanced and nutritive. There could be only one way in which the state of health became as it did. That was by the introduction into the system of some irritant. The smear test showed the red cells to be slightly stippled in appearance."

"What does that mean?"

"The child was showing signs of lead poisoning. But for your inopportune appearance that day I might have had time to make an examination to further my diagnosis. As it is I can do nothing. Mrs Holland refuses to see me."

The whole foul business laid bare in this detached manner made me say sharply, "You have a good idea who is responsible for Baby Holland's health, Doctor. Tell me and I'll get my husband onto it right away."

He shook his head in a kind of mild obstinacy. "Not yet. I must wait for proof. The child may have been sucking some lead toy. It has happened before."

I snorted in exasperation. He smiled at me deprecatingly.

"You don't understand, Mrs Matheson. If I go to the police or let you use your influence as you suggested, my position will be made more difficult. My present status is not too secure. I have no desire to be suspected of murder."

"Who would do that?" I demanded.

He gestured towards the receipt I still held in my hand.

"Your husband or Sergeant Billings certainly will follow that up sooner or later. My difference of opinion and ultimate quarrel with Mr Holland will then come to light. The motive put forward will be that I silenced him to save my professional reputation. I was actually in the vicinity of the Hall at the time of the murder."

"Oh!" I said slowly. The thought flashed through my head that Doctor Trefont might have been playing ball with me up to a certain point in the hope of bluffing his way out. An ingenious trick to place all the cards on the table and retain the one that would prove him a murderer.

"I was on my way back from the hospital when my car broke down outside the grounds. I had considerable difficulty in starting it. It backfired once or twice."

Immediately his words clicked with something I had been retaining at the back of my mind.

I asked quickly: "Your car backfired? Are you sure it was twice?"

He looked surprised.

"It might be important," I said. "Please try to remember."

"It may have been only once. It was a still, heavy night. The sound seemed to reverberate."

"Only once," I repeated thoughtfully, half to myself. I had heard two noises. If what Doctor Trefont said was correct, the other sound must have been the gunshot. And I was all for changing the time of the murder to an earlier hour. I gave a small sigh.

I felt very tired again. Interest in the doctor's story had superseded nervous exhaustion for a while. But the disappointment regarding the time of the murder caused me to slump once again. I did not care if Doctor Trefont was the killer himself, as long as he drove me home.

However, in the car my thoughts were aroused once again. This was accomplished by a reference to Connie Bellamy. Doctor Trefont repeated his request that I should go to see her.

"Try and rid her mind of the obsession that she was deliberately pushed," he urged.

"You don't believe her, Doctor?"

"It is not good for her to have the idea," he parried.

We were passing the Hall gates. There was no light showing, neither in the Lodge nor through the poplar trees from the house.

I said: "You are quite right. The shock of the fall is bad enough. I had a nasty spill myself, coming down the drive there."

There was a small glow from the dashboard, just enough for me to watch the doctor's face for a change of expression. He felt the sidelong glance and turned his eyes from the road for a minute.

"You must be very careful," he said gently.

The remainder of the journey passed in silence. I was thinking hard. I had found a common denominator in this stumbling business. The Cruikshanks. In fall one, in the Hall drive, the estate agent had been near at hand. In the crowd waiting for the bus after the pictures that night was his sister, Maud. It was not pleasant to remember the expression on their faces that day at the shop, when I first knew that Cruikshank had come back to Middleburn.

IV

John gave one or two ostentatious sighs. Finally he asked, in the grudging tone of one who has been awakened and wants only to go back to sleep, if I had enjoyed the show. I almost said: "What show?"

"Yes, thanks, quite good," I told him.

It was fortunate that his interest in films was negligible. I would have found it difficult to recall any particular part of the programme. My mind was full of the subsequent events of the evening.

Thoroughly wearied both mentally and physically, I tried to put them out of my head to be dealt with in the calmer light of day. The memory of Connie Bellamy's trembling voice asserting that she had been pushed was very strong. I tried to forget it.

All right, she was pushed. Leave it at that until morning. Wait until you have had some sleep. Think of something else not quite so grim.

I thought of Doctor Trefont and his revelations concerning the Holland baby. An extraordinary story. So strange that in my exhausted condition the knowledge he had imparted seemed almost fantastic. A feeling of vacillation took hold of me. I was unable to reach any decision regarding Doctor Trefont. Did I trust him or not? Was he playing a quixotic game or one entirely for his own benefit?

I turned to Connie again and a more personal disturbance shook me. That fall of hers was closely allied by its continuity to my own in the Hall drive. The underlying suspicion that she had been mistaken for me gave rise to horrid meditations.

In spite of my endeavours to banish these thoughts and to concentrate on more mundane matters, they kept rolling around in my head. I dropped off into an uneasy sleep. There seemed to be no dividing line between wakefulness, sleep and the suddenness with which I became fully conscious again. An indefinable apprehension increased with each stage. A fear, which developed to a superlative degree when I realized what had awakened me.

It was Tony's voice. A pitiful sobbing of terror such as adults rarely experience in the same way as children. I sat up at once groping for the bedside light. Tony may have had a nightmare and was calling out in his sleep. But my own state of mind was still so overwrought that I could not go back to sleep without making sure.

John raised himself on one elbow, blinking into the light.

"Tony!" I said, "something is wrong."

John muttered something but I did not catch what he said.

I ran down the passage switching on the lights. "Coming, Tony," I called loudly. "Coming." I did not feel like a sane person just then. I had had enough to bear earlier in the night. Tony's terror was communicated. When I reached the nursery door, the sight that met my eyes sent me into a frenzy.

The room was a muddle of pulled-open drawers. Little boy clothes and toys were scattered everywhere. Tony sat bolt upright in his cot, his eyes wide open with the unreasoning fright of childhood. At the foot of his cot a black-draped figure was bent almost double, rummaging amongst the bedclothes.

I went completely overboard and began screaming for John. That was my last coherent thought. The rest was just a confused jumble, in which I could not bear John or Tony out of my sight. The sense of loneliness and fear that they were coming to some harm nearly drove me mad.

Gradually I pulled myself together somehow. It was mainly owing to John, his firmness and his gentleness. He put Tony into bed with me and I clung to the child, trembling from head to foot.

Presently, when I was calmer, John left me. I think he went to make a telephone call. Needless to say, the black figure, as I thought of the person who had entered Tony's room through the low window, had got away as soon as I appeared on the scene. Later I remembered it as odd that the exit was not made when Tony began calling. I know now that the person was desperate in a search for something and risked capture until the very last moment.

Tony fell asleep, his warm, round body snug against my own. I thought how poorly I had lived up to his conception of everything that was secure. All I did was to stand in the doorway of the nursery and shriek my head off. I had not even the good sense to switch on the light and endeavour to recognize the black-cowled shape.

John came back after a while with a tray of tea. His face was set and stern. He is a man slow moved to wrath, my husband, the type all the more to be feared when in anger. Perhaps it was just as well that the intruder was not caught that night. John might have found himself in a ticklish position of investigating a murder when he himself was a killer also.

I smiled at him and held out my left hand. Tony slept with his head on my right shoulder. My hand was gripped so hard that the ring cut into my finger. He bent across me to look into Tony's face.

I murmured against his ear: "Tomorrow he will have forgotten all about it."

John turned a hard inquiring glance on me. His anxiety was too great for him to ask, "And you? What about you?"

I wriggled free of Tony and said in a would-be matter-of-fact voice, "Is that tea for me? I'd love some."

The reflection in the dressing-table mirror of the pair of us prosaically drinking tea was a crowning touch to the nightmarish incident. The snack was reminiscent of those highly uncomfortable midnight feasts of school days—which, after all I had gone through during the last few hours, was ludicrous. It had the good effect of resurrecting my sense of humour and proportion.

All the same I was glad when John said as we settled down at last, Tony still at my side: "I am not going to worry you now with questions, Maggie. Just forget everything. We'll deal with things in the morning. I promise you that there will be no repetition of tonight's performance."

CHAPTER ELEVEN

I

John's promise took a concrete form. A metaphorical description that could be almost literal. Constable Cornell, to whom he had assigned the job of watchdog, was not unlike a lean slab of putty-coloured stone. Inquisitive remarks made no impression on his smooth hard surface.

Early the next day this police constable put in an appearance at the back door.

"Hullo," I said.

"Morning. Constable Cornell," he announced, running the words together. I had difficulty in separating and defining them. "'Spector sent me."

"Did he? What for?" I thought John must have forgotten something. He ignored my question. "Mind if I sit here?" asked Constable Cornell from the back porch.

"Not at all. Like a cup of tea?" Constable Cornell's peculiarity of speech persuaded imitation.

He accepted John's large breakfast cup with a laconic word of thanks, and sat down with it on the steps.

"Er—are you staying long?" I asked this stray cat who had landed on my doorstep.

"Dunno." He took a loud sip from his cup and stared down the yard to the row of golden poplars. His taciturnity was irritating.

"I have to go out presently," I said, knowing full well that I did not.

"Oke," he replied. "Where can I change?"

I gaped at him.

He waxed a little more eloquent. "Get into civvies. People don't like being followed by a uniform."

Light broke at last. It was not a stray cat that had adopted me, but a watchdog.

"Inspector Matheson sent you," I said triumphantly.

"Th's right."

Very nice of John, I thought to myself. But I don't know how I am going to like being shadowed and watched all day and every day. It might prove a source of embarrassment. I was glad that Constable Cornell saw part of my point of view, in so much that he undertook to change out of his blue uniform. Walking through Middleburn trailing a policeman behind me would be worse than having a string of dogs at my heels.

I showed him to the small tool-room at the end of the porch. "You needn't get ready yet. I'll let you know when I am going."

"Oke." Then he spoke at the greatest length I was ever to hear from him. It was an overture he used with all his shadowees. "Shan't worry you. Won't notice me after a while. Never lost a body yet. Don't intend to start."

I caught an underlying warning. I was not to try any funny business with Constable Cornell, like attempting to give him the slip.

"You seem the pick at your kind of job," I said politely. Constable Cornell nodded, quite in earnest. He was the best. There was no need for him to proclaim it in words.

The knowledge that someone was waiting my pleasure gave me the fidgets. I dithered about the normal household tasks like a newly-wed. Now and then I went into the kitchen to glance at Constable Cornell through the window. He remained on the steps, staring vacantly at the poplars. His attitude of having nothing to do and all day in which to do it was soothing. If he was content, why should I worry?

I was glad of his company when it came to tidying the nursery. I had not fancied going into that room with the remembrance of the previous night still vivid in my mind. I noticed that Tony had been avoiding his room too, and worried a little. A child's memory might be short, but impressions often last until late in life. I knew I would have to overcome my reluctance in order to remove any subconscious fear that might lurk in his small brain.

I went to the nursery according to schedule with as much nonchalance as I could muster. Out of the corner of my eye I watched Tony hesitate in the passage. I opened the door, whistling loudly. John had made a cursory clean-up. The screen had been replaced in the window, and the drawers and cupboards closed. A few articles were still scattered on the floor, while Tony's cot was a jumble of bedclothes.

I opened the window wide as though to cleanse the room of a foul odour, and began to pick up the scattered clothes. Tony watched me from the door in silence. I continued my tuneless whistling.

By the time I came to stripping his bed he had advanced into his room and had started pulling at the drawers. I turned around and grinned at him. He relaxed still further and began to roam about the nursery. He even paused to stare out the window. I heaved a faint sigh of relief as I swung the mattress over. In so doing something fell onto the floor between the wall and the cot. Tony heard it and got down on his hands and knees to crawl under the cot.

"What is it, fellah?" I asked, remaking the bed. He came out flushed and with a piece of fluff on his hair. He held one hand behind his back, eyeing me obstinately.

"Show," I commanded, holding out my hand.

Tony gave a small sigh and brought his hand round. I opened his fist and stared down at a baby's dummy. It took me a minute to remember how he came to have such a thing. I took it from him, closing his hand over a sweet in compensation.

Holding the dummy gingerly by the yellow string attached through its handle I thought very deeply. I remembered its first appearance rather than when it turned up again. The yellow string had a familiar look. It was the same dummy I had taken from Yvonne Holland's baby and thrown away over the golf course. That was the day of my visit to the Middleburn Community Centre. The dummy had lain in the grass of the fairway unperceived.

Then Tony's sharp glance lighted on it during our walk. It took his volatile fancy. I remembered how Daisy Potts-Power, to my mortification, had laughed at him. That was the night the Bellamys came to dinner. The night Tony developed an unusual and inexplicable illness, and the Holland baby a similar complaint.

Tony had kept the dummy all that time. And I had not known about it until then. The morning after someone had entered the nursery through the long low window to make a desperate search.

I examined it closely, and then went quickly to the bathroom. In the medicine chest was a jar of malt extract, the comforter smear I had confiscated from Yvonne. Tony clamoured for a taste as I unscrewed the lid. The jar was now more than half empty. I wrapped up both articles with shaking hands. Now that I had a plan in mind I no longer dawdled. I told Constable Cornell to be ready in ten minutes and hurried Tony back to the nursery to dress for outdoors.

We strolled down to the village as casually as I could manage. I tried to resist the urge to keep glancing over my shoulder to see if my policeman was still there. Being shadowed took some getting used to. The High Street was crowded with housewives doing their shopping. It wasn't so bad when we mingled with them. My watchdog had more chance of looking unobtrusive. But each time I chatted with someone I knew, I felt that they must guess who the man staring into the window ten yards away was. I imagined their eyes going over my shoulder curiously and waited to hear it said: "My dear, don't look now, but I'm positive that man over there is following you. He has such an odd look about him."

I ran into Mrs Ames and paused to comment on the weather. As usual she kept her face averted. I followed her into the local pharmacy and pretended to glance through the trade magazine as she was being served. I wanted a completely clear coast before I stated my requests.

She spoke in her usual flat, toneless voice, but the words were unintelligible. They sounded the jargon only a physician or a chemist would understand. Like the weird hieroglyphics on a doctor's prescription. I was surprised to hear a lay person speak the language of medicinal formula.

The chemist came back from his dispensary with a sealed bottle. He handed this to Mrs Ames.

I nodded good-bye and watched her out of the shop.

"What on earth was that all about?" I asked, as the chemist bent one discreet ear towards me.

"The lady who has just gone out? She always does that. It saves such a lot of time when the patient can repeat the formula. I just whip into the dispensary, whip up the medicine and out again without any waiting. I think she must have been in the business at one time."

I saw someone outside the shop and hurried into my unorthodox request. My standing as the wife of a police officer stood me in good stead. The chemist eyed me with a curiosity which belied his discreet tones, and agreed to my proposal. I passed my little package over the counter quickly.

It was only just in time. Constable Cornell passed across the doorway throwing in a casual glance. I hurriedly snatched up a tin of patent baby food that Tony had long since outgrown. The chemist told me to come back later. He would see what he could do in the meantime.

I went to kick my heels for an hour in the village. It was not worth going home, so I betook myself to the lending library to browse amongst the books. I felt sorry trailing Constable Cornell in that selfish way, but the suspicion that he was spying on as well as guarding me salved my conscience. I was planning a few cutting remarks to be directed at John, whose idea Constable Cornell was, when I was bumped into the road. It was accidental that time, I was certain. But it came as rather a shock when I recognized Mr Cruikshank. He had catapulted out of his shop and I had not been heeding my surroundings. He muttered an apology. I said the first thing that came into my mind.

"You and your sister seem to make a habit of knocking me over, Mr Cruikshank." The agent shot me a quick terrified look. He glanced left and right and then retreated into the shop.

The library had been my objective so in I went. Constable Cornell was near at hand so I felt quite safe. I was tired of playing the game in the dark. It was time someone attacked in the open. In the broad light of day with my guardian watching every move, I was more annoyed than frightened at the remembrance of the string in the Holland drive and the affair at the bus stop. I felt an urge to be nasty.

Cruikshank put the counter between himself and the onslaught. The fact that the library was empty only deepened my desire for a fight. The stage seemed set for the purpose.

I made certain of receiving a bedspread I had left to be cleaned before I started. I watched him wrap it up and saw his fingers shake and fumble with the string.

"By the way, Mr Cruikshank," I said, putting a firm hand on the parcel. "How is the sick aunt? Any more attacks lately?"

He muttered something inaudibly.

I went on scornfully: "It was providential that she demanded your presence at her bedside at a time when the late Mr Holland was checking up on your position as his agent."

He was silent. His eyes darted now and then towards the door. I leaned over the counter.

"How quickly she recovered! You were able to return just after Mr Holland's death when Middleburn was no longer a place of embarrassment. I think you follow me, Mr Cruikshank," I added quickly as he started to make some protest. "Mr Holland had you sized up. He knew your little games, just as the police do now."

"The police!" The agent looked terrified.

"Certainly," I said, throwing discretion to the wind. "They have known all the time. They are waiting for the opportunity to tie up your disappearance with Mr Holland's murder. It is never wise to run away, Mr Cruikshank. Flight draws instant suspicion. You have a much better chance if you stay and try to bluff your innocence."

He shook all over as though with a sudden ague. "Will you leave my shop!" he whispered. "You don't know what you're saying."

"Oh, yes, I do, and I am not leaving until I have finished my piece. I don't like murder, Mr Cruikshank. I am married to a man whose job it is to solve such crimes. I wonder what he would do if he knew that his wife was nearly another victim of the Middleburn killer? I doubt whether he would stop to complete that tie-up I mentioned."

The agent's face was livid. His voice rose. "You're mad. I don't know what you are talking about."

"It is fortunate that I do. There are several things you and your sister," I added, noticing Maud peeping round a bookcase, "will have to explain to the police sooner or later. I am warning you now just in case you are both planning another string across my path or a convenient bus to push me under. I trust I make myself clear?"

Cruikshank opened his mouth again, and shut it quickly as his squeaking door was opened. I had finished what I wanted to say. I even had the satisfaction of the last word. I was about to pick up my parcel from the counter, when someone from behind tossed down a book to be exchanged. I noted the title automatically, as do all bookworms.

Then a familiar, flat voice spoke my name. "Mr Jenkins said he was ready for you, Mrs Matheson."

It was Mrs Ames again. I frowned in a sudden uneasiness. Her words had startled me. Jenkins was the chemist. He must have completed the job already. But Mrs Ames had been served in the shop before me.

My heart began to beat hard. For some reason I was nervous.

Mrs Ames still stood alongside me. She had made no move to wander around the bookshelves. Cruikshank was quiet behind the counter, but his eyes, alive with malice, were on my face. Even Maud Cruikshank had come out from her shelter to watch me. Now that I had satisfied my anger I felt lost and bewildered. I was just the right material for fear to invade.

I tried to jerk my head away from those watching faces, but could not. I could hear Tony's voice calling from the pusher outside the shop, but I felt unable to get out to him. I was frightened—frightened lest something was going to happen to me before I reached the door. I dared not move until I had broken free from the influence of those three people.

Then the door squeaked again. I could not look around, but I felt an overwhelming relief. The noise of that unoiled hinge meant safety from some intangible terror. Constable Cornell stood beside me at the counter. He gave no hint of recognition and addressed Cruikshank. He wanted some envelopes. I remember wondering why he wanted to buy them and not a writing pad. Mrs Ames moved away and Cruikshank turned his back to search the shelves behind the counter. Curiously limp and tired, I left the shop.

II

I made my way back to the pharmacy, my mind vague and far away. I did not know what it was I had experienced, but I felt very alone and lost again.

It took Mr Jenkins four explanations to succeed in bringing me down to earth. Technically, each explanation of the test he had made was well above my head. When I realized that the gist of it coincided with my own suspicions, I became more practical.

"Will you do me a favour?" I requested. "Make up what you have told me into a written report and hold it until I ask you for it. Keep the dum—"

"Brhp," said Mr Jenkins ostentatiously.

I turned round. Constable Cornell stood beside the weighing machine set near the doorway. He held his packet of envelopes in one hand, while from the other dangled the parcel I had left on Cruikshank's counter.

Cornell said in a polite stranger's voice: "Left this down the road, didn't you? They said it was yours."

I thanked him in an even politer and more distant voice. I did not care for Constable Cornell's habit of popping up at opportune and inopportune moments so readily. When he asked Mr Jenkins for a packet of envelopes my misgivings deepened.

"That will be all for me, thank you, Mr Jenkins," I said in a clear frank voice. "I'll let you know when I want those things."

The chemist nodded in a casual manner. Between us we would not have deceived Tony, let alone a member of John's squad. Cornell was weighing up the merits of different paper as I left.

I felt very satisfied with the morning's work. The emotional disturbance in the library was only a ripple on the surface compared with the evidence I now held and the pleasure I had had in haranguing Cruikshank.

I saw Daisy Potts-Power and smiled at her warmly instead of trying to avoid her eye. She kept me in conversation for some time which I made no attempt to limit, out of pure malice. Constable Cornell was obliged to stare at a window full of ladies' lingerie for ten minutes. However, he showed no sign of embarrassment or impatience.

Daisy asked me when I was going to call on "poor mother" again. I made a vague promise and then changed it to an interested: "Very soon. Tell her I am looking forward to concluding our conversation."

Daisy was puzzled by the cryptic remark.

"Mrs Matheson," called a voice from the kerb. I turned my head. The sister in charge of the Health Centre had drawn up in her car. The engine was still running.

I cut Daisy off quickly and went over to the car. Sister Heather looked disturbed.

"What is it?" I asked at once. She switched off the engine.

"I went along to your home but you were out. I was hoping I'd catch you in the village. I want to talk to you."

"Just a minute," I said, and parked Tony against a shop window which would keep him entertained for a while. Sister Heather opened the door of the car and I climbed in beside her.

"Yes, what is it, sister?"

She regarded me long and earnestly before she spoke. "Mrs Matheson, you are very friendly with Mrs Holland, are you not?"

"I don't know about the 'very.' I have seen her quite a deal since we moved to Middleburn. Let us say I am very interested in her and her baby."

My companion spoke drily. "Yes. You succeeded in bringing her down to the Centre." The remark was as cryptic as the one I had made to Daisy Potts-Power, but I was not puzzled by it. I waited for her to continue.

Sister Heather waited for Constable Cornell to pass the car before she spoke. "You have influence with her. I am asking you to use it. Persuade her to leave the Hall at once."

I gave the nurse a quick, searching glance. "That would require a great deal of influence on my part. Do you think I am qualified enough?"

She nodded.

"Why do you want her to leave?" I asked bluntly.

Sister Heather spread out her hands wearily. "Does the reason matter? I think you have guessed it, even if you do not know for certain already."

"I might," I agreed, with caution. "Supposing I do persuade Yvonne Holland to leave, where is she to go? She has no relatives."

Sister Heather was quite unembarrassed as she made her suggestion. "I want her to stay with you. You have plenty of room at your place to put her up."

"Here, I say!" I protested. "I admitted I was interested but I didn't say we were bosom friends. I can't take strange mothers and their children in just because they are being persecuted. Ten to one she wouldn't come, anyway."

"I think you could make her come, Mrs Matheson."

"Influence, sister?"

"Amongst other things. She won't see me or—or Doctor Trefont. You are the only other one who has any working knowledge of the Hall. If you were to talk to her frankly, I don't think there would be any difficulty."

"If that is the case," I replied, "I will be the first person to talk frankly. I am a great believer in the unvarnished truth. It gets you somewhere, whereas innuendos only leave you to struggle along to the same vague goal."

Sister Heather turned her ignition key. "Then I take it you'll do as I ask?"

I opened the door and slid one leg out. "I suppose so. You speak as though the responsibility was all mine."

Sister Heather gave me a troubled look. "It is, Mrs Matheson. Believe me, it is. Please do your best."

"OK," I replied negligently. "I'll let you know how I get on."

I did not go straight to the Hall after this interview. Tony wanted his dinner and Constable Cornell's lean and hungry look had become more evident. After all, one should feed the household pet as well as the son and heir. Tony had his meal first. I put him into his cot for a nap and then sat down to lunch with Constable Cornell in the kitchen.

He was as unobtrusive a guest as he was a shadower. At first I thought it might be embarrassing sharing a salad with a strange policeman without John there. Cornell's position in my household was out of the way. One could not class him as a casual labourer like a gardener and pass the luncheon through the kitchen door to be eaten on the porch. On the other hand, it would have been absurd for me to feed in lonely state in the dining-room, while he ate in the kitchen where I usually had meals in John's absence.

Constable Cornell, however, was not in the least put out. No doubt he was accustomed to adapting himself in his particular line of police work. He ate with solemn satisfaction, neatly avoiding any curious questions on my part without appearing rude. I gave up after a while and we talked on everyday topics. Cornell was chary with words, but I found myself mentally filling in the gaps, and lunch time passed quite pleasantly.

"When the boy wakes I want to go over to Holland Hall," I said, watching him closely.

He nodded into his third cup of tea.

"How will you get on?" I asked. "It was all right this morning, but you will be more noticeable in a private house."

He disdained an answer to such a foolish question. He merely asked how long before we started. I tried to match his superiority by pointing out that children must have their day sleep. Our departure depended entirely on Tony.

I took a childish pleasure in the fact that Tony again slept over his usual time. But still Cornell showed no impatience. He seemed quite happy to sit on the kitchen porch and stare at the back fence. I longed to know what went on in his mind, or whether it was as concrete in consistency as his appearance. I had offered him a magazine or two, but though he thanked me politely, they remained unread at his side.

I was curious to see how he would get over his position when I was at the Hall. Would he desert me at the gates or plod along behind the whole time I was seeking Yvonne out? But he deserted me even earlier than that.

Tony awoke, calling for me. I dressed him and led him through to the kitchen.

"I'm ready, Mr Cornell," I called. Instead of hearing his laconic "Oke," there was no reply. I opened the wire door but the porch was empty. I shrugged and turned back. The magazines I had lent him were neatly placed on the kitchen table. I called his name through a window in the front of the house thinking he might be waiting at the front gate. But there was still no reply.

"Come along, Tony. Our watchdog seems to have got off the chain. We'll go on ahead. After all it is his job to mind us, not we him. I don't anticipate needing his protection this afternoon."

I kept a look-out for Constable Cornell all the way to the Hall. His presence had worried me in the beginning. Now I noticed his absence and felt incomplete without my attendant.

Old man Ames sat smoking on the tiny porch of the Lodge. I waved to him and he answered it by taking his pipe from his mouth and describing a circle with the stem. As we passed, the door of the Lodge opened swiftly and Robin rushed out calling Tony's name. Tony pulled his hand away and darted forward. Perforce I had to follow, whereas I had no desire to stop and chat with the old man.

He asked me if I was going up to the Hall. The children could play together for a while. He would look after them. Robin and Tony were watching me with anxious eyes, so I accepted the offer.

The Hall door was wide open. Before I could ring, Mrs Mulqueen came down the passage. She did not see me waiting on the threshold until I spoke her name.

She came forward. I noticed she looked ruffled and out of temper. Her manner was rude when she asked what I wanted.

"When are we going to get rid of all these curious policemen?" she complained, following me along to the stairs. Yvonne, I had been informed, was in the nursery. She spent most of her time there nowadays.

"It is unpleasant," I agreed, wondering if I came within that category, being the wife of one.

"I thought we'd finished with them," she went on. "No one has been near us for a day or two when in came one just now. He said he was sent to look over James' rooms. As if that hasn't been done a dozen times already, I am going to make a complaint to your husband, Mrs Matheson. A picture from my sitting-room is missing. We can't have these strange men wandering around the house."

"I am afraid it is one of the evils that naturally follow on murder," I told her, backing up the stairs.

"I still won't believe my brother was murdered," she asserted with a toss of her head. "He had been worried and upset for months—"

"I know," I interrupted. "But the fact still remains it was murder, despite any wishful thinking as it is termed nowadays. It used to be called self-deception."

I made a swift ascent after this Parthian shot.

I identified the door of the nursery. I had not been on this floor by day. It seemed quite different with the sun streaming in at the window at the end of the passage. Before I had time to knock, the adjoining door opened and Nurse Stone came out. The woman's face was flushed and her breath stank.

"So," she muttered in a nasty voice. "The busybody has put in another appearance. The baby is asleep. He is not to be disturbed."

"I have no wish to disturb him," I said, trying to speak calmly. "I understand Mrs Holland is in the nursery. I came to see her."

The nurse stepped in front of the door. "No, she isn't. She has gone out. So you can just go too. I heard all about you the other night. I am in charge of the baby, and I won't have any interference from you or anyone else. So you can just go, my fine lady. And keep away or it will be the worse for you."

I caught the sound of footsteps the other side of the door. The significance of the woman's low tones had not escaped me.

"Is that you, Yvonne?" I called clearly.

"Mrs Matheson?" said an uncertain voice.

"Get out," said Nurse Stone, raising her voice and still blocking the way.

"I want to see you, Yvonne."

The nurse looked at me savagely. I moved aside in haste. Her fist was clenched and her arm half-raised when a door further along the passage opened. Out walked Constable Cornell. The woman dropped her arm as he stood still in the passage watching the scene with incurious eyes. Nurse Stone, realizing he was a representative of the law, could do nothing but retreat. I slid through the half-open door of the nursery. I had overcome one obstacle. Now Yvonne.

"What is it you want?" she asked, after I had locked the door behind me. I bent over the baby before I spoke. He looked pale and wasted.

"You," I said, turning to answer her question, "and Jimmy, of course. How would you like to come and stay with me for a while?"

She looked both surprised and startled.

I raised one hand. "Before you answer, I want to say a few things. Speak frankly, in fact. I seem to have been doing quite a bit of it today. I think it pays."

Yvonne sat down in a chair near the cot, while I perched myself on the arm of the chair and looked out the window. I wanted to marshal my forces.

"I am not sure how much you realize, Yvonne," I began, "but you do know or suspect that Jimmy is in deadly danger in this house. I have been advised by good friends of yours, although you will not for some reason recognize them as such, to persuade you to take shelter with us for a while. My husband"—and I crossed my fingers under a fold of my skirt; I did not know what John's reaction would be—"will be delighted to have you stay."

Yvonne's eyes had widened with fear. She turned to the cot. "Is he really in danger?" she whispered.

"I think so. In fact, I know it. I have evidence to prove it. I am not sure why, but I could tell you how. It would frighten you to death."

"I didn't know," she said, in a low tone.

"Didn't know!" I echoed. "But you did, only you were suspecting the wrong person."

She looked both puzzled and troubled. "I don't understand you. Really I don't."

It was my turn to frown in bewilderment. "But I heard you," I said. "You accused your father-in-law of trying to do Jimmy an injury. Don't you remember I told you? I overheard you accusing Mr Holland of child murder."

"But that hadn't anything to do with Jimmy," Yvonne replied, taking the initiative. "That was something else."

"What was it?"

She looked down at her hands as a slow colour deepened in her face. "I can't tell you. You wouldn't understand."

"You'd better tell me. We won't get anywhere if we stay at cross-purposes. I am a pretty understanding person and not easily shocked."

She bent her head even lower. "All right!" she agreed after a hesitation. "You see, I have had a certain operation. Even if Jim, my husband, had not been killed in his plane, we could never have had any more children."

"I guessed about the operation," I said gently. "Go on."

She raised her head. "It wasn't my idea," she declared with vehemence. "I didn't know about it until afterwards. Mr Holland arranged for it. When his son, my husband, died, he didn't want me to marry again. He thought that would stop anyone from wanting to marry me."

My brain seemed to tighten. For a moment I felt a surge of anger and disgust. James Holland seemed to have recognized in himself some higher authority over life and death.

"It was never spoken about," Yvonne went on, "until one day when we quarrelled. Someone had been paying me attention and Mr Holland didn't like it. He never did like having his plans upset and he had other ideas for this person."

I guessed she meant Alan Braithwaite, but held my tongue.

"He told me the matter was to stop. He said if I didn't discourage this man's attentions he would tell him I had had that operation. No one would believe that I had nothing to do with it. That was when I said what you overheard. I told Mr Holland he was a murderer.

That he had destroyed the life of children I might have had. He struck me in the face. He was like that, you know. He was used to running people's lives his own way. He could arouse such fear that no one ever questioned his authority. That was why I was glad when he died. It was the only way to stop him."

I did not like the way Yvonne spoke the last sentence. Her voice was weary and fatalistic, as though she might have been admitting to murder herself.

On impulse I asked: "Do you know who killed him?"

Her head darted up instantly. She was on the defensive again. "No!"

"But you can guess," I said shrewdly.

She clenched her hands together. "No, no," she said wildly. "It is impossible. He wouldn't have done it, even for me."

"Alan Braithwaite?" I asked at once. "Do you mean him?"

Her head fell forward after her foolish words. She really hadn't the stamina of a mouse. Any trained interrogator could have wormed her thoughts out of her after five minutes, if he had not already guessed them.

"Tell me about it," I suggested. "I may be able to help. He has no alibi for the time of the murder, but then neither have you nor anyone else. Why are you worried about him? I know you rang the other day to warn him. Tell me, Yvonne. There might be no need to worry. The police are not quite satisfied as to the time of the murder in spite of the shots that were heard."

"Shots?" Her eyes questioned me. "I only heard one. I thought it was a car backfiring until later when we were told about Mr Holland."

I wrinkled my forehead in perplexity. This business of the shot and the car backfiring! It had me completely puzzled. I stubbornly maintained that there were two sounds. Yet everybody else declared there was only one and that might have been a car backfiring. Then there was Doctor Trefont's statement that his car had backfired near the Hall.

"We won't discuss that now," I said, shelving the problem. "Tell me exactly where you were before dinner and what happened."

Alan Braithwaite, it appeared, had arrived early on that fateful evening. He and Yvonne had taken a stroll round the gardens. It was such a beautiful night.

"You must be in love, my girl," I told her. "It was beastly damp. I was worried about the state of my hair."

Presently Alan darted off, leaving her alone. He did not say anything. He just started to run. Yvonne did not know what toward. She retreated to the terrace to wait for him. He was away quite some time. That was when she heard the noise of a car backfiring. Braithwaite came back presently. He had seen a figure skulking round the house in a suspicious manner but did not want to alarm her. That was why he had left her so precipitately. He had lost the suspicious figure.

"I didn't think about it until afterwards," she told me in a strained voice. "Then I became worried, and when you talked about alibis I rang Alan to warn him. I knew he hated Mr Holland and I thought—" She broke off and eyed me fearfully.

"You thought," I continued, "he dashed through the wood to meet Mr Holland by appointment and killed him. Is that right?"

She bowed her head again. "Why did Alan Braithwaite hate him? Because of you? The way you were treated?"

"Mr Holland was always being offensive to someone. He was trying to order Alan to marry Ursula. Naturally Alan did not like being managed, and there were words between them. I think Mr Holland was going to remove his business from Alan's firm if he didn't fall in with his wishes."

"After seeing what happened to you after marrying into the Holland family, I can't blame Alan for not wanting to ally himself with Ursula. Tell me, if it is not an impertinent question, how did you come to marry the Squire's son?"

She smiled wearily. "No, it is not a rude question. In time Jim would have been just like Mr Holland. I thought I was in love with him once, but I was not sorry when he died. Of course it was a great tragedy. The plane smash, I mean. Mr Holland couldn't resign himself to the fact that it was an accident. He wanted to blame somebody."

I nodded. "He even suspected foul play. There was a letter my husband found. Was there any talk of it?"

"Not that I know of," she said, looking startled again.

"Forget it," I said, with a wave of my hand. "Go on about your husband."

"That's about all. Only"—her voice took on a brittle quality—"I learned that I was chosen to marry a Holland for just one reason. To provide an heir. After that I was to be quietly banished into the background. I told you I had no relatives.

"Mr Holland wanted someone who would bring no outside influence with her. I don't mean that the operation would have been performed after my baby's birth even if Jim had lived, but there was a chance it might have. Once I was a Holland's wife there was to be no risk of me becoming anyone else's. Mr Holland's own wife left him. He was not going to have a similar thing happen to Jim. Hence I was selected as the best available material to work on."

"Just as if you were a cow," I said, glancing at my watch. "Here! We have been yarning long enough. Get some things together and we'll go. Are you willing to come?"

Yvonne got up and faced me. "I would like to ask you one question. Who are those friends you spoke of? The ones you said I would not admit?"

I had not wanted this difficulty to arise. Yvonne was just as likely to dig her heels in and refuse to budge. "Doctor Trefont and Sister Heather. Their concern is not so much for you as for this fellow," I indicated the baby.

She stammered: "But Doctor Trefont! He was one of them at the operation."

I sighed. "I know that too. But he was in as much ignorance as you were. He too didn't know about it until afterwards. That is why he has always been so interested in your baby."

III

I got Yvonne out of the house without encountering any direct opposition. I had expected another scene with the nurse. Beyond sitting at her open door and eyeing every move we made as Yvonne put a few clothes in a suitcase, she made no attempt to argue with her. I never learned who was responsible for the locking of the closet door on the ground floor where the pram was kept, but I rather suspected Nurse Stone of a malicious intent.

I was willing to go back upstairs and wrestle for the key, but Yvonne begged me not to, almost hysterically. She was more anxious now than I was to leave the Hall.

Ames came along the passage. I saw his eyes pass from Yvonne holding the baby wrapped in a shawl to her case in my hand. They were quite expressionless, but as usual his attitude forced an explanation from me. I told him as casually as I could that Mrs Holland was going to spend a few days at the Dower. Yvonne was agog to go. I think she felt that some of the influence she had ascribed to her father-in-law remained vested in Ames.

But Ames spoke pleasantly enough. "By the way, Mrs Matheson, someone has been calling your husband several times during the afternoon. I think it was Mr Cruikshank, the estate agent. The voice was familiar, but he wouldn't leave a message."

I wondered at once what Cruikshank wanted so urgently, and if any words of mine had inspired him to get in touch with John. Unfortunately I did not know where John was, although a call through to headquarters might have contacted him. I wished afterwards I had taken the trouble to do just that. It might not have been too late even then.

Constable Cornell materialized half-way along the road. Yvonne noticed him first. She was forever glancing over her shoulder as though some hand might reach out and pull her and the child back to the Hall.

"Maggie, there's a man following us. He came out of the woods."

"That," I stated, "is not a man. It is a watchdog. There is no need to be agitated. He won't bite. Let's wait for him."

Cornell did not hasten his walk when he saw us pause. When he came up he held out his hand. "Carry the case?"

I passed it over thankfully. Babies' paraphernalia becomes heavy after a while. I introduced Yvonne and said that in future he would have the two of us in his charge. He regarded the extra work with a dispassionate eye, but I could wager he was glad when John came home and he went off duty.

John took Yvonne's presence in the house almost for granted. This was surprising. As a rule he was not enthusiastic about overnight guests outside the family. Furthermore, I had thought he would be mystified about the necessity to protect Yvonne and Jimmy. Not that any discussion on the matter arose, for I did not want him to learn of my activities; but he inferred that it was good for her to be at the Dower. Evidently he had his own ideas on Yvonne's position in the case, although we had mutually refused to compare notes. He treated her as though she had every right to be present at our dinner table. He even inspected Jimmy. It was such a close and interested inspection that I became more and more suspicious of those ideas of his.

John talked a great deal about the case that evening. This, also, surprised me. As a rule his reticence amounted almost to rudeness. It encouraged Yvonne to open up on several impressions, as was his intention. She did not observe it, however. That night I learned of two steps that had been made.

The first was the matter of the gun found in Mr Holland's hand. John explained its make and usage with a wealth of ballistic detail which made little impression on me, whatever it might have done to Yvonne. It all boiled down to the fact that a bullet from the same gun was the one that had killed the Squire. An interesting point was that Sergeant Billings had traced its licence and the place of purchase. It was one of a pair that had been bought in Mr Holland's name. This, as John remarked, might or might not be important. The next move was to discover what had happened to the twin gun.

Yvonne was unable to help him in this regard. She admitted to complete ignorance of firearms. She doubted whether she had ever seen the first gun. "Though, wait a moment."

John and I waited patiently as she wrinkled her brow in an effort at remembrance. John was sitting on the couch beside me, having dutifully given up his favourite chair to the guest. I felt his muscles tighten and wondered what he was so excited about.

"It was some time ago," Yvonne said. "Mr Holland was away. Mrs Mulqueen thought she saw someone on the terrace and rang through to Ames at the Lodge. I remember he went all round the house but found no one. I think he had a gun with him that time."

John's muscles remained tense. I shot a quick look at him and saw his eyes gleaming. That and the way he changed the subject so carefully started me thinking.

He told us something else Sergeant Billings had unearthed.

It was the result of a tedious job: that of tracing Mr Holland's movements before he died.

The Squire had spent several days in Bendigo. During those days he made several trips to outlying towns. The purpose of these trips seemed to be entirely to visit the local Bush Nursing Hospitals. John offered no comment with this information. Yvonne looked frankly puzzled and did not offer any suggestions. I tried not to look wise. I had already guessed that Mr Holland had been searching for positive evidence of his erring wife's death.

Then the climax of the evening arrived. It had all been so safe and cosy in front of the fire. I was happy in the knowledge that I had done my duty by Yvonne and Jimmy. John seemed satisfied with the way the case was developing.

Yet during that time another crime had been committed. I blamed myself for it bitterly. It was such a careless mistake, due chiefly to my negligence. It was not so much what I had done, but what I had left undone.

A ring came at the front door. The sudden sound did not startle me, so wrapped up was I in mental and bodily comfort. I did not even have that much warning. John came back with a familiar-looking man who walked on one leg with the aid of crutches. I recognized him after a moment as the Middleburn postmaster.

He looked rather excited, and did not keep us long in explaining the reason for his call.

"I wouldn't have come at all," he said, "but I saw Miss Cruikshank pass the house. I couldn't understand what she was doing back so soon."

At the name my hand went to my mouth to still a gasp. Cruikshank, so eager to get in touch with John. I had forgotten to give him the message.

"You see," went on the postmaster, "there was a telegram earlier this afternoon addressed to her. It said that her aunt was seriously ill and wanted her to come and stay. I remember sending the boy over with it to the library at once. It was marked urgent. Miss Cruikshank came over to me in a flurry and sent a wire back to say she would be there on the four o'clock train. The aunt lives about sixty miles out of the town.

"When I saw Miss Cruikshank tonight I started wondering. I remembered thinking something was odd about that wire after Miss Cruikshank sent hers back. I went into the office to check up on it and I found this."

He passed over a duplicate sheet to John. "See here?" he pointed out. "Miss Cruikshank's aunt lives sixty odd miles from Melbourne and yet this wire bears the stamp of Ashton post office. Queer, don't you think, Inspector?"

"John," I said. My voice shook. "I'm terribly sorry, but I forgot to tell you. Mr Cruikshank has been trying to contact you all the afternoon."

I hardly dared meet his eyes as he raised them slowly and frowningly from the duplicate wire. Both Yvonne and the postmaster realized something was wrong, but they did not share the foreboding John and I had.

I do not think John blamed me even then, but I remember saying forlornly to Yvonne, after he had left the house: "He didn't say good-bye. He always does, even though it might only be for a short time."

Yvonne was the strong one that night. Our positions were reversed. She did not realize the significance of what the postmaster had told us. In fact, she had no idea why Cruikshank's name should concern us so much. She supported as best she could my doubts and fears as we waited for news from John. Once or twice I tried to reassert my authority and order her to bed, but she shook her head and put another log on the fire.

I was wandering restlessly around the room when John came back. He only stayed a few minutes to tell us what had happened and to allay any anxiety I might have felt concerning his whereabouts. He knew my powers of endurance, but he glanced hard at Yvonne before he spoke.

"What is it?" I whispered. "Cruikshank?"

He stood against the door watching me. I read a certain anger in his eyes and wondered briefly if I was the cause. "Yes, he's dead. He left a note."

"Suicide?"

John said deliberately: "I found him in a cupboard under the stairs. He was hanging by a cord around his throat from a hook."

CHAPTER TWELVE

I

There were a thousand questions to ask, but John was gone again before the first numbness of shock passed. It was only at the end when all the gaps were being filled in that I learned precisely what had happened. Although my knowledge just then was incomplete, it is chronological to give the facts now. The recital might seem a little bald, as it is second-hand, and John is never one to give rein to impressions.

After the postmaster had brought the copy of the two telegrams to show him and I had admitted my forgetfulness, John drove straight down to the library in the postmaster's little runabout. The postmaster was agreeable to tag along. I do not think for one minute that John was apprehensive about his own personal safety. After all, what could a man hampered by a crutch and hindered by the lack of one leg do in the matter of defence? The postmaster's presence was more in the nature of an excuse for calling on the Cruikshanks. If all was well and there was to be nothing gained by the call, it would be easier to concoct some story about the wire in order to satisfy any sudden suspicion the Cruikshanks might have.

There was no light showing from the Cruikshanks' flat above the shop, but that and the lateness of the hour did not deter John. He knocked and rang at the shop door. After some time Miss Cruikshank put her head out the window above and called: "Is that you, Arthur?"

John gave his name and asked her to come down. After a few moments she appeared, hugging an ancient red dressing-gown around her spinster shape. John carefully removed his eyes from that, and the sight of her thin, colourless hair done up in curlers.

Her manner was nervous and she seemed more than naturally pale. Assisted by the postmaster, John questioned her and learned that the wire, as had been suspected, was a hoax. Aunt was never in better health. She had been astounded to see Maud, and from what John gathered not particularly delighted. Miss Cruikshank was on her way back to town within half an hour. She got back to the shop about nine thirty that evening, seething with righteous indignation and burning to tell Arthur all about it, only to find the place in darkness and her brother out. As she did not know where he was or how long he might be, she bottled her story to keep hot for the morning and went to bed. She had been there until that moment.

John thanked Miss Cruikshank for all this information. He then told her about her brother's efforts to contact him. He asked if she knew what it was about. She said "No" almost before he finished the question. She seemed to become more agitated, although she strove to hide it. John then asked formal permission to look round the place.

Assisted again by the postmaster, who was thoroughly enjoying his role of policeman, they searched the flat and the shop. Luckily it was John who opened the cupboard underneath the stairs. He was in some ways hardened to the sight that met his eyes. He shut the door quickly and told Miss Cruikshank to wait upstairs until he came to her. His casual manner deceived her. She went upstairs obediently, while John and the postmaster, whose enjoyment dropped suddenly to zero, cut down the rigid dead body of the estate agent. He was as cold as mutton and not as pretty a sight.

John said on the face of it, it looked then like a suicide. Especially as he found a note addressed to himself in one of the pockets of the black sateen apron Mr Cruikshank always wore on duty in the shop.

I was glad I did not see that note until afterwards. It would not have been pleasant thinking I had hounded a man into taking his own life, no matter how criminal he was. It took the form of a confession to the murder and was signed with Cruikshank's name. When Maud Cruikshank was asked to identify the writing she did so through such a blind of tears that it deceived her. Luckily there are experts at Russell Street who make short shrift of such forgeries.

John did not return home until well into the early hours of the next morning. I was still awake, but he sank into bed dead tired and without a word. I was still full of imaginings that he blamed me for my forgetfulness, and one or two tears stole down my face in self-pity at his neglect.

I thought I had overcome resenting his unapproachableness during one of his cases, but it seemed I had not. However, the self-pity had a good effect. It relaxed my taut nerves and presently sent me off to sleep.

He was off again early next morning, with a farewell peck that made me ashamed in front of Yvonne. I had rather wanted to demonstrate the ideal husband to her. The self-pity started again during lunch when the telephone rang. I started up, thinking it would be John. A man's voice asked for Yvonne. She came back to the table after a long time with a confused but not unhappy look on her face. Alan Braithwaite, she announced, and tried to go on with her meal.

I remember that afternoon very vividly. The weather was one of delicious warmth and clear air. A somnolent autumnal calm that gave no hint of what the night would bring to me. Armed with garden chairs and knitting, we went down to the back of the garden and the shade of the poplars. Jimmy lay on his back in Tony's outgrown pram. For a while Yvonne seemed on edge lest he start crying, but the peace of the day and the good meals I had supervised into his little stomach had good effects. By and by she relaxed and even began to play with Tony in the sandpit.

Constable Cornell retained his position on the back porch despite two or three invitations to join us. He kept his gaze fixed vacantly on the trees above our heads until I longed to give him some knitting to do.

This lasted until afternoon teatime, when I went into the house to prepare orange juice for the children. When I was searching in a cupboard for uncracked cups to do honour to my guest, my eye fell on some packs of cards. I presented one to Constable Cornell along with his tea. It was a happy inspiration, for he immediately opened up into an intricate patience.

Very soon the warmth of the sun started to wane, reminding us that after all it was autumn and not summer. I was about to suggest going indoors when Tony made his discovery.

He had been digging like a puppy in his sandpit when suddenly out of the corner of my eye I saw him pause and shoot a quick glance to see if I was watching. I pretended not to be, but continued to keep an eye on him. His busy fingers pulled something out of the sand. It was dropped into his bucket with a hard rattle. The noise was very pleasing and he rolled the bucket around to continue it. Presently he came up to my chair and I stole a look inside.

There was no mistaking the small object Tony had been playing with so blithely. Even if you have never seen a bullet before, your imagination does not need much to identify one.

"Look!" I said to Yvonne. "Tony found it in the sand. Now how on earth would such a thing get into the pit?"

Yvonne looked and then raised startled eyes on my face. I had been going to treat the bullet as a curio until her anxious look. It was extremely unlikely that the bullet had been delivered along with the soil. And as John had only completed the sandpit a week or so, the scavenging of time would scarcely account for its presence.

I turned it round in my fingers gingerly.

"I hope it is not likely to go off," I said.

The bullet in Tony's sandpit meant something. Of that I was sure. Where had it come from? Why should anyone fire a gun into the sand? I turned my head slowly from one side to the other. Constable Cornell's interest was still in his patience. I observed him as my eyes swept a circle searching for some place where the person who had fired the bullet might have stood.

A bullet meant a gun or some sort of firearm. The first and last time I had heard a gunshot was the night Mr Holland was found dead in the wood with one in his hand. And that gun John had said was one of a pair.

237

What did the bullet in Tony's sandpit mean? As far as I could see there were more guns and bullets than the actual noise of their explosion.

I dropped my knitting into my lap and sat back, thinking hard. I closed my eyes, pretending to Yvonne that I was dozing in the sun while all the time I was reliving that day. The day and night of James Holland's murder.

I turned over each direct or indirect contact we had had with our landlord. The period between our arrival in Middleburn and his death had been so brief. Up to the day of the murder there had been no positive communication between us.

For my part that decisive day had progressed smoothly, even enjoyably until—

Suddenly my mind was alert to a small feeling of disturbance. The first hint of a strange reaction on the day of the dinner-party. I fumbled for the underlying significance.

I came home from golf. It was late. Nearly six. I had lost a ball? No, that wasn't right. That lost ball came into the picture later. What was it, then? Begin again.

I was late. It was a scramble to get dressed for the dinner-party and to put Tony into bed. Tony? Not Tony alone. Tony and Robin and Mrs Ames. When I came in they were having their meal in the kitchen. They had been out at the sandpit the whole afternoon and had just come in for tea.

And up in the lounge-room I could sense some strange occupation. Mrs Ames has been exploring the house. No, not Mrs Ames. Although it was natural enough at the time to presume so. James Holland!

Without evidence, even without a tangible clue I was convinced James Holland had called into the Dower House before setting out on his last walk through the wood.

The time on the duplicate telegram was the correct one. The Squire had been due to arrive at Holland Hall at five, and not, as the police were led to believe, at seven when the shot was fired.

The same sound of an exploding gun to which I alone bore obstinate witness, and which I had in an endeavour to shirk the responsibility checked and rechecked. Why, oh why, hadn't John of all people distinguished it more clearly when to me it was like a bang in the ear?

A bang in the ear! I sat up suddenly and my eyes fell on Yvonne's anxious ones. She had not been deceived by my somnolent pose. A bang in the ear! A tiny thread started at the back of my brain and started to weave itself strongly to the front. I had it. I nearly had it. Then quite simply everything was clear. I knew what had happened. I knew what the bullet in Tony's sandpit meant.

I glanced quickly towards Constable Cornell. He was shuffling the cards, his eyes once more above our heads. I waited until he had opened up another game of patience.

"Yvonne," I said softly. "I need your co-operation. Come inside for a moment. The children will be all right here."

She got up obediently and followed me indoors to John's study. She made no comment of surprise when I presented her with a steel-lined riding crop and indicated a leather upholstered chair. She promised to remain within earshot of the study while I was gone. I found myself loving Yvonne for the way she did not ask questions.

II

I chose to go to the Hall through the wood. I did not want my red-hot idea to lose any of its warmth by a tedious walk round by the road and up the drive. Neither did I want Constable Cornell dogging my footsteps.

The track through the wood helped me to develop the timing and execution of the crime more clearly.

I entered the house quietly through the conservatory door. There was no point in attracting attention. I had no legitimate excuse for being there. I hoped to accomplish my task unnoticed.

The place seemed empty in spite of the unlocked door. The gathering of the autumn mist which hid the sinking sun rendered it gloomy and just a little frightening. I had made up my mind not to be nervous. Should I meet anyone, I could say Yvonne had forgotten some clothing or invent some similar excuse. Once I had accomplished my objective there would be no need ever to set foot in the Hall again.

I think I would have preferred to see someone. The unnatural stillness of the Hall amused every instinct of my fertile imagination. Anyone's company, no matter how hostile, would be better than this isolation in an alien house.

For the first time I was conscious of James Holland's domination. I had an eerie feeling that I was bending to his will. My remembrance of him, his appearance and his character became strangely vivid. Unseen, he seemed to be commanding me to bring his murderer to justice.

I tried to shake off this uncanny influence. Justice for the unjust man? Revenge for one who sought only revenge on others in life? I could find nothing to admire in that vivid remembrance, and more to hate from what I had subsequently learned of James Holland.

I lifted the receiver from the switchboard at the foot of the stairs. The dial tone of the open exchange line seemed extraordinarily loud. I cut it off at once and threw a hasty glance up and down the passage. There was still no sign of life.

I connected the key of the Hall with the extension to the Dower and, pressing down on the ringing key, turned the handle once. Yvonne answered immediately. I repeated my instructions to her and hung the receiver on the hook which I had jammed with my handkerchief. Then I moved away towards the door of the drawing-room and waited. The sound of the steel-lined riding crop striking the leather chair came over the wire, but it was not quite satisfactory. In spite of my ever-growing apprehension I wanted the experiment to be perfect if it was to be considered successful. It meant a few more minutes in the deepening lonely gloom.

I went back to the switchboard, my ears alert for any disturbance either from behind me or above on the stairs. I fancied I heard sounds, but put them down to my own edginess. I had to keep calm.

"Try again," I whispered over the line to Yvonne. "Harder— harder, and hurry. I'm getting the jumps."

My fingers fumbled as I readjusted the handkerchief to hold the line open and placed the receiver back. My hands shook in the need for haste. I wanted to get back to my position near the drawing-room before Yvonne raised the whip again. I was only a step away from the stairs as the noise came again. This time it reverberated across the line. The sound as of a gunshot broke the silence of the Hall.

"Again, Yvonne," I spoke clearly. The success had made me reckless. I stepped back along the wall. The crack came again. I felt sweat trickling down my body and my heart thumped almost unbearably. I was right. What a plan it was, how clever! But I could smash it.

I need never set foot in this horrible house again. It frightened me. I owned to it now. If I remained there much longer I would start screaming with a mad and unreasoning terror. I had to get out now. At once.

In every shadow I saw someone looming up before me. At every footstep I took someone was following me. After a journey of dire anticipation I reached the conservatory door. It had been my goal. It meant safety. But fear, worse than the previous imaginings, struck me again.

I had left the door ajar ready for a quick getaway if the need arose. Now it was shut. I tried the handle. It slipped under my wet hand. With the handkerchief I had used at the switchboard I covered the palm of my hand and tried again. It was locked.

I had left it ajar. I knew I had. I remembered that clearly because I had deemed it advisable. You must get out, said a steady voice over and over in my brain. I pushed the voice away, in order to think. How could I get out? Why wasn't there someone in the house? Someone other than the person who had played this horrid trick of locking the door where I had planned my exit?

There was only one thing to do. The last remaining reasonable corner of my mind told me what it was. I must retrace my footsteps and go down that length of gloomy hall. I could let myself out the front door.

There is no point in making a mad dash. The journey must be undertaken calmly and quietly. There is nothing to be gained by panic.

That reasonable corner of my brain told me these things, but it seemed to be growing smaller and fainter in sound. I had to hang on to it in order to follow its directions. My skin felt wet all over now.

I reached the foot of the stairs again. I dared not look up into the gloom that swallowed them from sight. My eyes were fixed on the dull-coloured glow from the leadlights on either side of the front door. They were such a long way ahead. I crept by each door. Those doors which I had passed that first day when James Holland sent me to find Mrs Mulqueen. At every one I expected it to widen and some evil thing to come leaping out. I could scarcely believe it when I reached the front door. It did not seem possible that I could get out of the house with my experiment a proven success without some opposition.

The relief was almost ludicrous as I stepped out onto the terrace, pulling the heavy door to behind me with a carefree bang. I felt the same sense of embarrassed relief as one does coming out of a theatre after seeing a "horror" film. After all, it was only the imagination at work. There was nothing really concrete to be scared about. Only the overwhelming importance of the news I could give John had caused me to think these things. I had worked myself up into a state all for nothing.

Nothing? What about the locked door of the conservatory?

I dismissed it with a reckless shrug. I got out. That was all that mattered. Maybe the conservatory door had an automatic lock and a draught blew it shut. So I deceived myself, while all the time I knew that there was no breeze in that autumn mist to send the door to, and that the door itself had an ordinary old-fashioned lock.

I was persuading myself out of sheer bravado, for I still had the trip down the drive to do. The scene of another uncomfortable experience. I needed all the courage I could muster.

It could be said that night had fallen, although the time was that of twilight. The mist was growing thicker and the close growing poplars made the hour seem later. However, it was still light enough for me to distinguish a woman's figure coming up the drive to meet me.

I kept on steadily, well in the centre of the interlacing poplars. The figure's approach was not a stealthy menacing one, in spite of my sudden alertness for danger. Indeed the woman's eyes were on the ground and were only raised when I was a few feet away. It was Elizabeth Mulqueen.

She gave an exclamation. I believe I almost frightened her, when I was the one ready to be intimidated.

"I've been to get something for Yvonne," I said, not caring about the contradiction of my empty hands. Mrs Mulqueen did not notice it. She was not interested in the explanation of what I was doing at the Hall. Her eyes were over my head, staring in puzzled surprise at something beyond me.

"How is dear Yvonne?" The question was conventional and mechanical.

"Quite well. Jimmy seems to find the change to his liking." I sidled round so as to face the same way.

For a moment we stood side by side in silence. Suddenly Mrs Mulqueen grabbed my arm. The light in the tower flashed on and off.

"I thought I wasn't mistaken," she remarked in a complacently triumphant voice which was quite different from my own emotions.

That the tower light should signal at that particular moment seemed unbelievable.

I let her clutch my arm, although I disliked it intensely. I wanted to make myself realize Elizabeth Mulqueen was standing in the drive and not in the tower sending amorous messages by the medium of the light. I had considered that problem solved. One mystery seemed to develop into another. Was my red-hot idea about the switchboard to merge into a similar position? I was almost desperate. I could not let my solution fall through.

The light in the tower continued to go on and off.

III

I made a quick decision. I broke away from Mrs Mulqueen and hurried back to the Hall. I had to know who was in the tower. The need for satisfaction was so urgent that I ignored the probable resurgence of fear I had thought to leave behind me forever. Someone other than Elizabeth Mulqueen was in the tower and I had to know who it was.

I had no exact idea of the approach to the tower, but made for the top floor. I climbed the stairs breathlessly, pulling myself up by the banisters. Speed was important. It was my intention to cut off the signaller's retreat if possible. The tower was situated towards the front of the building. In order to save time I tried to reason ahead the most likely room. I got it right the second door.

The light pressed on under my hand as I fumbled around the jamb to find the switch. Steep steps arose straight from the centre of the room. I glanced up to the trapdoor in the roof. It was wide open, a black square against the white ceiling. Very cautiously I began to ascend the stairs, gripping the railing either side with my hands. I thought I knew what to expect if someone was up there in the darkness above my head, and listened for sounds to betray the exact position. I was prepared for swift action if the need arose, and felt quite calm when so near to grips with an enemy.

I pulled myself head and shoulders into the darkness of the tower room, resting my elbows either side on the floor.

"Who is there?" I asked clearly. The room was perfectly still. I listened again for some faint noise, even breathing. The silence was as heavy as the mist that pressed against the windows. The tower room was empty.

"Mrs Matheson!" said a voice from below. I withdrew my head and glanced down. Ursula Mulqueen stood at the foot of the steps. She looked bewildered and just a little frightened.

"Mother sent me to find you. I heard someone running along the passage. It was you?"

I stayed on my perch. "Did you see anyone? Where have you been all this time?" I asked.

"In my room, reading. I haven't been out of it all day. I only knew you were here when Mother told me. What are you looking for?"

"The light in the tower room. Where is it?"

Under Ursula's directions I climbed in and found it. I moved eagerly about the room now bathed in a powerful light. It was barely eight feet square, empty except for an old telescope in one corner. I had hoped to find some small forgotten mark, betraying the identity of the signaller. But there was nothing—no conveniently dropped handkerchief and no cigarette and no lingering perfume.

I switched off the tower-room light and descended the steps. Ursula stood in the doorway. She seemed undecided what to do or say. She was puzzled about something and I guessed what it was.

"Your mother and I," I told her gently, "met in the drive. We saw the tower-room light flashing as though someone was signalling. I thought it was worth an inspection."

Ursula's mouth fell open. "Then it wasn't—couldn't have been—"

"No, it wasn't and perhaps never was." I don't know why I said that. Perhaps I wanted to destroy that disillusioned cynical look Ursula always wore when speaking of her mother.

We went down to the ground floor together. The Hall seemed alive with light and people now, a striking contrast to the lonely gloom I had crept through not an hour previously. Mrs Mulqueen was talking to Ames in the passage.

She glanced towards me. "Did you see anyone?" she asked.

I shook my head.

Ames said: "Inspector Matheson just rang for you, Mrs Matheson. I did not know you were here. He insisted that you were."

"What did he want?" I asked, at once agog. Yvonne must have told John of my experiment,

"His dinner," said Ames without a change of expression. "If you go back to the Dower through the wood he will meet you on the path."

How very prosaic of John! I was indignant that he should treat my investigations so lightly. There was no mysterious significance to be read in his message at all. Merely that the man was hungry and that it was my place to go home and feed him.

Elizabeth Mulqueen saw me to the conservatory door. I frowned when I saw it was ajar; almost as I had left it. Had I given way to panic so much that my own senses had been deceived? But that did not matter now. Soon I would meet John and present him with some facts that more than compensated for those horrible moments.

What a fool I was just then! I can never work out how I happened to become so gullible. If only I had stopped one moment to think and to analyse the position. But I was still rebellious at having to go home and get a dinner instead of continuing uninterrupted on an exciting pitch to the conclusion of the case.

I entered the wood carefully, for there was but little light left to see the path. The trees were likely to make it practically indistinguishable further on. My progress was slow. Now and then I gave the whistle which was John's own signal to me.

"I only hope the man has the sense to bring a torch," I said aloud, stumbling over a root and pausing to steady myself.

It was during that pause that something John had said flashed into my head. "Promise me, Maggie, you will never go through the wood alone."

My breath caught in my throat. But this meeting had been John's own idea! It was rather inconsistent of him certainly, but Ames had said—I whistled again and again. But no answering notes came to my ears. That same fear I had felt in the gloom at the Hall was somewhere inside me. I checked it, but it was there.

I was deep into the wood now. Where was John? I peered ahead through the darkness imagining I saw a flashlight and heard a faint call. There was not the faintest gleam of a light. Just the wood smothered into a deeper silence and darkness by the mist. I clung to a tree, breathing heavily and trying again to quell the rising panic. It was stronger now. For out of the depths of that deadly quiet someone was stalking me.

I was alone, but for an unseen enemy. I did not imagine the stealthy footsteps coming along the path, nor the brushing of the leaves and branches. Those steps were too real. They kept time with the thud of my heart, as I waited still clinging to the tree. There was no use now in whistling or peering ahead for John's light. I knew now. John would not come. He had not sent that message.

Some wild and desperate hope made me think of Constable Cornell. Perhaps the footsteps were his. What was it he had said? "Never lost a body yet. Don't intend to begin." Odd the way he called his charges bodies. It had a sinister ring. The same hope braced me for a moment. The footsteps had paused.

"Cornell?" I asked sharply, trying to distinguish a figure through the darkness.

I will never forget the answer to my query. It was a deep and malicious chuckle. The sound seemed to continue for seconds while my fingers scraped the bark of the tree as I fought for the last remaining threads of control. If only the person would say something so that I could recognize the voice. It was ignorance of what I had to face that was so unnerving.

I strove to speak through the choking fear, to sound as normal as I could. "You mustn't show how frightened you are," said that small reasonable part of my brain with me still.

But my enemy spoke before I could test my strength. The voice was as malicious and evil as that low laugh. "I frightened you, Mrs Matheson? I apologize."

It was a slightly familiar voice, a woman's voice, but still I did not recognize it. "Who are you?" I asked. "Who are you? And what do you want?"

I forced myself to advance in the direction of the voice. It was better to measure the woman up face to face than to remain clinging in terror to a tree which would be of no assistance at all.

A whiff of human breath came to my sharpened senses.

"Nurse Stone?"

"Yes, Nurse Stone, Mrs Matheson. I followed you. I hoped we might have a little talk together." I was standing only a few steps away from the woman now.

"What is it?" I repeated. "I am on my way home. My husband is expecting me."

The woman laughed again, but I had a check on that panic. "Is he, now? And Yvonne? Is she expecting you too?"

I guessed at the woman's emotions. She was in a fit of drunken jealousy. Jimmy was at the root of the trouble: I had taken him away from her charge.

"Yvonne is well," I answered in a conciliatory manner. "Jimmy seems better. Why don't you come and see him tomorrow? You are very fond of him, Nurse Stone?"

My guess had been accurate. She started to weep in a maudlin fashion. It was disgusting and rather alarming, alone with the foolish woman in the middle of the wood, but it was better than the panic I had felt before. I had the upper hand now. I was no longer on the defensive.

"I don't believe you," she whined. "He was all right. I looked after him well. He is mine. You have stolen him away. I have always looked after him."

I felt sorry for her. "But he wasn't well," I said gently. "Surely you knew that. He needs a special diet and care."

This angered her. "What do you know about it? You modern women who call yourselves mothers! All books and fancy foods. I had charge of Jimmy's father and I know how to care for his son. Give him back to me."

There was nothing to be gained in pursuing an argument with a tipsy jealous woman.

I said: "Come to the Dower tomorrow. We'll talk things over then when you feel better."

It was a tactless remark and only served to inflame Nurse Stone further. She came up very close, thrusting her face into mine. The smell of her breath sickened me.

"I know what you're thinking. You think I'm tight. Well, I'm not. I'm as sober as you are, you busybody. How dare you suggest I drink!"

I moved back a step or two and turned away. "I really must go, Nurse Stone. My husband will be waiting. Come and see me tomorrow."

I started to move along the path. There was a mad rush behind me. I could not see where the blow was coming, but I swerved sharply. Something, I think it was only the enraged woman's clenched fist, caught me on the shoulder. I was sent reeling against a bush. I tried to regain my balance but stumbled against a root, and for the next minute lay sprawling on the ground. Nurse Stone came towards me.

The woman's gait was none too steady. As she blundered forward I put out a foot and tripped her, dragging myself upward. Down the path I could see the faint thread of a light passing over the track.

"John," I yelled, hurrying along. "Here I am."

Nurse Stone must have seen the light too. I heard her grunting as she got to her feet. She made off in the opposite direction at once. I was thankful that there was to be no ugly scene. The woman was not responsible, and I was in no mood for further brawling.

"Whose idea was this?" I asked, when the light was flashed into my face. "I thought you forbade me to go through the wood? You won't need an extracted promise to keep me away in future. I've been grappling with a drunken woman."

The encounter with Nurse Stone had left me shaken even more so than the fall. I was dazed, so much so that it did not occur to me at first that John was very quiet. The light played on my face unswervingly.

"Turn that damned thing off me," I said irritably, "and let's get home."

Very slowly the torch was swept round in a semi-circle. It lighted up the trees and the path which faded away into a dark hole beyond its strength. Then it was held steadily on the face of its owner.

IV

The breath drew back sharply in my throat. In that face exposed in the blinding light was something that I recognized before the woman herself. You can see people day after day, and unconsciously think you will know them anywhere. Then the time comes when you catch them from an untried angle and observe a subtle unfamiliarity.

On this occasion the face of Harriet Ames was presented in a different aspect. It still had the contours of the woman I knew, the red stain across one cheek. But now the primary feature was the familiar look of another person. I recognized in Harriet Ames another woman's expression I had learned by heart from a portrait. A likeness which was verified by the long lobe of her ear.

I knew too that Mrs Ames was not illuminating her own face so deliberately without some purpose in mind. Nurse Stone was not the enemy I dreaded in the darkness of the wood. It was this silent, bitter woman who stood before me like an unscaleable wall. It was not Nurse Stone who had aroused the feeling of panic, but this young woman whom I had always dismissed because of her blank eyes and expressionless voice.

I did not speak either. There was nothing for me to say. I was up against my enemy at last, and the sudden shock of revelation stilled my tongue. I could not pretend when all the time I recognized Harriet Ames as such and she knew that I knew. There was no question of this being a surprise encounter. It had been planned deliberately, just as carefully as James Holland's murder. I knew too much. There were many gaps in the story I could tell, but I still knew too much.

Mrs Ames turned the light aside at last. She spoke courteously as she always had. That was the frightening part. Her manner was normal even in the midst of the abnormality.

"I have a gun, Mrs Matheson. Please walk ahead of me."

I passed her and walked just behind the torchlight she flashed in front of my feet. I walked quite steadily too. I was proud of the fact, even though some part of me said: "This is not you. This is just a dream. A nightmare where one always picks on the most inoffensive person to be the villain of the piece, and awakes to smile at the absurdity of it all."

"One moment, Mrs Matheson. Stand still, please." The courteous voice was as hard as steel. Odd how I had never noticed the possibility of such a quality before.

I stopped. Was she going to indulge in a little rhetoric and postpone the business ahead? Was there going to be the hope of time on my side? John would have arrived home by now. Surely Yvonne, even in spite of her promise of secrecy, would have become disturbed and told him where I was and what I had been doing.

"I am sorry about this, Mrs Matheson, believe me. But you have left us no alternative. We did warn you indirectly to stay out of our affairs."

We? Us? Where was Ames? Did he leave his wife to do the dirty work alone?

She was continuing: "I could of course shoot you dead, but unfortunately such a death might arouse your husband's suspicions."

So they were going to have another attempt to make murder look like suicide. It would have to be ingenious to deceive John. I concentrated on that grain of comfort.

Suddenly my silence seemed to anger Mrs Ames. She wanted tears and pleadings in order to test out the temper of that steely quality in her. But I was too proud and beyond such trivial emotions to afford her satisfaction.

"You fool! You damned fool! What did you hope to gain from your prying?"

I found my tongue at last. "I don't regret it," I answered. "What information I have will help my husband make his conviction."

She laughed softly. "You don't deceive me. He knows nothing of your doings. Don't think I haven't been observing you all these weeks. Why else should he set that policeman to watch you? No, Mrs Matheson, you can't get out of it like that."

"Very well," I said. My tone implied that I did not care whether she believed me or not. It was still true.

For a brief space I thought my bluff might succeed. She paused and I held my breath. Not that I realized for one moment that Mrs Ames was going to kill me. It just wasn't possible. Even the dangerous game of prying and my insatiable curiosity over the last weeks did not seem enough justification to come up against the real thing. That was the trouble. I had made too much of a game of crime without realizing what deadly consequences would come about. I was still convinced that John would arrive to rescue me as he had once before. I had forgotten all about that other occasion in time. Time had softened the memory of those few grim minutes just as these would be forgotten. I was inviolate.

I was strangely calm when I should have been terrified. I find myself more frightened now, when I remember that scene in the wood with Harriet Ames. At the time I was deceived by her matter-of-fact attitude. Something more like Nurse Stone's attack might have jolted me out of the fictional state of mind.

My attempt at a bluff gave Mrs Ames time to think, but she still remained in deadly earnest. She spoke with the faintest hint of a sneer in her flat voice.

"If you are living in hopes of your husband or that attendant of yours turning up at the eleventh hour you are doomed to disappointment. Your husband phoned the Hall that he would be delayed at the office and we arranged for Cornell to be called into town on other urgent business. So you see we have the coast clear to deal with both you and Yvonne, not to mention that brat of hers."

I said over my shoulder: "You can't possibly hope to get away with it. If you are planning a wholesale slaughter of myself, Yvonne and the baby you haven't got a chance."

Harriet Ames was not a half-crazed unreasonable person like Nurse Stone. She spoke confidently. "Wait and see. But what a pity you won't be here to see the success of our plans. Keep going, please, Mrs Matheson, and obey my instructions. If you do not I will shoot you now and then continue to the Dower and kill your son."

A primitive fury shook me when she spoke of Tony. Once I had left him in her charge. He and that beautiful child of hers had played together with the utmost happiness. And now she was holding the price of Tony's blood over my head. It was inconceivable that a woman with a beloved child of her own could make such a threat. I longed for a genuine passion of revenge that could make me wish ill for her child.

There was nothing to be gained by turning on her. I had enough sense to see that, even in my insane anger. Time was the only chance I had. Hope had been long since taken from me. But whatever happened, life for Tony was the greatest bequest I could leave to him.

Time! I did what I could to stretch out that horrible trip through the wood. I tried to work out the hour as we went, and to estimate the chances of John's return. Sometimes he would stay at headquarters until late at night and it could not be more than seven-thirty now. But Cornell! What about him? I was none too sanguine about him recognizing a wild-goose chase quickly. He looked the type of man who was excellent in his own sphere but a blockhead out of it.

I dawdled as much as I dared and pretended to stumble once or twice. But my adversary was an intelligent, desperate woman, and I was forced on with a prod of her gun in my back. It was an unpleasant feeling, and while I still had life I fought instinctively against a repetition.

I shrank from the sight of the Dower House. It came all too soon, even after what seemed like a long trek through the wood. A single light shone from one of the windows. It winked evilly through the mist and seemed the epitome of disaster. Just as the lantern of a wrecker must have appeared to mariners of other times.

Mrs Ames guided me through a hole in the hedge and along the side of the house.

"Stop, please, Mrs Matheson."

I halted right outside the nursery window.

"This is your son's room. If I stand here I can shoot through the screen exactly to where he is lying asleep. You will now go to the front door and get Yvonne to let you in. Then go through to the kitchen and open the back door and come back here. It should take you about two minutes. Any longer and I will fire straight at your son's cot. Do you follow me?"

My mouth was dry. I could only nod as Mrs Ames shone the torch for a brief moment in my face. I wanted to beseech her for more time, to make allowance for some possible delay in Yvonne answering my ring. I would do anything she wanted if she would only promise not to level the gun through the wire at Tony's cot.

I half-ran, half-stumbled around to the porch. My legs felt stiff and refused to do the bidding of my desperate brain. The climbing rose caught at my clothes. I wrenched myself free and heard the material tear. The flagged path which John had complained about so often caught the heel of one shoe and held it fast. I tried to wriggle my foot free.

Had one minute passed? Had Harriet Ames stepped up to Tony's window, gun in hand? I bent down to drag at my ankle, but the heel was firmly wedged. My fingers fumbled at the shoelace. It broke under a suddenly acquired strength, born of desperation. I left my shoe there and fell on my knees on the porch step. I did not pause to get to my feet until I had crawled to the doorway. I rang on the bell as firmly as my cold and trembling hand would allow. It jumped under the pulse in my thumb and I brought my other hand onto the wrist to steady the pressure.

I called Yvonne by name, battering at the door with both fists and imploring her to open at once. Minutes seemed to pass before she came. My eyes strained anxiously. If Mrs Ames could only hear my earnest endeavour to obey her instructions surely she would not fire.

Hurry, Yvonne! My mind was so occupied with Tony that I did not consider what the opening of the door would mean to her and Jimmy. I was to pay the penalty too. But not Tony, whose only fault was being my son and taking a fancy to a dummy which was evidence against the killer.

Yvonne opened the door under my pounding fists and almost fell over the threshold. She put out both hands to catch me and I felt her slight body brace against my weight. Her eyes were wide open in her pale face, the usual timid look accentuated by an underlying expression of bewilderment. Her hands were on my wrists. In spite of her air of fragility they felt like iron bands to stop me passing. Had I suddenly grown so weak when I thought I had acquired an abnormal strength to help me face this crisis?

Then I became conscious of being held from behind. Yvonne's eyes were over my shoulder. Her mouth had fallen open awry but no sound came from it. I struggled in the grasp of someone who had stepped from behind the door to hold me. I wanted to explain about the two minutes that must be passing. Before I could open my mouth to plead for release a hand came firmly down across my jaw. I saw John's face over my shoulder. It was hard and pale and a line of sweat was gathered on his upper lip as he struggled to hold me still.

I put all the pleading I could into my eyes. Didn't he know that our son's life was in jeopardy? If only he would release his cruel grip on my jaw. Was he willing to stand by and risk Tony's life? His eyes were not those of Tony's father. They belonged to some cruel relent-less stranger. I hated John in that moment. He was killing my child. Tony was all mine then. John had no claim on him.

There was no word spoken although I made desperate imploring noises in my throat. My strength was ebbing quickly under the sheer brute force John was exerting. I knew it was nearly all up with me. When the shot sounded I gave one jerk and then fell completely limp against him. I was still conscious but everything was dark and thick. I knew just one thing. The two minutes had passed. Harriet Ames had carried out her threat.

John removed his hand and picked me up in his arms. As he car-ried me down the passage I gazed at his averted face with a dull loathing. I did not know where he was taking me. I did not care. I said "Tony," over and over.

CHAPTER THIRTEEN

I

My memory of that night when John made his arrests is still confused. But I do recall feeling resentful when John slapped my face as I laughed to hear Tony crying for me. Then he dried my eyes with his own handkerchief and went out of the room. The next and last coherent thought I had was when Doctor Trefont was pinching my arm. I asked him why he wanted a blood test from me. I was going to be shot, not poisoned. His gentle laugh accompanied me into a deep sleep.

When I awoke the following morning John had gone. I lay there thinking what it was I wanted urgently to tell him. My head was heavy and my body felt bruised. A knock sounded at the door and Yvonne Holland came in bearing a tray.

"Hullo," I said, struggling to sit up. "Great hostess I am. Are the children all right?"

Yvonne put the tray on my knee. "Daisy Potts-Power has taken them out for a walk. She was so anxious to do something. You are to stay in bed until the doctor comes."

She gave me a timid look, scared lest she had given me an opening on a forbidden subject. I shuddered at the fried egg, covering it up hastily, and poured out some black coffee.

Yvonne wandered around the room arranging chrysanthemums Daisy had left.

"Get me a cigarette, like a dear girl," I requested. She glanced at me doubtfully.

"If you don't," I said, flinging off the bedclothes in a threatening fashion, "I'll get up and find one myself."

The look of doubt was joined by a weak smile as she searched for my case.

I took a deep inhalation. It made my head sing.

"Sit down," I ordered. "And don't look apprehensive, Yvonne! It makes me irritable. All I want you to tell me is what happened last night. No more, no less. I'll get someone else to fill in the gaps. You won't get into a row from telling me that much, will you?"

Her hand fiddled with her waistband in her old habit.

"Doctor Trefont said—" she began.

I interrupted her by wiping the doctor out of the conversation in one short sentence.

"Your husband," Yvonne tried again.

"Quite another matter," I said. "If only John would stick around for a while, I would soon find out everything. Come on, now. What happened?"

Her hand fell away from her belt and began to trace a pattern on the arm of the chair. I considered it a hopeful sign and waited patiently.

"It was all rather confusing," said Yvonne. "I didn't know quite what was happening. I still don't know why you wanted me to hit that leather chair with the riding crop."

"An old trick of noises off. The sound came over the extension like a gunshot. When we found that bullet in the sandpit, I wondered if it might have something to do with the shot I heard the night Mr Holland was killed. I was looking around trying to figure out where it was fired from when I saw a tiny casement window. It juts out from the study directly in line with where we were sitting that afternoon. Then I remembered that John's desk was very near that window, and on John's desk was the telephone. The combination of the shot and the telephone made me remember more important details. That I had been standing near the switchboard at the Hall and had been the only one to hear the shot clearly. In fact, people seemed to infer I had been hearing things. Also, that the keys of the Dower and the Hall on the board were connected.

"And speaking of Tony, I don't know if it was sheer coincidence or whether he is the remarkable child every mother imagines her son to be, but the following morning he imitated the sound. He must have awakened when Mrs Ames fired her gun through the study window.

"That same shot, which I heard over the extension, was to be passed off as the one that killed your father-in-law. The killer had an alibi for that time. Actually James Holland was murdered at least an hour earlier. That," I finished with a sidelong glance, "should clear up any doubts you had about Alan Braithwaite."

Yvonne flushed and said uncertainly: "I never thought for one moment—"

"Didn't you? Go on with what happened."

"Well," she continued, "after you rang off from the Hall I went back to the children."

"Was Cornell still there?" I demanded, stubbing out my cigarette and making no pretence about having enjoyed it.

"Oh, yes. He remained on the porch until the call came for him."

"What call?"

Yvonne wrinkled her brow. "That's just what I don't quite understand. Someone rang. He wanted to speak to Mr Cornell. I went out to get him. Then I went and brought the children in. It was getting late and Tony was asking for his tea. When I looked out the kitchen door there was no sign of Cornell—I didn't know where he had gone."

"On his wild-goose chase. Mrs Ames said she had arranged for his removal."

"And yet," Yvonne suggested, "he was there when Mrs Ames was arrested."

"Cornell is evidently too old a hand at his game to be put off by a false telephone call," I said. "Go on with your part. Did Tony wonder where I was?"

"He asked for you once or twice. He really started me getting worried about you. You were away such a long time and it was getting dark. I got Tony undressed and put him into his cot, but he wouldn't go to sleep until he saw you or his father. Then after feeding Jimmy I put them in the same bed together. By the time they had gone to sleep I was terribly nervous. I didn't know what to do. It was so late and I was by myself. I nearly screamed when your husband came in quietly by the back door. He apologized for giving me such a fright, but he had not wished to be seen. He didn't ask where you were, which I thought rather odd. I wanted to tell him but he stopped me. He told me what he wanted me to do."

"And what was that?"

"I was to move about the house quite normally and to answer the door and any phone rings as if nothing had happened. Your husband kept out of sight somewhere. Tony wasn't to know he had arrived home. Then you came. I was terrified when you rang the bell and started thumping on the door. Then you looked so queer. I couldn't understand why you struggled with your husband."

"Mrs Ames said she would shoot Tony if I was any longer than two minutes in opening the back door. She was standing outside the nursery window with a gun ready in her hand."

Yvonne was very pale. "They were coming to kill us, weren't they? Your husband told me later."

I nodded. "I was in for it too. I knew too much. As long as I could swear to the time of that shot over the phone without realising how I heard it, I was safe. But I became too curious. I was to be removed along with you and Jimmy."

"Inspector Matheson told me their plan was to use Nurse Stone as the scapegoat. She drank, you know. She was terribly jealous of anyone who interfered with Jimmy."

"Don't I know it!" I said ruefully. "I mistook her for my true enemy. She gave me a nasty moment or two in the wood. I thought she was after my blood then. But how was Nurse Stone to be saddled with the deaths of the three of us?"

"I think the idea was that she killed us in a fit of drunken jealousy."

"Easy enough to plant some incriminating evidence on a tipsy woman," I remarked thoughtfully. "It might have worked. I wonder if she was to be blamed for your father-in-law's death after the abortive attempt to give Cruikshank that role?"

Safe and cared for in my own house, I could now view Mrs Ames' plan in a detached fashion.

So much for the final scene. I did not pump Yvonne for any further information. Just then I did not consider it necessary. I thought I knew who had done the actual killing, the murders of Holland and Cruikshank; who was the brilliant organizer of the whole affair. The partner to whom Mrs Ames had referred without actually mentioning a name. All I wanted to do was to fill in the gaps and make the whole picture complete in every detail.

II

Another piece of the jigsaw puzzle was supplied that very morning when Sister Heather called. She was followed by Doctor Trefont himself. My rude health left him rather at a loss for something to say. As Connie Bellamy had warned me, he had no bedside manner. He did not indulge in any of the usual time-passing tricks of his trade such as pulse-taking or respiration. Some medicos test your heart if you complain of a pain in your big toe. We exchanged pleasantries for a while, but I seized the opportunity when he began to talk of the trouble he was having with his car.

"Backfiring again, doctor?" I asked slyly. He looked blank a moment before he read the reason for my significant tone.

"I fear I owe you an apology," I went on. "I didn't trust you. But it was your own fault, or perhaps I should have said your car's. If you hadn't admitted being in the vicinity of the Hall the night Mr Holland was killed, I would never have had the slightest doubts about your integrity. On top of that admission, you and Sister Heather seemed to be playing a too discreet game with me."

Sister Heather gave me her gentle smile. "It wasn't so much that we were being discreet, Mrs Matheson. Unfortunately, our part of the game, as you term it, was being played in the dark."

I said to the doctor: "You suspected someone wanting to harm the Holland baby. Wasn't that person Mrs Ames?"

He nodded: "It was. But suspicion and proof are poles apart."

"My fault," said Sister Heather. "I couldn't give Doctor Trefont more help than an odd notion I had got into my head. I have a very good memory for faces and people's characteristics. When Mrs Ames called for the first and only time at the Centre, I was struck by a sharp memory of an obstetric case I had once attended. I was only a probationer at the time, but it had always stuck in the back of my mind. It happened years ago at a Bush Nursing Hospital. A woman was brought in late one night in labour. It was the first delivery I had witnessed. I remember the child was a girl. Although as I have said I was only training and therefore on the lowest rung of a nursing career, the doctor and midwife called me over to see the child. The poor little thing had a terrible birthmark on one cheek."

"Where was this hospital?"

Sister Heather told me the name of the town. I recalled it at once. It was one of the many outlying towns Mr Holland had visited during the last few days before his death.

"Do you remember the mother's name?" I asked Sister Heather.

"Not specifically. It was Smith or Jones or one of those similar names, so obviously assumed. I learned, however, that the woman was a bit of a mystery character. She had appeared from nowhere only six months before the baby's birth and taken a house in the town. No-one knew who she was or where she came from. She lived very quietly. Although she was friendly enough, it was impossible to get her to unbend about herself. Of course there was a bit of talk after the baby arrived, but she didn't seem to care. However, it all came out after her death a few years later that her morals were quite in order and that the baby had no stigma on its name."

"These small towns!" I said with feeling. "What happened to the child?"

"It was sent away when the mother knew she was dying. I never heard any more about it until—"

"Until the day Harriet Ames walked into the Health Centre," I supplied.

"That's right. I was interested when she told me where she came from. But she shut up like a clam when I tried to question her further, and never repeated her visit. I got in touch with a friend of those early days. After a length of time and trouble I learned that the mystery woman's real name had turned out to be Holland. I became troubled. You see, it was just then that the Holland baby started to get sick. I had heard a rumour about Mr Holland and how it was suspected that his wife had left him. It was impossible not to start wondering and worrying what was going on at the Hall. If the Holland baby was to die, it meant that the child Mrs Ames brought for my inspection that day at the Health Centre would be old Mr Holland's heir.

"I knew Doctor Trefont of old. He had once attended Yvonne Holland. I went to him and told my story, thinking he might be able to do something."

The doctor threw out his hands. "As you know, Mrs Matheson," he said ruefully, "I could do nothing. I was in complete disfavour with both Mr Holland and Yvonne."

"You took a blood test of young Jimmy and diagnosed lead poisoning," I said with approval.

"That's as far as I got, I'm afraid. I still don't know how Mrs Ames was administering the stuff to the baby, or even how she got hold of it."

It was my moment. It always makes one feel good to be able to tell someone else their own business.

"The dummy!" I announced in triumph. "Nurse Stone belongs to the old, old school and insisted upon it. The poison was mixed with a malt extract and smeared on the bulb. Mrs Ames did all the catering for the Hall."

Sister Heather looked disapproving. "I didn't know Mrs Holland permitted one of those things to be given to her baby." Doctor Trefont asked: "What made you think of the dummy?"

"It didn't require very much cleverness on my part," I admitted. "It was rather thrust at me by a stroke of luck." I told them how I had thrown the comforter away over the golf course.

"For a while Jimmy seemed to pick up. I bet Mrs Ames was sore at my interference. However, Nurse Stone played into her hands by asking her to get another one, and the fun started all over again. Then by some extraordinary chance Tony picked up the original dummy. He took a fancy to it, and helped himself to the jar of comforter smear I had confiscated from Yvonne. His precocity frightens me still. Mrs Ames learned of its whereabouts through Daisy Potts-Power, who saw Tony with it in his mouth. Daisy was taking a golfing lesson from Ames that day. When Tony was off-colour she became frightened and tried to get the dummy back.

"Actually she gave herself away. For it was only after I was searching for some reason why anyone should break in and turn the nursery topsy-turvy that I chanced on the beastly thing. I took a sample of the malt to the local chemist, who arranged an analysis. It was on the same day that I came to suspect Mrs Ames. I overheard her ordering a prescription in a very professional manner. On looking into her record, it might be found that she had made a study of pharmacology."

Doctor Trefont was tremendously interested. When I told him that the chemist still had the jar of malt and a copy of the report, he made no apology about cutting his professional visit short and departing to confer with Jenkins. Sister Heather gave me a sedative and ordered me to settle down for another nap. I could get up after lunch.

I was just feeling warm and drowsy and ready to relax into a deep sleep when Ernest Mulqueen put his head in the window. I sat up with a start.

He raised one hand. "Don't be scared. It's only me. I had to see you for a minute."

"Do come in," I invited.

Ernest Mulqueen shook his head. "Don't think I will. I wasn't made for a sick room. I'll stay here if you don't mind, and say my piece through the window. Do you remember the last time I saw you?"

I drew my brows together. So much had happened that I was in no position to work out riddles.

"The day after the old man was shot. In the wood. Before I landed in jug," he explained quite happily. I was glad to see that "jug" had not robbed him of his old bounce. Indeed, the experience appeared to have made him more buoyant.

I remembered at once and realized why his sudden appearance had startled me out of all proportion. At our last meeting Ernest Mulqueen had looked as though he wanted to strike me.

"What about it?" I asked cautiously.

"I could have belted the hide off of you for your cheek," I was informed quite without rancour. "I want to say I am sorry now. I was worried that day. I'd talked too much. I always do. A bad habit, but I'm a plain man and I talk straight. You knew about the agreement I had with the old man. I thought you'd put your hubby on to it."

"You mean the document you told me you had signed giving up your farm?"

"That's right."

"You've no need to worry," I assured him. "They couldn't find it."

He grinned slyly. "Of course they couldn't. I stole it."

I looked at him half-fearfully, half in amazement at his candour. His next words were to startle me more.

"You see, I came across the old man dead. I could have told the chuckle-headed police that he wasn't shot at the time they said. Sorry again. Forgot about your hubby; no offence meant."

I said in my most disapproving voice, forgetting my own lapses: "It was your duty to report your finding at once to the police."

"And get myself arrested instead of detained? Not me! Anyway, I wasn't sorry to see the old man dead. The gun in his hand didn't deceive me either. James thought the world would stop turning if he wasn't in it to give it a spin or two. It suited me better to keep quiet. I had other things to attend to."

"Tell me," I said curiously. "Was it you slinking up the drive that night? We saw someone amongst the trees."

"I didn't want to be seen. As a matter of fact that pansy chap Yvonne and Ursula are so mad about chased after me. But I was able to give him the slip. I knew where I could find the agreement. It was up in the old man's bedroom. Then I remembered about Ursie. She'd been playing for some extra cash, and I didn't blame her much. She never had much to splurge. The old man believed in keeping us all more or less dependent on him. I tore out a few pages of the account book and took them along with the agreement to be destroyed."

"Your wife nearly gave the show away," I told him. "She heard someone in Mr Holland's room and thought it was he. But of course after he was found dead it couldn't have been."

The roundness of his jolly face suddenly hardened into a square shape. The change was fascinating. I could well imagine the same transition taking place when he came across Elizabeth Mulqueen with Nugent Parsons in the wood.

I had been tactless in mentioning her name. The little man left me abruptly. Although there was nothing more to be said—he had spoken his "piece"—I could have done with more of his bracing conversation.

I lay back again, trying to recapture the warm drowsy feeling Ernest Mulqueen had terminated so abruptly. My mind turned idly from speculating on the future relations between Ernest and Elizabeth Mulqueen to a relative subject. That of the signal light from the tower. Mrs Mulqueen was the inaugurator of the idea, and Harriet Ames had adopted it. She had recognized in it an admirable means of communicating with that partner of hers, whose name was ever in the back of my mind but about whose actual identity I was still in error.

That some of my movements had been the subject of the signalling I had no doubt whatsoever. It had been Mrs Ames who had stalked me that night at the Hall when I had gone to answer Yvonne's call to see Jimmy. It had been she who had listened to me talking to John concerning the time on the telegram and who had watched me as I studied the portrait of Olivia in Elizabeth Mulqueen's sitting-room. Thinking I might return to study the picture again and recognize a likeness either to herself or Robin, she took it away to destroy. She had observed all my movements from the very beginning and had estimated at every one how much I had learned. My curiosity became dangerous. With the breaking of the time of the murder known to the police, my presence, which had once been necessary for the killer's alibi, was regarded as a menace. The string across the Hall drive was hastily prepared. I was to be frightened off the scene. When Mrs Ames found I was not so easily deterred she made another attempt, this time more ruthless than the first.

III

I learned my mistake from Connie Bellamy when she called that afternoon. Stunned and grieved by the revelation of the second person John had arrested, I was helpless against Connie's vicarious excitement. She was completely untouched by the reality of the Middleburn crimes. With an envious eye she regarded me in the same light as one of her long-suffering screen heroines.

"My dear, how frightfully odd that you did not know. I heard that your husband actually arrested him here in this house. He was coming to kill you. How marvellous that you escaped, but I daresay your husband would have caught him just the same. I was speaking to Marion over the phone. Of course, you remember Marion Parkes, our dramatic coach at the Community Centre, don't you, Maggie? Well, she thinks it a marvellous idea if you could make the whole thing into a play. Marion would produce it and of course you could have the leading part. What do you think?"

"Connie," I said. "Please go now. Forgive me, but I have a shocking headache."

"My dear, let me get you something. It may be your eyes, Maggie, you know. Do you eat carrots? Such a potent source of vitamin A. I hope Yvonne is managing properly. I'll pop in and give her a few tips as I leave."

I caught my breath and started to laugh silently. "Connie, you're impossible."

Connie's eyes goggled at me in apprehension. "I hope you are not going to be hysterical, Maggie. So unlike you, my dear. Perhaps I had better go now. I'd love to stay and chat, but you know how I must avoid everything unpleasant just now."

I saw her out and then went back to the lounge-room again. I was sitting in front of the fire when John came in. I jumped up at once, but he stood in the doorway watching me. He looked thoroughly weary, but relaxed and unconcerned.

"Hullo," I said. "I had something to tell you this morning, but you'd gone."

"What was it?" he asked, taking off his coat and scarf and throwing them on to the nearest chair.

"I don't hate you, after all."

"That's good."

"In fact, I like you—very much."

"That's better still. Sorry I was brutal last night." He came over towards the fire.

"You nearly broke my jaw—and my heart."

John gripped my outstretched hands tightly.

"Tell me about the case," I said presently. "It was old man Ames, wasn't it? Connie told me. I was so certain it was his son."

John began to fill his pipe with his free hand. "The case goes back a long way, Maggie. The foundation of the Middleburn crimes was laid when James Holland's wife, Olivia, left him. Or perhaps even before that. The killer was someone who belonged to the same generation as the Squire. Charles Ames was the originator and organizer of the whole plan, but he had a worthy accessory in his daughter-in-law, Harriet."

I lifted my head. "Do you mean to say Harriet's husband knew nothing whatsoever?"

"It is hard to credit, but if you stop to consider Robert Ames' character you will know why. There is a superficial quality in him. As we know, he does most things well; perfect, but without imagination. There is no broad vision in his mind. Every move Robert made that seemed incriminating was at the suggestion either of his wife or his father. Had Charles Ames confided in him he probably would have been shocked by any suggestion that the positions of the two families should be reversed. For that was Charles Ames' ambition right from the beginning. For years he had been jealous of James Holland's position and wealth and the influence he wielded. He could not see why the Squire and his descendants should have more of this world's gain and power than his own family. So when Olivia

Holland appealed to him for friendship out of sheer desperation and lack of anyone else, there began the first glimmerings of a plan to achieve ascendancy over Holland.

"Although not in love with Olivia, he despised James Holland's attitude towards his wife. Ruthlessness was completely foreign to his own intelligent approach towards ambition. No matter how insignificant their position, people could always be put to some use by a superior brain.

"Olivia had started a second child. She made up her mind to leave James Holland's despotism and bring it up by herself. Charles Ames helped her run away and hide herself in the country. Later when she was dying, Olivia communicated with Ames and he came and took the child, Harriet, to be cared for elsewhere. Whether in later years it was persuasion, propinquity or a happy chance that caused a daughter of Holland to bestow her hand on his son, I do not know.

"Although I say that the foundation of the crimes was laid years ago, it was not until recently that the actual temptation came Charles Ames' way. Fate seemed to be forcing him along when James Holland's son was killed in a plane smash. He knew what the old man's will would be. The money and estates were to go to the nearest male descendant. Between the Ames family and the Holland position and wealth was a puny, delicate baby, Holland's other grandson. Harriet Ames undertook to remove that barrier."

"Did you know about that all the time?" I asked crossly.

"Not as soon as you did," John said in a soothing voice. "Thanks for getting the stuff analysed. Cornell picked up the report after you left the chemist's shop."

"Never again will I play amateur detective. Go on."

"Affairs were going well for Charles Ames until he was forced to take in another partner. If I ever turn to crime, which is the silliest thing anyone could do, may I never make the mistake of joining forces with an accessory after the fact. It invariably leads to more strife than one is guaranteed or willing to weather. The partner in this instance was Cruikshank the estate agent.

"Cruikshank had been playing around with some of the Holland interests. When James Holland had him up for an account of his stewardship, he tried to blackmail his way out of it by threatening to expose the old scandal of Olivia's flight. He even hinted that Olivia had had another child. Cruikshank was one of those village busybodies who always know more than is good for them. His hint was enough to send the squire off to trace this mysterious daughter. Cruikshank, on the other hand, was none too happy about the outcome of his attempted bluff, and when Ames offered him a hideout he welcomed it with open arms. Ames did not want him to spread the rumour about the daughter any more than he wanted Holland to trace his child to his very Lodge.

"Fate again was pushing him along. The telegram announcing Holland's homecoming was taken over the telephone by Harriet Ames, who withheld the exact time of arrival.

"This is where you and I came into the game. Getting the Dower was an extraordinary piece of luck for us. I am inclined to think it would never have come about if you hadn't given Holland my official card. It occurred to him how useful it would be to have the police on his doorstep and thereby under his influence. He could do a lot with the police on his side. I forbear comment on these, his probable thoughts.

"James Holland had always been dissatisfied with the verdict of his son's death. Someone must be made to pay for it.

"The plane smash could not have been a mere accident. An enemy must have organized it in an attempt to sabotage the Holland plan of life.

"Then Cruikshank spilled his story of Olivia's daughter. It came as a shock to Holland—but no more than that. He was not interested in females; not enough to make him leave all to search for his missing daughter and bring her into the bosom of the family. But he brooded on Cruikshank's information. Suddenly it occurred to him that she might consider herself heiress to the Holland fortune. This was out of the question by the ruling of his will, but this elusive daughter would not know that. Supposing she had engineered her brother's accident, and was waiting the time to step in and claim the Holland estate.

"The longer Holland brooded, the more he became convinced that his daughter had deliberately caused Jim Holland's plane to crash. Here at last was someone to blame! Someone on whom to be revenged.

"His first move was to get in touch with me. Unfortunately I was out when he rang. Cruikshank must have had information as to where Olivia Holland went after her flight, and told this to James Holland to lend support to his story.

"The Squire went off at once to trace his late wife's movements. I think he must have dashed off a letter first, asking me to look into the matter also. Charles Ames or Harriet saw to it that I never got the note. That is the only way I can account for my name on the blotting-pad.

"That letter was the starting point from which Ames built up his alibi. It had been spread about that Holland would be home at seven. He wired to Holland in my name to call in at the Dower on his way home, hinting that I had something of importance to tell him concerning Jim Holland's death."

"I remember that wire when I was checking messages at the Post Office," I interrupted, with some chagrin. "I thought the postmaster was joking when he said you had sent one to the Squire."

"I am afraid you could almost be considered an accessory too, my pet. The offer of a game of golf was your undoing. Tony didn't matter, but you had to be removed out of the Dower when the Squire called."

"I wonder what they said to each other," I remarked thoughtfully. "Father facing strange daughter."

"Harriet Ames refuses to talk about it," John answered. "But she detained him here for as long as the plan necessitated. Mindful of his dinner party and the fact that he could see me later, Holland then started on his walk through his artificial wood.

"This is where I take my hat off to Ames for his cleverness. He had to supply an alibi for himself and Mrs Ames in case of accidents— the death was to look like suicide. He allowed a minimum of time in which to do the actual murder by setting the stage so as to avoid delay. This was accomplished by using Mulqueen's fox-trap. A silencer was affixed to the gun stolen earlier from James Holland's study, then removed, and the gun placed in the dead man's hand. The other gun of the pair Holland had bought and which Robert Ames kept at the Lodge was used to fire the shot you heard relayed over the extension telephone line between the Hall and Dower House; about which time Charles Ames was playing chess and Harriet Ames had gullible, vague Maud Cruikshank for company.

"So far, so good. In fact, it was just about perfect. The only snag was Cruikshank. Was he to be trusted? Evidently not.

"After a while Cruikshank realized he had bitten off more than he could chew. It was one thing to go pinching another man's money, but quite another to become involved in the murder of the same man. Ames kept a strict eye on his unwilling partner."

"I saw him one night at the Lodge," I interrupted again.

"Cruikshank's feet became colder and colder. When Ames suspected him of wanting to turn informer after his several attempts to contact me, Cruikshank had to leave the happy partnership. This second murder was clumsier than the first. It too was meant to look like suicide but it would not have deceived a child. Ames did not have the time to conceive a better plan. His alibi for that night had as many holes in it as a colander.

"He had started to consider the police easily duped. The greatest mistake is to consider the police fools, Maggie. Our methods may not be as dramatic as fiction would have them, as we don't play to an audience.

"Criminal investigation can be systematized just as much as debits and credits in a ledger. A certain amount of investigation is mainly paperwork. Items of information actual and suspect are all amassed. Unfortunately in this case suspicion was one thing and proof quite another. And that is where, though it hurts me to confess it, you did a grand job.

"I told Cornell to let you have a free hand, but always to be on guard. Your inimitable capacity for meddling helped us to set the trap."

"Just the bait," I commented without rancour.

We watched the leaping fire for a while in silence. It grew brighter as the daylight faded and the mist came up from the creek to end another perfect autumn day.

"And he quoted Tennyson at me," I said. "The old hypocrite."

"No, Maggie, you are wrong about Charles Ames. The old man really thought a new order at the Hall would be better. The Squire had corrupted enough of Middleburn."

The door of the lounge-room opened. I sat up quickly as Yvonne, flushed and smiling, came in. Behind her was Alan Braithwaite, bearing a tray of glasses in one hand and a gold-topped bottle wrapped in a white cloth in the other.

"This has a wedding atmosphere about it," I remarked, and saw Yvonne's flush deepen. She nodded happily, slipping her hand through Braithwaite's arm.

"Champagne always tastes like vinegar and water to me. Is there any beer?" John asked, as he took the long envelope Alan held out to him.

"This is an important occasion," I said, frowning at him. "Yvonne and Alan are engaged. What's this?" John had taken a document out of the envelope and put it on my knee. "That," said John, "is for being a good girl. The title deeds of the Dower House."

THE END

AN INTERVIEW WITH JUNE WRIGHT (1996)

Lucy Sussex

I interviewed June Wright in 1996, when working as a researcher for Stephen Knight's history of Australian crime fiction, Continent of Mystery. *At the time, she seemed a relic from another era. Of her contemporaries, the Australian crime writers active when she began writing in the 1940s: Arthur Upfield, Carter Brown, A. E. Martin, the Goyder sisters (who wrote as Margot Neville), June Wright was the only one still alive, and very much kicking. The previous month I had written to the Goyders' nephew and received a long and informative letter about his aunts. But it was nothing like meeting the living, talking writer. Here was an opportunity not to be missed.*

As June Wright had not been active as a crime novelist for thirty years, I was not quite sure what to expect. It did not help that my car misbehaved on the freeway, so I arrived rather bothered as well as nervous. The lady who answered my knock belonged to the category of the elegant elderly—well coiffed and, as I would find, as sharp as tacks. She was instantly identifiable from the PR photos of decades earlier, although she introduced herself by saying I probably wouldn't recognise her. "I recognised your nose," I said, not altogether tactfully. She laughed: "Horse-faced!" We got on just fine after that. I began by asking June about her background and early history.

LS: I know from an interview in the *Post* (28/3/48) with Frank Doherty that you were born June Healy. Doherty remembered you from school as a 'shy little girl'. Was this true?

JW: Well, it's nice to be known as a shy little girl. I think I was rather a pert little girl, from memory.

I was born in 1919 and I will be seventy-seven within the next couple of weeks. Born in Melbourne, and lived most of my life in Melbourne—Malvern. I had two brothers, one sister. I was the youngest of four. My father was in the public service, in the Audit Office. I started off in the Brigidine convent in Malvern, and then we went to Adelaide, because my father was moved there. I went to the Loreto convent in Adelaide, and then when we came back I finished my schooling at Mandeville Hall.

There's been a tremendous upheaval in Australia and I've been witness to the extraordinary changes that have been taking place, from my young days to the present time. To visualise that world that I was born into and grew up in and went to school in—it's absolutely at variance with today's society.

LS: Do you recall the crime fiction you read when young?

JW: Agatha Christie, Dorothy Sayers, Marjorie Allingham—the women. [Mignon] Eberhart was a favourite: she was rather a romantic crime writer, but very entertaining. There was a series called the Crime Club, either Collins or Heinemann ran it. If you went to the library, you'd look for a book with the sign 'Crime Club Book', because they published only good crime writers.

LS: When did you start writing?

JW: I wrote my first story when I was about four . . . I think I always wanted to be a writer. One of my grandfathers, who died before I was born [Daniel Newham] . . . he was the son of the first Church of England clergyman at St Peters, East Melbourne. I came across a manuscript that he had started. It was obviously going to be the great Australian, definitive novel, but he didn't go on with it. That was an inspiration. I always thought to myself, now I'd love to be able to justify his ambition by finishing something myself *and* having it published. But I never dreamt that I *would* get it published.

LS: In the *Post* interview, you said you came across the advertisement for Hutchinson's novel competition [which closed in June 1944] in a newspaper while wrapping up vegetable scraps.

JW: It was really a stroke of luck. I'd written this manuscript and one night I was preparing the dinner—my husband and I, we lived in Ashburton—and I was putting the potato peelings and the pease pods and things into a sheet of paper. All of a sudden there was a little paragraph. Hutchinson's of London were offering a competition for all stages and types of writing and there was a section for crime. And I thought: well, this is it! I'll have a crack at this. So I sent the manuscript over to them.

I wrote it in longhand, I can't think onto a typewriter . . . I've still got the original manuscript here, actually. In those days it was wartime and it was very difficult to get anything typed, but I managed to hire a typewriter. It had a very, very faded ribbon on it, so consequently I had to bang each key terribly hard. It was very badly set out but whoever read it . . . Evidently it caught the reader's fancy. In time I had an air letter from London. It was the most thrilling experience of my life to get this letter!

LS: In the 1940s, when you began to be published, there were a few other Australian women writing crime. Margot Neville [the sisters Margot Goyder and Ann Neville Joske] turned to crime writing in the 40s. Did you know about these writers? Read them? Ever meet them?

JW: Margot Neville, I know that name. I don't remember them.

LS: Also Jean Spender, who was the wife of Sir Percy.

JW: Oh really? That's interesting, that's why she was asked . . . I went to Sydney for publicity purposes. At that time—this was just after the war—there was a certain Lord Mountevans who came out here with his wife—he was Evans of the Broke, who went down to the South Pole. And Mr Spender was there, and so was his wife. I've got a photograph somewhere or other, with me standing alongside them. I didn't realise that was who she was. It was a very formal luncheon, really it was in honour of Lord Mountevans. I was alongside . . . the publicist was getting a little bit of publicity for me. That was how it was. He was the star attraction.

LS: She was a very striking looking woman, from the photos.

JW [*emphatic*]: She was a pretty woman, yes.

LS: You've said that the idea for *Murder in the Telephone Exchange* came while you were working in the Melbourne exchange, because people said 'you could write a book about this place'.

JW: It was, it was quite remarkable.

LS: Why did you write about it using the form of detective fiction?

JW: Aha! Here comes the answer. And it is true, too. The Exchange, I found, was a very exciting place to be in, because all sorts of dramatic things could and did happen. I was there when, at the beginning of the war, there was an aeroplane accident and we lost several very important men, including army commanders . . . I was there during the very bad bushfires of 1939. We were involved with all those dramatic events. So I thought the best way to convey that sense of drama and urgency was to put it into the context of a murder story.

LS: The other Australian women crime writers I mentioned earlier were Sydney-based, but you're definitely a Melburnian. And proud of it.

JW: Very!

LS: There's a very strong sense of place in your writing, similar to Fergus Hume's *The Mystery of the Hansom Cab*.

JW: Actually this same grandfather I mentioned knew Fergus Hume. See, Melbourne was a very small place—even in my day. We knew everyone and everyone knew everyone else, or knew of them, or knew the family.

[*Here I bring out a photocopy of a page from the 1985 edition of* Bookmark *(the annual publication of the Australian Library Promotion Council), which reprints two of June Wright's book covers and also a quote by the author, part of which she reads aloud*]:

[June Wright believes that Australian novelists] should not be self-conscious about giving their stories local settings . . . Good heavens!

LS: Did you say that?

JW: Oh yes. Especially then . . . this was late 1940s, early 1950s, and the writing in those days *was* self-conscious.

LS: They were a bit precious, dragging in the kookaburras?

JW: Yes, kookaburras and kangaroos down Collins Street. Instead of writing about something and its background, people would almost apologise for the background, or for the setting. In my book I considered that you just want to write absolutely naturally, and if people don't know what the background is, they can jolly well find out for themselves. And that's how it should be.

We were an evolving nation, becoming more sophisticated, more open to world ideas. I tried to introduce that note, that we were on the world stage, as much as any other country.

That's another thing that one should always do, you really should write about the things that you know. There's a story in everyone's life.

LS: You published *Murder in the Telephone Exchange* in 1948, *So Bad a Death* the following year, and *The Devil's Caress* in 1952. Was that all from the impetus of the original acceptance, or did they contract you to write more?

JW: The contract was for three books, with Hutchinson's.

LS: What were the terms of that contract?

JW: I can't remember now. The money was lovely, because it came out in English pounds . . . the rate increased by a quarter or a half or something at the time. That was very welcome.

LS: Your first detective is Maggie Byrnes—single, working at the telephone exchange. She gets mixed up in murder and ends up marrying John Matheson, a policeman. In *So Bad a Death*, they're married, with a small son, trying to buy a house in the suburbs . . .Was that a particular suburb, or just any outer suburb?

JW: No, it was Ashburton. During the war all building stopped, so consequently Ashburton then was more or less an isolated township. The railway line wasn't there—to get there we used to have to get to Camberwell and take a small train, which travelled across the empty paddocks, which is now Jordanville, all those places. Out here to Glen Waverly, which was the last [stop] on the line. Asburton was the last village really, on the outskirts of Melbourne. It was terribly hard to find a house. Very difficult for young people who got married after the war.

LS: The striking image in that book is the old estate, very British-style, which is being encroached upon by suburbia.

JW: That place still exists, in High Street Road. If you drive down, you'll see a square tower. That was once the homestead for a big area. How I knew about it originally was that many many years ago when I used to go horseriding, they had a riding school there, three sisters called Desailly used to run it. And all that area, for acres and acres surrounding, was just open paddock, around this big house with its square tower. It's very hard, even in my mind's eye, to remember all those wide open paddocks.

LS: Did you feel that Maggie as a protagonist could only go so far, fictionally? You abandoned her after two books.

JW: Yes. Maggie had come to the end of her useful life. It was [her] use-by date. It was also time to take it out of the first person into a broader canvas, using various other characters. *The Devil's Caress* was my first attempt in broadening the writing.

[*June Wright asked me to turn off the tape off this point, while she told me she got tired of people assuming Maggie was autobiographical. That said, she let me turn the tape on again.*]

LS: Good title.

JW: Rubbish!

LS: When I took your books out from the library, the checkout assistant said: 'Good titles!'

JW: 'Doubt is the Devil's caress.' I don't know where I came across that quotation. Funnily enough, I've always found [it] rather hard to think of a good title.

LS: Shakespeare.

JW: Or the Bible. *So Bad a Death* was a title from Shakespeare.

LS: I understand it was originally called *Who Would Murder a Baby?*

JW: They didn't like that title.

LS: *The Devil's Caress* is the interim book between your two series characters, Maggie and Mother Paul. You have a young woman doctor as protagonist. Did you research that medical background?

JW: Yes. At the time I had a woman pediatrician for my children, she was a wonderful doctor. She became very interested in what I had written. She gave me quite a lot of help.

LS: Stephen Knight described the book as a psychological thriller.

JW: It was supposed to be, too. I was taking myself a little bit too seriously at that stage.

LS: I got the impression it was written more hurriedly than the other two.

JW: Possibly it was, because I had a few more children at that stage. I had to fulfil a contract with the publisher and hurry it along.

LS: So *Bad a Death* must be the only novel in which poison is administered via a baby's dummy. There's a lot of talk in it about the correct way to rear a child—was this the era of officious childrearing?

JW: Doctor Truby King reigned supreme in those days, and we were all very conscientious mothers, bringing up our babies and caring for our children according to the book. No doubt that was reflected in the story.

LS: This leads to your family. You wrote your first three novels despite having four children under six.

JW: Four children under *four*. I had a son, and a daughter, and then twin boys. And then after a space of eight years I had another daughter and another son.

LS: Several times you've commented that writing murder fiction was a good way of dealing with homicidal impulses towards children.

JW: That was another line I used to shoot. Instead of wringing the children's necks, I'd take it out on the typewriter.

LS: You had roughly the same number of books as children.

JW: Six books, six children. Six brain children, six physical children.

LS: Kathy Lette has stated that every time a woman writer has a baby, she loses one or two books, in terms of time and energy. What do you think of this comment?

JW: Oh I agree. I agree wholeheartedly, because your vitality as a mother is used on your children, and a similar vitality is needed for writing. It's an exhausting business. Writing is almost as exhausting as looking after children. It's an emotional exhaustion.

LS: In the late 40s and 50s, you had some news coverage in which the journalists seemed quite incredulous that you could write and manage a family at the same time.

JW: The press was always very kind to me, actually. There was only one occasion when I got bad press and that was a reviewer in Sydney—at one point of the review of the particular book, he suggested it would be a very good idea if I went to bed and let the children have the typewriter. But in those days you didn't reply to your critics, which I think is good policy. It deprives the public of a lot of fun, of course—witness the Darville/Demidenko saga—but if you don't reply to a critic they have nothing more to go on, you don't feed them any more information. My minder wouldn't let me reply. I was highly indignant, I was going to write a letter demanding an apology, but my minder at the time, he said: 'No. You don't reply.'

LS: This was the PR person for Hutchinson's?

JW: Hutchinson's had an office here in Melbourne, and this man was handling all the publicity. He pointed me in the right direction and stood on my toe if I was saying something out of place.

LS: Did you do any radio work at all?

JW: Oh, quite a lot.

LS: Did you appear on radio or write for the radio?

JW: I appeared on the radio, just interview stuff.

LS: So they were publicising you quite a bit. And you, despite saying that writers should be read and not seen . . .

JW: . . . Not seen, nor heard, just read.

LS: But you managed to do it?

JW: Yes, but it was always an effort. I was on television a couple of times. I was on *Tell the Truth*. It was an American program in which there were three people, and one of them is the real person. There was a jury and they had to question the three people and find out which was the real writer. That was rather good fun, really, because all I had to do was sit there and look dumb, which wasn't a difficult job, and these other two women, who were on with me, they lied like mad, you see, and I had to tell the truth. And we won, too.

LS: Did you tuck this information away for use in *Make-up for Murder*?

JW: Yes, quite a lot, because I also did a couple of interviews on Channel 2 and Channel 7. Oh yes, I picked up a bit of background information.

LS: In your early interviews you described how you wrote—in the evening, after dinner, washing up and putting the children to bed.

JW: I would sit down and write, or rather struggle to write. It would have been [five days a week]. It's very hard to remember now. I think I used to set myself a certain number of words every night. See, *Murder in the Telephone Exchange*, the first one, I ran hot on that. I wrote that in six weeks. But the others became more laborious, and my time was at a premium, so I had to pace myself, give myself so many words to write.

LS: That would be after a full day of housework, cooking, childcare, which started at 6.30 every day, except for washday, when it was 5.30, you said.

JW: Deadly dull, when you come to think of it. Which was all the more reason why I wrote, because of that secret world. Wonderful!

LS: After *The Devil's Caress*, it was six years before *Reservation for Murder* appeared, in 1958. What happened? I notice you had a different publisher.

JW: Actually it was the same. Hutchinson's split up into various subsidiary companies, and John Long was the one looking after the crime writers. So it really was the same.

I wrote one [book] and they knocked it back, it wasn't suitable. And then I tried somewhere else with it, but I couldn't get it published. It really wasn't good enough, and I knew it wasn't good enough. And then I let it go for a couple of years and then I started on Hostel for Homicide, which was *Reservation for Murder*. Hostel was a much better title, I thought, but the publishers wanted Reservation. They thought [mine] was too American-sounding. Homicide, of course, has become a commonplace word now.

LS: Were they interventionist, asking you to rewrite a lot?

JW: Not a lot, but there was a certain amount of rewriting. I remember after the twins were born, I sat up in bed in St Vincent's maternity hospital, and did the revision there. It was a wonderful opportunity, actually, plenty of time. Plenty of uninterrupted time. That was the great drawback with children, finding the uninterrupted time.

LS: *Reservation for Murder* introduced Mother Paul, your nun detective. The first nun detective was introduced by Anthony Boucher, writing as H. H. Holmes, in the 1940s.

JW: Oh really?

LS: Julian Symons described Mother Paul as 'Father Brown's niece'. Had you been reading G. K. Chesterton?

JW: No, I hadn't.

LS: Mother Paul is a great character.

JW: She was a dear. I was sorry that I stopped writing, because of her—because it would have been a very interesting time to write about nuns, especially the transition from the enclosed orders out into the outside world, with these feisty nuns that there are around today.

LS: Nuns can be tough characters.

JW: And the modern day nun is even more so, because she's highly intelligent, highly sophisticated—in the right sort of way—and has knocked around a bit in the outside world, and yet she's retained a certain innocence and integrity that probably is part and parcel of belonging to a religious order.

What led me into that was that I read an interview with Arthur Upfield. He said that for any mystery story writer, one of the pre-requisites would be to select an unusual detective. He had Napoleon Bonaparte. And I thought to myself: Right! I know nuns, I'll make a nun a detective.

LS: You seem a very female-centric writer, finding drama in mother's clubs, hostels, school committees. *Reservation* was described as 'fresh and original' in its setting, a hostel for businesswomen. Was it a case of writing about what you knew?

JW: Writing about what I knew.

LS: Symons called Mother Paul 'very readable'—high praise for him.

JW: A very nice comment.

LS: What were your reviews like?

JW: They were all good. There was a man who used to write for the *Herald*, he used to do a crime book review every Saturday. A. R. MacIlwain. He was very rigid in his ideas of how a detective story should be constructed—the reader should be able to solve the crime along with the writer. One book I had something or other—forget what it was now. He took umbrage at this and he wrote me a letter, more in sorrow than in anger, that I'd used a trick. You should never, ever trick the reader. He had his ideas.

LS: Do you have any favourites among your books?

JW: Mother Paul, because she was a composite of many nuns that I knew.

LS: Can you talk a bit about *Faculty of Murder?* Did you have a Melbourne University connection? Were your children going to the university?

JW: That's where I got it all from. A friend of mine who wrote for radio, she lived in a college. St Mary's Hall.

LS: I read that you said you deliberately set the site of your college in the middle of the Melbourne General Cemetery.

JW: That's right, on Cemetery Road. Newman College I called Manning College. There was Cardinal Manning and there was Cardinal Newman, so . . .

Actually that one went down very well with men readers. I was surprised.

LS: It was an early academic mystery, certainly the first in Australia, I believe.

JW: I would say it was, and honestly, I'll have to confess that reading Dorothy Sayers' *Gaudy Night* was partly inspiration for it.

LS: It's set in a fictional college, but I note it looks like Ormond College on the cover.

JW: Well it is. They went to immense trouble in England, whoever did the jacket got pictures of all the colleges around Melbourne University and that's what they did.

LS: So they went to a lot of trouble with the packaging of that one.

[*JW brings out a copy of* Faculty for Murder *and the associated publicity material—including a dagger book- mark, complete with blood on the blade and a bloody fingerprint*]

JW: That was the publicist's idea. We had a literary luncheon at the old Oriental Hotel in Collins Street and all the guests at the luncheon got a bookmark. It was a publicity stunt.

LS: But nobody got stabbed in the book! Were you pleased about the packaging—covers, designs—of your books?

JW: Oh yes. Always. I didn't think *not* to be pleased. The first book that came out, it was just unbelievable. Little me, writing a book! Published! People are going to read it!

LS: Why did you stop writing?

JW: My husband had a bit of a breakdown, and then he thought he'd try to run a business, a cleaning business, because he had worked as an accountant for a cleaning firm. You never make money writing—publishers do, but writers never make very much money. So I thought to myself at the time, now which is it going to be? There's a good chance we could make quite a bit of money, as against pursuing a craft which is very hard and very demanding, very difficult to do—I wasn't finding it at all easy. So I just made a conscious decision that I would give the writing away, and concentrate on helping him establish this business. Which we did and he made a big success of it and we were just in it at the right time. I used to do the books and he used to manage it. We had quite a big staff, so we made quite a comfortable living. And he died in 1989, when we had just sold the business, and left me to enjoy the fruits of it.

LS: You said to me over the phone that you didn't regret giving up crime writing.

JW: No I don't—because I've got back to writing, and writing gives me immense pleasure. And I can afford to publish it myself!

LS: Read any women's crime writing recently?

JW: No. It's a bit like busman's holiday. If you drive a bus you don't take a holiday on a bus.

LS: You said earlier that you thought you wouldn't go back to crime writing.

JW: If it was easy I would, but I've got other interests now. I like writing family history. . . at the moment I'm doing my own memoirs, and I find that's enough. I do a bit of travelling, I play golf. I have a wonderful life, in fact.

MORE FROM JUNE WRIGHT

The earlier adventures of Maggie Byrnes
. . . and a previously unpublished gem

MURDER IN THE TELEPHONE EXCHANGE

When an unpopular colleague at Melbourne Central is murdered – her head bashed in with a buttinsky, a piece of equipment used to listen in on phone calls – feisty young "hello girl" Maggie Byrnes resolves to turn sleuth. Some of her co-workers are acting strangely, and Maggie is convinced she has a better chance of figuring out the killer's identity than the stodgy police team assigned to the case, who seem to think she herself might have had something to do with it. But then one of her friends is murdered too, and it looks like Maggie is next in line.

Narrated with verve and wit, this is a mystery in the tradition of Dorothy L. Sayers, by turns entertaining and suspenseful, and building to a gripping climax. It also offers an evocative account of Melbourne in the early postwar years, as young women like Maggie flocked to the big city, leaving behind small-town family life for jobs, boarding houses and independence.

(336 pages, with a new introduction by Derham Groves)

DUCK SEASON DEATH

June Wright wrote this lost gem in the mid-1950s, but consigned it to her bottom drawer after her publisher foolishly rejected it. Perhaps it was just a little ahead of its time, because while it delivers a bravura twist on the classic 'country house' murder mystery, it's also a sharp-eyed and sparkling send-up of the genre.

When someone takes advantage of a duck hunt to murder publisher Athol Sefton at a remote hunting inn, it soon turns out that almost everyone, guests and staff alike, had good reason to shoot him. Sefton's nephew Charles believes he can solve the crime by applying the traditional "rules of the game" he's absorbed over years as a reviewer of detective fiction. Much to his annoyance, however, the killer doesn't seem to be playing by those rules, and Charles finds that he is the one under suspicion. *Duck Season Death* is a both a devilishly clever whodunit and a delightful entertainment.

(192 pages, with a new introduction by Derham Groves)

PETER DOYLE

Peter Doyle's crime novels, featuring irresistible antihero Billy Glasheen, brilliantly explore the criminal underworld, political corruption, and the explosion of sex, drugs, and rock'n'roll in postwar Australian life, and have earned him three Ned Kelly Awards, including a Lifetime Achievement Award in 2010. Two titles are currently available from Dark Passage, with a new novel, *The Big Whatever*, scheduled for 2015.

THE DEVIL'S JUMP

August 1945: the Japanese have surrendered and there's dancing in the streets of Sydney. But Billy Glasheen has little time to celebrate; his black marketeer boss has disappeared, leaving Billy high and dry. Soon he's on the run from the criminals and the cops, not to mention a shady private army. They all think he has the thing they want, and they'll kill to get hold of it. Unfortunately for Billy, he doesn't know what it is . . . but he'd better find it fast.

> "Peter Doyle does for Sydney what Carl Hiaasen does for Miami."
> —Shane Maloney

GET RICH QUICK

Sydney in the 1950s. Billy Glasheen is trying to make a living, any way he can. Luckily, he's a likeable guy, with a gift for masterminding elaborate scenarios—whether it's a gambling scam, transporting a fortune in stolen jewels, or keeping the wheels greased during the notorious 1957 tour by Little Richard and his rock 'n' roll entourage.

But trouble follows close behind—because Billy's schemes always seem to interfere with the plans of Sydney's big players, an unholy trinity of crooks, bent cops, and politicians on the make. Suddenly he's in the frame for murder, and on the run from the police, who'll happily send him down for it. Billy's no sleuth, but there's nowhere to turn for help. To prove it wasn't him, he'll have to find the real killer.

> "An absolute gem . . . a marvellous read and a truly distinctive piece of Australian crime writing."—*Sydney Morning Herald*

> "Think of a hopped-up James M. Cain."—*Kirkus Reviews*

ALSO FROM DARK PASSAGE BOOKS

G.S. MANSON – *Coorparoo Blues & The Irish Fandango*

Written in the spare, plain-spoken style of all great pulp fiction, G.S. Manson's series featuring 1940s Brisbane P.I. Jack Munro captures the high stakes and nervous energy of wartime, when everything becomes a matter of life and death.

BRISBANE, 1943. Overnight a provincial Australian city has become the main Allied staging post for the war in the Pacific. The tensions – social, sexual, and racial – created by the arrival of thousands of US troops are stirring up all kinds of mayhem, and Brisbane's once quiet streets are looking pretty mean.

Enter Jack Munro, a World War I veteran and ex-cop with a nose for trouble and a stubborn dedication to exposing the truth, however inconvenient it is for the -powers that be. He's not always a particularly good man, but he's the one you want on your side when things look bad.

When Jack is hired by a knockout blonde to find her no-good missing husband, he turns over a few rocks he's not supposed to. Soon the questions are piling up, and so are the bodies. But Jack forges on through the dockside bars, black-market warehouses, and segregated brothels of his roiling city, uncovering greed and corruption eating away at the foundations of the war effort.

Then Jack is hired to investigate a suspicious suicide, and there's a whole new cast of characters for him to deal with – a father surprisingly unmoved by his son's death, a dodgy priest, crooked cops, Spanish Civil War refugees – and a wall of silence between him and the truth, which has its roots deep in the past. Friends, enemies, the police – they're all warning Jack to back off. But he can't walk away from a case: he has to do the square thing.

"Great historical detail of wartime Australia mixed with the steady pace of sex and violence . . . keeps the pages turning."—*Brisbane Courier-Mail*

"Rough and gritty, but also vital."—*The Age*

DARK PASSAGE BOOKS
CHECKLIST

❏ **PETER DOYLE**: The Devil's Jump $14.95

❏ **PETER DOYLE**: Get Rich Quick. $13.95

❏ **G.S. MANSON**: Coorparoo Blues & The Irish Fandango . . . $13.95

❏ **ARTHUR NERSESIAN**: Gladyss of the Hunt. $14.95

❏ **JUNE WRIGHT**: Murder in the Telephone Exchange $15.95

❏ **JUNE WRIGHT**: So Bad a Death $14.95

❏ **JUNE WRIGHT**: Duck Season Death. $12.95

also available as ebooks

darkpassagebooks.com
facebook.com/versechoruspress